RECORD OF WRONGS

RECORD OF WRONGS

ANDY STRAKA

FIVE STAR
A part of Gale, Cengage Learning

GALE
CENGAGE Learning

Detroit • New York • San Francisco • New Haven, Conn • Waterville, Maine • London

GALE
CENGAGE Learning

LIBRARY OF CONGRESS CATALOGING-IN-PUBLICATION DATA

Straka, Andrew.
    Record of wrongs / by Andrew Straka. — 1st ed.
        p. cm.
    ISBN-13: 978-1-59414-652-7 (hardcover : alk. paper)
    ISBN-10: 1-59414-652-7 (hardcover : alk. paper)
    1. Young women—Crimes against—Fiction. 2. African American men—Fiction. 3. Judicial error—Fiction. 4. Murder victims' families—Fiction. 5. Murder—Investigation—Fiction. I. Title.
    PS3619.T733R43 2008
    813'.6—dc22   2007037454

First Edition. First Printing: February 2008.

Published in 2008 in conjunction with Tekno Books and Ed Gorman.

Printed in the United States of America
1 2 3 4 5 6 7 12 11 10 09 08

To the innocent,
wherever they are.

ACKNOWLEDGMENTS

For help in bringing this book to fruition, I'd like to thank, as always, my patient wife and children. I'm grateful as well to Deputy Commonwealth's Attorney Rick Moore, writers, friends, and critique artists extraordinaire Debby Prum, Lucy Russell, Jennifer Elvgren, Charlotte Crystal, Anne Raustol, Tom Nolan, Mara Rockliff, and Dave King. My editor, Hugh Abramson, and agent, Scott Miller, also deserve special nods, as do John Helfers, and all the special folks at Five Star. Any errors, of course, are my responsibility alone.

Love keeps no record of wrongs.

—1 Corinthians 13:5

ONE

They came for him a couple of hours before dawn. Only two of them this time: the bloated, baby-faced guard everyone called Ray the Inferno, and Elder, the night-shift supervisor with his mortuary eyes, pock-marked neck, and uniform starched so crisp you'd swear it could stop a knife.

The super managed a thin smile through the bars. "Liberation day, Price."

"Yes, sir."

Quentin knew better than to smile back. A head taller than the biggest of the guards, he knew better than to glower down at them either. He relaxed his shoulders into his submissive pose, kept his voice low, his brown eyes staring straight ahead.

"Don't be leaving any of your stinking paraphernalia behind," the Inferno said. "I got better things to do than clean up after your mess."

Quentin patted the tall canvas sack on the floor next to him. "Got everything right here."

"Good."

The bag was old army issue. He had crammed it full of his books, toiletries, clean shirts and pants, underwear and socks to go with the new suit they'd bought him. Those and a couple of old Wilson Pickett CDs were the sum of his worldly possessions—at least in here. He glanced around his cell. It may have been a Spartan existence, but a part of him realized he would miss the perverse security of imprisonment.

With a rattle that reverberated through the cell, the Inferno unlocked the small portal between the bars. "Wrists."

Quentin complied by pushing his hands together through the opening. Steel cuffs snapped around his skin.

He moved back to stand by his bag.

Elder slipped a different key into the side lock, and the electronic mechanism began to slide open the cell door. Steel ground against steel, a whisper of tubes until the bars hit the end of their run with a muted clank. Quentin wrestled the sack over his shoulder with his manacled hands and, without looking back, strode through the open door.

The Inferno methodically patted him down.

"All right then," Elder said. "Let's go."

In the semi-darkness the three men walked down the row of cells. Some of the other convicts were already awake. On the outside, word might not have leaked to the media yet about the unusual hour of his release, but in here it had spread like wild fire among the Main Line.

They passed beneath the catwalk. Before he knew it, they had slipped around a corner, through two more sets of locked doors, and down a narrow hallway into an air-conditioned, windowless room where a technician in a white smock, a chubby man with a long, salt and pepper beard and oversized glasses that made him look like he'd just beamed in from Woodstock, sat at the keyboard of a large machine that looked like a combination computer and commercial copier.

"Top of the morning to you, gentlemen." The technician, grinning, almost appeared to be chained to his machine.

"Hurry it up," Elder said. "And make sure you get it right this time."

The technician signaled Quentin.

He let his bag slide off his shoulder to the floor and stepped up to the computer. He'd already been fingerprinted a few months before with this gizmo. It was connected, he'd heard, to some FBI database in the sky that held his file along with thousands of other convicted felons. Now they would match his prints one more time to make sure they weren't releasing some imposter.

The tech took him by the hands. "You know this would be easier without the cuffs."

"Rules are rules," Elder said.

With a sigh, the tech wiped Quentin's fingers with alcohol, rolled each one in turn on a glass plate, and, when satisfied with each curlicue image on the computer monitor, pounded something on the keyboard and clicked a box on the screen with the mouse.

"Done?" Elder said finally.

"Done."

"All right. Pick up your bag again, Price, and let's go."

Quentin did as ordered and let the two guards lead him out through another locked door. They continued on past a large open area and through another locked door, arriving at the interchange desk, where a female guard perched behind a sliding glass partition, her eyes glued to a bank of video screens that monitored the entire block.

"Wrists."

Quentin set his bag down and held them out. The super undid the cuffs; the Inferno produced a set of scissors, snipped the plastic prisoner ID bracelet off of Quentin, and handed the bracelet to Elder.

"We'll be saving this for your encore," Elder said with a wry smile, as if he were communicating some universal truth of life.

Not anytime soon, Quentin wanted to say, but didn't.

"Be seeing you, partner."

The Inferno chuckled and the two guards turned and walked

back the way they had come, leaving Quentin to stand alone before the silent unblinking monitors and the officer on the other side of the glass.

His first whiff of freedom.

Her name tag read HERNANDEZ. She stood, unlocked the partition, and slid it open.

"Mr. Price. Right on time."

"Yes, ma'am."

"Think you're ready for the outside world again?"

"I hope so," he said, beginning to dare to believe that it was finally going to happen.

She smiled. "I'll bet."

She was one of the better badges in the place, her voice always calm but not dispassionate. He'd once seen her single-handedly head off a potential fight in the yard without even raising her baton.

She sat back down in her chair, fished a key from her trouser pocket, and opened a locked drawer below the desk. She pulled out a white number-ten envelope with his name written on it and placed it on the counter between them.

"State of New York says you're entitled to all of your personal effects, which you've already received. Plus you get forty dollars gate money and a bus ticket to your county of conviction. In your case, that would be Broome, City of Binghamton."

He took the envelope, lifted open the flap and peered inside. Four crisp ten dollar bills and the bus ticket winked out at him.

"Normally, we'd have someone drive you up to the station in Syracuse. But the bus from there to Binghamton doesn't leave until eight, and it takes over three hours with all the stops. You can still do that if you want." She looked down at some notes on the desk in front of her. "Only there's an individual supposed to be waiting for you outside who apparently has an interest in your case. Says here they'll drive you wherever you want to go."

An individual?

No one from his family, that was for sure. Quentin had never married, had no brothers or sisters; his mother had died two years before, and his grandparents were all dead too. His bum of a father, who lived somewhere in California, had ignored him his whole life. An uncle still lived in Binghamton, which was where he hoped he might be able to land for a while, but the uncle didn't own a car. A reporter? No, he'd specifically been told they'd kept the media out of the loop about the timing of his release.

"You can decline the ride, of course," Hernandez said. "But if you do, you're looking at spending an entire morning on Greyhound."

"Do you know who it is?"

She shrugged. "No one bothered to say. Guess you'll just have to see for yourself. If you decide you don't want the lift, come on back to the gate, and we'll go get one of the vans and drive you on up to the bus station."

Probably another lawyer. Some shyster in a flashy suit looking to make a name for him or herself. Not to mention a possible fortune by latching on to him and mounting a campaign of wrongful incarceration lawsuits against the state and anyone else they could sink their greedy talons into. He'd already received a stack of legal correspondence on fine stationery. Who were they to put a price tag on his rights? Besides, he already had a lawyer who had worked hard to get the DNA testing that had finally set him free. Christine Shackleford had been planning to escort him from prison, but when they changed his release time at the last minute she sent a message that she couldn't make it. He was to meet her at her office back in Binghamton instead. If it was another lawyer, Quentin would just tell them to get lost.

"Okay," he said.

Hernandez fiddled with a larger set of keys attached to her belt to unlock a switchboard of sorts in front of her. When the console lit up, she pressed a glowing red button, and a heavy steel door to Quentin's right swung open revealing the outdoors and a covered walkway leading toward the prison's wall and the outside gate.

A clean breath of warm night air washed through and drifted over him. Spring in upstate New York. It didn't really show until May, but when it finally did, you appreciated the green grass and flowers all the more.

"That's it then?" he said.

"That's it. Best of luck to you, Mr. Price."

"Same to you."

Another male badge appeared like an apparition at the door, this one brandishing a pump-action shotgun held at port arms. Quentin didn't recognize the man, but that was no surprise. Maybe he was a new jack, or maybe he only worked the late shift and he and Quentin had never crossed paths before. Quentin picked up his bag and followed his new escort through the door.

Outside along the walkway, a pair of generators emitted hollow electric moans. The wind stirred, bringing with it the faint smells of the town beyond the wall. Auburn was still a Finger Lakes destination, where people came for rest and rejuvenation, even if the grim edifice of the prison at its heart was a constant reminder of a starker reality.

His armed attendant accompanied him to the Wall Street gate, where they found a figure whose sober face was a few shades darker than Quentin's, waiting for them in a pool of light.

Warden Hallorhan.

A reflective sort with tight gray curls that clung to the sides of his head, the prison chief always seemed to look right through you, as if there was something more interesting in the distance. He usually wore a coat and tie, but this morning he was dressed only in slacks and a sweater.

With a nod Hallorhan dismissed the gun-toting guard, who promptly disappeared back the way they had come. "Nice morning for freedom."

"Yes, sir."

"Then again, I suppose any morning is."

Quentin said nothing.

"I came to give you something, Quentin."

"Sir?"

The warden stepped toward him, lifting a book he'd been holding at his side. He held it out for him—an oversized leather-bound Bible Quentin instantly recognized.

"It belonged to your mother."

"I know. I wondered whatever happened to it."

"Apparently, when they settled her estate after the expenses of the funeral . . . well, as you know there wasn't any money. This is what she wanted to leave you. Her instructions were clear. She wanted it given to you only on your release from prison."

"My release?" Maybe he could have used it more while doing the time. He looked at the thick book, its cover worn and discolored with age. "But how did she—?"

"I wanted to personally make sure it got to you."

"Thanks."

He took the book from the man's hand. In the sudden transfer of weight, Quentin felt as though someone were handing him a vital piece of his mother's soul. Running his finger along the spine brought back memories of all the times his mother had read to him when he was young—the mechanical

Andy Straka

click of the clock on the mantle, the gentle tone of her voice, the strength and warmth of her hand. He could see that the pages were well used.

"She always did believe I was innocent."

The warden nodded. Then he pulled a set of keys from his pocket, turned, and unlocked a double steel door built into the big gate.

"You take good care of yourself out there now, Mr. Price." He pushed open the hatch. "Bad side of the world hasn't gotten any smaller while you've been locked up in here."

No sorry-for-what-happened acknowledgement, one black man to another, commenting on the injustices of the system. No waste of words. What for? Inside had its own system of regulations, its own primeval justice.

Quentin looked the warden in the eye. "I'll do that."

Hallorhan shook his hand. The man's grip pulsed in his for a moment, like a stone claw, before letting go.

Quentin heaved his bag through the open hatch. Then he stepped through it himself into a puff of outside air.

Freedom.

As the door clanked shut and locked behind him, it occurred to him how mundane the movement was. All that had physically separated him from the life outside for the past ten years had been the ability to make that one simple step.

This time of year, the wind usually died after dark, magnifying the clamor of crickets and katydids, but the sound amounted to little more than a muted din, often barely discernible from inside the walls. Here, it seemed to ring louder than he'd ever heard it before. He paused to take a better look around.

Blue-collar Auburn. Sleeping bungalows in the shadow of blinding lights from the prison that flooded the street in both directions. Cars and boats in driveways. From somewhere the barking of a dog. They called it Wall Street because of the prison or maybe some upstater's idea of poking fun at lower Manhattan. Across from the high wall, a hundred yards or so down the sidewalk, Quentin saw a pair of amber parking lights defining the dark shape of a vehicle parked against the curb.

He wanted to take a minute to flip through the worn pages of his mother's Bible, but knew he'd better wait. He tucked the book with the envelope containing the money and bus ticket into the top of his satchel, shouldered the bag again, and strode off down the center of the street toward the car.

He'd walked only a few paces when its engine sprang to life. A pair of headlights flicked on and the vehicle began to roll slowly toward him. It was a fifteen- or twenty-year-old Chrysler, its front tires coated with dust, one missing a hubcap. A loose belt whined and from the rumble of the exhaust, a new muffler was in order. Who in the world?

He kept walking. The car continued toward him, bouncing through a pothole.

As it drew closer, he could make out a slender white woman behind the wheel. Middle-aged, a cigarette dangling from her lips, her hair a disheveled blaze of curls, vaguely familiar. She appeared to hurry the cigarette from her mouth as she neared, leaning over to crush it out in an ashtray on the dash.

He stopped, dropped his bag again, and waited while the woman braked to a halt and rolled her window the rest of the way down.

The face. The eyes. It all came back to him then, of course. Ruth Crawford.

"Hello, Quentin," she said. "Remember me?"

Quentin stared at the woman and her ugly car. "You expect me to forget?"

Her put-on smile faded a bit. "I know this must seem a little out of the ordinary."

Out of the ordinary? Caviar in the prison mess would have

been out of the ordinary. This was freaky.

"You could say that," Quentin said. "Since I'm supposed to be the animal who raped and murdered your daughter."

TWO

Quentin eyed the woman, trying to see her angle. Ruth Crawford, among others, had helped fast-track him into Auburn because the Man said someone had to pay for what had happened. Though she hadn't exactly perjured herself on the stand. There had been no need to. Did it even matter now, almost ten years later, that the nearly all-white jury had already been certain beyond a reasonable doubt that Quentin was the one to blame?

"What do you want?" he asked.

She coughed, clearing her throat. "Why, I, umm, I came to offer you a ride back to Binghamton."

Not an answer. He looked at her some more. "Surprised they let you."

She glanced at the wall and the brightly lit compound beside them. "I went to grade school with the head correctional officer in there. He arranged it."

Elder. Figured. This place, this whole part of the county was incestuous, everybody knowing everybody else, or thinking they did.

Quentin turned his head to take a broader look—his last he hoped—at the prison. Framed against the semi-darkness, it looked like some Hollywood horror movie vision—medieval castle meets twentieth-century nuclear bomb shelter. The concrete walls, even more massive than you could appreciate from inside, were framed by high-tech guard towers interspersed around the perimeter. You'd have thought they were housing exotic wild animals in there.

Before dark, late on winter afternoons, tens of thousands of wild animals actually did appear in town: roosting crows, one of the largest flocks in North America, drawn by the warm waters of the Owasco Outlet. Some said they were harbingers of death. Auburn was where they'd first used the electric chair.

"What do you really want?" Quentin asked.

"Just to give you a ride, like I said. And maybe to talk a little. To apologize."

"Forget it." He picked up his bag, turned, and, as much as he hated to, began walking back toward the gate.

"Wait." The car rumbled along, keeping pace. "I was wrong and I'm sorry. I know it's probably way too late to say that now, Quentin, but I was convinced you were guilty. I didn't know you, you see? I believed what I wanted to believe."

"You don't know me now either."

"You're right," she said. "I don't. But I'd like to."

He stopped and turned to look at her again. "Why?"

She seemed to think for a moment. "For Gwen's sake."

A picture of her daughter arose in his mind. Not the vision captured in the crime-scene photos that was almost loving. He'd been pushing that image from his thoughts for such a long time, it no longer haunted him. It was the girl's reflection in the glass, laughing at something funny he'd said to her one time when he'd shown up after closing at the college library. He was there to lock the doors. She worked late four nights a week because she was on financial aid and needed the money.

Much had been made at trial about Quentin's relationship with Gwen. Most of the students at Merryweather—located in the town of Hamlick outside of Binghamton, not exactly a high-crime burg—either tolerated or ignored the security staff. Gwen was different. She went out of her way to be friendly, especially to Quentin. He couldn't remember now, though, what he'd said to make her laugh that night.

"Forget it." He shook his head.

"For your mother's sake too."

"My mother's?" He glared down at the car. "I'm looking at a crazy person."

"You're finally free from this place. You don't want to spend all day riding on a bus, do you?"

He said nothing.

"Are you just going to stand there?"

"No." He began to walk again.

She kept pace. "I can have you back in Broome County in less than ninety minutes. That's where you want to go, to Binghamton, isn't it?"

It was true, but beyond meeting his lawyer and going to his uncle's place, he hadn't really given the details much thought. Not looking too closely at the future protected him, kept him insulated from disappointment. How many other options did he have with no money and no job?

Maybe a few.

He furrowed his brow. "What's your angle?"

"No angle. It's the least I can do for you, after all you've been through."

He reached into his coat pocket and fingered the bus ticket and the forty dollars. "I don't need your charity."

"I know. And anyway, as you can see . . ." She pointed at the dashboard of the Chrysler. "I don't have much to give."

He stopped again, stepped behind his bag, still undecided, and looked away.

She tilted her head a little and caught his eye again. "Come on. What, you think I'm packing a machine gun in here or something? It's just a ride back home."

Home. With his mother gone, there was no real home left for

him there, no place with any permanence.

The last time he'd seen Binghamton had been at her funeral. Two guards accompanied him in the van from the prison. The temperature was in the forties and the ground not quite frozen yet. He stood at her gravesite in his shackles. The wind had made his hands and feet throb.

The legal winds, though, had started to blow in his favor by then. The lawyers told him it was only a matter of time before he'd have his chance at vindication. It had turned out to be nearly three more years.

As if she could read his mind, Ruth said, "You know I got to know your mother pretty well before she passed."

"You what?"

Ruth's smile was disarming in the same way Gwen's had been. They didn't really look all that much alike, he decided, except for that.

"It's true," she said. "Carla sort of took me under her wing for a while. She and a bunch of her friends from her church used to come in every Sunday to the diner where I work. Most of them still do."

He could run. Head on over to the bus station and try to have his ticket changed, see how far that and forty bucks would take him. Then hitch a ride with a trucker driving West. Chicago. L.A. maybe. Someplace new.

"I've got an idea," Ruth said. "Let's just pretend you forgive me for your mother's sake. What do you say?"

"Huh."

He really didn't want to have to go knock on the gate and ask to be let back inside, if only for the time it took to arrange another ride. Maybe he could even cash in his bus ticket once they got to Binghamton. What did he have to lose besides his pride?

He listened to the night sounds of the sleeping town again. "Okay," he finally said. "But just a ride."

THREE

Knee deep in a tangle of briers, Detective Garnell Harris lingered under the klieg lights and watched as the crime scene techs freed the young woman's arms. They began to bag her hands. Careful with the fingernails, he thought, almost as if they were preparing her for an expensive manicure.

Sad. Especially sad since she appeared to be a working girl and therefore vulnerable.

No ID, of course. Pretty Asian features, even after the beating she'd obviously suffered. Spiked heel pumps made for street-walking. Slender thighs that had been on full display beneath the hem of her mini-skirt but were now twisted in an unnatural way like some broken porcelain doll. Her pantyhose had been crushed into a ball and stuffed into her mouth, the final indignity.

Nothing new about that. Nothing new about any of it.

Garnell pulled his sport coat a little closer around him and buttoned it in front. The air still held a chill as dawn broke over Mott Haven and the Manhattan skyline in the distance. One of the techs began using a pair of tweezers and a tape strip to collect stray pieces of hair, pubic and otherwise, and any loose bits of fiber to be found on the body.

"Hey, Gar. Someone's on the horn for you."

His partner, Jane Pappas, had appeared without a sound at his shoulder, still munching on an egg biscuit and sipping her coffee. They'd both been called in on their weekend off to this shit hole of a park near the Grand Concourse.

"What do you mean? Why didn't they call me on my cell?"

Pappas finished her bite and dabbed at the edge of her mouth with the corner of her sleeve. "You're not going to believe this. It's the deputy AG."

"The what?"

"The deputy attorney general. The one based up in Albany. His name is Bollinger. He's on the phone in the car. I confirmed it with the captain on my mobile line."

"The deputy AG wants to talk to me."

"That's what the man says."

"At this hour of the morning?"

Pappas shrugged. "You go on. I'll take over here."

Garnell stared at her for a moment, saw she was serious, turned, and trudged back to the unit parked at the curb.

What in the world would the DAG want to talk to him for? Something to do with internal affairs? He sure hoped not. Besides, IA would have contacted him directly.

"Detective Harris?" a voice said when he picked up the phone.

"That's me."

"Stewart Bollinger up in Albany."

"Yes, sir. You're up early, sir."

"Always have been an early riser. I know this may seem a little unusual, calling you out of the blue like this, but we have a special situation brewing up here and I need your help."

Okay, this guy sounded as slick as they came. "What kind of situation?"

"You grew up in the Binghamton area, did you not?"

"That's right."

"Went to college at Binghamton University, class of eighty-nine." He was obviously reading off a resume. "BA in psychology. Graduated magna cum laude."

"You didn't call this early in the morning to recite my

background."

"No, detective, I didn't. Have you heard of Quentin Price?"

"Price?" He searched his memory but came up blank. "Nope. Should I?"

"The case has gotten a fair amount of press. Price was doing life up in Auburn for raping and murdering a Merryweather coed back in ninety-six."

Of course.

Garnell was suddenly back in high school in the early eighties. Quentin Price was the hoops phenom from St. Anthony's who had blown out his knee. A sad story. He heard Price had joined the army, but he also recalled reading about the murder trial a decade before.

"I remember who you're talking about now," he said.

"Good. Here's the situation. The case against Price was apparently airtight. Still mostly is, according to all concerned, jury only deliberated a few hours. Except that there was some DNA evidence that was never analyzed. Price went and got himself a lawyer, the folks down there at the innocence project in the city took an interest in his case, and the rest is—"

"Price is sprung?"

"That's the long and the short of it. Turns out the DNA they were finally able to extract from the minute semen sample wasn't his. Of course we all know there could have been any number of other explanations for that. The girl's body wasn't even discovered for more than a week, which the lab people say is really pushing the envelope for gathering semen evidence. Probably why it wasn't part of the case on the first go-round. Took too long to get the test results and they didn't need it."

"So where do I fit in?"

"I'd like you to go on up there and review the case. Poke around a little bit, see what you can find out. The DA in Binghamton is an old buddy of mine named Randall Tischler. I've already told him you might be coming."

"But I've already got a full caseload. I'm looking at a fresh homicide as we speak."

"Already cleared it with your captain. Your partner and some of the other detectives in your precinct will cover for you until you get back. I don't expect it'll take more than a week or so."

Garnell took a deep breath. His wife, Monique, for one, would be upset with him if he took off for upstate, no matter what the reason. He already worked too many unholy hours as it was. They had a nine-month-old baby and Monique was about to begin her final year of law school.

"If you don't mind my asking, what exactly are you expecting me do, Mr. Bollinger? You can't retry Price for murder, can you?"

"Not on that exact charge, no."

The line was silent for a moment or two. Garnell had been around the NYPD long enough to know a rat when he smelled one. This one had a different odor than most though. The state must have been looking at a hefty lawsuit on behalf of the lucky Quentin Price now that he had walked, but that wouldn't carry enough juice to put the DAG himself on the phone with some lowly NYPD detective early on a Saturday morning.

"Is this a request or an order, sir?" he asked.

"Right now it's still a request," Bollinger said.

"All right. I'd like to think about it, talk to my wife. How long do I have?"

"How about until 5 p.m.?"

"Today?"

"Today."

"What, someone going to turn into a pumpkin or something by then?"

"I'm not screwing around with this, detective. I want someone on this case ASAP."

"I hear you, sir." Loud and clear.

Forget that it was a weekend. Forget that Monique was premenstrual, that the baby was still a little colicky, that Monique's sister in Queens was planning a birthday party that afternoon for their brother-in-law.

Bollinger gave him his private mobile number with instructions to call him before the day was out.

"Just one more thing, sir, if you don't mind my asking," Garnell said.

"What's that?"

"You've obviously had a good look at this case."

"Yes, I have."

"You think Price did it?"

There was another pause on the line, just long enough to make Harris wonder.

"I have no earthly idea," the DAG said. "I need your decision by five o'clock."

FOUR

They had left Auburn behind and were winding south along the lake toward Cortland and the interstate. Summer leaves swelled the darkened birches and maples. Theirs were the only headlights at this hour.

Ruth was a cautious driver. Either that or her beat-up old Chrysler had trouble sputtering along at anywhere near the posted speed limit. The car smelled of cigarettes and some kind of flavored lipstick. Quentin didn't really care if the woman smoked cigars or used perfume or did heroin, just as long as her junk set of wheels held together long enough to get him back to where he wanted to go.

"How's it feel?" she asked, as the dark surface of the lake filled a wide swath of real estate out her side of the car.

"What?"

"You know what I mean. To be out after all this time."

"Too soon to tell," he said.

"Mmmmmm."

So what did she really want? To coax from him some kind of admission? To smoke out whether he really killed Gwen? Maybe all she really sought was the repair of an old wound, one that would most likely never be healed. Despite what the police and prosecutors alleged, Quentin had never once come on to her daughter. Gwen sought him out, not the other way around. She confided in him, telling him about her troubles with her mother—with whom she hadn't spoken in months—problems with various boys, problems with her studies. She admitted she'd tried weed, hinting she knew others who were into more serious drugs. That was the way it had been. And maybe Gwen's mother finally sensed this.

But it wasn't his job to fill in the gaps for Ruth Crawford. He leaned his head against the window, feeling the vibration of the old snow tires, and closed his eyes.

"You know," Ruth said. "Some people thought it odd, your mother and me getting to be friends after what happened. But I always told them they didn't know Carla."

He opened his eyes to stare at the road, hoping she'd soon run out of conversation.

"She really was a wonderful person. One of the kindest people I've ever known."

"Mmmmm."

"She used to tell me all about how you'd played basketball for St. Anthony's and led the region in scoring. How you'd just about been assured of a scholarship before you hurt your knee and all. I know a little of that came out in the trial, but—"

"Ancient history."

"Of course."

Lights appeared from around a curve and a tanker truck on its way to Auburn blew past them. He wondered if it would be making a delivery to the prison.

"Anyway," she said. "Carla was always convinced you were innocent. But I'm sure you already know that."

"She make you believe it too?"

Ruth smiled again. "What she wouldn't have given, I'm sure, to be here right now."

It was another non-answer, but he smiled too, dwelling for a moment on her words. Still, he couldn't escape the notion that his mother dying when she did was just one more cruel irony in his life. Fate working against him, as it always seemed to.

Or time. He'd gotten to know time in Auburn. You don't just do time in the Grey Bar Hotel, he had learned. You breathe it. You swim in it, you sweat in it, you drink it, you dream in it. So far his life seemed out of sync, the pacing a little off—from the breakdown of his knee to the breakdown of his alibi ten years before. Life wasn't like playing hoops in his prime when everything seemed to flow together on the court the way it was supposed to.

"It must have been terrible back there," Ruth said, meaning Auburn.

He looked out the window. "Wasn't fun, I'll tell you that."

"I knew another guard who used to work there. I grew up near Skaneateles. Gwen's grandparents, my parents, still have a place there."

"Probably no one else you know has ever been a convict though, have they?"

"No," she said. "I can't say that they ever have."

Quentin had become a no-shit guy on the block. Actually, he'd been a no-shit guy during his stint in the army, after he'd rehabbed his knee as far as the knee was going to go. No, it had started even earlier, back when he was only six years old and his father left his mother and him for good. Overnight, he found himself the male figure in the family. Brave little man.

His clearest memory of his dad was a hollow-eyed, drunken face and a big black hand that bought him a Mounds Bar on his fifth birthday at a Korean grocery store in Flushing. He remembered the hot, bustling, ethnic tenor of the place and days spent playing in the small back yard of their tenement.

"You have any plans?" she asked, apparently determined to keep talking. "For the future, I mean."

He shrugged. "Get back to Binghamton. Talk to my lawyer. Look for a job. Start from there."

"Where are you planning to stay?"

"My uncle owns a house on Front Street. Figured I'd see if he might let me crash there for a while."

"Does this uncle of yours know you're planning to come home today?"

"He sent me a letter a couple of weeks ago, wanted to know when I might be getting out. I wrote back, said I didn't know for sure, but I told him it might be somewhere around now."

"I should have written you a letter or something myself before showing this morning. I'm sorry."

"It doesn't matter," he said. "If you did, I'd have told 'em to put me on the bus."

They reached the interstate. Ruth merged the Chrysler into traffic at a more reasonable speed to keep pace with the big rigs and the newer cars. Quentin had never been much attracted to stylish automobiles, but he gawked at a gleaming new charcoal colored BMW with its recessed grille that whizzed past them, its driver deep in conversation on a wireless phone. Had anything during the last ten years prepared him for changes moving so fast? He'd thought about trying to pick up some computer skills while inside, but with all the restrictions they had and his situation so uncertain, somehow he'd never gotten around to it.

They were between Cortland and Marathon, had just passed a sign reading BINGHAMTON 30 MILES, when the car began to vibrate. Seconds later, it escalated to a violent shaking.

"What's going on?"

"I don't know."

The steering wheel pulsed in Ruth's hands. She fought to keep the car under control.

"Pull over."

"I'm trying."

She swerved into the passing lane directly in the path of a tractor trailer. The trucker hit his brakes and lay on his horn.

She finally managed to pull the Chrysler back into the right lane and onto the shoulder, where they pounded to a stop beside the guardrail.

She pushed an errant strand of hair from across her forehead. "Whew. That was close."

"Looks like you've got a flat." The fender on Quentin's side of the car was dipping precariously toward the pavement.

"Great. That's just great." Ruth shook her head.

At least the interstate had a wide enough shoulder to try to remedy the problem.

"You have a spare?"

"I think so."

"How much do you drive this thing?"

"Not that much. Every day to work, but that's it. Bertha's never let me down like this before."

"Bertha?"

"Yeah." She patted the dashboard. "That's what I like to call her. She's usually a good old girl."

"Nice name. Sounds like some fat old woman." He pushed his door open. "Let's see what you've got."

Ruth climbed out too and walked around behind the car to meet him. Amazingly, the trunk light still worked when the lid was lifted. The spare lay tucked in a compartment beneath the carpet; it was nearly full size and looked like it would work okay.

"Can I help?" she asked, peering into the trunk beside him.

"I've got it."

"You sure?"

"I'm sure."

He found a jack and a tire iron in the compartment as well. Lucky thing. The last thing he needed right now was to be stranded here with this woman. He stowed his suit coat in the back seat on top of his bag, rolled up his shirt sleeves, and went

35

to work. It had been years since he'd changed a tire, heard the squeak of lug nuts loosening and felt the shiver of the wrench in his hands, but it was the kind of thing you didn't forget.

He bounced the spare out onto the shoulder.

Ruth stood to the side and lit up a cigarette, watching as he positioned the jack by the reflected glare from the headlights.

"This kind of stuff always seems to happen to me," she said.

"Oh, yeah?"

"My ex-husband used to call me the 'crap-magnet.' "

"That why he's your ex?"

"Partly."

She offered nothing more and Quentin wasn't about to ask. Gwen had talked to him some, not just about her troubles with her mother but about her parents' divorce. Her father, Jack, had been a cop up in Syracuse. Quentin remembered him from the trial, sitting in the gallery each and every day, a brooding, dark-haired mass of a man with bulging forearms and judgment eyes.

Cars and trucks roared past them, blowing Ruth's hairdo to smithereens and her smoke down the guardrail into the distance.

"Gwen's grandfather was a mechanic. She ever tell you that?"

"Nope," he said groaning under the strain of lifting off the wheel with the flat tire. "She didn't."

"Worked on cars, buses, tractors—you name it—for more than fifty years. That man could fix almost anything."

Ten minutes later, Quentin had them back up and running down the road.

"I really appreciate your helping me out like that," she said. "I should pay you something."

"Don't worry about it." He said, wiping his hands with a handkerchief she'd provided. "The ride's enough."

Mercifully, she let him doze for a while after that and before he knew it, they were approaching the outskirts of Binghamton.

The sun, just beginning to rise over the hills east of the city, made him open his eyes. The lean, gray industrial town where he and his mother had made their escape from Queens rose out of the bottomlands at the confluence of the Susquehanna and Chenango rivers. A place mostly filled by people of English, Irish, Italian, Polish, Russian, or Czechoslovakian descent. Quentin and his mother had always moved effortlessly, if never invisibly, among them, as long as they never tried to raise their heads above the blue-collar status to which they—and for that matter most of their neighbors—seemed destined.

Ruth had reduced her speed again, perhaps out of fear of damaging the spare, but also, maybe, because she meant to draw out her time with him. Whatever her motives, the woman still made him nervous.

"Bet you never thought you'd be riding back into Binghamton with me."

Not in his wildest dreams.

"Mrs. Crawford—"

"Ruth. For God's sake, call me Ruth, will you?"

"Ruth then. Just what is it that you're really wanting from me?"

She turned her neck, angling her eyes to look in her rearview mirror and at the thickening tangle of cars ahead of them. "Traffic's picking up a little. Must be early rush hour."

"You're not answering my question."

"I know. I know."

Bright sunlight angled across the hood of the Chrysler.

"Seems to me I'm entitled to some answers. You drive all the way up to Auburn in the middle of the night, sit outside the wall there waiting by yourself, not even knowing for sure if I'd even accept a ride from you."

She said nothing.

"What am I, some poor underprivileged minority project for

you or something?"

"No. No, no." She laughed bitterly. "Believe you me, Quentin, I've taken on enough projects in my life and you're not one of them. Gwen's father was one, he . . . well."

She followed a UPS truck off the next exit for downtown.

"Gwen," he said. "This is about Gwen, though, isn't it?"

She nodded. "Of course. Of course it is."

They came to a light.

"Where do you want me to take you?" she asked.

"Nowhere. You can just let me off anywhere around here. The next corner if you want."

She turned right and headed into the nearest parking lot, a strip mall with a convenience store, a dry cleaners, a sub and pizza place, and a gift store. Only the convenience store was open this early. There were a couple of pickups, a commercial van, and three or four sedans parked in front.

"I wish I didn't have to leave you like this," she said.

Okay, here it finally came. He said nothing.

"If you remember from the trial, Gwen and I weren't exactly getting along at the time of her death."

"I remember."

"Well I suppose I was just hoping you might be able to help me out a little with that."

"You think 'cause Gwen was talking to me before she died that I might be able to fill in a few of the gaps for you. Is that it?"

It was cruel of him to say. He knew it as soon as the words escaped his mouth. But ten years of his life had come and gone as if they'd been nothing more than a blink of the eye for the rest of the world. He'd long since passed beyond caring.

"Why, no," she said. "I mean, I do want you to help me . . . to help me understand better who she was and all. It just that I—"

"Everything I told that jury ten years ago was true. Every word of it," he said, staring.

"I believe you now," she said.

"Yeah, well, not everybody does, you know."

"That's okay."

"Why do you believe me now when you didn't before? Because of the DNA?"

"Maybe. I don't know." Her eyes clouded over. "You were just so much more convenient than facing reality, I suppose. I know it sounds awful, but it's true."

"You mean I was an easier way out for you than dealing with your pain."

She nodded. "That sounds about right."

Of course, Quentin's presumed guilt had been more convenient than the truth for a lot of people, not just Ruth.

"I've been talking to the district attorney," she went on. "Trying to find out where they are with the investigation into Gwen's murder. You know, if they've made any new discoveries, any more progress."

"What, you want to question me about that again now too, is that it?"

"No, I—"

Quentin pushed his door open and climbed out, pulled open the door to the back seat. He slipped on his suit jacket and took out his oversized sack, then closed the doors again.

Leaning over the front door frame, he looked over the roof at the cars rushing past on the road across the lot. The air was still chilly, but the sun was striking the tops of the buildings behind him now. He looked back through the open window.

"I can't heal you, Mrs. Crawford. Can't bring Gwen back."

"Of course." She sniffled once and reached up to wipe a tear from her cheek with the back of her hand. "I'm not asking you to."

He could see in her eyes this was going all wrong for her. He felt sorry for being so blunt. But not too sorry.

"I appreciate the ride." He turned to leave. "I gotta go."

"Wait."

He looked back. "What?"

She slid her hands around the steering wheel and gripped it harder, as if to gather her emotions. "You want to know what I want, Quentin? You want to know what I really want?"

"What's that?" A couple of empty school buses roared past on their way to pick up children for the day.

"I want someone to start taking me seriously," she said. "I want someone to help me find out who really killed my Gwen."

FIVE

The morning sun burned through the haze to shimmer on the surface of Cazenovia Lake, calming Jack Crawford's raw nerves. He angled his Seville into the driveway of the stately Victorian home. Years ago, when he'd been married, Jack could hardly have imagined himself doing what he was doing now. Fantasize maybe, but not seriously imagine it. He parked in his usual spot in back of the garage. Hannah met him on the screened-in porch. She wore a midlength summer print dress beneath her sweater and stood on tiptoe in her bare feet to kiss him.

Other than his work as private investigator, nothing was more important in Jack's life than his adulterous relationship with Hannah Marx. He hated to think of her in such terms, hated that in his line of work he'd busted his share of philandering spouses. He ran his fingers down her back to the hem of the dress and felt the warm softness of her thigh, pulling her in to him.

They went inside to the spare bedroom, where she'd already drawn the shades, and made love on the four-poster bed that had been handed down to her by her mother. She was beautiful, her skin as smooth as ivory. She was everything Jack had ever wanted. It almost made him forget.

They lay together after, her blond hair tucked beneath the fold of his chin.

"What's bothering you?" she asked.

"You can tell?"

"Of course I can tell."

He reached across the bedside table to where he'd stowed his .45 Beretta and checked to make sure the safety was still on. "It's nothing."

"You're lying," she said.

He smiled, more of a wince really.

"Today's the day, isn't it?"

"The day for what?"

"The day they let Quentin Price out of Auburn. I had forgotten until just now. You told me you thought it was going to be today or tomorrow."

"Uh-huh."

"You don't have to talk about it any more if you don't want to."

He shrugged. "What more is there to talk about?"

"You still think he's guilty, don't you?"

"Of course."

"What about the DNA?"

"I don't want to get into this with you right now, sweetie. The DNA is just one piece of evidence. It doesn't change the fact that Price did the crime. Remember, I was there ten years ago. I sat through every single minute of testimony."

"So you're saying you think there's another reason that wasn't Price's DNA?"

"Obviously."

"Which means Price is getting off on a technicality."

"Basically, yes."

"Well, there's nothing anyone can do about that, is there? It's the system."

Jack rarely found himself at a loss for words, but such a deep river of emotion welled up from inside of him, he could only manage a nod. She lifted her face to his and kissed him softly on the cheek, then dipped her head into his shoulder again. He kissed the top of her hair and buried his face in it.

"It'll be okay," she said.

"Yeah. Maybe."

"Does your ex-wife know about Price's release?"

"I can't imagine that she wouldn't."

"You haven't talked with her about it?"

"I don't remember the last time I talked to Ruth about anything."

The divorce was just one more arrow in Jack's quiver of grief, one more inexplicable chapter in his life. Ruth was selfish, simple as that, too absorbed in her own problems to see how police work had taken a toll on him, to be on his side when the depression hit. Maybe he had lost control of his emotions for a time, but that was long since behind him. He'd matured, he'd prospered, and he had Hannah. It was she, not Ruth, who seemed to understand his mood swings and the dark ogre of violence that continued to haunt him.

Hannah kissed him again. They lay still for a minute or two, absorbed in one another's presence. For a moment he almost forgot again about Quentin Price.

"Look," he said finally. "I've got to get to work."

He slid out from beneath her and began to pull his arm into a sleeve and his shirt over his broad shoulders.

She pulled the covers up, propped her head on the pillow, and turned on her side to watch him. "I'm worried about you, Jack."

"Don't be."

"You shouldn't let this thing about Price keep eating away at you."

"The only thing eating away at me is this drop-dead gorgeous blonde." He gave her a wink. "She's turning me into some stereotypical TV private eye who solves the case and beds the woman."

Hannah's husband, a prominent art dealer and acrobatic philanderer, had originally hired Jack to help trace a potential forgery. The case had been relatively straightforward. A kid working in Marx's warehouse suddenly grew bigger ambitions. But after Jack and Hannah met, nothing had been the same for either of them. That Hannah and her husband were the parents of a teenage son complicated matters, but not too much.

"You work too hard," she said.

"My only other mistress."

"It better be."

He finished putting on his shoulder holster and slipped on his sport coat.

"When will we see each other again?" she asked.

"He still leaving town on Wednesday?"

"As far as I know."

"Why don't you come on up to my place for a couple of days. It's more anonymous."

"I'd like that."

Half an hour later, Jack was behind his desk at his office in East Syracuse. The schedule promised tedious work on a handful of reports he'd let slip too long. There was a certain art in distilling all of the information he gathered into a concise summary, and Jack was pretty good at it. Good enough to make sure his clients got what they were looking for and to make certain that he got paid.

When it came to money, the last two years had been especially kind to him. He'd managed to close several big cases, one of which had led to a huge settlement for the client of one of the attorneys he worked for. From that case alone he had earned nearly as much money as he made in a typical year.

Sitting behind his oversized desk, staring out at the pond behind his office, he couldn't help thinking his good fortune must be happening for a reason.

He stood and walked over to the wall where an array of black and white photographs were arranged in neat rows. Each photo, whether a portrait or a landscape, revealed aspects of the subject that showed that Gwen had had a real sympathy for whatever was in front of her. She had been a talented photographer with an eye for detail, balance, and texture.

These were just a few of her signature pieces. Ruth had the rest packed away in storage, over a hundred in all; some had even been displayed at a gallery in Binghamton following Gwen's death. Jack was no art critic, but looking into the images his daughter had seen through her lens had come to offer him what he imagined was a window into her soul.

He conjured up memories he hadn't dared visit for a while.

Gwen, captured on video blowing out the candles on her third birthday. Falling over and over again but not giving up until she had learned how to ride a bicycle. Goofing around and laughing with a couple of her middle school friends on the giant carousel at the state fair.

How many more photos might she have taken? How might her work have evolved? Would she have even had children of her own one day?

He thought about Quentin Price's murder trial, about all the witnesses and evidence presented, the give and take between the defense and the prosecution, the judge's stern admonishments and the looks on the juror's faces, how sad but satisfied he had felt after the conviction. He thought about the high walls of Auburn, about fancy, high-priced lawyers, some of whom were his customers, and all that had transpired since then.

Since he'd first heard of the possibility of Price's release, seeds of a vague idea had begun stirring in his mind. Now he allowed them to come into clearer focus and to begin to bloom.

It wasn't the same sense of satisfaction he had felt ten years before, but it came close.

He picked up the phone.

Six

She hadn't realized just how much she'd left the apartment in shambles.

Bleary-eyed and disgusted with herself for having made such a mess of her morning, Ruth shuffled in through the front door and dropped her purse and keys on the shelf by the phone. The kitchen smelled stale and empty. Petrified oatmeal remains in a cereal bowl sat atop yesterday's newspaper, which was scattered across the table. A stone-cold cup of black coffee. The hollowed out rind of a slice of cantaloupe. A pair of blue jeans that she'd rejected for the trip to Auburn, and a clean blouse that had been equally nixed, formed the beginning of a crumpled trail of clothes from the bedroom that ended with her nightgown and dirty panties.

She needed to tame the chaos.

First thing, she half filled the sink with suds as much to smell the lemon scent and feel the warmth of the water on her hands as to wash the dishes.

How could she have been foolish enough to think the man imprisoned—falsely it now appeared—for murdering Gwen would have any interest at all in helping her? She hadn't even gotten to the important part: her evidence. There hadn't been time and he had seemed so different from what she'd expected. Maybe it would have been better to have waited until a few days after his release. But how could she have even been sure she could get in touch with him? In that sense, at least, the trip hadn't been a total waste.

She rubbed the back of her neck, felt the dull pain of a creeping headache coming on. She longed for rest. Her bed, still unmade, was waiting for her. But would she even be able to get back to sleep with everything spinning through her mind?

She thought of Gwen and the look on Quentin Price's face when they had talked about her. In her heart, she realized now, she had always found it hard to believe a man like him had actually done such horrible things to her daughter. Or had she really? Was she that good a judge of another's inner canvas? Like Jack, who knew what kind of monsters Quentin Price kept locked beneath the surface?

Maybe her guilt over Gwen's death was finally beginning to chip away at her reason. Was the idea that the condolence notes she received every year had come from Gwen's killer merely a figment of her imagination? The police certainly thought so. By now they seemed to have written her off as an anguished parent gone over the edge, so crazed by grief that whatever she told them needed to be taken with a grain of salt. Not for the first time she wished Carla Price were still alive. Carla would have been able to help her make sense of things.

Finished with the dishes, she floated toward the bedroom, picking up the clothes as she went. She almost wished it wasn't her day off. At least work kept her mind occupied.

She glanced through the blinds at the morning sunlight breaking through the trees of the garden apartment complex. Too early yet for most people. But, this being a Saturday, a father was throwing a football with his son, who looked to be about six or seven. The boy ran down the sidewalk past the parking spaces filled with cars. The father lofted a short pass over the youngster's head, and at the last instant the boy reached up to catch the ball the way he had probably seen on TV, to the whooping approval of his father.

She shouldn't. She knew she shouldn't, not again.

But as the boy and the father disappeared from view, leaving her with only the vacant morning light, she reached for the bottle of Seagram's Extra Dry on the counter.

SEVEN

The last time Quentin had seen his lawyer had been three days before when she had marched into one of the cramped visiting legal counsel rooms at Auburn to give him the news.

"In accordance with New York state statute 440.30, motion to vacate judgment and set aside sentencing procedures in the case of Quentin Abraham Price has been granted."

And that was it. Quentin was to be released from prison, this time for real.

Christine Shackleford may have been no more than five-two, but she packed a powerful punch. With long black hair, red fingernails, fiery eyes, and a face hardened by nearly two decades of doing battle as both a public defender and a private defense attorney, she had a reputation for brashness and a quick wit among her colleagues. With Quentin though her manner was almost always quiet and deliberate, as if she were handling a Faberge egg. No doubt his case had become the most significant, symbolically at least, of her long career. Quentin hadn't had much use for criminal defense attorneys until he had met Shackleford.

"So this is it then," he said to her through the glass partition, not quite daring yet to believe the news.

"This is it. Congratulations." She smiled, one of the few

times he ever remembered her doing so. His lawyer was not one to crow, especially in a place like this, perhaps because she was all too aware that such victories were often short-lived.

"And they can't come back at me."

"Not for these charges." She shook her head. "Double jeopardy."

"How soon?"

"As soon as all the paperwork is completed and the preparations are in order. Most likely by the weekend."

He nodded, his eyes nearly welling with tears.

"Anybody you want me to let know you're coming home?" she said.

He thought about it. He'd already written his uncle. "No thanks. Will you be coming to get me?"

"I'll try, but I can't promise. I'm in the middle of another court case and we're down to crunch time."

"Sure." He remembered back to his own case years before and what he considered at the time to be the feeble efforts of his original attorney.

"If I can't make it, I can send someone from the office."

"It's okay, don't worry about it. I'll manage."

"Either way, I want to meet with you in my office to discuss the options. I know you're not a big fan of litigation, especially when it comes to money. But the bald truth is—as I've told you before—you've got a hell of a case for wrongful incarceration here. The state is expecting us to file. I've already received overtures about a settlement."

"What about the murder case?"

"What do you mean?"

"Are the cops still going to try to find out who really killed Gwen?"

She shrugged. "Not our concern. My advice is to distance yourself from that as much you can. Which of course includes staying out of Hamlick and away from Merryweather College."

"I'm planning to stick around," he said. "At least until I figure out where I want to go and what I want to do. But no problem about the college."

"Good."

Hamlick was only ten minutes on the interstate from Binghamton, but except for the occasional scandal such as Gwen's death, it might as well have been on another continent as far as most of the city's residents were concerned. Now, in his first few hours of freedom back in the city, Quentin realized he was going to have to be careful. Meeting Ruth Crawford had dredged up a lot of the old fears. She'd seemed genuine enough, but if she still had so much passion, what about everyone else involved in the case? What about the rest of this town?

He thought seriously about skipping the appointment with his lawyer, with her wrinkled skirt and sincere demeanor. It wasn't that he didn't trust her or feel she had his best interests at heart. But Christine Shackleford's office was in the old Security Mutual Building on Exchange Street, an eclectic Romanesque revival that helped anchor the area around the Broome County courthouse and the city's power structure. By now he'd developed a certain revulsion to such venues. Call it prison fatigue, post-traumatic stress, whatever, but even more than when he'd stood outside the walls staring at Ruth Crawford in her car, he felt the urge to run.

But he didn't. Not yet, at least.

The decorative carousel horses along Court Street looked like they might be ready to run. Binghamton billed itself as "The Carousel Capital of America," Broome County being home to no less than six giant antique carousels. It was an electric blue morning with a breeze stirring the new leaves on the trees. In his craziest hopes he had never thought he might be standing here again on the streets of this town as a free man.

Quentin thought of calling Uncle Nelson, but the old man liked to sleep late, so that could wait. His appointment with Shackleford wasn't until nine. Since it was still well before eight, he ducked into a downtown bakery, rich with the aromas of fresh pastries and real coffee, a far cry from tepid prison blend, and ordered an English muffin to go with his tall steaming cup.

The place was nearly empty. The elderly woman who filled his order did so with practiced care and compassionate eyes.

He sat alone at a table in the back and for the first time in a long time tried to simply take in the sights and sounds of a morning—the shadows of the buildings outside framed by the brilliant sunshine, the hum and swish of a street cleaning machine moving somewhere down the street. Two businessmen in shirts and ties sat at a table near the front, apparently debating approaches to a pending sales presentation. The only other customers were a couple of teenage girls bent over a ream of loose-leaf notes, one of whom pounded away on a laptop—cramming for finals or doing last-minute term papers.

With his new suit and clean-shaven look, Quentin could have passed for a banker or a stock broker, even a lawyer. He felt like an alien dropped from another dimension.

No one was watching so he pulled his mother's Bible from the top of his bag and began leafing through it. He'd heard the gospel according to King James before. Was the book just a family keepsake, or was there some message his mother had wanted him to absorb? He would have to look more closely when there was time.

He tucked the Bible back in his sack and found a *USA Today* on an adjacent table.

As usual of late, there were headlines about the War on Terror, the fighting overseas in Afghanistan and Iraq. Not for the first time, he wondered if any of his old army buddies were serving in either theater. But he'd lost track of them all long ago. Prison had made him a forgotten man.

He began to run through a mental checklist of things he would need over the coming days. First and foremost was gainful employment, if that was even possible. Then . . . a new set of shoes would be nice. His black prison loafers might be fine for some kinds of work, but they still had that institutional look and reminded him too much of life inside.

A cell phone would be nice too. He'd noticed one in Ruth Crawford's purse. But he was getting ahead of himself. Right now, his most important need was for a place to stay. He'd see if his lawyer had anything to say about other prospects. The men in front packed up and headed out the door. More customers came and went. Traffic began to pick up outside. Forty-five minutes and a couple of coffee refills later, he stood, stretched, and began gathering up his things.

He was just about to head out the door for his appointment when he noticed the copy of the day's local *Press and Sun Bulletin* that someone had left folded across a table behind him. His photo was on the front page. It was a dated image, back when he had longer hair, from when he began work at the college almost fifteen years before. The headline said it all: MURDER AND RAPE CONVICTION OVERTURNED. LOCAL MAN TO BE RELEASED TODAY.

So there he was: practically a local celebrity again. Even if he did have more hard mileage on him than the old photo implied. He tried not to hover over the article, glanced around the bakery to see if anyone might have possibly made the connection. But if they did, no one seemed to show it.

He turned to go, leaving the paper where it lay.

Though he knew the building, Quentin had never actually set foot in Christine Shackleford's office. He was unsure about what to expect, but wasn't surprised by what he saw. The lobby ceiling was ornate, an impressive collection of murals ringing its circumference. There was a security desk, and a paunchy guard with an attitude who gave him the stern once-over and asked him if he needed any help.

"Got an appointment with a lawyer, Christine Shackleford."

The guard nodded, pointed to a clipboard on the counter. "Sign in here. Fourth floor. Elevators to your right." He flipped a visitor's badge with a clip-on attachment onto the counter as well.

Quentin signed the sheet, picked up the badge, and climbed into the elevator alone. It reeked of some kind of floor polish. He pushed the button and waited for the door to close.

He hadn't wanted to think about it anymore, but his mind drifted to the possibility of the settlement money as the elevator rose.

"Don't be some dumb nigga, let them take you for a fool," Antwone, who worked laundry detail with him, had said to him the week before, when they were folding towels.

"Hey, I'll tell you what a real fool is," he said. "Anyone who gets a bunch of money in a hurry and lets it spoil them. Like some of those big lottery winners you read about."

He could still see Antwone's big grin. "Could come and let it spoil me all it want."

To hear Shackleford tell it, the money was almost there for the taking. But even she, at times, showed some wariness. Like Quentin, she'd obviously seen her share of winners and losers come down the pike and knew that money in the wrong hands was worse than no money at all.

The elevator doors swished open again. He found himself in the middle of an empty corridor, doors on ether side. After some searching, he found a glass door with her name stenciled on it at the end of the hall. An attractive, dark-skinned woman with a nice smile looked up from behind a reception table when he entered. "You must be Quentin Price."

"I am."

"I'm Sierra Lathrop, Ms. Shackleford's new assistant. I've typed up the latest briefs and correspondence related to your case."

He nodded. "Nice to meet you."

She extended her bare-sleeved arm across the counter. He set down his bag and took her hand and shook it. Man, she was fine. Her fingers were slender and cool to the touch.

"Ms. Shackleford's on the phone at the moment, but she ought to be done in just a couple of minutes. Can I get you something to drink, some tea or coffee?"

"No thanks. Just spent the last hour down at the coffee shop."

"Ms. Shackleford felt terrible about not being able to come up to Auburn to meet you. Did everything go all right?"

Looking at the woman and seeing no big ring on her finger, he found himself wishing he'd taken up his lawyer on her offer to send someone from her office. "Everything was fine."

"We're in the middle of another court battle. Our client's being charged with felony assault and battery on her husband, if you can believe that. He's still a student at the university, been working on his PhD for forever, while the client's been supporting both him and their child. It's a real mess."

"Sounds like it."

"You're our real star though. I've haven't been here all that long, but I've never seen Ms. Shackleford so thrilled with a court action as when she got word of the judge's decision in your case."

"Only wish it had happened a long time ago."

"I'm sure. You see the article about you in the paper this morning?"

"I had a glance at it."

"That old picture doesn't do you justice."

There was something in her eyes. He'd been away from women so long, he didn't know he could still respond to it. "Maybe I'm like wine, getting better with age."

"Kind of makes you wonder how many other people there are out there like you, serving time for crimes they didn't commit."

He nodded, said nothing. He didn't think any of them were among the other cons at Auburn he had gotten to know. Most didn't believe he was really innocent either, even after word spread about his pending release. He'd bucked the system and beaten the man, that was all. There were only two realities in stir: inside and out. Only the where counted. No one gave much credence to the whats and whys.

"Oh, my gosh, you made it." Christine Shackleford burst into the room, her normally stern face beaming. "I was afraid you were going to be stuck on the bus for hours and wouldn't make it back until this afternoon. I still don't know why you wouldn't let me send Sierra after you."

"Kind of wish I had," he said, nodding at the younger woman, who smiled back. "But I caught some luck and hitched another ride."

Shackleford clutched his arm as she shook his hand. "Luck must be shining down on you from all over, Quentin."

"I guess you could say that."

"Why don't you leave your bag out here. Come on in to my office. We've got a lot to talk about."

He began to follow her through the door to her office. Glancing back over his shoulder, he thought he saw Sierra giving him that look again.

The lawyer turned to her assistant. "Sierra, please hold any calls, unless it's Bill Morton about the Druckenmuller case."

"Of course, Ms. Shackleford."

They entered a small but stylish office, with a view of the

river and the courthouse. Shackleford was into plants apparently. There must have been close to a dozen of them, none of which Quentin could name, in colorful planters lining the bookshelves and the windowsill, even one gargantuan palm-like specimen filling a huge floor pot by the door.

"Welcome to my jungle," she said.

"It's nice."

"Have a seat." She gestured toward a soft-looking wingback chair set at an angle to the desk so that her clients could best enjoy the view. Quentin did and immediately noted the stacks of manila folders, law books, and other papers crowding her work space.

"Sorry about the mess." She sat down behind her desk. "As usual, I'm up to my eyeballs with work. But you, my friend, are worth more than all the lines of bullshit—excuse the expression—those in my chosen profession have ever churned out."

He almost smiled. Her self-deprecating honesty was one of the things he'd liked about her from the start.

"You must be feeling like you've gotten a new lease on life."

"I hope so," he said. "I feel lucky just to be sitting here."

"We've come quite a ways together, haven't we?"

"You could say that." Another Auburn inmate had given him Christine Shackleford's name. It was she who had gotten the ball rolling for the appeal. She who, working with the innocence project attorneys, had found out about the DNA evidence that had bought Quentin his freedom. She who had agreed to work pro bono up until now and who deserved some sort of payout. He might decide to sue the county and the state just for her sake.

"The truth is," she said, "I don't put my faith in luck. I put it in justice, and at least you're finally starting to get a measure of that."

"Thanks to you."

She brushed him off with a wave of her hand. "The question is, where do we go from here. Not many people ever get the chance to hold the government's feet to the fire like you have."

"I suppose."

She looked him over for a moment. "You know I'm no money grubber, Quentin."

"I know."

"I said when we started this whole appeals process the objective was to see the right thing done and to see your conviction overturned. Well, we've done that. But shouldn't the state also be held accountable for keeping you locked up these past ten years?"

He shrugged, then nodded with a frown.

She leaned forward, put on the reading glasses she wore hanging from a chain around her neck, and reached across the desk to one of the stack of folders. She pulled the top one off and opened it. "I've already prepared the necessary documentation for a filing. The good news is that New York is one of the few state that provides statutory compensation for wrongful incarceration and there's no limit to the punitive damages. You understand what that means?"

"Sure. Lawyer-talk for a big pile of cash."

"Well it should be, shouldn't it? We start with the basics, which include your several years of lost wages at the college among other things. But as I said, once we get into the punitive phase, damages will amount to a lot more than that. You could be looking at a settlement that approaches seven figures."

"A million dollars."

"If not more. I recommend we ask for as much as we can, just as in any negotiation."

A million dollars. What would that mean for his life? What would that have meant for his mother's life had she still been alive?

"I don't know. I need to think about it."

"What's there to think about?"

He hesitated. "I don't know."

Shackleford took off her glasses, closed the folder, and leaned back in her chair. "Of course. May I ask, are you talking to any other attorneys about representation?"

"Oh, no. Just you . . . I just . . . I don't know, I need to think about where I'm going with my life now, and all. Have to start looking for a job."

She eyed him for a moment, as if she were considering how far to try to push him. "I understand," she said. "How are you set for cash?"

"I've got the gate money they gave me and my bus ticket and the few things in my bag. That's it."

"Well, I'm tiptoeing on an ethical border here, but I can give you the name of a bank that sometimes advances money to people in your situation. But their terms aren't the best, I'm afraid."

He considered the idea. Banks meant immediate scrutiny.

"That's okay," he said. "I'll let you know if I'm interested."

"How can I get a hold of you? Where do you plan to stay?"

"Not sure, exactly. I'm hoping to hook up with my uncle, who still lives here in town. Maybe crash at his place until I get settled."

"All right. But remember, if you decide to move forward, I think you've got a very good shot at a settlement."

"But don't we also have to show that the cops or the prosecutors did something wrong?"

Shackleford smiled. "You've been doing your homework."

Quentin shrugged. "Lot of jailhouse lawyers up at Auburn."

"Oh, I'm sure. But you let me worry about any mistakes that may have been made."

He liked the fact she wasn't trying to guarantee him anything.

She coughed into her hand and looked down at her notes. "That brings up one other thing though, Quentin, that I'm obligated to make you aware of."

"What's that?"

"I got a call yesterday from Randall Tischler."

"The DA?"

"That's right."

"I thought you said they couldn't come back at me for this."

"They can't. But Tischler would like you to voluntarily come in for further questioning. 'Just to clear up some issues as they reexamine their investigation,' he said. I told him I'd pass on the request but that I would advise against it. And I do. He's obviously on a fishing expedition. No way should you go out of your way to help him or the police."

"They still think I did it."

"So what if they do? I told Tischler in no uncertain terms they needed to start focusing their investigation elsewhere. Not that the DA's office has ever been inclined to take my advice."

He thought about Ruth Crawford's earnest plea again. "What if I decide to go?"

His lawyer pursed her lips. "I wouldn't advise you to even consider it."

"Sure. But what if you tell them I want to think about it for a little while?"

"I don't know, exactly. What's the point?" She eyed him with a hint of suspicion. "What possible good can come of it as far as you're concerned?"

"I'm not sure."

"You want them dredging up that old misdemeanor sexual misconduct conviction of yours from Queens again?"

"No."

"It doesn't matter that it was consensual and you were only eighteen and the girl was sixteen or whatever, you know. It's still on your record. And I've read all the transcripts from your case up here. Tischler managed to make you out to look like a serial rapist."

Quentin remembered it all too well. His mother had warned him about having sex before marriage, especially with a young white girl whose hotheaded father would go through the roof if he found out, which of course he did.

"My mom and I wouldn't even have ended up in this town if that hadn't happened," he said.

"No, but it did. And even though you didn't rape and kill Gwen Crawford, it helped the prosecution make it look like you did."

"Gave the local sportswriters something else to write about too."

"Yes, it did."

There were other things he couldn't tell his lawyer, other things he hadn't told anyone.

"I don't care," he said. "Go ahead and tell them no for now. But don't close the door."

"You trying to play games with the prosecutor?"

"No."

"Believe it or not, I have a good working relationship with the DA's office. I'm not about to go in there to taunt them."

"Just tell them."

"They could be looking for something else to indict you on, you know. Or some piece of additional information to convince the appellate court to order a new trial. I know I told you they can't try you again for Gwen's murder, but double jeopardy isn't entirely impenetrable."

He shrugged.

"Cooperating with them won't get you any more money. You're already holding most of the cards."

"I'd still like the chance to think it over."

"Okay." She tapped the pile of papers on her desk. "You're the boss. And you're sure now about the wrongful incarceration filing?"

"I'll probably go ahead with it, but just give me some more time to get used to the idea."

"Ten years wasn't enough?"

"You're the lawyer. Isn't there some merit in letting the powers that be twist in the wind?"

She smiled. "That depends. But I guess you know what you're doing."

"Yes."

"All right, I'll do as you ask . . . on both counts. But remember, you're playing with fire." She closed the file in front of her, replaced it on top of the stack of folders, and turned to look out the window for a few moments. "By the way, who was it you caught a ride home with from the prison?"

He followed her gaze to look at the sunlight streaming in through the window and the river and the city below.

"Nobody," he said. "Just a friend."

EIGHT

Garnell sat on the edge of the sheets in the apartment's darkened bedroom. The sound of classical music—a piano concerto, he thought—filtered in through the door, playing softly on the living room stereo down the hall. The room was warm and smelled of perfume and baby powder. Monique lay with her back to him, breastfeeding Ivy, their three-month-old little girl, who had just awakened from her midday nap.

"Okay," he said. "I know you need some time to absorb all this. But I've got to make this decision today."

"Why does it have to be you?" Monique said. "Why can't they get somebody else?"

"They probably could, but they wouldn't get someone who knew the territory as well as I do."

Monique adjusted the baby and tried to keep her voice low. "That's not it. Whoever prosecuted the case up there must have screwed up. Either they convicted the wrong guy or they left a loophole a mile wide for the defense team to drive through."

They'd done a Lexus/Nexus search of the story together while the baby had been napping. Monique had special access through her enrollment at Fordham.

"Yeah, well maybe one of your law professors can create a new course around it. In the meantime, I'm the guy stuck holding the bag here."

"The way I see it, it's lose-lose. If you confirm that the guy is guilty, all you're doing is reinforcing what everyone apparently already believes. If you find out otherwise, then you're liable to stir up a hornet's nest."

"Maybe."

She said nothing.

"I saw Price up close a couple of times, you know. I was still a kid, but I remember there was something different about the guy."

"So?"

"He was a really big deal for awhile. B-ball phenom. The way he wrecked his knee . . . most guys would have folded up and quit or come back down here and hit the streets."

"What are you saying?"

"I'm saying I'm not sure the Quentin Price I saw back then could have ever done what he was convicted of doing."

She sighed, switching the baby to the other side. The child kept right on feeding.

"Are you sure?" she asked.

"Sure enough that I'd like the chance to go up there and try to find what really might be going on."

"What if he really did it?"

Quentin drew in a deep breath through his nostrils. "Then I'll nail his ass just like every other perp I've ever had to."

"But his conviction's already been overturned."

"I can sure as heck help the DA up there find another way to jam the guy up again."

She was quiet for a moment. Then, "We're due at Jaclyn's house for Nate's birthday cookout later, you know."

"I remember."

"What am I supposed to tell them?"

"Tell them you're married to superman or something. I don't know."

She was silent again for a moment, but he could see the side of her cheek rise in a half smile. He lay down on the bed gently so as not to disturb the baby, spooned up behind his wife and ran a finger through her dark hair.

NINE

At the Greyhound station on Chenango Street, all Quentin received in exchange for his unused voucher was a refund on the Syracuse to Binghamton portion of the trip, not the shuttle that would have taken him from Auburn to Syracuse. Plus, good old Greyhound assessed a fifteen-dollar cancellation fee on the ticket, so that the net cash in Quentin's pocket came out to only eight dollars and fifty-four cents—barely enough to have paid for his breakfast.

This for a guy whose lawyer was angling to make a rich man.

Whatever, he would put it to good use.

He deposited a dollar to stow his bag in a locker at the bus terminal and walked the two and a half blocks down to the junction on Hawley Street to catch a white, blue, and yellow BC Transit bus out to Endicott. Like the carousel ponies, things hadn't really changed much downtown in the time he'd been away. His mother's old apartment building still looked the same. He thought of stopping by just for old time's sake, maybe checking out her floor to see if any of her old neighbors were still there. But he didn't want to cause a stir or start any rumors flying. Not yet, at any rate.

On the ride out to Endicott, he had the bus mostly to himself. He caught the driver, a man with dark hair and no neck, glancing at him on several occasions. By the time they reached his stop at the Friendly's on Main Street, he was glad to be rid of the man.

The walk to Roundtop Park was pleasant enough. A quiet neighborhood. An old man mowing the grass. He looked for signs that anything might have changed—new construction, whatever—but it was mostly as he remembered it.

The park itself rose to over twelve hundred feet above the city and the brownish gray water of the Susquehanna snaking into the distance below. There was a newly remodeled picnic area at the summit, but that didn't really concern him.

He walked the curving entrance road for a bit, then cut off into the trees, following a rough path along the slope. Except for a lone jogger farther down the hill, no one else seemed to be using the park at this hour.

The trees had grown some, but he had committed these woods to memory, going over it nearly every night in his cell. The trail soon merged with another larger, better groomed one, but Quentin veered off, sticking to the older, now almost overgrown path. After another hundred and fifty yards or so, he came to a large rock outcropping.

Okay. Here was the spot.

He looked down through the forest canopy at the city and all around him, making sure that he couldn't be seen. Then he turned and climbed uphill from the trail. He began counting his steps as he grabbed saplings and smaller tree trunks to support himself on the steep hill.

And there it was at last: the remains of the stone wall, even more weathered and moss covered but still the landmark he remembered.

He glanced around him one final time. Searched for and found a sturdy enough branch to poke at the dirt. He squatted down and began probing with the piece of wood. In less than a minute he'd located the metal box, buried beneath the weeds.

"All right. Let's see what you've got."

The day was growing warmer. Quentin's suit, while it made

him look respectable, wasn't made for traipsing around Round-top Park or digging in the dirt. He took off his jacket and hung it on a nearby branch. He began scraping with the blunt end of the stick and soon had freed the entire box.

It was an old file container, made for 8×10 index cards. Its beige enamel surface was speckled with rust, but it was in better condition than he'd feared. He pushed on the latch and pried open the lid.

He smiled.

Ten years and it was still all there: more than three thousand dollars, in hundred and fifties, wrapped in paper towels inside an airtight plastic bag. They smelled musty, but the bills were still basically dry.

He fished a coin from his pocket and used it to pry along the edge of the floor of the box, the false bottom he'd carefully cut from a second discarded file box. It popped up. Inside the shallow compartment was another plastic bag, this one containing the photos. Speckled some by time but still mostly intact. He replaced these and refit the bottom into the box.

He stuffed the money in his jacket pocket, then reburied the box, covering it up with dirt and moss and weeds again as best he could. After wiping his hands off with his handkerchief, he slipped his coat on, headed back down to the trail, and made his way out of the park, still wary but feeling more sure of himself.

They were waiting for him back at the bus terminal: a young woman with a handheld tape recorder and notepad, and a short, middle-aged man with a goatee carrying an oversized Nikon digital camera. They approached him as he pulled his bag from the locker.

"You're Quentin Price, aren't you?"

The reporter couldn't have been more than twenty-five. She

had anxious stringer written all over her.

"I am. Who are you?"

"Kelly Miller from the *News & Record*. I'm working on another article about you."

She extended her arm to shake his hand, but he ignored it and continued pulling his bag from the locker. "Good for you."

"If you have a few moments, I'd like to ask you some questions. You know, to get your side of the story in print. It isn't every day someone like you gets let out of prison."

"It isn't every day I get reporters bothering me either. I don't have a few moments, and even if I did, I'm not interested in helping you. Sorry."

The man with the camera raised it to his eye and began clicking a few shots.

Quentin thrust his hand at the lens. "Hey. I said I'm not interested. You understand?"

The photographer stopped shooting and lowered the camera. "Okay. Just trying to do my job here."

"Mr. Price," the woman said. "I understand your reluctance to want to speak to the press after all that's happened. But we're not out to paint an unflattering portrait. We just want our readers to get a chance to understand how such an injustice might have occurred."

"Lady, if anybody knew that, we wouldn't be having this conversation, would we?" He pulled the bag up over his shoulder, turned, and headed for the door.

"But don't you feel wronged by all this?"

He kept going.

"Are you planning to sue the city, the state?"

He still kept going.

"Don't you think it's odd when the police say that they don't have any other suspects at this time?"

He pushed out through the glass door of the bus station, didn't look back.

Ten

Corcoran's Brewery Restaurant near Government Plaza in Binghamton was one of the few decent places left to eat downtown.
Aged wooden beams ran lengthwise across the ceiling. The lighting was dim and the furnishings seemed to soak up conversation.

By this hour in the evening, the tables and booths were usually filled with cops, lawyers, and others who worked in and
around the courthouse. Jack Crawford shook the two detectives'
hands, slid into a booth across from them, and ordered a beer.

"You've trimmed a few pounds since the last time we laid
eyes on you," George Hollister, the bigger and older of the two,
said.

"Still working out at the gym," Jack said.

The other detective, Sean King, said, "The PI gig must be
good for your health as well as your pocketbook."

"Sometimes."

His beer arrived in an icy mug. He clicked glasses with the
two, who'd obviously had a head start and were almost through
theirs.

"Some day, huh, Jack?" Hollister said.

"Nothing to celebrate."

"I'll say. We put the right people down, only to have them
pop back up again like weeds."

"Not the first time."

"No. But most cons are lucky enough not to have Jack Crawford dogging their ass."

Jack nodded and glanced beyond the bar toward the street outside where the light was beginning to turn to azure.

"You know," Hollister said, "when I got your call, the first thing I thought was, this just makes sense. Hell with everything else. For once, here's something that makes real sense."

"Long as we all just do our jobs," Jack said.

Hollister bobbed his head then shifted his eyes around the restaurant for a moment.

"What's the DA saying?" Jack asked.

"Gloves off, but we're going to have to be real careful," King said. "Everything is years old now and if we screw up, Price's attorney will be on us like a fly on shit."

"So what do you think? He had an accomplice?"

"I don't know, but something may be going down even now," Hollister said.

Jack felt his heart began to race a little. "Oh? That quick, huh?"

"I didn't think this would happen, but we got lucky right out of the chute. Tailed him when he took a bus to Endicott this afternoon, and on foot to a place called Roundtop Park."

"What was he doing over there?"

"We lost him for a little bit when he went off the trail, but we picked him again when he came out of the woods. Figured whatever it was must be important, so we let him go on his merry way and checked it out. Spent a couple of hours searching, but we finally found some signs of him digging. And we came up with this."

Hollister reached down next to him on the bench seat, pulled out a paper shopping bag, and set it on the table. Jack peered inside. It was a rusted metal file box with a broken latch, the kind a kid might use under his bed at his home. And it was empty.

He didn't waste any more time looking at it; he lifted the bag off the table and set it on the booth seat next to him.

"What do you think was inside?"

Hollister shrugged. "Drugs? Money? Who knows? Whatever it was, it could be additional evidence and now he's got it with him."

"I knew it," Jack said. Price was dirty, even if it hadn't been his semen they found. He felt events beginning to spin forward, gaining new momentum. What could they do with this information? Probably not much. Not yet, anyway.

"We're going to stay all over this, needless to say."

"Any other angles?"

"Nothing solid yet, but we're working on a couple."

"If you can't get him for killing Gwen, what else can you get him for?"

"There may have been additional crimes. If it's there, we're going to find it."

Jack appreciated the sentiment, but he knew Hollister was blowing smoke. Back when he'd been working the street in Syracuse, he'd taken a lot of heat for bucking the system. It was one of the reasons he'd gotten out. Working on his own—besides being a lot more lucrative—allowed him to skirt up a little closer to the edge now and then.

"Sounds like you've made a promising start," he said without enthusiasm.

Hollister shot him a look. "Don't go running some kind of mental game on us, Jack. We've known you now for what, almost eleven years?"

"Ever since the trial."

"Exactly. So you know these things may take some time."

"Time."

"I don't like it any better than you, but if you go off the reservation, you could find yourself fucking this thing up for everyone, and that sure as hell ain't going to do the memory of your daughter any good."

He nodded. New photos she might have taken could have been hanging again in that gallery a few blocks from here. Where was the place? Maybe he'd take a run by there after he left these two just to refresh his memory. He took another sip of his beer.

"There's something else," King said.

"Yeah? What's that?"

King looked at his older partner. "The captain talked to the DA," Hollister said. "Apparently their hands are tied. The folks up in Albany have ordered an outside investigator to come in here and take a look at things, see if he can help us out."

"What? Who?"

"Some NYPD homicide hotshot," King said.

This was not good news. Other players meant more potential problems. "That doesn't sound too hopeful."

"At least it's not the Feds trying to shut us out," Hollister said.

"When's he supposed to get here?"

"Tomorrow. Monday at the latest. The DA's also floated a request to Price's attorney, asking if Price would be willing to come in for further questioning. Not that anyone really expects him to."

"All right." Jack had drained about three quarters of his mug. He didn't want to drink any more on an empty stomach. "You guys will keep me informed, right?"

"Every step of the way."

"I really appreciate it."

Darkness was gathering rapidly outside. He had at least an hour's drive ahead of him to get back to Syracuse, not counting swinging by the art gallery or the stop he'd make along the way to grab some fast food for dinner. He felt a little better just being here, hearing the news about Price's suspicious activities, knowing the investigation was ramping up again, having Hollister and King on the inside to keep him informed. But he was still uneasy.

"We've got to shove off," Hollister said.

"Me too. The beers are on me." Jack was already whipping out his billfold.

"We'll call you in a day or two, unless something else comes up between now and then."

"Fair enough."

"Go home, have a nice dinner, and get some sleep, Jack. Don't worry. We're in motion over this."

Jack nodded. They'd better be. He figured he'd give them forty-eight hours.

ELEVEN

Fog muddied the Chenango Valley as Garnell drove down the hill into Binghamton. He switched off the cruise control on the unmarked Caprice and rubbed his eyes. US 17, skirting the edge of the Catskills all the way up from Middletown, was a tiring road to navigate, especially before the sun was up, but he'd wanted to make an early start of it.

A trip down memory lane. His father had worked at the IBM plant in Endicott for years, helping to build the Model 4300 processors that had been Big Blue's mainstay for more than a generation. Binghamton had grown up as a company town—first with shoe manufacturer Endicott Johnson and then, starting in 1914, by a hard-charging former National Cash Register salesman named Thomas Watson, who moved to town to run Computing-Tabulating-Recording Co. and eventually transformed it into the enterprise that would come to be known as IBM.

Tischler, the Broome County DA, had promised to meet Garnell at the district attorney's office downtown at eight before heading to church. Later on, Garnell was to meet with the detectives who had originally worked the Price case, both of whom were still on the job. He wasn't exactly expecting a hearty welcome in either case.

He punched in the pass code he'd been given and drove into the empty parking garage behind the old Press building downtown. The only other vehicle parked there at the moment was a gray Ford Explorer that must have belonged to the DA.

A tall man in a handsome black suit was waiting between the buildings. The man came over to where he was pushing open his door.

"You must be Detective Harris."

"That would be me."

He extended his hand. "Randall Tischler."

The DA had heavy brows and bulldog eyes that protruded from a forehead made more prominent by a receding head of graying hair. The line of his mouth curved slightly, as if the whole of his face were shifted slightly off center. Garnell pegged him at maybe late fifties early sixties. Athletic—probably a tennis player.

"Sorry we had to meet so early," he said. "Not much traffic getting out of the city at four o'clock on a Sunday morning."

"No, no. That's just fine. I appreciate your initiative in coming so soon. Let's head on in."

Garnell locked his car with the remote, and the DA led him through a covered walkway in the alley around to the street side of the building.

They went in through the front door. The old Press building had once housed the city newspaper. Someone had done paintings on the walls depicting its rich history. They climbed into the elevator together.

"Bollinger tells me you're a Broome County native."

"Born and raised. Graduated BU. My dad was an IBMer."

"Good for him. Wish we still had a few thousand more of those jobs. But your dad's probably told you all about the cutbacks."

"Just about every other time we talk. When he's not railing about his pension."

Tischler gave him an obligatory smile. "Where's he live now?"

"South Carolina. Plays golf every day."

"I'll bet."

Garnell's dad was proud of him too, he knew, proud of his shield and his rapid rise to detective, although when he told the old man about some of the cases he had to deal with, the elder Harris would just shake his head and sigh.

The elevator doors opened and he followed the DA into a reception area and office.

"I also hear you're quite the superstar down there in the city."

"Really?"

"You and your partner have one of the best solve rates on the force."

"We've had a lot of help."

"Yes, well, as I'm sure you know from having grown up here, our homicides, thankfully, are a lot fewer and far between. Work many cold cases like this one?"

"Not really."

The DA led the way into a small conference room with a computer and a workstation. He beckoned Garnell to one of the hardback chairs around a table, upon which sat four size-able cardboard boxes.

"Come on," the man said, "let's pull some of these files and get you started. Sorry I can't stick around."

"Were you the original prosecutor on the Price case?" Garnell asked.

"That's right."

"Any changes in your thinking about it now?"

The DA smiled. "You mean have the DNA results caused me to think we screwed up?"

"More or less."

"Before I answer that, would you like some coffee?"

"Sure, why not?"

"Let me put a pot on for you. I'll just be a minute."

He disappeared through the office door and Garnell was left to stare at the boxes on the desk. They had little labels on their corners—the typed letters read QUENTIN PRICE PROSECU-TION along with stamped dates.

Here was the collected record of a man's wrongs. Either a paper trail of justice served or the progressive deconstruction of an innocent person's life. The depositions, motions, briefs, arguments and counterarguments, witness lists, presentation of evidence—it all amounted to a calculated assault on a sometimes fragile fortress: the presumption of innocence. At least, as far as Garnell was concerned, the system got it right the vast majority of the time. Was he looking at one of the times when it hadn't? A black man being railroaded? In the projects down home, some of the bangers on the street called him U.T. Five-O, Uncle Tom cop; he'd grown use to the insults. What would they call him back here in Binghamton?

The single window in the room looked down on the street and across to the courthouse. Vertical blinds obscured the view. An air conditioner kicked on somewhere and a puff of cool air settled around his shoulders. The top box closest to him was already open. He stood to peer inside when he heard Tischler's steps returning from down the hall. He sat back down.

"Coffee should be ready shortly," Tischler said, appearing through the doorway.

"I appreciate it."

"Now . . ." Tischler cleared his throat and took a chair beside him. "You wanted to know if I have any second thoughts about prosecuting Price."

"That's right."

"The answer is both yes and no." He patted one of the boxes. "As you'll see, the case is otherwise pretty substantial. We have several witnesses who saw Price talking to the girl the night she disappeared. We found pieces of the rope used to bind her in his garage, even a receipt from Home Depot where he bought it. The plain fact is Price is still guilty as he ever was, as far as I'm concerned."

"But—"

"I know what you're going to say. We should've shared everything we had with the defense, including the old semen, even if the medical examiner hadn't considered it significant. It was a gross oversight. I take full responsibility for the error."

"Any clue whose semen it was then?"

"That," Tischler said, "would be the question of the moment, wouldn't it? No match from either the state or FBI database of prior offenders."

"How'd the city pick up the case if the murder took place out in Hamlick?"

"Her body was found near the railroad yard in the city."

"That where she was killed?"

"Near as we can tell."

"And she was missing nearly a week before the body was found?"

"Yes."

"So he gets her in the car and drives all the way over here from Hamlick. Why?"

"Who knows? Maybe she went willingly."

"No, I mean, why bring her here?"

He shrugged. "Any number of reasons."

"So basically what we've got is new questions on a cold case."

"Frigid is more like it."

"If I bring you something new, you're going to consider it?"

"I suppose I have to."

"You aren't going to mind me getting in your hair and poking around?"

Tischler offered him an even stare. "Bollinger and his people in Albany want you here. What I might mind is irrelevant."

"What about the detectives who worked the case?"

"Hollister and King. Yes, you're meeting with them later, aren't you?"

"That's right."

"I can't vouch for how they're going to feel about the situation."

Which meant they were just as pissed off as Tischler appeared to be, once you scratched beneath the surface. Great.

"You think Price could have had an accomplice with the rape? That would explain the DNA."

"Nah. There was a big party going on that night at the college. I'd say it's more likely Ms. Crawford got it on with some other guy before Price got hold of her."

"And that person's never come forward?"

Tischler put his hands on his desk. "Would you?"

He thought about it. "Maybe not. Especially if I were the real murderer."

Tischler ignored the suggestion. "I've also contacted Price's lawyer to ask if he'll volunteer to come in for further questioning. But I wouldn't count on it. His attorney's too smart for that."

"So why am I really here, Mr. Tischler?"

The DA looked at him evenly for a moment or two. "Who knows? Maybe Albany's looking for a rubber stamp on our office's conclusions."

"Or to solidify the state's position if Price sues for wrongful incarceration. If I think he's still guilty too, that strengthens your case for having held back the semen evidence."

"There is that, yes. Doesn't let me off the hook though, if it comes down to it."

"Your job on the line?"

"Maybe so. I hope not." The DA looked at his watch. "Look, I'm sorry, I've got to run." The man patted the top of one of the boxes again. "It's all here. Take all the time you'd like. Just be sure the door locks behind you when you're through."

"Can I take these boxes back to my hotel?"

"We've got copies of everything. I don't see why not. As long as you know you're responsible for them. Where are you staying, by the way?"

"Holiday Inn."

"We'll know where we can find you then."

"Thanks again."

"Oh, and one other thing. You did know about Gwen Crawford's father, didn't you?"

"No. What about him?"

"Name is Jack Crawford. He's from Syracuse. Divorced from Gwen Crawford's mother. Works as a private investigator, but back then he was a cop."

"You mean when his daughter was killed?"

"That's right," the DA said. "Gwen Crawford was one of our own."

TWELVE

Garnell awoke from a sound sleep eight hours later, manila folders and papers spread out all around him on the hotel bed. Outside it had begun to rain. Through the opening in the curtains, he watched the water piling up in puddles around the storm drains in the parking lot.

He smacked his lips. His mouth was filled with the pasty aftertaste of the delivery pepperoni pizza he had downed for lunch. He glanced at the clock. Almost time to go meet Detectives Hollister and King. He sat up, stretched, and yawned.

Where had the day gone?

Nowhere interesting, that was for sure. The reams of material in the boxes—autopsy reports, crime scene photos, witness statements—almost all of it pointed to Price's guilt.

Okay, there were a few phone log messages that someone might have done a better job following up on. And of course there was the reasonable doubt introduced by someone else's DNA being found on the victim. But in the end, the record forced him to agree with the DA. Why had they let this guy free?

Trust some zealous defense attorney out there to find the loophole.

He found himself wanting to talk with Price though, if nothing else to confirm that the man was indeed a murderer and a rapist, to try to understand what had led him from such promise to such pain.

He sprang from the bed and stripped off his clothes. A hot shower revitalized him and ten minutes later he was heading out through the hotel lobby into the rain.

It was a short drive out to Vestal. King and Hollister had agreed to meet him at the Denny's across from the university. By the time he pulled in to the restaurant, the rain had tapered to a drizzle. He slid into a booth by himself and asked for an ice water with lemon. No sign of anyone resembling his image of Hollister or King. He hadn't been seated too long though when two men came in through the door and made a beeline for his table. Maybe a well-dressed black man in Binghamton stood out. Either that or they must have made his Caprice parked in the lot.

The bigger of the two spoke first. "Detective Harris?"

"That's me."

They introduced themselves. He stood from the booth and they all shook hands. Of the pair, Hollister was clearly in command, but Garnell sensed a restless urgency in his younger partner.

"You're a long way from home," King said after the waitress gathered up their menus and flitted away.

"Not exactly," Garnell said. "I grew up around here."

"That a fact?" Hollister said.

He gave them the particulars.

Hollister nodded, apparently impressed. "You must know then we don't see murders like the Gwen Crawford case every day."

He nodded.

"But we think we do a pretty good job."

He nodded again, but that remained to be seen.

"What kind of crime are you seeing around here these days?" Garnell asked.

Hollister shrugged. "Oh, you know . . . like a lot of other places, we're seeing more meth."

"Folks seem to be cooking up the stuff everywhere."

"White trash cocaine," King said.

"You must remember from growing up around here. What you've basically got with us is a pretty safe place to live. Way below the national averages in just about every category of violent and nonviolent crime."

"Not like all the shit you get to deal with, huh, Harris?" King said.

Garnell didn't take the bait. "You two sound like you're running for office."

"Christ." Hollister snickered. "That'll be the day."

"You gonna visit the Crawford crime scene, reinterview all the witnesses, that sort of thing?" King asked Garnell, focusing his attention back on the matter at hand.

"I don't know yet. I spent all day reading through the DA's files. Looks like you people had a pretty solid case."

"Damned straight, we did."

"No other physical evidence, besides the rope, to link Price to the crime scene though?"

"No," Hollister said, "but what else did we need? He was seen in conversation with her that night and had no good alibi. He had the motive."

"Which was again?"

"Simple. He wanted a romance or at least sex. Gwen Crawford didn't. He pushed too far and things got out of hand. Price had a prior statutory rape record, you know."

"Yeah, I read that. It was consensual though—sexual misconduct. Still . . . crime of passion, she does something that sets him off. Why did he have the rope with him?"

"What do you mean?"

"The rope was found in his garage along with a receipt. It must have been in his car that night. Suggests premeditation."

"Price drove an old pickup. He had a bunch of other junk in

the back of it. We figure he cut off a length and was carrying it around with him for some other purpose. It happened to be handy."

"Nothing else found in the truck though. No blood, fibers, anything."

"Right. Nothing conclusive."

"Didn't that bother you?"

Hollister stared at him for a moment. "Not enough to discount all the rest of the evidence."

The waitress brought their food, a cheeseburger and fries for King, chicken sandwich with potato chips for Hollister, and a fish sandwich for Garnell. They ate in silence for a few moments.

"What do you think's got the deputy attorney general interested in this case anyway?" King said between bites.

"Politics," Garnell said flatly. "And money, probably. What else?"

"You got that right," Hollister said. "Word is Price's lawyer plans to sue the state for a cool couple of mil. Probably get it too."

"I met with the DA earlier when I picked up the files," Garnell said.

"Tischler?"

"Yeah. His butt in the sling over this case?"

"Probably," Hollister said. "Ours too."

"He told me he's asked Price to come in for further questioning."

"Right. Fat chance. The guy's probably planning to laugh all the way to the bank."

"The press been sniffing around at all?"

"Yeah, but we aren't about to talk to them. Tischler's office put out an official press release, the usual bullshit, once we got word Price's conviction had been vacated."

"Just for the record, I didn't know when I agreed to come up here that Gwen Crawford was the daughter of a cop."

Hollister glanced at his partner. "Okay."

"You must have talked to the father some during the investigation."

"That's right."

"I understand he's a private investigator now."

Another glance, a shrug. "So I hear."

"You think he knows anything that might help us?"

"I doubt it. If he did, we'd probably have it by now."

Garnell plucked the last of his chips from his plate and held it in front of his mouth. "Just wondering. That's all."

"You want to take a look at the spot where the body was found?" King said. "I mean, for what it's worth now that so much time has passed."

"Maybe."

"It's down between the river and the railroad yard in East Binghamton. Hasn't changed all that much, judging from the last time I passed by there. We could meet you out there in the morning in the better light."

"The ME determined it was the crime scene, right?"

"Yeah," Hollister said. "At first, we thought the body might've been just dumped there, but the scene told a different story."

"Guess I ought to have a look then," he said. "How far is it from the campus where she disappeared?"

"Maybe eight, ten miles."

"Close enough to die for," King said.

According to the files, Quentin Price had only one living relative left in the Binghamton area: his uncle, Nelson Root. Before they parted ways, Garnell had set up a time to go visit the crime scene with Hollister and King the next morning, but there was still some light left in the day. So what if the prosecutor didn't expect Price to voluntarily come in for questioning? That didn't mean Garnell couldn't give it a shot. He eased his car along Front Street toward the uncle's neighborhood.

Not the nicest area of town, not the worst. Mixed residential and commercial, bungalows and ranches, mostly well cared for. He thought about how he would introduce himself to Price, played through the potential conversation. The man was bound to be wary of cops. The man could have also decided to move in somewhere else.

Unfortunately, today was not going to be the day to find out. Root's place looked dark and deserted as he pulled up. Or was it? He noticed a piece of paper with writing on it taped to the door.

He pulled in to the curb, shut down the engine, and climbed out. He bounded onto the porch of the house as if he belonged there and quickly scanned the paper. It was from Price's uncle, addressed to Price. Which meant Price was still elsewhere.

He walked back and climbed in his car.

THIRTEEN

Nights were always the worst.

Ruth lay beneath her covers in the stillness of her room, the window air conditioning turned on low. She'd only had a couple of drinks after coming home from work, the gin leaving her stomach with the pleasing warmth she needed. Today had been far better than yesterday, a day when she could crawl into a hot shower, pour strong coffee into her, and drive the short distance to the restaurant where her shift began at noon.

The church crowd descended on the place soon thereafter as they always did, in their dresses and sports coats and ties, kids running everywhere, the parents sometimes laughing, sometimes more somber, depending perhaps on the sermons they'd just heard. Every table filled by twelve thirty, with Ruth and the other waitresses scurrying to keep up, the kitchen on overdrive cooking up batches of pancakes, eggs, and sausages for Sunday brunch. A couple of them said nice things to her, said they'd seen the newspaper article about Price and that they were praying for her, which was sweet. But apart from a passing reference one of the cooks made regarding the news story, none of her coworkers mentioned anything about Gwen. She could forget for a while.

But here with the sound of the summer crickets outside and the shallow emptiness of the night descending, she felt herself drifting into half sleep and the realm of dreams her dead daughter too often inhabited.

Tonight Gwen was only three years old—her hair in brown pigtails, riding her tricycle with a proud, determined look on her face. Her trike was bright pink with white tires and pedals, pink and white streamers sprouting from the handlebars. Gwen was going too fast. She hit a break in the sidewalk and was falling forward off the trike. Ruth was running after her, reaching out to catch her, never quite catching up, powerless to help.

She woke in a sweat beneath the blankets. Glanced up at the dimly lit display of her radio's digital alarm clock. Three a.m.

She climbed out of bed and slipped on her bathrobe. Went to her closet, slid open the door, and pulled a large cardboard box from inside. Kneeling on the floor, she opened the lid and began to rifle through the box's contents, a set of file folders neatly organized. She finally found what she was looking for: a thin manila folder containing a handful of notes and business cards.

She pulled the card of the Binghamton Police Bureau detective from the stack.

FOURTEEN

"Telephone call."

Quentin awoke with a start. "Huh?"

The man at the Salvation Army shelter was knocking on the wall outside his cubicle, his gravelly voice making Quentin think for a moment he was back in prison. Quentin struggled off the cot and pushed aside the curtain that served as a door.

"Phone's for you." The bespectacled shelter manager held out a dusty cordless phone. "Woman says she knows you."

Saturday, Quentin had spent the rest of the day in and around Otsiningo Park, wandering along the river, shouldering his bag of belongings. He wanted to clear his mind, feel the open air on his skin again, breathe in the essence of a spring day with the freedom to just sit and think or do nothing. He was committed to beginning something new. He wasn't sure exactly what it was.

He'd even taken some time to leaf briefly through his mother's Bible, noting the worn pages and the occasional marginal notes on particular passages in her careful hand.

By the time he'd finally gotten around to catching another bus out to his uncle's place, it was nearly dark. When he arrived, the place was locked up tight and he found a note taped to the door that said Nelson had had to take a trip down to Pennsylvania for a couple of days, and where was Quentin?

He'd scribbled a hasty reply, promising to return on Monday. Money in his pocket or no, he needed to keep a low profile, so he caught another bus back down here to the shelter where'd he'd been told he could find a clean dry place to sleep for a night or two.

Sunday, he'd spent the dreary afternoon moving around town, filling out applications at various stores and fast food establishments, most of whom had told him either they weren't hiring or he'd need to talk to the regular manager during the week.

He thanked the man from the shelter and put the phone to his ear.

"Quentin?"

It was Ruth Crawford.

"Oh, you again."

Right now he needed coffee, not another dose of Gwen's mother. His eyes felt like they were rimmed with sand.

"You were expecting somebody else?"

"Never mind. Why do you keep bothering me? How'd you know where I was?"

"I stopped by your uncle's place, and from the newspapers and mail stuffed in the box, it didn't look like anyone had been there in a couple of days. So, I decided to try down here."

If it was that easy to track him down, maybe he should consider spending some of his cash on a hotel room. He checked to make sure the money roll in his pocket was intact, shook the cobwebs from his head, and revisited his surroundings. A narrow, coffin-like room, with a dormitory-style window enshrouded in dark curtains. The cot looked and felt like something kept in a closet and brought out only for emergencies. Overhead, a pair of fluorescent bulbs buzzed to life as he flipped on the light switch and stared at grease-stained panel walls. The bathroom down the hall offered a single shower stall to be shared by all those forced to use the shelter. If anyone knew the kind of money he was carrying . . . He needed to get out of this place. It was too much like Auburn.

"If this is about Gwen again, I told you, I'm not your man."

"I'm not going to argue with you about that," she said. "But don't you care that the authorities apparently still believe you killed Gwen?"

"Not really. Not anymore."

"You don't want to at least try to clear your name?"

"It's already clear enough, far as I'm concerned. They can't come after me again."

Or could they? He knew better than to believe everything a lawyer told him, even a lawyer like Christine Shackleford.

"You know as well as I they'll make you a marked man, even if you sue the state and win a bunch of money. You want to live the rest of your life like that?"

"It's better than being in prison."

She said nothing. And to his surprise, he found that he was worried about her.

"No offense, ma'am. But you know what's good for you, you'll let somebody else figure out who really killed your daughter. You go and start talking to a whole bunch of people, you're looking for trouble."

"That's why I could use your help."

"What, you feel I owe you some kind of protection? You feel I owe you anything?" He heard a hardness in his voice he hadn't really intended, but there it was.

"You hungry?" she asked.

"I just woke up."

"I've been waitressing at a restaurant ever since they laid me off at the factory. Place called McGinnis's. You know it?"

"Never heard of it."

"It isn't much, more of a diner really, but the food's pretty good. I can probably stir you up a free meal, let your uncle sleep in a little longer this morning, if you want."

Now what exactly was this woman up to?

"Look. Haven't you and me been through enough already? All I wanted was a ride. Remember?"

"I know. I just thought that—"

Down the block, a street sweeper was beginning to make its noisy way toward him.

"Don't you have to go to work?" he asked.

"No. Saturday and Monday are my days off."

Uncle Nelson should be home by now. But he didn't want to pull him out of bed so early. He didn't want to have to ask the man, who moved around the house gingerly on a hand crutch, to cook for him either.

"If I eat with you, will that get you off my back?"

"I promise."

"All right," he said. "I'll go have some breakfast. But let's leave it at that."

On the curb in front of the shelter, the air felt scrubbed clean. The sun was attempting to break through low clouds as Monday morning traffic moved along the street at a brisk pace. When Ruth appeared, Bertha the tank looked every bit as unroadworthy as when she had dropped Quentin off a couple of mornings before. Ruth was still driving around on the spare tire.

"Car must have nine lives," he said, tossing his duffel over the seat and climbing in beside Ruth. She was wearing a sky blue wraparound skirt this morning along with a white blouse and a hint of eye shadow. There was something else about her eyes he hadn't noticed before. They were red-rimmed and sallow. A drunk's eyes.

She patted the dusty dashboard. "Don't listen to him, Bertha. He just got up on the wrong side of bed this morning."

"You going to get that flat tire fixed?"

"When I get time."

"You're not supposed to be driving around on the spare forever, you know. Ain't made for that."

"I know." She shrugged as if there were more important things to worry about and started off into traffic.

"At least we don't have to worry about getting stuck in the rain." He rolled his window down and let his elbow rest along the door.

"Aren't you the cheery one. What did you do all day yesterday, if you don't mind my asking?"

"Looked for work."

"Any luck?"

"Nope. It's a little hard to know what to put in that section on the application that asks if you've ever been convicted of a felony, not to mention the part that says 'most recent experience.' "

They crossed the river and drove out Vestal Avenue, stopping for a light. Puddles of rainwater from the night before still dotted the edges of storm drains and parking lots. Trees shed droplets of moisture like diamonds spitting into the breeze.

"I could put in a word for you to my boss," she said. "Seems like he's always hiring someone new, to bus tables or whatever."

He'd have to be pretty desperate to work in the same restaurant as Ruth. Who knew what he might have to put up with? Maybe he should give Christine Shackleford a call. He should have thought of that the other day. His lawyer might be able to help him find work.

"I'll think about it," was all he said.

Ruth was driving slowly again today. She glanced in the rearview mirror to check her lipstick then took her foot off the gas. A semi driver that had been bearing down on them from behind shot them a blast on his air horn before swerving around them. The big truck's wake shook the car.

"Never a cop when you really need one," he said.

She smiled. "Nice to see you haven't lost your sense of humor. Your mother always said that was one of your better qualities."

"Right. Auburn was a blast too. Better than the comedy channel."

"Well, just for your information, I spent a little time on the phone yesterday, talking to a couple of Gwen's old classmates."

"Stirring up trouble, I'll bet," he said under his breath.

"Pardon me?"

"Nothing. Good for you."

"I took a lot of notes. You never know what might be of help. A lot of them mentioned you, of course. Not all of them had heard you were getting out."

"I bet they were comforted."

"Most of them don't know what to think, I guess. If someone else killed Gwen, then it could even be one of them."

"What do you plan on doing, checking every single one of them out?"

"That won't be easy. They're scattered around the country. Most of them are married and have families. Her old roommate lives here in Endicott though. I may go try to talk with her. And Gwen's old best friend, Kristin. Remember her?"

"I remember." Kristin Brodsky. Overweight and badly in need of a seminar on how to cut down on the mascara.

"She lost seventy-five pounds and works in Washington for some federal agency or another. Married a senior Senate staffer and they have twins."

"Great. At least we know she's not the killer then."

McGinnis's occupied one corner of a busy intersection on the Vestal-Binghamton town line, a long low building with a flat roof and a brick façade. A sign out front read FOOD YOUR MOTHER WOULD APPROVE. The parking lot was nearly full of cars, vans, and trucks.

"It's always busy in the mornings and Monday's payday," Ruth said. "C'mon, you'll see what I mean about the coffee."

He hadn't realized how hungry he was. As he climbed out of her car, the smells of lilac and new grass mixed with fry-fat smoke from the building's kitchen exhaust made his mouth water. He remembered his mother's kitchen in their apartment and the savory meals she served.

"What about . . . I mean, what if someone in here recognizes me?" The last thing he needed was another newshound showing up or any undue attention. He'd earned the freedom to be anonymous.

"Don't worry," she said. "As long as you're with me, anybody knows you, they'll keep their mouths shut."

He hadn't even thought about it until now, but she was right. Being with Ruth shielded him in some ways from judgment. He was going to have to get used to being looked at as an ex-con: the sideways glances, the slightly higher pitched voices, the nervous smiles.

They circled behind the building past piles of plastic milk crates, a large emergency generator, and a rust-speckled Dumpster. He followed her through the back door. Inside, the aroma of bacon, ham, and eggs was nearly overpowering. A short hall led to the kitchen entryway, where a stocky man with white hair and a neatly trimmed beard worked with a calculator behind an old steel desk in a tiny cubicle. Stacks of papers littered the space around him. He wore a plaid shirt over khakis and an oversized pair of running shoes. Reading glasses on a chain gave him an incongruous schoolmarmish appearance.

"Well if it isn't the breath of summer herself."

"Don't you start in on me, Walter. I just came in for my check. I'm not even working today."

"I know, I know. I was just noticing how pretty you looked

this morning, Ruth Crawford." He chuckled, turning in his chair and thumbing through a stack of windowed envelopes to pull one out and hand to her. "Who's that you got with you?"

"Uh, well." Ruth cleared her throat. "You might remember him from a few years back. This is Quentin Price."

There was an uncomfortable silence. The man pulled off his glasses, letting them drop gently to his chest, and stared at them as if he were seeing a ghost. "But how'd you—?"

"You know the DNA caused them to throw out his conviction. He was just released from prison."

"You don't say."

"Quentin, this is Walt Oriskany. He owns this place."

"Pleased to meet you," Quentin said.

"Right. Of course." Oriskany stood awkwardly and shook hands with him.

"If it's okay with you, I thought I'd get him a little breakfast . . . since he's just, you know, trying to get reacclimated to civilian life and all."

Oriskany folded his arms across his chest. "Sure. I mean, okay."

"I appreciate it," Quentin told him.

"Don't mention it."

"I told him we serve the best coffee in the Southern Tier and the food's not half bad either," Ruth said.

"You better keep lying like that too, you want to keep a paycheck coming." Oriskany smiled and winked at Quentin. "Don't worry. We'll try not to poison you."

"The back corner booth still available?"

"Was last I knew."

"Thanks again, Walt."

The man nodded, sat down again, and went back to his work.

They turned to pass through the busy, steam-filled kitchen, but not without Quentin feeling Oriskany's appraising stare on the back of his neck. Yeah, there was going to be a lot to get used to. They found the empty booth just outside the swinging kitchen doors that led to the dining room.

"Maybe this wasn't such a good idea," he said. With a little money from his stash he could easily buy breakfast somewhere else.

"Don't worry about it. Walt just gets jealous of me spending time with anybody but him."

"Are you and he—?"

"Nah." She waved her hand. "But he'd like it if we were."

Their table was as private as he could ask, the last in a row along the wall of an alcove. Three of the other booths were occupied, but no one paid them any attention. They were blocked from the view of the main dining room and there was a bank of windows to the side opposite the booths. A waitress came and poured them both steaming cups of coffee and took their meal orders.

"Thanks, hon," Ruth said to the other waitress as she prepared to leave. "Looks like we're even busier than usual this morning."

"Senators are playing Bridgeport at the arena tonight, first round of the playoffs," the other woman said. "We've got a bunch of folks in from Connecticut."

"Hope they're good tippers."

"Me too."

If she knew who Quentin was, she didn't show it. Maybe she and Ruth were good enough friends that Ruth had already told her of her plan to pick up Quentin and bring him in for breakfast.

The coffee was as good as advertised. The waitress took their orders and spun off to another table.

"Hockey," Ruth said. "You ever go to any of the games?"

Quentin shook his head. "Always seemed like more of a white

man's sport."

"You should check it out sometime. You never know, you might like it."

"Maybe."

"So . . . I don't want to pry, but you already said you were looking for work. What are your plans now that you're back here in Binghamton?"

There was more than a little suggestion that he reconsider her proposal about helping her investigate Gwen's murder. He decided to ignore it. "What do you mean?"

"Do you plan to hire a lawyer to sue the state?"

"I already have a lawyer."

"You should at least make someone pay for putting you in jail for so long."

"Wouldn't really change anything except for the money."

Even with money in his pocket, he'd find some kind of work. Didn't matter whether you were in Binghamton or Biafra, there were almost always jobs waiting for those willing to do what no one else was willing to do. His mom had taught him that back in Queens when he was barely a teenager. It kept him off the streets and probably, he realized years later, saved his life.

"Maybe if the police and prosecutors had to pay up it would even get them to really try to. . . ." Her voice trailed off as if she were uncomfortable finishing the sentence.

He had to get her off this line of thinking.

"Look," he said, lowering his voice a little. "I appreciate you want to know what really happened to Gwen, but—"

"Don't you want to know yourself?"

"Yeah. But I'd like to be kept out of the process. Send me a postcard if you or the cops come up with something."

She looked a little nervous. "Of course."

"All I want to do is get settled in with a place to stay, find work, and be left alone to go about my business. That seem fair enough to you?"

"Of course." She nodded and looked out the window for a moment then back at him. "You think your uncle will let you stay with him then?"

"Yeah."

"He the only family you've got around here?"

"All I have left."

"No long list of girlfriends?"

"Listen, let's just leave the past alone."

"I guess I'm just surprised you didn't at least keep in touch with more people."

"Not much need for pen pals in the stir when you think you may be doing Buck Rogers time."

She looked confused but too polite to ask.

He sighed and folded his hands on the table. "An inmate in the Grey Bar Hilton who knows he's never coming out."

"Oh, right. I'm sorry."

He shrugged. "I'm moving on now though, aren't I? Making new friends. You want to be one, don't you? Not like you're picking me up and feeding me breakfast 'cause you want something from me, right?"

"I'm sorry, I do want to be your friend. I know it seems like I'm badgering you. It's just . . . it's just hard to let go."

He said nothing.

The waitress arrived with their steaming breakfast plates and refilled their coffees. The food smelled delicious. Quentin dug into his eggs.

He felt talked out. He wished they could just finish their meal in silence and she would take him and drop him off at his uncle's house and he would be done with her. She must have sensed what he was thinking because she didn't speak again either while they ate.

He was almost through eating when she finally broke the silence.

"I'm sorry, but I'm going to need a smoke. I'll just step out back."

"What, and leave me here by myself?"

"It'll just be for a minute or two."

"They won't let you smoke in the restaurant?"

"Not anymore. Have to take it outside."

"No problem. I'm ready to go anyway." He began to push himself out of the both. "My uncle should be getting up pretty soon. I don't care if you smoke in the car."

"Okay, but . . . I'm sorry, Quentin, but I've got a confession to make . . ."

"What?"

A panic button went off in his head. While they'd been talking and eating, he hadn't noticed that the rest of the booths in their private area in the back of the restaurant had all been vacated.

He heard a chair scrape somewhere behind him.

Turning, he saw them stroll around the corner: two men in coats and ties. One of them was grim-faced, the other smiling. Detectives George Hollister and Sean King. Ghosts from his dreams.

FIFTEEN

The morning Quentin was arrested for murder, a squad of uniformed officers drove up in front of the house he was renting in Johnson City in blue and white cruisers. They were followed by Detectives Hollister and King in an unmarked car. Before he realized what was happening, they had read him his rights, cuffed him, and bundled him into a cruiser, where he sat while uniforms and crime scene types invaded the place, searching.

He tried not to think much about those things anymore. Prosecutors had believed none of his story then and neither, for that matter, had Ruth. She told the jury she had been certain Gwen was afraid of something or someone, and she wouldn't have been at all surprised if that someone had been Quentin Price.

"What the hell is this?" He glared at Ruth.

She gave an embarrassed shrug.

Should have known better. He started to slide from the booth.

"What's your hurry, Price? We don't bite."

Ghost number one, the smiling Sean King dragged a chair along with him in front of the booth and sat down.

He was tall and lean—not as tall as Quentin but well over six feet. His hair was flat, blond, and lifeless, same as Quentin remembered. He had a narrow pointed chin and eyes that seemed made to try to calm you. Hollister was a different story. Unlike Quentin, whose physique had grown leaner and added more muscle while in prison, the elder detective had put on at least twenty pounds since he'd last seen him, all of it in the midsection. But the man still had the same crew cut, still wore the same hangdog look.

Quentin focused on Ruth. She was fumbling for a cigarette, at the same time trying to extricate herself from the vinyl bench. "I, uh. I got to go outside to catch that smoke," she said.

Quentin shook his head. "I don't believe it."

"I'm sorry, I'll, uh, I'll be back. It'll only be a minute or two." She looked at the two detectives. "Then I'll take you, Quentin, and drop you off wherever you want to go."

"You're nothing but white trash. You can go to hell."

"Hey, that's no way to speak to a lady." Hollister moved toward Quentin.

"Leave him alone." Ruth pulled herself from the booth and stood between them with her pack and lighter in hand. "Detective Hollister, can I speak to you in the back for just a minute?"

Hollister nodded and the two of them disappeared for a moment through the swinging kitchen door.

Quentin almost followed her but figured his best move at the moment was to stay put. He sat still and stared out the window. King drummed his fingers on the chair.

"Quentin, listen. We only wanted to stop by and say hello is all. For old times' sake, you know?"

"Yeah. 'Cause we're such good homies."

Hollister came back through the door and took up position behind King.

"Anyway, you're a free man, now, aren't you?" King said. "That's all that matters when it comes right down to it. The courts have had their say."

"I'll be calling my attorney," Quentin said.

"What for?"

"I told her to tell the DA I didn't want to talk to any of you right now."

"So we hear."

All of a sudden the idea of a lawyer and a lawsuit didn't seem like such a bad plan after all. Get these cops and this crazy woman off his back at least.

Thing was, believe it or not, he'd actually liked King and Hollister back when they'd first talked to him the morning after Gwen's body was found. Even later when they'd gone deeper into his interrogation, when King had done everything but slam Quentin's head against the wall, he didn't blame them. Fact is, a part of him still believed he'd deserved it.

He'd known the moment they hit his driveway that morning that the whole affair might go down badly for him. He'd known it while waiting in his holding cell. He knew it even after talking to his original attorney, an aging friend of his mother's named Zane Fortune who occasionally defended small-time drug users and gang bangers and, it turned out later, was already dying of prostate cancer. But he hung on, convinced even during the trial that everything was going to turn out okay for him in the end. Right up until the time the jury handed down their decision and he realized the prosecutors and the police had never been his friends.

He wasn't about to suffer through a repeat performance.

"I've got nothing to say to either of you," he said.

"Well, of course you don't," King said. "I'd feel the same way if I was in your shoes."

"Be pissed, that's for sure," Hollister said.

"I'm free to walk out of here then?"

"Of course. We just wanted to say hello, like Sean said, and have a little chat with you about what kind of pickle we find ourselves in now that this ten-year-old murder investigation has been thrown wide open and back into our laps again."

He stared at them. "What do you want to talk to me for?"

"What for? Well what do you think?" Hollister said. "Ruth here is Gwen's mother. Why'd you get in the car with her the other day?"

"She offered me a ride."

"That's all?"

"Seems to me you guys should be asking why she drove all the way up to Auburn to offer me one."

The detectives said nothing.

"I've been over this with you guys a million times. Focus on somebody else. I've paid my price and that's all I have to say about it."

Hollister was staring at his fingernails. "What if . . . oh . . . what if we told you we had some new evidence that shows you were up to no good."

A pinprick of fear bubbled up inside him. What if they decided to frisk him? He fought the urge to check the wad of money, some of which he'd hidden in his bag but the rest of which he still carried in his coat pocket.

"I don't care what you say you've got. As far as I'm concerned, I'm done with this and I'm done with you."

He started to rise up from the booth, but Hollister stepped toward him and put one hand on the table, speaking in a low voice.

"You may have wiggled off the hook this time, Price, but as far as I'm concerned, you're still right in the center of this thing. I've been over all the old files two or three times now. We've even reinterviewed a couple of the old witnesses. And for the love of Christ, I just can't help but coming back to the same conclusion we came to ten years ago."

"Like I said, that's not my problem."

"No? I've got a pretty good hunch you know a lot more than you've told so far about what happened to Gwen Crawford that night ten years ago."

Quentin shook his head.

"If I was you," King said, "and I knew anything more that could help us nail down this case, anything at all, I'd want to get it all out in the open."

"You're barking up the wrong tree. I've already told you everything I know." Quentin started to rise from the booth. "It's time for me to move on."

Hollister held out his arm to block his path. "All right then, but remember this, hombre. You may have been freed by one piece of evidence. But that's all it is—just one piece."

"What are you talking about?"

"I'm talking about the fact that every cop out there has seen cases where other factors and additional evidence hold more sway. No matter what some judge says."

"It's somebody else's DNA."

"Maybe one of your buddies'."

Quentin sighed. "So you two are going to keep dogging me, is that it?"

"Afraid so."

"Maybe you should be hearing from my lawyer then."

It became quiet in the little alcove at the back of the restaurant for a few moments. Hollister looked out the window while King looked at his watch.

"All I have to ask you is this," Hollister said. "Somebody raped and killed that girl ten years ago. If it wasn't you, then who was it?"

"Like I told you back then," he said. "I have no idea."

"No idea." Hollister looked away from Quentin out at the parking lot again. "You've had a long time to think about things though, haven't you?"

"That's right."

"Hey, Sean. Ten years up in Auburn. That seem like enough

hard time for rape and murder to you?"

"Not hardly."

"Doesn't seem like enough time to me either. And even after taking those criminology classes, Mr. Wannabe cop here can't help us figure out who else might've done the deed if it wasn't him."

"You guys are treading real close to the line here," Quentin said.

The door to the kitchen swung open and Ruth swept into the room. Hollister coughed into the back of his hand and pretended not to notice her. Quentin stared at her along with King. Ruth looked calmly at the two detectives as she squeezed by King in his chair.

"All right, I've had my smoke." She bent over the booth, picked up her purse, which she'd left lying on the bench, and turned to Quentin. "You ready to go?"

King stood and spun the chair around and slid it back where he'd gotten it from, then headed back toward the entrance of the restaurant. Hollister followed, still eyeing Quentin.

"Be seeing you around, buddy, okay?" he said. "We'll be watching."

Quentin should have just walked out when he had the chance.

A minute later, he and Ruth were standing back outside alone in the lot.

"You set me up." He tried to keep his voice calm and deliberate, but it still came out as a hiss.

Ruth looked surprised. "What?"

"Don't try that. You sandbagged me with those two."

"I did no such thing. I told you I'd been talking to the police."

"Are you kidding? You knew they'd be here this morning. You practically invited them to come back and harass me."

Ruth took out a tissue and dabbed at her nose.

"Well?"

"Well, I, I just thought . . . after the other day, I mean . . . I just thought if you could see firsthand what I'm up against."

"What you're up against. What about what I'm up against?" He looked around the outside of the building, afraid to say anything else here in this place.

"You just don't understand," she said.

"I don't have to."

"Quentin, she was my only child. And to have thought all these years . . . to have never had the chance to . . . to make things okay. To never have the chance to see her again. To . . ."

Tears flooded her eyes. She began to tremble, rubbing her nose with the tissue again.

He looked away at the parking lot and through the windows at the people still eating breakfast inside.

"Your car unlocked?" he asked.

"What?"

"Are the Chrysler's doors open?"

"Yes."

"I'll go grab my bag then." He'd be lucky if his money hadn't been stolen. He started walking toward the car.

Ruth followed. "I thought I was going to—"

"I'll find myself another way to get where I need to go."

"Quentin, listen. I didn't mean to . . . You don't need to—"

Her face looked as if it were about to dissolve. He didn't know what to believe, but the last thing he needed right now was to get involved with this woman any further, especially when the cops were still out to slam him. He'd already done whatever penance he'd been due. Maybe Ruth was still trying to earn hers, but neither of them could rewrite history.

He stopped to look at her again. "I've very sorry for the loss you suffered," he said. It was the best he could do.

She stared at him. "I guess I was wrong about you then."

"Say what?"

"Didn't you care anything about what happened to Gwen? Don't you want to see justice done here?"

"You've got the cops' attention again. Let them try to get some justice for you."

"So you're just going to walk away and give up."

"Call it that if you want." He stepped to the car and jerked open one of the rear doors.

"You can make that choice now because you're free," she said.

"That's where you're wrong, lady." He started to slide his bag from the car. "The way it looks to me now, I ain't never going to be free."

Sixteen

Jack pushed away from his desk on his rolling executive chair and closed the office door so his secretary wouldn't hear the conversation. His ex-wife calling him out of the blue was bad enough, but when she told him what she'd been doing with Quentin Price, he nearly lost control.

"I didn't know what else to do, Jack. No one seems interested in taking me seriously when it comes to looking for a different killer."

"You're talking about overturning an entire investigation. Months, maybe years of work. Why should anyone take you seriously?"

"But what if Price really didn't do it? What if Gwen's killer is still out there and has gotten away with it for all these years?"

"Look, Ruth, I don't care what kind of cop TV you may have been watching, but just because Price's DNA didn't match doesn't mean he's innocent. And you say you even asked him to help you find out who the real killer is? Are you out of your mind?"

"Well, I didn't ask him that in so many words."

"You're a joke, Ruth. That's all. A joke."

"I—"

"I don't hear from you for years and this is what you decide to call me about?"

"It's not like you've ever called me either, Jack."

He glanced again at his daughter's photos on the wall. Each

time he heard Ruth's voice, he heard echoes of Gwen's: the alto pitch, the soft inflection of uncertain sophistication. Of course he hadn't called her.

"You're delusional," he said.

Silence on the line.

"You hear what I'm saying?"

"I didn't call you up to be insulted."

"I'm not trying to insult you. I'm just trying to get you to face the truth."

"What, that the man who killed our daughter is walking around free because of some lab test?"

"That would be it in a nutshell."

"I don't believe it."

He shook his head at the phone. "You think judges and the courts don't make mistakes? Ever hear of O.J.? Where you been the last twenty years?"

"I have a feeling Quentin Price is innocent, and not just because of the DNA."

"Oh, you have a feeling. That settles it then."

"What about all those cards and notes I've gotten over the years? I got one again last spring, you know. And Gwen's birthday's coming up again."

"You've talked to the cops about them, right? What do they say?"

"They still say it's nothing."

"They're right, Ruth. You're dreaming."

"If we could just talk sensibly for a change, maybe discuss some other possibilities. Maybe you and I—"

He couldn't listen anymore. "Why are you really calling me? To rub my nose in this shit again? To explain to me one more time what a neglectful father I was? Not that you were Mrs. Apple Pie Mom."

He didn't know why, but they always seemed to end up this

way. Maybe it was that echo of Gwen's ghost, guilt interlaced with a dread so deep he was afraid to even go near it.

"You haven't changed," she said.

"Thank God."

"I don't know why I even bothered to phone you."

He could feel his anger rising, a jagged edge of pain, like an internal knife working its way up from the depths of his emotions. "I'm warning you, don't screw around with this situation, Ruth. It's bad enough as it is. You'll only end up getting yourself and maybe a lot of other people hurt."

"Hurt doesn't begin to describe where I am right now, Jack," she said, "and you're no help."

Later, a once-a-week ritual for Ruth.

Cemetery in the sunlight above the river. Finding Gwen's stone by memory. Walking as if floating. Talking to the dead.

Carla had come here with her once, a day not unlike today.

"It'd be sad," Carla had said, "to let the memory of your daughter and the love I feel for my son stand between the healing I know Jesus is trying to do."

"You really believe that?" she had asked.

"Of course I do."

"I stopped believing in God the day I heard Gwen had been murdered."

"That's all right, honey. He ain't never stopped believing in you."

As she stared at Gwen's stone now, Ruth wondered. Maybe God was still out there. But if he was, he was certainly biding his time.

Seventeen

Gwen Crawford had died on an embankment of cinder and stone. Littered with shards of glass, it was backed by a narrow strip of grass flanking a little-used spur of the Canadian Pacific Railway yard in East Binghamton. The view from both the road and the tracks was blocked by a large electric utility shed and, now as when the murder had taken place, weeds and the stalks of wild plants, which explained why the body had gone undetected for so long.

Gwen had been found lying supine, her head twisted to one side. The crime scene photos were positively haunting. In them her eyes were closed, the almost innocent look on her face belying the horror of the rest of the scene. Nearly a week's worth of decomposition and the work that scavengers and insects can do had taken their toll as well. The ligature marks and bruising on her neck made it all too clear how she had died.

"You've already had a chance to look through the pictures, I assume," Hollister said. He was decked out in a three-piece suit today, clean shaven and sober looking.

Garnell nodded. "The setting doesn't look like it's really changed much."

"Nope."

Garnell was trying to imagine the girl's panic, knowing this was no lover's lane, realizing that this patch of ground, this dirt and grass, was probably the last thing she would ever see. The autopsy report had made it clear that she may have fought initially, but that after she was bound she may have been drugged. Too much time had elapsed before the body was discovered for a good sweep for trace evidence, but no such paraphernalia, residue, or link to Quentin Price was ever found at the scene. Another curiosity.

"Cause of death was strangulation?" Garnell said.

"Yes."

"And she was found by a railroad worker, right?"

"Poor guy blew chunks all over the grass. Said he'd been in Vietnam, but he'd never seen anything like it."

Garnell nodded.

"We suspected Price all along, of course, especially with so many witnesses reporting they saw the two of them talking together at the party. After finding the body and the rope, we knew we had a murder on our hands. We executed a warrant and when we found the rest of the coil of rope at Price's place, we knew we had him cold."

"Why here?" Garnell asked.

"What?"

"Why do you think Price brought her here?"

Hollister shrugged. "Didn't want to be seen so he left the college and drove her way over here, I suppose. We figured he knew about this place, living here in the city and all. He picked a good spot, too. We'd have found her sooner if it weren't for the shed and the weeds."

"How far is it from here to the house that Price was renting?"

"Three or four miles. But if you're thinking of taking a look around there too, you can forget it. The place was demolished a couple of years ago. State's running a new highway interchange through there."

"I drove the route a few times just to get the feel of it back during the investigation," King said. "The right time of night, it's only about ten minutes."

"You said at first the case was just a suspicious disappearance, right?"

"Sure."

"Were you guys watching Price during that period?"

"We had surveillance on him, yes."

"He ever drive over this way then?"

"Nope. Be nice if he had. Would have made our job even easier."

"Wouldn't have made any difference as far as the vic was concerned," Hollister said.

"No, I guess not," Garnell said.

They kicked around in the grass and stared at the spot for a few more moments.

"I don't see much lighting in the area. Must get pretty dark around here at night."

"Pitch dark. That hasn't changed much either."

"Either of you guys into trains?"

The two local detectives shook their heads.

"I was, back when I was a kid. In fact, I can remember my dad bringing me down here a couple of times to watch the locomotives work. Of course it was a much busier place back then."

"I'm amazed they're even still in business," Hollister said. "What with all the problems they've had, government subsidies and the like."

"You're thinking about the passenger business. Freight lines are thriving. Most of 'em at any rate. Still the cheapest way to ship a lot of bulk from one place to another."

Hollister smiled. "You're still into trains."

"That rail worker still around?"

"Who's that, the guy that found the body?"

"Yeah."

"I don't know. I suppose we could try to look him up. What do you want to talk to him for?"

"I don't know. Sometimes the years have a way of fine-tuning people's memories."

"If they don't fog them out first, especially in a guy his age. But what the heck, we'll see if we can run him down. Worse comes to worst, you and he can swap train stories."

"I appreciate it."

Hollister looked at his watch. "We've got other business pressing. You seen everything you wanted to see here for the time being, detective?"

Garnell bent down and scooped up a handful of cinder from along the border of the track bank.

"Yeah," he said. "I think I've seen everything there is to see here for now."

EIGHTEEN

There was no way to be certain, at least not yet. Still, Quentin could almost swear someone had been watching him from the moment he left Ruth Crawford in the parking lot of the restaurant where she worked. Paranoia? Maybe. Still, he hadn't survived Auburn for nearly ten years by ignoring his instincts.

He needed to hide his money. He didn't feel comfortable walking around with so much cash. And unless it had changed, there was only one safe place he knew. He hoisted his bag over his shoulder and caught a bus back downtown.

Half an hour later, he walked in the front entrance of the apartment building his mother had called home for the last fifteen years of her life. No mansion in the sky, but it was no roach motel either. In the lobby, a terrazzo floor and dark-paneled walls flanked a reception/security desk that was always unmanned. His mother had lived on the fifth floor, in a comfortable two-bedroom layout with a nice view of the city and the surrounding hills.

Other than an elderly man reading a newspaper who glanced up only briefly at his entrance, the lobby was empty. He stepped to the bank of elevators, pushed the UP button, and waited. If someone were watching from the street, they would have seen him get on and the elevator move upward until the lit numerals showed it reaching the fifth floor. What they wouldn't have seen was Quentin stepping off the elevator, turning to his right, and, finding the hallway empty as he had hoped, making his way to the back stairwell of the building where he hustled down six flights of stairs to the basement.

Here was the same dim corridor he remembered, the same laundry room. One of the machines was running, but fortunately no one was there to keep an eye on it. And beyond, through a small doorway that was unlocked just as he hoped it might be, he found the boiler room where a huge furnace sat idle at this time of year.

The place he was looking for—the one he'd discovered moving furniture out of storage years before—was now covered over by a loose piece of plywood leaning against the wall. All the better. He pulled the wood away, found the loose brick, placed all but three hundred dollars of the money in the empty space behind it, replaced the brick, and slid the plywood back. Without stopping to think, he hurried from the room, crossed the laundry area, and bounded back up the stairs to the fifth floor.

It was quiet on his mother's old hall, except for the sounds of a baby crying, muted by the walls. Apartment 5E had a new and unfamiliar nameplate. He considered knocking, but before he could move, the door opened to the apartment beside his mother's and a short, middle-aged man in a coat and tie stepped out.

He looked at Quentin with alarm. "Can I help you?"

"Mr. Ambrose?"

"Who are—Quentin? Oh, my gosh, it's you."

"It's me."

"I saw an article on you in the paper. How are you?"

"Okay."

"What are you, uh . . . I mean, what are you doing here?"

"Just thought I'd come by to check out Mom's old place."

"You know the people who live here now?"

"No."

"Yuppie couple named Hendrix. Only finished earning their

degrees a couple of years ago, but they're already moving next month into a fancy townhouse. He works in a bank or something. She's a nurse. It ain't like it was when your mom was around, Quentin. This building misses her. No more than you do, I'm sure."

"Mr. Ambrose, when my mom was still living . . . in the last month or two before she died, you remember her having any special visitors?"

"Oh, she had lots of visitors. Your mom had so many friends from her church and all over, it seemed."

"You don't remember anyone different though? Someone from out of state, maybe?"

"Like who?"

"Like my father."

"Oh, no. That is, I don't ever remember someone like that. Why, are you trying to find him?"

"No. Just curious, that's all."

Though his old man had disappeared forever from his life, he still held out some sliver of hope that the guy would at least turn up for something as big as his mother dying. But it was a false hope and he knew it. His father might even be dead too, for all he was aware. The man had been as good as dead to him for a long time.

"It's all totally redecorated and everything, but you want me to see if I can find the super to maybe let you in and have a look at your mom's old apartment?"

"No thanks, that's okay. Just being here and talking to you is good enough."

"All right. I was just headed out to an afternoon class. I started teaching part time at Broome Community again, you know."

"Hey, that's great."

Mr. Ambrose turned to lock his door with his key. "Yeah,

well, it keeps me on my toes and puts a few extra dollars in the old bank account every month."

"Thanks very much for the information."

"Oh, you know what? Come to think of it, there was one thing that happened around the time your mother died."

"What's that?"

"A man showed up wanting to talk to her, but it was pretty late in the game, and I guess she must not have been up for talking. I poked my head out a couple of minutes and I saw him taking a picture with one of those little digital cameras in the hallway. Thought it was a little odd. The visiting hospice nurse turned him away."

"Do you remember what the man looked like?"

"Short guy. Older than you. A dark beard."

"Did he say anything to you?"

"Nope. Just disappeared into the elevator, but I do remember the last thing he said to the nurse when she was shooing him off."

"What's that?"

"Told her he was working for a private investigator," he said.

NINETEEN

It had all been a huge mistake. Ruth had known it from the look on Quentin's face the moment he'd caught sight of Hollister and King the morning before. After all her years as a cop's wife, after all that she'd been through with Jack, she should have known better. She'd known Quentin would be bitter, of course, how could he not? She had even anticipated he'd tell her no when she asked him to help her find out who really killed Gwen. But she'd hoped that by bringing in the two detectives and telling them just enough to whet their curiosity about what he was like now, she could shock Quentin into getting on board with her.

But her plan had backfired. Now back at work, she was afraid she'd done just the opposite. She twirled the cigarette nervously in her fingers as she passed by Walt's office.

Her boss looked up from his work. "Ruth, you got a quick second?"

Oh, no, here it came again. The what-are-you-doing-hanging-out-with-that-kind-of-guy lecture.

"Yeah. Real quick," she said. "I was just about to light up."

Walt hoisted himself out from behind his desk, stepped around, and stood in front of her. "I know you're a big girl and everything, Ruth. And far be it from me to try to tell you your business. But do you think it's wise cozying up to this guy the minute he gets out of prison? I mean . . . innocent or not, he's—"

"An honest and decent human being from everything I can tell."

"I know he may seem that way to you, but—"

"Did I tell you he changed my tire for me? Bertha had a flat on the interstate. He just took care of it in his suit and everything. Didn't hardly break a sweat."

"You shouldn't be blind to certain basic realities though, Ruth. People who've spent time in prison—good or bad when they went in—well, most of 'em come out of the place changed, if you know what I mean. It's not exactly a prime environment for personal development."

"Look, Walt. You're sweet and I appreciate it. But I can take care of myself, okay?"

"It still hurts, doesn't it?"

"What?"

"You know what I'm talking about. Gwen. Ten years and it still hurts you like hell. I've see you on the phone with the cops and the lawyers and all."

She nodded, said nothing.

"Thing like that happens—it must still tear you up inside."

"Yeah. Thank you for noticing."

"I just want you to know I'm here, you ever need me, Ruth."

He reached out to put a hand on her arm, but she sidestepped it.

"I know," she said. "And thank you. Gotta go catch that smoke."

He shrugged. "All right."

"You know what though?" She stopped and turned back to her boss. "There is one thing you might be able to do."

TWENTY

The fourth floor of the parking garage was filled with empty cars, dark and silent. Jack had the radio tuned to classic rock, Jim Morrison crooning "Love Her Madly." Through the girders he could make out the gray monolith of the federal building and Government Plaza presiding over Binghamton's downtown. When they came into view, he flashed his lights, cut the music, and pushed the button to unlock the Seville.

"You missed your calling, Jack." Hollister brought the warm outside air in with him as he heaved his bulk into the front passenger seat. "Should've signed up for the CIA."

King did the same in the rear behind them. "Yeah. What's with all the clandestine shit?"

Jack smiled, said nothing.

Hollister ran his hand along the smooth leather seat. "Yeah? Well business doesn't seem to be doing too bad for you these days."

"I keep telling you two turkeys the government dole ain't where it's at. What have you got for me?"

King pulled a narrow loose-leaf notebook from his jacket pocket. "Not that much, really. After our opening fun in the park, our boy's been pretty quiet."

He gave Jack a cursory summary of Price's whereabouts and movements since they'd last talked.

Jack waited until he was through. "Is that it?"

"Yeah."

"Why can't you tell me something I don't already know."

"Well jeez, Jack," Hollister said. "I hope you weren't expecting the guy to start running around slashing people right out of the joint."

"I suppose." He shook his head.

"We're trying to build some kind of different case but it isn't going to be easy. Not after this much time. May take a while."

Jack didn't have a while.

"What about the guy they brought up from NYPD?" he asked. "Is he going to play ball or try to pull a Sidney Poitier on us?"

Hollister sighed. "Harris seems like a decent cop. He'll follow the evidence wherever it leads. Just like we all will."

"How about if your hands are tied? What if the pricks we got for judges and DAs these days won't let you close whatever loops you need to get the job done?"

Hollister shrugged. "I don't like it any better than you do, Jack."

The three of them watched as a Binghamton City van drove past them and went through a gate to enter the official side of the garage.

Jack shifted some in his seat. "All right then. Let's just go ahead and call it off."

Hollister's forehead flipped into a mass of wrinkles. "What?"

"Forget it, I said. I'll deal with this thing by myself."

"Whoa, hold on there now, partner. We talked about this before. You go off the reservation and we—"

"I'm not talking about going off the reservation. But I've got talents and resources I can bring to bear on this situation you guys can't touch. We should be able to help one another."

"Like what kind of resources, for instance?"

He smiled and held up his hands. "C'mon, fellas. You don't

expect a man to go revealing all of his proprietary secrets, do you?"

Hollister gave him a dark look. "I told you what happened at the restaurant when Sean and I tried to lean on Price. He went straight to lawyer talk."

"Yeah, I know."

"You go breaking any laws here, and you're going to royally screw this up for everybody, and I mean everybody."

"My specialty is tiptoeing around the edge of things. You guys know that. Think of me as a big snitch."

"A big snitch with an axe to grind."

"Which they all have, one way or another, don't they?"

It was silent in the car for a few moments.

Hollister glanced back over his shoulder at King. "All right, Jack. We'll play it your way. For now."

"Cool."

"I don't want you mucking around with witnesses though, not without my say so. You got that?"

"You won't even know I'm there."

"And you better keep us in the loop."

"Absolutely."

The two cops were already climbing out of the car. Hollister leaned back down to look at him. "We still get paid for the work we've done, right?"

"Of course."

"You be in touch then."

"You bet. Like I said, we ought to be able to do each other some good."

Twenty-One

A gray Toyota sedan had been shadowing him ever since Quentin had left his mother's apartment building earlier that afternoon. The driver was good. If Quentin hadn't been on the lookout, he might never have picked out the car.

When the bus dropped him off three blocks from his uncle's address, he took off walking and rounded a corner only to glance back and see the Toyota edge up to the curb and stop at the corner a few seconds later. Should he lead him to his uncle's house?

Whoever the driver was, chances were he already had Uncle Nelson's address. Someone had probably been tailing him when he came out here a couple of days before as well. To hell with it. Let 'em watch for now. As long as he could watch them back. They might even begin to tell him something.

Nelson Root, his mother's younger brother, lived in a brick bungalow set back from the street, a nondescript house in a row of similar dwellings with an abandoned car wash at one end and an auto parts store at the other. The row of colorful flags in front of the parts store awning stirred in the sun. Quentin wondered why they all hadn't been stolen. Maybe they only put them out in daylight.

Nelson's front porch was just as he remembered it, a rust-stained concrete slab with wrought iron railings that were perpetually in need of a new coat of paint. A small pile of leftover fall leaves blocked the doorway. He didn't know exactly what time it was, probably after three by now. He set his bag down on the concrete and pressed the yellowed doorbell.

A loud woof sounded from somewhere in the house. Nelson always kept a dog, usually a big one, but there'd been no sign of the canine when he'd visited the house a couple of days before and found the note. He could make out the brown-black outline of what looked like a German shepherd through the living room curtains, pacing back and forth, its tail swishing. A paw scratched at the window as the dog barked another alarm.

"Get down, boy. It's all right, Ringo. Hush your racket."

After ten years he still recognized his uncle's gravelly voice through the door. The thump of the old man's cane fell against the carpet, followed by the clatter of a deadbolt and chain. From somewhere inside he could hear the sound of a television news announcer. The door squeaked as it was cracked open.

"I do believe I see a sight for sore eyes." The door opened to reveal a barrel-chested man in a maroon bathrobe leaning on a prime piece of black walnut. He clutched the collar of an enormous dog who was obviously none too happy about the situation.

"Good afternoon," Quentin said.

"Good afternoon? That all you got to say to an old man been waiting on you to show up all these years?" His uncle's face broke into a grin. "I got the note you left in the door the other day."

"Yeah. Sorry, I would have come by sooner, but—"

"Don't worry about it. Get over here and let me hug that big mug of yours."

The dog whimpered some more. Nelson let the shepherd go, steadying himself for a moment on his cane. Quentin stepped into the old man's one-armed embrace.

"Don't mind the dog. He's only killed a couple of mailmen so far this year."

"Good thing I'm not still wearing my prison regs then."

His uncle studied his face. "It's good to have you back."

The shepherd, finally realizing Quentin was friend not foe, began to dance around.

"Where you should've been all along, of course," Uncle Nelson said. "But let's not get into that right now. Come on in. Come in and put your bag down. I just poured myself a bowl of cereal back in the kitchen. Don't usually take a nap this time of day, but I was pretty tuckered out after my trip."

Quentin stepped into the living room and lay his bag down on the threadbare carpet.

His uncle thumped in behind him. "Where you been staying the past couple of nights?"

"Salvation Army shelter."

"Shoot. If I'd have known, I could've told you where I keep the spare key and you could've stayed here. I read the article in the paper. How come I didn't see a big story with footage on the television when they let you go?"

"Auburn wasn't exactly advertising it. They let me out of there before dawn, a couple of hours before they told the press I'd be leaving."

"You don't say?" Nelson turned with his cane and began a slow limp toward the back of the house. Quentin and the dog followed. "The cops just don't want nobody seeing your face on the TV again, that's why. Makes them look bad."

They reached the kitchen where a folding Formica table stood propped against one wall between an ancient refrigerator and a grease-splattered gas stove. A chrome-rimmed kitchen counter was stacked high with cereal boxes and condiments, jars of peanut butter, and canned vegetables and fruits. A small color TV was tuned to Fox News.

The shepherd nuzzled at Quentin's fingers. He reached down

and patted the dog's head, stroking his ears. "Nice dog you have here."

"Oh, he's just an old mutt I picked up from the SPCA, but he sure is loyal. Sit down, Ringo. Go, sit."

The shepherd moaned and curled up in corner next to a food and water dish.

Uncle Nelson picked up a remote on the table and turned the TV sound down. "Sorry for the mess. Its easier when I got stuff to eat close at hand. Plus, you know me. Never been much of a housekeeper."

"That's fine by me."

"They let you out before dawn you say? You must have spent half of Saturday on the damn bus." Nelson pulled out a chair from the kitchen table and, obviously in some pain, began to sit down in front of a bowl of corn flakes.

He moved to help the old man into the seat, but his uncle waved him away.

"Actually no," Quentin said. "Someone showed up to give me a ride."

"A ride?" A smile played across Nelson's face. "Now who might that be? Some lawyer? Or one of your old female admirers?"

"Not my lawyer, and she was female all right, but she wasn't any old admirer. It was Ruth Crawford."

"Ruth Crawford." His uncle scratched his chin and stared at him for a moment. "You're not . . . uh . . . talking about that, you know, that girl's mother, are you?"

"One and the same."

Nelson started to shake his head. "Whoa, boy. You haven't been out of the big house less than a day and you're already asking for trouble."

If he only knew the half of it.

"What did that whore want?" Uncle Nelson said.

"She said she wanted to give me a ride and to say she was sorry and to make amends."

"Oh, please, not some do-gooder liberal charity." Now the TV was blasting images of some obnoxious car commercial. Nelson picked up the remote again and shut the thing off.

"No. Nothing like that."

"What then?"

"This morning she called me where I was staying down at the shelter, came and picked me up and took me to breakfast."

"Now ain't she in a generous mood."

"Not exactly. We'd barely finished eating when the same two detectives that took me down for her daughter's case showed."

"What? They both still cops?"

"Looks that way?"

"I told you that woman was trouble."

"Yeah, well, the two dudes made it pretty clear they still think I did it. And apparently they're not the only ones."

"Why that's nothing but pure harassment, Quentin. You need to sic your lawyer onto that bitch. This isn't the Jim Crow South."

"That's not what it was all about. I mean, it was and it wasn't. Not for her."

"What do you mean?"

"The two cops want to bring me down, that was for sure, but I think she just wanted me to see what they were thinking."

"What in the world for?"

"Because she wants me to help her find out who really killed her daughter. Says I'm the only other one who knows I didn't do it."

Uncle Nelson, who'd begun eating his corn flakes, stared open-mouthed for a moment with the spoon paused in front of his face. Then he started to shake his head. "That's about the stupidest thing I've ever heard in my life."

"Maybe."

"I hope you told her where she could stick that idea."

Quentin shrugged. "Not in so many words, but yeah."

"That woman's got some kind of balls asking a man just come out of prison to do something like that. Even if she did lose her daughter."

"Yes."

His uncle stared at him for a moment. "You're thinking about doing it though, aren't you?"

"The thought passed through my mind." Quentin couldn't tell his uncle he was just thinking of sticking close to Ruth for safety's sake.

"It's got to be kind of hard on the woman. You getting out and all and her not knowing what to think about who committed the crime."

"I've thought of that too."

"You do what you want, but I hope you stick to your guns. If it was me, I wouldn't have nothing to do with Ruth Crawford."

He nodded.

"So they fed you over there at that diner this morning?"

"Yeah."

"How about lunch?"

"I picked up a burger. I'm fine."

"They give you any money to take with you when you left the prison?"

He thought about the sudden extra money he was carrying. Not that he worried about Uncle Nelson going through his pockets while he was asleep or anything. But prison habits died hard. "Forty dollars. Gate money."

"You got any savings?"

"Nope, I'm afraid that's it." He hated lying to his uncle but it had to be done. "Cost me more than two thousand to bury Mom and that tapped me out."

"Yeah, you know I'd of helped out and come to the funeral if I wasn't in the hospital then myself."

"I know you would have, Uncle Nelson. I know you would have."

"She was the only one of my sisters ever amounted to anything. The rest of them ran away down South or whatever, I wouldn't give two cents for them. They all of them dead now of course. But your momma, she was one strong Christian woman. Strong in the Lord."

"I know."

"Well, you can plan on staying here for as long as you want—until you get back on your feet again or whatever. We might have to move a few boxes, but I've got a spare bedroom."

"I really appreciate it."

"Shoot, ain't that much to appreciate. But at least you'll have a roof over your head. What are your plans?"

"I'm not sure exactly. Figured I could get a job working fast food or something, just to tide me over. I don't think anyone around here's going to want to hire me anymore for security. Not right away at least. I finished my associates degree up at Auburn. Might even start working on my bachelors."

"College, huh? You'll be older than every one of 'em."

"I suppose so."

"You going after the state for putting you in jail like they did? Seems like they ought to be paying you a boatload of money."

"Possibly. Got a lawyer who has the paperwork all ready."

Uncle Nelson nodded and grunted between bites of his flakes. "You're crazy if you don't, after everything you been through. Things ain't easy these days. You need to really give that some thought."

"We'll see," he said.

He spent the next couple of hours helping Nelson tidy up the place. He moved boxes, cleaned the toilet, sink, and shower in the bathroom; swept the kitchen and ran a vacuum cleaner across the carpets in the rest of the rooms. He even worked a dust rag over the spare room that would be his for the time being, remembering as he did the potential danger from the man in the car outside and that he couldn't stay here for long.

Uncle Nelson gave him the weekend newspaper he'd saved with all the classifieds so Quentin could keep looking for work. After a little TV and dinner, the old man was clearly spent.

"Time for my evening siesta." The dog trailed after him toward his bedroom like an honor guard. Quentin was finally left alone to unpack his bag in his room.

A single bed took up much of the space, but there was a desk and a dresser and window looking out the back, where Quentin could see an old charcoal grill rusting against a chain link fence and a lawn in need of spring raking.

He sat down on the bed, untied the cord at the top of the bag, and lifted out his mother's Bible again. Somehow it seemed larger, heavier than when the warden had handed it to him by the gate. The old leather cover, frayed at the edges, felt almost like dry parchment.

The book was an authorized King James version of the Old and New Testaments, "Produced expressly for Sears, Roebuck and Co. by The National Bible Press of Philadelphia, Pennsylvania." There were maps of the Exodus and Paul's Missionary Journeys in the end papers, fine color paintings reproduced on some of the pages—the crossing of the Red Sea, Daniel in the Lion's Den, and Jesus praying in Gethsemane. In the New Testament all of Jesus' spoken words had been printed in red ink.

From as far back as he could remember, his mother would hoist this Bible out from its place of honor on a little stand beside the window once a week or so and read to him. He mostly paid attention to the pictures when he was young. By the time he was old enough to read himself, his interest waned, and he simply let her words roll over him, marking the time until he could go out to play.

Now he opened it up and was drawn into page after page of underlined passages and notes inscribed into the margins in his mother's feathery handwriting.

The basis for everything God does and everything he allows is love
Source of love and forgiveness
Sacrifice on the cross
Glory not to man but to Jesus
Deliverance
Equality between man and woman does not mean sameness

He remembered similar words from Sunday school and going to church with his mother years before. Her notes went on and on and on throughout the entire Bible. It would take him a while to digest all of their meaning for her.

He had no idea why, but he felt his eyes begin to well up with tears as he turned the pages, seeing his mother there, hearing her patient voice again. Her pride for him as a young man, followed by her ultimate pain and frustration at his arrest. He hoped she believed in her heart that what the police and prosecutors alleged wasn't true. But always the slightly worried expression, the seed of doubt put there by a system that had almost but never quite managed to strip her of her faith.

She hadn't lived to see her prayers for him answered, but the book he held in his hands was the solid evidence of her devotion. Not just the record of his wrongs, but the testimony of his potential for redemption.

He lay back on the bed, suddenly bone weary. The impact of the last couple of days washed over him in a dark wave of foreboding. He wasn't even sure he could summon up the energy to unpack the rest of his belongings.

He was just about to shut the Bible and try to catch some sleep himself when a half-opened page caused a small slip of paper wedged deep into the fold to flutter open before his eyes. He looked at it absently.

Ruth Crawford's name was at the bottom.

He sat bolt upright. It couldn't be.

The mattress coils squeaked in protest as he swung his legs off the bed. There was a reading lamp on the corner of the desk. He snatched up the scrap of paper and carried it over to the lamp, switched on the light, and held the paper up close to its yellow glow to make sure he'd read his mother's words correctly.

In her spidery hand was some kind of spiritual to-do list:

Learn better patience
Hold your tongue
Find Samantha Grimes after church and apologize
Help Ruth Crawford

Quentin didn't know if he believed in God anymore. Auburn had a way of squeezing the faith out of you. But it was hard to look at this list and not see it as a message.

He heard the phone ring in the other room. His uncle picked it up. He heard him murmuring for a moment or two. Then the sound of his uncle's cane hitting the floor followed by his footsteps as he climbed out of bed and headed toward Quentin's room.

He was up and out of bed before Uncle Nelson reached the door.

"It's for you," his uncle said, cupping his hand over the portable phone. "And it reminds me. Some newspaper reporter's trying to get a hold of you too. Called this morning."

"Wonderful. Who's on the phone now?"

"It's that woman again." The old man's face was set in a look somewhere between anger and aggravation.

"Ruth Crawford?"

He nodded.

"What's she doing calling me here?"

"Claims she's found you a job."

TWENTY-TWO

Jack stretched his shoulders, jiggling the tumbler of scotch and ice in his hand as he stared at a new newspaper photo of Quentin Price.

He had converted part of the second floor of the upscale contemporary he'd bought the year before into a home office. In an alcove with a narrow window covered by a roman blind, he'd created what he'd come to think of as his war room. There was a bulletin board with maps and photos tacked across the wall, a white eraser board, arrows pointing to key bits of information, a timeline of the case—everything he'd been able to glean from the police, prosecutor, newspapers, and any other source about Gwen's murder.

But even more than that, there were reams of information about Price—his background, his conviction, his incarceration. Ruth had shocked him with her contact with Price, but of course she'd known the Auburn supervisor, Elder, from high school.

He didn't trust Ruth. Gwen hadn't even thought enough of her mother at the time of her killing to be on speaking terms with her. Maybe though, he'd be able to use whatever connection she forged with Price to his advantage.

He examined the picture, part of an article on Price's release. Not a bad-looking guy really. Jack took another sip of his drink. He could almost believe that Gwen, younger by a few years, might have developed a crush on the man. The two of them together—wouldn't that have been ironic? A storybook rather than a tragic ending, him walking down the aisle one day to give his daughter away.

It made no difference to Jack that Price was African American. What mattered was that the man whose image glared back at him had managed for some reason known only in his own warped mind to twist the potential good of a friendship with Gwen into something evil. For that there was no forgiveness, never could be.

What to do about it was really the only question. Beyond the surveillance and potential harassment he'd put in place already, that was. Whenever Price breathed he'd be there; if not physically, then virtually through someone with whom he'd contracted or through someone, like Hollister and King, who also had some skin in the game. Was there anything more he could do?

He set down the paper and ran his fingers across the metal box he'd gotten from Hollister and King. The two cops had wanted to detain and search Price to find out what he'd retrieved from his buried cache in the woods. But they needed probable cause. And anyway what would it gain them?

A small stash of drugs perhaps. Maybe a short stint back behind bars for the murderer. Jack was after something bigger, much bigger. He wanted to cause Price the kind of pain he had felt ever since his phone rang the morning they'd found Gwen's body. Searing, Richter magnitude, and worse, the kind of hurt Price would carry with him forever.

He would need to move soon though, before Price and his lawyer filed some outrageous suit against the state and the media dropped the crown of bleeding heart sympathy on Price. What did Price want now? The tape from the bug he'd planted in the lawyer's office had told him it wasn't necessarily money.

He drained the rest of his drink. The sound of the phone jangled him from his thoughts.

"Jack?"

"Speaking."

"Doyle Fletcher."

"Mr. Fletcher. Long time no see. Nice of you to return my call."

"Sure, Jack. It's business, right?"

"You bet. How's life down in Binghamton?"

"Same as ever."

"Still working crime scenes?"

"Yeah . . . and for the newspaper."

He glanced through the door at the hallway wall and yet another example of Gwen's own photographic prowess, an outdoor winter scene. "Good. I've got a special job for you."

"What kind of job?"

"I want you to start keeping close tabs on someone and when the time comes we may need to make a move on him to persuade him to tell us things."

"And who might that be?"

"Quentin Price."

"Not the one who—"

Jack could sense the other man smiling through the phone. "That's him," he said. "He was just cut loose from Auburn."

"I know. I snapped a bunch of pics of the guy yesterday. I told you I was still freelancing. There's a reporter chasing around after Price."

"Perfect."

"You're looking to shake the guy down?"

"Maybe."

"You want me to bring in a couple of guys to get rough?"

"I've got some ideas. For now just keep a close eye."

"What about costs? I might miss some work."

"I'll take good care of you. Results are the issue."

They agreed upon a figure. It was more than Jack wanted to

pay but not really more than he'd expected.

"I see only one problem," Fletcher said.

"What's that?"

"You sound pretty emotional about this, Jack."

"Well, Christ, what do you expect?"

"Makes me nervous working with people who are too emotional."

"Look, you just do your job and I'll take care of whatever I gotta do on my end."

There was a long pause. "Okay."

"That's what I wanted to hear." He felt better knowing he wouldn't have to shop around. He'd hired Fletcher a couple of times before, had more of a string on him. "I don't want any surprises, Doyle."

"I'll try my best."

"Do."

Jack broke the connection. He turned back to squint at the photos, maps, documents, and timelines laid out on the walls and the desk before him, found some measure of solace there.

Twenty-Three

Merryweather College in Hamlick was a few light years from the Bronx streets Garnell normally plied. From the faux-Victorian lampposts to the manicured lawns, to the futuristic glass and steel science center, the place looked idyllic. There was even a brick and cobblestone archway at the entrance.

At its founding in 1879 and for nearly a century thereafter, the school educated young women—predominately the daughters of New York and Philadelphia high society sent away to the country to be schooled in the classics, far from the temptations of the metropolis. But since Merryweather had gone coed more than forty years before, it had taken on a decidedly hipper quality. Exclusively bohemian was more like it. Garnell and his classmates at Binghamton University, no stranger to bohemianism themselves, used to refer to Merryweather as Woodstock on the Susquehanna.

He was surprised to learn that Quentin Price had ended up working here. After Price's knee injury and disappearance from the local sports pages, Garnell had assumed that he had moved back downstate to make his way in the broader spectrum and chaos of the Big Apple. He looked forward to finally meeting the man, guilty or not. He wondered what might have turned him into a killer.

He had arrived just in time for his appointment with the head of campus security, a woman named Beatrice Tover. Her office was housed in the basement of the main administration building. Since it was summertime, the dormitories and academic buildings seemed mostly quiet, except for some kind of language camp evidenced by prominent banners strung around the campus.

"Not too often we get an NYPD detective showing up in this neck of the woods." Tover beckoned him into a side chair and sat down across from him in her closet of a work space—barely enough room for a desk and a computer. She was a semi-attractive redhead in her forties who reminded him a little bit of his partner, Jane Pappas. He'd already declined her offer of coffee.

"When was the last time?"

"Actually, this is it."

He suppressed a smile.

"You said you wanted to talk about the Gwen Crawford murder?"

"That's why I'm here."

"What's the NYPD care about the Crawford case?"

"We don't. But the deputy attorney general in Albany seems to have developed a keen sense of curiosity about the matter."

"I see." The security chief gave a knowing look. "The Crawford murder is not, as you might imagine, the most popular topic of discussion around here."

"I can understand that. Were you head of security at the time?"

"No, but I was working here as a guard."

"So you knew Quentin Price."

She nodded. "We all knew him."

"Did you think he was guilty?"

"As much as it looked like he was, I think it was still hard for a lot of us to believe he could've done such a thing."

"He was well-liked then."

"Yes. He was."

"Did you also know Gwen Crawford?"

"Not really. I knew of her."

"Was she a good student?"

"Above average."

"Popular?"

"Above average in that department too, I guess. She worked for the campus newspaper. An art major—she was really into photography."

"All the other possible suspects were well vetted at the time, fellow students, professors, and the like?"

"As far as I know. But then, once it became a police matter it was out of our hands. We're too small. We don't employ investigators."

"But as a guard you might have heard something, rumors, whatever, that might have corroborated Price's guilt."

She shook her head. "Most people were just in shock, especially after they found Gwen's body over in Binghamton. Quentin Price was immediately suspended and eventually terminated of course."

"Who was the security boss at the time?"

"A man named Clyde Watford. He's retired, lives in Arizona now. Phoenix. You want his number?"

"I can get it later." He looked at a poster Tover kept on her wall. It was one of those motivational sayings superimposed over a photo of a rowing team, an eight-woman boat, pulling for all they were worth, the wet tips of their oars gleaming with the water as they rowed into a rising sun. "Do you happen to know if Gwen Crawford had much contact with anyone beyond the campus, someone from town maybe?"

"Sorry, I wouldn't know."

"Were you working the night she disappeared?"

"No. It was a weekend. My husband and I were out of town."

"According to the police reports, there were several witnesses who saw Price talking with Crawford that night."

"That sounds about right. That's what I remember being told too."

"Where would Price and Crawford have been speaking?"

"Outside at the entrance to the party that was going on, I suppose. That's normally where security would be stationed."

"Which Quentin was supposed to be working."

"Yes."

"But no one actually saw Gwen Crawford leave with Quentin Price?"

"From what I understand, no one saw her leave at all."

"Right. The theory was that she left by herself and drove first to her apartment, where the dress she'd been seen wearing that night was found on the floor by her closet, then went back to the party where her car was found, most probably to meet Price."

"That sounds right," she said.

"So Price was having a relationship with her?"

"I suppose, but I don't think it was any kind of romantic relationship. At least not before that night. You should understand, this is a small school, in a small town. Some students get to know the security guards pretty well, especially the kids on financial aid like Gwen Crawford, who work in the dining hall or as building monitors."

"So you're saying they were just friends."

"That was the way I understood it. Maybe a better description would be close acquaintances."

"Do you know if Gwen Crawford slept around?"

The security chief crossed her legs. "No more so than a lot of her classmates. But like I say, I didn't know her."

"So she didn't have a reputation."

"No, not to my knowledge."

"She worked in the library, was it?"

"That's right."

"Where was the party held that year?"

"Same as always, in the main student union."

"That the big brick building with the cupola I passed on the way in?"

"That's it."

"So the parking lot is pretty visible."

"I'd say that it is."

"Yet no one saw Gwen return the night of the party or leave with Quentin Price after his shift was through."

"Apparently not. Of course it was dark. The lighting in the parking lot has been improved considerably since then."

"I'm sure it has." He could just imagine the letters and emails Merryweather administration must have received from parents after the news broke about the Crawford murder. "Can you show me the building?"

"Of course."

She fished a set of keys and a computerized access card from her desk. She stood and he followed her out the door.

"You need to understand, the Crawford murder was a total aberration around here," she said as they navigated the picture perfect walkway between the administration building and the student union. "Our entire student body is only a little over twelve hundred. We don't get all the major problems with rape or drugs that you have at some larger campuses."

"No problems at all then?"

"Oh, we have our share. Drinking. Fighting. Some drugs, mostly pot. But by and large this is a safe place to go to school. It's an open campus—sororities were abolished back when the school went coed and fraternities never existed."

"Any other violent crimes since the Crawford case?"

"None."

He looked out across the campus lawns at the quiet arches,

pristine grass, and manicured planting beds. The air was warm and sweet with the smell of new mowing. Working security at such a place wouldn't be such a bad job, if you could keep yourself from going stir crazy. Was that what had gone wrong with Quentin Price? A warrior sent to guard a candy castle?

The main entrance of the student union was open. "For the language campers," she explained. They ducked inside. There was a large mailroom, walls lined with aluminum boxes, a snack bar, the booths and tables of which were mostly empty at the moment, a computer room and game room.

"What about race relations?"

"You mean because Quentin is black and most of our students are white?"

"Just curious."

"You went to BU down the road, right?"

"That's right."

"I'd say our standing as far as race relations go is pretty similar to the situation you have over there."

"Cordial but not intimate."

"In most cases, yes."

Tover pushed the security card into a slot to open an electronic lock in a door that led to a back section of the building, obviously not in use during the summer. The air conditioning was off and the darkened hallway on the other side smelled stale. She flipped on a line of lights overhead and went and opened a door with a key that led to a large open foyer.

"This is the ballroom." She crossed the dim expanse to turn on another bank of lights, then opened one of a pair of double doors. They entered a large hall with high ceilings, oversized tapestries decorating the walls, and a long row of French doors leading to a patio alongside the building. At this time of day, enough natural light filled the room that there was no need to turn on the overhead chandeliers. "The end of year party, the same one that was taking place that night, is always held here."

"Is that the patio where Gwen was last seen talking to Price?"

"That's right."

They walked over to the doors and gazed out through the glass. Not much to see really. An empty expanse of flagstone bordered by a metal railing. The building was built into the hillside and a moderate slope dropped toward some woods in back.

"Both faculty and students attend the big end of year bash?"

"Just about everybody. The faculty presence tends to keep the general rowdiness to a minimum."

"Most of your students are from privileged backgrounds, from what I understand."

"Many are, yes, but the admissions department has made a concerted effort over the last decade to build a more diverse student body."

He nearly smiled at the recruitment-flyer prose. "Still more girls than boys?"

"The ratio last year was sixty-forty."

"What was it when Gwen Crawford was a student?"

She shrugged. "I can't say exactly. But there were definitely more girls back then. Why?"

"Just thinking. Have any of your other male guards ever been disciplined or dismissed for improper contact with female students?"

"I see where you're going, yes. We have had a couple of other relatively minor incidents. None recently."

"So Quentin Price was, as you say, an aberration?"

"Yes. I'd say that he was."

"Was that why you were shocked at his arrest?"

The security chief turned and checked a side door to make sure it was locked before turning back to Garnell. "Not entirely. Quentin was a straight arrow . . . No, it was more than that.

Whenever you talked to him, you just got the feeling that he was meant for bigger things."

"Bigger things than working here?"

"Yes. He was taking classes at Broome Community."

"Classes in what?"

"General subject leading toward a degree and also criminology."

"He ever talk to you about his long-term plans?"

"Not in so many words. But you knew they were there."

"What about other romantic interests in his life? He have a wife, a girlfriend?"

"I think he may have at one time, but I'm not sure. He was pretty reserved."

"Sounds like you think he had a lot to lose by abducting and murdering Gwen Crawford."

"I'm saying he wasn't just some young thug drifting through life who happened to be filling in the gaps working security at a cushy college where he could ogle the coeds."

"Which is how the prosecution painted him."

"From what I read in the newspaper, pretty much."

They began moving back toward the door through which they had entered.

"If it was a crime of passion like they say, that pretty much trumps everything else though, doesn't it?" he said.

"I suppose it might."

"You think the new DNA results are a good thing then?"

"It doesn't matter much what I think. But yeah, I've always had my doubts about Quentin's guilt. At least, I never thought it was the open-and-shut case they made it out to be."

"If you're right, justice has been a long time coming."

"I suppose. You through looking in here?"

"Yes. Anyone else I should be talking to on campus? Faculty?"

"Possibly. But you may have a hard time finding most of the

professors—they seem to scatter to the four winds come sum-mertime. I think Gwen's old faculty advisor may be in town though. At least I think he was her advisor. I saw him at the post office yesterday."

"Can you get me his contact info?"

"Of course."

"Do you have some kind of alumni directory where I could try to get in touch with any of Gwen's old classmates?"

"Sure. And I promised to get you Clyde's number out in Phoenix."

They made idle talk about the history of the college as they headed back over to the administration building. He was trying to imagine Gwen Crawford here as an undergraduate, her petite figure and attractive smile packaged in blue jeans, moving as any other student might among the buildings and grounds of this supposedly safe haven of academia.

"Oh, I almost forgot," Tover said, "if you're interested there's a memorial plaque to Gwen, donated by her graduating class. It's in one of the gardens in back of the upperclassmen dorms. I can tell you how to get there if you'd like to swing by and take a look at it."

"Okay," he said. "Thanks."

The heat from the morning sun had not yet built to a peak. Insects buzzed and a pair of men from the buildings and grounds department fired up grass trimmers around the edge of one of the dormitories as he passed. The painted trellis in the garden was interwoven with climbing roses. He stopped to look for a moment. At its base a tasteful granite marker read simply IN MEMORY OF GWEN CRACE CRAWFORD and the years spanning her shortened life.

Twenty-Four

Maybe it was a long way down from where he'd dreamed he'd one day be, but busing tables at McGinnis's was a start on the way back up. At Auburn, Quentin had worked in the laundry, had helped build government furniture, always worked more than one job, wherever they could find a place for him, sometimes two or three. Work felt good.

"You're a demon on these tables, Quentin, I got to give you that." Patting his circular stomach, Walt Oriskany slipped around the corner of the near-empty dining room. "You clear 'em twice as fast as the last fella I had in here. And he wasn't half bad."

"Thanks."

"I'm going to take off now. Leave Ruth and the rest of the evening crew to close the place up. As soon as you're done with the pots and pans, you can punch out."

"All right."

"See you tomorrow."

"Yes, sir."

Oriskany slipped a light jacket around his shoulders and disappeared through the back.

Only his second day on the job and Quentin had already proved his mettle in the man's eyes. McGinnis's was a busy place. Quentin calculated they must be grossing more than three quarters of a million a year. The waitresses were already beginning to tell him how much easier his speed and efficiency was making their jobs.

The only fly in the ointment was figuring out how to avoid Ruth Crawford. That and the continued presence of the gray Toyota he'd seen cruising past the restaurant earlier as he was wiping down a table in front.

A few minutes later, he was spraying down the last of the pans and setting them in the rack to dry for the morning.

"Half this place is already in love with you."

Ruth held a tray full of nearly empty salt and pepper shakers in her hands.

"I hope that's a good thing," he said.

"It is. Even Walt thinks so. He told me before he left he couldn't believe I had to talk him into hiring you."

Quentin said nothing. He pulled a paper towel from the dispenser and began drying off his hands.

"You need a lift home?"

"No thanks," he said. "I can catch the bus."

"Okay." She set down the tray of shakers. "About the other day, Quentin . . . I just wanted to say how sorry I am for letting those two ambush you like that. I just wanted to—"

He held up his hand. "It's okay. I know what you're trying to do and I know how you must feel."

"You do?"

"Yeah. I've never had a child, but if I did and someone . . . well, you know . . ."

She nodded. "Thank you."

He said nothing.

"There's something important I need to show you," she said.

"What's that?"

She looked around the kitchen. "Not here. Come on into Walt's office where we can close the door."

He didn't like the sound of this. "You sure that's okay?"

She went and grabbed something from her purse hanging on peg with the staff's coats in the hall. "Yes. Just for a second."

He followed her into the cramped office and she closed the door. In her hands she held a thick manila envelope.

"What have you got there?"

She slid two sheets from the envelope. "I should have told you about this sooner, before I went back to those idiot cops."

"Told me what?"

She unfolded one of the sheets of paper. "These are copies. I have several of them. The police still have the originals."

He glanced at them. "This looks like a condolence card."

"It is. Once a year, every year, on Gwen's birthday, I've been getting them. They're anonymous. No return address, although the postmark is always here in Binghamton. No signature of any kind."

"When's Gwen's birthday?"

"June first."

"Next week."

"And you've talked to the cops all about this."

"Of course. But they've never taken them too seriously. They just assume it's an old family friend."

"But you said they were anonymous. That doesn't sound like a friend."

"The first couple of years it happened I didn't really think much of it. But when they kept coming . . ."

He looked at the handwriting on the paper she was holding. It wasn't familiar, but it wouldn't be. "Anything threatening about them?"

"Not exactly. It's just a little creepy because I don't know who they're from."

"What about your ex-husband? He gotten any?"

"Jack? No. He thinks I'm crazy, like the police. He thinks I'm looking for a bogeyman where nothing exists."

She was a drunk, but was she crazy? He knew as well as any, there were bogeymen in the world. She seemed determined to keep pushing this. He thought of the note he'd found in his mother's Bible. It would be safer for Ruth if he could bring himself to stick close.

"You know, I've been thinking," he said. "About what you're trying to do and all."

"Yes."

"It's not going to be an easy web to untangle after all this time."

"Or course."

"You're going to have to try to go back through all the people who knew Gwen at the college or who might have had contact with her that night."

"Already started doing that, like I told you."

"That's a start then."

"But what if it was just some stranger? You know, someone passing through town."

"Could be, but the odds are against it. She went back to her dorm room and changed. Chances are you're looking at someone she would have known."

She looked at him for a moment, a glimmer of uncertainty in her eyes. "Does this mean you're willing to help me?"

He thought about everything his uncle had said and his mother.

"Yeah. I suppose it does."

She smiled, standing as still as a mannequin for a second or two. Quentin thought he saw another flash of her long-dead daughter, still-lifed behind the lens of her camera that night on campus. Shutter speed, the stain from Gwen's red lipstick marking the rim of the foam cup from which she had been drinking.

"Quentin?"

"Yes?"

"You looked like you'd seen a ghost for a moment."

"Sorry. It was nothing."

"Are you through working?" she asked.

"Just about to punch out."

"Me too. Ira and Wanda will stay to lock up. You sure I can't give you that ride?"

TWENTY-FIVE

The bar had a forgetful name. It was also in a seedier part of downtown Binghamton than he'd ever visited before, not that Jack's success of late made him above such places. He parked the Seville next to a pickup truck with oversized chrome bumpers, locked the doors, and went in through the front.

It was a place for serious drinking. Inside, the air smelled of sweat and beer. The dark wood of the bar itself was flanked by a row of booths and a kaleidoscope-like jukebox, and that was about all there was. The floor felt slick and Jack had to watch his step while searching the faces of the patrons.

He didn't have to search long. Doyle Fletcher was seated in a back booth with two companions. The booth closest to them was empty. Jack made eye contact and strolled their way.

"Moving up in the world, aren't we, Jack? Nice threads."

The dim light revealed an older-looking Fletcher than when he'd last laid eyes on him. The man wore blue jeans, a gray T-shirt with a Yankees cap, and sported a goatee. He was accompanied by a couple of larger, clean-shaven men wearing coats and ties. Fletcher introduced them as Mr. Paul and Mr. Troy, but Jack doubted those were their real names.

Fletcher slid further into the seat to make room for Jack. Jack set the briefcase he was carrying on the floor beside the booth and sat down.

"You want a drink?" The two other men were drinking bottles of beer while a nearly finished mixed drink, mostly ice left in the glass, sat on the table in front of Fletcher.

"No thanks. Not tonight."

"Suit yourself." Fletcher shrugged. "Service sucks here anyway."

"You know why we're here," Jack said, glancing around to make sure no one was watching them.

"You want to figure out how to extract a confession from Price."

"Exactly."

Fletcher lowered his voice. "There are people who would kill him, you know that. Why not just use one of them and be done with it?"

"I'm no murderer."

"Not yet, at least."

"What's that supposed to mean?"

"Just that once you start down that road, sometimes you come to the inevitable conclusion."

"I'm only looking for justice," Jack said.

"Okay. It's your money."

The two other men nodded.

"So you think you can handle this the way it needs to be handled?"

"I believe so," Fletcher said. "Did you bring that box you told me about?"

Jack reached down to open the briefcase by his side and extracted the small metal box he'd been given by Hollister and King. He handed it to Fletcher.

"What's the scoop with this thing again?"

"Price was observed digging this up from some hidey hole in a public park."

Fletcher raised an eyebrow and lifted the lid. He looked disappointed. "It's empty."

"Exactly. But I figure there must have been drugs or money

inside, which he now has in his possession."

Fletcher took a deep breath. "So you want us to use this to demonstrate to Mr. Price that his hidey hole wasn't so private."

"Pretty much."

"Okay." Fletcher smiled. "It might be useful."

"I suppose you want the first installment of your payment too."

"That would certainly be appreciated."

Jack reached into his coat pocket and extracted a billfold. He drew out a stack of hundred-dollar bills held together with a rubber band and tossed it on the table in front of Fletcher. Fletcher scooped it up and tucked it one of the breast pockets of his jumpsuit.

"You aren't going to count it?"

"Here and now? What for?" Fletcher winked. "We all trust each other, right?"

"All right then. I want you to keep me updated and I want to be able to get a hold of you when I need to."

"Not a problem."

"You see anything that Price does as suspicious, you notify me immediately, right?"

"You got it." Fletcher slid the box off the table and down on to the seat next to him. "And you let us know when you want us to make the move."

Jack shrugged, noncommittal, then stood from the booth, adjusting his coat.

"You're dressed too nicely for a joint like this, my man."

Jack ignored the subtle dig. "You know my daughter's birthday's coming up," he said. "She would have been thirty."

"No kidding? So what you're doing now and everything . . . I suppose maybe it's good timing."

"Yeah." He turned to leave.

"One hell of a way to have to try to make up for her life

though. You know?"

Jack turned back to look at the men in the booth. Yeah, he knew.

TWENTY-SIX

Kelly Miller ambushed Quentin again as he stepped out of Uncle Nelson's front door after sunrise. There was still a chill in the air. She must have been waiting in her car at the curb, a nondescript Chevy Cavalier.

"You don't give up, do you?" Quentin was annoyed. He had other plans this morning.

"No, Mr. Price. Not when I think you have such a compelling story to tell our readers." The young woman was hurrying down the sidewalk with her tape recorder, pad, and pen. Her smile may have been meant to be disarming, but it worked. Her earnestness reminded him a little of Gwen Crawford.

"I'm in a hurry."

"I can see that," she said. "I'm sorry. I don't mean to keep sneaking up on you like this. And I apologize for trying to question you in public like that at the bus terminal."

He said nothing.

"If you don't have time to talk now, maybe we could set something up for later this afternoon or this evening after you get off work."

"You know where I'm working now too?"

"It's my job. But let me assure you, people are interested in stories of exonerees like yourself. The system didn't give you a fair shake and folks can relate to that."

"Can they relate to Auburn?"

"Maybe. Maybe not."

"What did you say your name was again?"

"Miller. Kelly Miller with the *Press and Sun Bulletin*."

"You want to know my story?"

"Yes. In your own words."

Quentin grimaced. "I don't know."

"I promise you I won't try to misquote you or slant what you say. Listen, why don't I give you my card." She was pulling one out of her pocket. "Do you think we could get together later? I'd be happy to come by the restaurant if you'd rather talk there."

He stared at her for a moment. She seemed sincere enough. Like all those kids in law school working for the innocence project. "Why don't you let me think about it for a day or two?"

"Okay."

"Not everyone in Binghamton is so happy about me being out of prison, you know."

"So I've heard. All the more reason for us to get your side of the story out."

"I suppose."

"Will you give me an exclusive?"

"Why? You worried Oprah's going to come calling?"

She smiled again. "Depends on your story."

"Okay. Like I said, I'll think about it."

"Fair enough." She handed him her business card. "And will it be okay to bring the photographer?"

"We'll see."

"Call me anytime, day or night," she said. "If I don't hear from you, I'll try you again in a couple of days."

A half an hour later, he crested the hill into the cemetery, granite and marble monuments backlit by the morning sun. He had stopped in at a mall the afternoon before and bought new shoes. How much warmer it felt here than during his last visit, shivering during his mother's burial in his light prison coat and shackles. It took him a while to get his bearings. He should have expected the disorientation, having been here only once before. Then again, he'd always relied on some internal compass. Why should it fail him when it came to finding his mother's grave?

He finally came upon the plain stone marker in the shade of a sugar maple. He'd almost missed it—it lay practically flush with the ground. The neat trimming of the grass around the edges, the small Christian flag hanging limp in the morning dew—these looked fresh, however. Her friends and members of her church were faithful to the core.

Unlike several of the other monuments in the immediate area, hers stood alone. No overarching family moniker, no neatly laid out plots for various family members, husband and wife, mother, father, daughter, son.

It saddened him to think again that he and Uncle Nelson were virtually all she had had left of a family, save for his absent father and her southern sisters with whom she had little or no contact. Her church was her family, she was fond of saying. Her only son might have been sent up the river for rape and murder, but nary a soul had a bad word to say about Carla Price.

He bowed his head and offered up a brief, silent prayer, more out of respect for her than any real belief. When he looked up, the sunlight was angling differently through the trees. A dapple of mottled radiance was spilling over Carla's stone.

He arrived more than half an hour late for his appointment with Christine Shackleford. BC Transit had been behind schedule and, worse, they'd gotten stuck behind an accident and all the attendant traffic cops, fire engines, and other rescue vehicles.

At least he didn't need to be at work until noon. Sierra was typing on her computer again when he entered. She was wearing a light pink skirt and a close fitting white blouse this morning, he noticed.

"Quentin, we thought you'd forgot."

"Sorry, problem with the bus."

"Ms. Shackleford is on the phone. She was just preparing to leave for court."

"Bummer."

"You want me to let her know you're here?"

"Please. But before you do there's something I wanted to talk to you about."

She smiled. "Sure. What is it?"

"You do a lot of research here for Ms. Shackleford, don't you?"

"Yes."

"Computer and library searches, that sort of thing."

"Sure, of course."

"I need to look into an old matter that requires that kind of thing. Do you think you could help me?"

She glanced at her boss's door. "You mean outside the office here?"

"Yeah."

"Okay."

"Great."

She pulled out one of the lawyer's cards and wrote a phone number on the back. "I'm off tomorrow morning. Why don't you call me and we'll set it up."

"Thanks very much. I'll do that."

"Is that Quentin out there, Sierra?" Shackleford's voice boomed through the closed door.

"Yes it is, Ms. Shackleford."

"I've still got a couple of minutes. Send him back."

She smiled again at Quentin. "There you go then."

"Later," he said. "Thanks again."

"Don't mention it."

He found the attorney standing behind her open briefcase sifting through a ream of legal documents. She had already stuffed several inside.

"I haven't got much time," she said. "Due in court in less than half an hour. Hopefully we can deal with this quickly enough. Go ahead and sit down, please. Tell me what it is you want to do."

Quentin took a seat while she continued piling papers into the briefcase. "It's simple. I want to talk to the DA."

Shackleford paused for a moment to stare at him over top of her reading glasses. "We've been through this, haven't we? You told me to tell him no and I did."

"I told you to say I would think about it."

She continued sorting her papers. "That means the same as no in my book. At least it has the same effect."

"Okay, I hear you. But I've changed my mind."

"What are you trying to do, overturn our legal victory?"

"No, I just want to find out how their investigation is going."

"No you don't," she said. "You're looking for absolution and you won't find any from Randall Tischler. You're wasting your time."

"I'll take that chance. I'm not looking for Tischler's official forgiveness or anyone else's for that matter."

"What are you looking for then?" She finished with the papers and snapped her briefcase shut.

"The truth about who raped and murdered Gwen Crawford."

She pulled her briefcase to her side, came around the desk and sat down in the other client chair beside him, placing the briefcase next to her. "Quentin, please, for the love of God . . ." She removed her reading glasses and let them dangle from the chain around her neck.

"It's important," he said. "It's not just for me."

"You could end up unraveling your chances at a settlement."

"I won't."

"What about signing the papers for the lawsuit?"

"We will soon. Please. Just make the call and set it up."

She drew in a breath. "If you insist on meeting with him, I'm going to have to go with you of course."

"Naturally."

She shook her head and pursed her lips. "It's against my better judgment, I'm telling you that right now."

"I'm sorry."

"They'll try to put you into a position to incriminate you for something, anything else related."

"That's why you'll be there."

"You know they've brought in another investigator."

"Really?" It was the first he had heard about it.

"Some young hotshot detective from the NYPD to look over the case."

"That's good though, isn't it?" he said. "It means someone with a fresh set of eyes is looking over everything."

"Maybe."

"I want to talk to this new detective too, whoever he is."

"Oh, don't worry, I'm sure he'll be there, listening with all ears."

"Okay."

"Why this sudden urgency? Why this change of heart?"

He needed to be careful here. "Maybe I remembered some things that might help unravel what really happened."

"Do you have some further evidence you can present in the case?"

"Not particularly."

She stared at him. "What are you really up to?"

"Like I said, just trying to get at the truth."

"All right. I'll go ahead and make the call." She stood with her hand on her briefcase and lifted it off the desk. "But I still say this is crazy."

"Look," he said. "I'm sorry to make things so difficult. I know you haven't made any money yet from my case or anything."

"You know that's not what I'm worried about—"

"I know, but listen. I've got a feeling this will work out for the best."

"That depends."

"On what?"

"On what your precious truth turns out to be," she said and wheeled to head out the door.

Twenty-Seven

Garnell hung up the phone in his hotel room. DA Tischler had hardly been able to contain his anticipation, and who could blame the man? Garnell was finally going to get to meet the object of his investigation. Quentin Price was coming in.

Something odd was going on though. He could no more explain his intuition than tell Monique all the ways in which he loved her, the very sight of her, her smell, her touch, the lilting tremor of her laugh . . .

He picked up the phone again and dialed home.

"We're doing fine," Monique told him once he had her on the line. He could hear Ivy cooing in the background.

"Really?"

"Really."

"The baby's okay?"

"She's eating like a horse."

"But . . . in a lady-like way, right?"

Monique laughed. "I don't think she's too worried about such things yet."

He was quiet for a moment.

"Is everything going okay up there?" she asked.

"Yes."

"You lie like a rug."

"Yes."

"Did you expect it was going to be easy?"

"I hoped it would be. I was afraid it might not be. The fear's winning."

"Okay, how's it not easy?"

"This whole thing has a strange feeling to it, but I can't put my finger on it. It bothers me. I can say this though. If this had been my case, I would have gone after Price too."

"Even knowing what you know now?"

"Maybe so. But somehow it doesn't quite feel right."

"Maybe it's part of the nostalgia of being back home."

"I thought that might be it too, at first, but now I'm not so sure."

"There was a small article in the *Times* yesterday about Quentin Price. Have you met him yet?"

"No, but I'm about to. I was about to go find him to talk to him anyway, but his lawyer called the DA's office today and said he wants to come in and talk. It's all arranged. Tomorrow morning."

"You still think he did it?"

"Probably. Maybe. I hope I'll know better after tomorrow."

"The article made him out to be a victim of the system."

"He may be. If he is, I'd like to see the evidence for it though."

"You mean besides the DNA."

"Yeah."

"Was the original investigation clean?"

He sighed. "Appears to be. The cops up here seem honest enough, and I don't know why they would want to railroad Price."

"How about the prosecutor?"

"Tischler? So far, so good."

"He really blew it, withholding information about the semen sample from the defense though, you know."

"I know. He understands that. Believe me, he understands."

"Is his head on the chopping block?"

"Could be."

"Have you heard anymore from the DAG in Albany?"

"I gave Bollinger an update this morning. Wish I had something more earth-shattering to report."

They were both quiet for a moment or two.

"I miss you like crazy," he said. "And the baby. I didn't expect—"

"I miss you too."

After they hung up, he lay back on his bed in his hotel room and stared at the ceiling. It didn't surprise him that the media would make Price out to be a victim. Those were the kind of stories that sold newspapers—little guy against the system—even more so when there were hints of racism involved.

In his experience, that kind of thing almost never happened though. Way more often than not, the perps that got nailed for something—issues of race or creed aside—were guilty. Even on those rare occasions where they might not be guilty of what they were accused of, they were guilty of something just as bad or worse.

At least the A/C kept it cool inside his room. It had been hotter today, the late afternoon sun still baking the buildings outside and beating through the curtains. His plans called for changing into shorts and running shoes, hitting the weights in the hotel fitness center and maybe getting in three or four miles before dinner. Maybe even down along the river where it was a little cooler.

He had just finished lacing up his sneakers and grabbing his room key when his cell phone jangled. Monique calling back? He picked up the phone and glanced at the caller ID. It was Jane. His partner's number was locked into his brain.

"How's the little vacation?" she asked when he answered.

"Some vacation. It's hard enough trying to solve murders when they're brand new."

"Makes you feel for the guys on the cold case squad. On the other hand, they don't have a DA breathing down their necks."

"Yeah. How are things going down there?"

"The captain's got Sandusky and Grimes working with me till you come back. If you don't get back here soon, I'm going to die of onion and garlic asphyxiation."

"Serves you right for all those ice cream sundaes you eat in front of me."

"Can I help it if you've yet to develop an appreciation for the finer things in life?"

He paused. "What's up, Pappy? You didn't call to discuss gastronomics."

"Nope. More like genetics," she said.

"How's that?"

"Just took a call from one of our esteemed colleagues over at the Federal Bureau of Investigation."

"And?"

"You remember hearing about a rape-murder case five, six years ago, that Johnson and Keiper investigated where the body was found off the Hutch near Co-Op City but the vic was from upstate?"

"Vaguely. Not really."

"Victim's name was Santiago and they never solved it."

"Okay."

"But they took a rape kit."

"Sure."

"Well guess what?"

"CODIS came up with an identical DNA profile."

"Yup, in the SDIS, but more than that . . . The DNA from the semen found on Gwen Crawford, your vic up there in Binghamton . . . ?"

"Yeah?"

"It's a dead-on match."

TWENTY-EIGHT

Quentin and Ruth were in her car again. At least she'd gotten the flat fixed and the spare put back in its place. McGinnis's closed at nine o'clock. Ruth said she wanted to go by the spot near the railroad yard where they'd found Gwen's body, again, said she wanted to see the place in the dark like Gwen would have seen it before she died. She had always been afraid to go there by herself alone at night.

"You think going to talk to the DA is such a good idea?" she asked.

"Why? You got a better one?"

"I don't know," she said. "It just seems dangerous. I saw the way those two detectives were looking at you the other morning."

"You were the one who called them on me."

"I know. I know. I didn't realize—"

"Forget it. At least there's no doubt where they stand."

"So why do you want to go back in and subject yourself to scrutiny again?"

"Because they're professionals, and you and I are not. They might just reveal something important."

"But you used to work security. You were studying crime work—"

"And I got all the extra education I'll ever need up at Auburn, believe you me. But it's not the same."

"I wish I could go in there with you," she said.

"It'll be fine. I'll have my lawyer with me."

"Did you know there's a new detective on the case?"

"I heard."

"He called me. His name is Harris, with the NYPD. But he didn't ask me anything I hadn't already told Hollister and King before. He said he wanted to talk with me in person. You think his being here will help?"

"I hope so. Looking forward to meeting him myself."

Ruth babied Bertha along the street leading past the yard.

A diesel locomotive was pulling a long line of flatbed container cars along the tracks, each looking like a gargantuan breadbox on wheels. The lights on the tracks were flashing red and green. Across the river, headlights streamed along Business Route 17.

"You remember where it is?" she asked.

"Not exactly."

They'd brought him out here soon after he was arrested to pepper him with more questions. By then, of course he'd gone almost numb. The prosecution had brought the jury out here during the trial, too. In that case he and his attorney were brought along, as was the court reporter, since it constituted the taking of additional evidence. His memory of the event was cloudy. He was sick that day, had vomited from bad jail food. He'd blocked most of the rest of the trial from his mind as well. At least after a certain point.

Ruth stopped the car and he followed her gaze out across the tracks into the darkness. What if he'd actually been here the night Gwen Crawford was murdered? What if he'd only dreamed of finishing work at the big party and leaving for home by himself? The idea had occurred to him once before, sitting in his cell at Auburn. People had hallucinations—mental breaks, what have you—all the time, didn't they? At least he'd read about such cases.

"There's a flashlight in the glove compartment," she said.

He opened it and found the light, encased in an aluminum housing. You twisted it to activate the small but powerful beam. "All right. Let's go."

They exited the Chrysler, not bothering to lock the doors, and started across the tracks. A thin haze engulfed them with its spectral tentacles. It only added to the creepiness of the place as far as Quentin was concerned. Except for the last of the container cars, now receding into the dark distance like memories of the old Erie and Lackawanna, the yard seemed deserted. The air was perfectly still.

They moved across to the bank of tracks nearest the river and walked along it for a few moments. Quentin kept the flashlight beam trained along the ground.

"I think it's back over this way a little bit." Ruth said. She pointed down the tracks in the opposite direction. "You know, a thought just occurred to me. Whoever killed her might just live somewhere around here."

He said nothing. They set off in the direction she had indicated.

"If he does, it might make it easier to find him," she said.

"Unless he's moved."

They had walked another fifty yards or so when he glanced back toward their car along the shoulder of the road, a hundred or more yards distant, and he didn't like what he saw.

"Hush up a second." He killed the light.

"What is it?"

The gray Toyota was making its way slowly up the street toward the railroad yard.

"That car coming along there. By where we're parked," he said.

"I see it."

"It's been following me off and on since Sunday."

They crouched low, peering over top of the embankment and the tracks. The car appeared to be moving steadily but cautiously. When it drew even with the Chrysler, it slowed nearly to a crawl, then sped up again as it continued on past the rest of the yard.

"Who is it, do you think?"

"Good question."

"The police?"

"I don't think so."

He could feel her gaze upon him in the dark.

"Can I trust you, Quentin?" she asked.

The words were her own, but the question could have risen up from the depths of her daughter's grave. Ever since their eyes first met in the courtroom years before. Had he, Quentin Price, done something, anything wrong when it came to her daughter?

Yes. But not what she thought. And now he could make it right at last.

"Yes, you can trust me," he said.

"Why would someone be following you?"

He shook his head and shrugged. The car had turned the bend and disappeared along the river.

"I don't know why, but I suddenly feel like this is all wrong," she said. "Being here, I mean."

"How's that?"

"Not sure. It seems whatever happened here turned this place evil for me."

"If there's any evil here, it's the evil he put here. The one who did those things to Gwen."

"I guess I thought coming over here would give me some fresh perspective. But instead it's brought back the same old fears. The same old guilt."

"You mean about not talking with Gwen?"

"Yes."

They stood in silence for a moment. Quentin switched on the flashlight again, training its beam along the edge of the bank below the tracks. He had to agree with her. There was really nothing more to see here anymore, just memories and ghosts, inventions of their own imaginations.

He tried to conjure up an image of Gwen, what she might have been thinking here in her last moments. But none of it squared with the Gwen he knew, full of life, with so much to look forward to.

"Do you think whoever is in that car is out to harm you or me?" she asked.

"Maybe somebody doesn't like the idea of me being set free. Or maybe it's just the cops being nosey."

"I have another confession to make," she said.

"Uh-oh."

"I called Jack, Gwen's father."

"When?"

"After I dropped you off downtown the other day. I know I shouldn't have. I guess I was afraid."

A cold resentment stirred in him, but for the first time in a long time it was coupled with acceptance.

"Don't worry about it," he said. "Ten years in max, you learn what it is to be afraid."

She nodded.

He followed her gaze back across the line of tracks.

"What if whoever killed Gwen is in that car?"

"That would be good."

"That would be good?"

"It means he's close. It means he's so confident he's not afraid to risk showing himself."

"But if he doesn't think you know he's here . . ."

"He knows I know he's here. If he's paying attention, he does."

His words seemed to hang in the air for a moment, echoing back to him from the dark.

"C'mon. Let's get out of here," she said.

TWENTY-NINE

Garnell stared at the clock on the district attorney's conference room wall. Almost eight a.m. He'd been up at five, here working since before six, and in this meeting since seven. Price and his attorney were due in a little more than an hour.

Seated around the table were the Broome County district attorney Randall Tischler, the state assistant attorney general in charge of criminal prosecutions from the Binghamton regional office—a woman named Betty James—not to mention Detectives Hollister and King of the Binghamton Police along with their captain, a diminutive man with a bald spot on top of his head named Bernie Dolanski. The politics in the room was almost palpable. The governor had stopped short of appointing the attorney general's office to supersede the DA in the matter. At least for now. A large whiteboard propped on an easel was filled with words, arrows, and checkmarks. Topic A was the SDIS match.

"If we're talking some kind of serial killer, it still doesn't necessarily let Price off the hook," Hollister was saying.

"Why?" Garnell said. "You think Gwen Crawford just happened to have sex with a serial rapist the night Price killed her?"

"Price could have had an accomplice."

"Serial rapist working with an accomplice would be extremely rare," Tischler said.

"Like the D.C. sniper case was extremely rare. Look, I know Price knows more than he's said. And I still think he was up to something the night she died. Hell, he might be up to something even worse now."

"That brings up another issue," King said. "Who knows how many other cases we might be missing?"

Garnell was a little mystified by Hollister and King's stubbornness about Price's involvement in the murders. Did they know something more than they were revealing? The group had talked round and round the possibilities for the better part of an hour and still seemed no closer to making any real progress.

"I'm not sure what to think anymore," said Tischler, who'd been leading the discussion standing beside the whiteboard, magic marker in hand.

"Can I make a suggestion?" Garnell asked.

"By all means."

"I think we need to basically go back to square one. Throw out just about everything we think we know except for the DNA information. Start looking for new evidence."

"But this is a ten-year-old case now, detective. Seems pretty unlikely we're going to be able to come up with anything truly new at this stage of the game."

"That depends where you're looking."

Garnell pulled a fresh fax of a weathered photocopy Jane Pappas had sent to him that morning from his folder. It was a copy of a cash receipt from a diner on Route 17 in Roscoe, between Binghamton and New York City. It had been found near the body in the Santiago case. The victim, Mariana Santiago, was from the Bronx but she'd been visiting her aunt and uncle at their house up in the Catskills when she'd disappeared, and the investigating detectives had speculated at the time that their perp was most likely from somewhere upstate. Garnell had shared the idea with the group at the beginning of the meeting but produced the receipt again now for emphasis.

"There are only so many things in this case we know for

certain," he said, "and one of them is that it was linked with this case."

Detective King had been chewing on his pen. Now he spat it out. "But what about the rope? We know for certain she was killed with that. And we know for certain it was found in Price's garage." As if to counter Garnell's fax, he pushed a copy of a photo of the dead young woman's neck closer to the middle of the table.

Garnell needed to choose his words carefully here. He'd been on the phone earlier with DAG Bollinger in Albany and the consensus from afar now seemed to be that the locals had rushed to judgment. Of everyone in the room, Tischler appeared to sense this, perhaps because his job was on the line, but even he was resistant to any complete reversal in direction.

"But that was pretty convenient, wasn't it?" Garnell said.

No one spoke. A chair squeaked.

"Just what are you implying, Detective Harris?" Captain Dolanski asked.

"He's saying that someone from our department may have planted evidence." Hollister and Garnell shared a look with no love in it.

"Not necessarily," Garnell said. "Someone else could have."

"The murderer?"

"Why not?"

"You're supposing he was someone who knew Price and Crawford. That he might even have been there that night at the college party."

"Might even have been a cop and he knew Price would make a good target to frame." He had to throw the idea out just to see their reaction. He could see the questions playing through the eyes around the room.

"But we found the Home Depot receipt and the other items, not just the rope in Price's garage," Hollister said.

"Price also said during questioning that he kept the garage unlocked. And it was a cash receipt, wasn't it? The store kept no video checkout records at the time. There's no reason it couldn't have been someone else."

No one said anything.

"But if you'd been there and seen the way the stuff was stored and everything . . ." Hollister said.

"I'm saying it's possible, that's all," he said. "It's hard to imagine, but I suppose we can't rule it out." Tischler wrote on the whiteboard PRICE FRAMED followed by a question mark. "What else does anyone have?"

THIRTY

It was midmorning, the sun already well above the horizon by the time Jack found the old logging road cut into the state forest between Utica and Binghamton, not too far from the town of Pharsalia. He drove his old pickup, a weathered Chevy with a five-point-seven liter V-8 he used for hunting and camping trips. He had been waiting only about five minutes when he heard the roar of the other vehicle's engine. A few seconds later the gray Toyota ground to a halt beside him.

"Right on time." He shook hands with Fletcher, who had climbed out and come around to Jack's rolled-down window. Today the photographer was dressed in a crisp black jumpsuit to go with his trademark baseball cap.

"And you're early."

"Always." Jack peeled eight more hundred-dollar bills from a roll in his pocket and handed them over. "What more have you got for me?"

"Not much. He's mostly been going back and forth to work, riding the bus."

"Oh, he's got an honest job now, has he?"

"Busing tables at McGinnis's in Vestal. You remember? That's the place I told you I saw the two cops talking to him before."

"Yeah." The same place Ruth worked. He felt his blood pressure jump a notch. "So he's going to work at the restaurant. What else?"

"Nothing else that I can see. He works, goes home. So while

he's there, I've been checking on those two cops you wanted me to keep an eye on."

"And?"

"They don't seem to be doing squat since that first time I seen them talking to your boy Price in the restaurant. They haven't gone near the man."

"Figures. But it doesn't necessarily mean they're doing nothing."

The photographer slapped at a black fly that was trying to dive bomb his neck, said nothing.

"Where's Price now?"

"He rode the bus and went into that lawyer's office again first thing this morning. He came out with a woman, I guess the lawyer herself, after a few minutes. They got in a car and drove over to the district attorney's office."

"They've gone to see the DA?"

"Looks that way."

"Good. Good." Maybe Hollister and King were finally doing their job after all. Then again, maybe not. "That's it then? Otherwise, Price's just been going back and forth between his uncle's place and work?"

"Pretty much."

"What about the uncle?"

"The old coot doesn't ever seem to come out of his house."

"Okay."

Fletcher seemed to hesitate. "There is maybe one more thing."

"What's that?"

"The past couple of nights Price's been catching a ride home with your ex in that beat-up old Chrysler of hers."

"Has he now?"

Ruth again.

"And last night, they did something that seemed a little weird.

Drove out of their way and parked in a spot by the old railroad yard in East Binghamton."

"No kidding."

"They got out of the car and I saw them cross the tracks with a flashlight. Couldn't tell what they were doing though."

He had a pretty good idea what they'd been doing. He couldn't bring himself to visit the place anymore himself. The last time had been a few years before when he'd detoured off of I-81 on a trip down to Scranton on business. The pink rage it threw him into made him almost physically ill.

"Okay," he said. "Good job."

"You ready to move on this turkey yet?"

"You know what, Doyle . . . ? I think I am."

"Cool." Fletcher nodded, his expression unchanging.

Jack leaned across the seat and reached inside his glove box. He pulled out a plain number-10 envelope with the words FOR RUTH CRAWFORD written on the front of it. "My ex Ruthie's been getting notes every now and then from some mystery person and it's got her panties in a twist. Figure we can use that."

He handed the envelope to Fletcher. "Why don't you slip this under the wipers of her car at the restaurant before the two of them leave work."

"Okay."

"It's open. Go ahead and read it before you seal it. I think it'll put her and Mr. Price in a position where you and your friends can more easily begin to have a productive chat with them."

THIRTY-ONE

"Let's go over this one more time," Shackleford said. "When they ask you a question, what's the first thing you should do?"

"Think about it, and glance at you," Quentin said.

"Right. Of course, I'll jump in and speak for you if and when I need to. If they follow the usual script, they'll probably start out with some pretty innocuous questions. Don't be thrown off by that."

They were on the sidewalk in front of the old Press building. His lawyer looked ready to do battle. Her normally flat hair had been coiffed into a stylish cut. She wore a suit and stockings, the same as she'd worn for his release hearings. She wasn't the corporate executive type, Quentin thought, but she could almost pass for it.

He wore his new suit as well.

"You really think they're going to be able to trip me up at this point?"

"No reflection on you, Quentin, but we have to assume the worst. You've already had ten years of seeing how serious this can get."

Inside the lobby they took the elevator to the main floor reception area. They waited only a couple of minutes before being ushered into a windowless conference room where five people sat around a long table.

He already knew DA Tischler and his assistant as well as Detectives Hollister and King, of course. The new man was obviously the NYPD detective, but . . . Quentin thought he vaguely recognized him. How?

"Ms. Shackleford, Mr. Price, thanks very much for coming in this morning," Tischler said. "Have a chair."

They took seats next to one another at the opposite end of the table from Hollister and King, closest to Tischler.

"I believe you already know most everyone in attendance. Our one new face is Detective Garnell Harris with the NYPD. He's here to assist in our renewed investigation of the Gwen Crawford murder."

Harris, seated next to where the DA was standing, nodded at the two of them with piercing eyes. He was a good deal shorter than Quentin, but Quentin thought he looked like the type you wouldn't want to tangle with. And he was pretty sure now he had seen him somewhere before. On the street growing up in Queens? In Binghamton?

Tischler looked at Shackleford. "I'm assuming your client has already been made aware of all his rights in coming down here for questioning today."

"He has. I'm almost afraid to ask, since you've already lost the appeals battle in court, but is Mr. Price somehow still a suspect?"

Quentin nearly smiled. Go get 'em, Christine.

"Put your cards right out on the table, Ms. Shackleford," the DA said. "I appreciate that. And to show good faith I'll do the same. The simple answer is no. Mr. Price is no longer a suspect, as far as we're concerned, in the rape and murder of Gwen Crawford."

What? Quentin looked at Hollister and King, both of whom stared absently at the wall opposite.

Something was out of sync here. Two days ago, they'd practically been willing to rip his head off. He hadn't said anything about it to Shackleford and now he was glad he didn't, but he sensed he was in for a different kind of tactic, maybe a drawn-out version of good cop/bad cop.

Shackleford kept her poker face. "I'm happy to hear that."

"We still, of course, consider him an important material witness."

"Which means you'd try to get a judge to lock him up again if you thought he might flee to avoid further participating in your investigation."

The DA pulled out his chair at the head of the table and sat down. A conciliatory gesture. "I don't think it's going to come down to that. Besides . . ." Tischler looked directly at Quentin. "You're not thinking of going anywhere, are you, Mr. Price?"

He glanced at Shackleford, who intercepted the question.

"My client is already gainfully employed and residing here in the city. He has no plans to leave the area at present."

"That's good." The smile again from the DA Then he turned to Harris next to him. "Detective Harris? I know you have some questions for Mr. Price."

"I do."

Harris looked him straight in the eye and Quentin was struck by a memory of a basketball game years before—Union-Endicott versus St. Anthony's. Not many black faces in the stands at those games. But Harris, a much younger Harris but the same man who now looked at him across the table, had been one of them. So it was Binghamton after all, not Queens. And now Harris was a detective with the NYPD, no less. The kid had gone from those bleachers to the kind of job Quentin should have had.

"I've read all the trial transcripts," Harris said, "and gone over the tapes of your original interrogation, Mr. Price. Are you still sticking to the same story about where you were and what you were doing the night Gwen Crawford disappeared from the Merryweather College campus?"

A glance at Shackleford, who nodded slightly. "I am."

"But you were friends with this young woman, weren't you?"

Shackleford remained stone-faced. He took her passivity to mean it was okay to go ahead and keep talking. "In a manner of speaking."

"What do you mean by that?"

"I mean I wasn't friends in the way another student might have been her friend. I was . . . I was more of a big brother figure to her, I guess."

"Yes, you said that at trial. Did you ever have sex with the young Ms. Crawford?"

"Never."

His inquisitor hadn't blinked. Neither did he.

"I don't see what relevance that might—" Shackleford sat forward in her seat.

"Forget it." Harris held up his hands. "Sorry. Forget I asked the question."

Quentin waited.

"We know you didn't commit this crime, Quentin." Harris softened his expression and his voice. "In fact, we know that virtually beyond a shadow of a doubt. But somebody did. Someone grabbed this little college girl right from under your watchful eyes, took her and raped her and strangled her and left her down there in the weeds beside those tracks like a worthless piece of garbage."

Quentin blinked. He'd lived with that for ten years now, but it didn't get any easier.

"Detective Harris, no one feels worse or has suffered more because of what happened to Gwen Crawford than my client," Shackleford said. "He doesn't need to be reminded of the details."

Oh, yes he did. He needed to remind himself every day.

Harris was unwavering. He looked back at Quentin. "Are you

on board with us, here, Mr. Price? What have you got to lose? Don't you want to catch this cocksucker as bad as we do?"

"Detective Harris." Shackleford's tone was threatening now. "Mr. Tischler, I—"

Quentin held up his hand and she stopped. His stare was locked with Harris's.

"Okay," he said. "So you have some new evidence."

They examined one another across a gap of time and circumstance formed by dancing to separate but not all that dissimilar tunes, to the tides and prejudices of the man and their own expectations.

The rest of the room was silent.

"Why should I tell you that?" Harris said.

"Because I know this thing must be heating up now. Otherwise, our conversation wouldn't be headed in this direction."

They weren't going to be able to make him think they were taking him onto their team. The district attorney broke the impasse by flipping open a dark manila file folder on the table in front of him, lifting out a single sheet of paper, and pushing it down the table toward where Shackleford and Quentin sat.

"What's this?" Shackleford picked up the document and put on her reading glasses.

"It's a DNA match," Harris told them. "The profile from the semen sample taken from the Crawford case ten years ago matches the profile from another murder that happened five years ago. Only this time the body of the young woman was found in the Bronx."

"While my client was behind bars up in Auburn."

"So it seems." The NYPD detective turned his gaze on Quentin again. "Are you going to help us now, Mr. Price?"

He looked at Shackleford, who was shaking her head as she continued reading the report. Another killing? Another girl, maybe another like Gwen?

Hollister slapped a big hand on the table.

"I can't sit here and take this any longer."

"Excuse me?" Shackleford said.

"We had a good case ten years ago. As solid as any I've ever been on." His eyes lasered in on Quentin's. "There's something squirrelly about this whole damn deal, Price, and I think you know what it is. I know you know what it is."

Quentin looked at the big sad-eyed Binghamton detective and felt sorry for him for a moment. How can you ever go back? How could he explain?

"You might just as well have killed her yourself." Hollister pulled a pencil from his ear and threw it on the pad of paper in front of him.

"That's enough of that," Tischler said.

Shackleford pushed away from the table. "That's it. We're done." She looked at Quentin and shook her head.

"Ms. Shackleford—"

"As far as we're concerned, this interview is over." She buttoned up her briefcase and replaced her reading glasses around her neck. She pushed the DNA report back across to the table at the DA Motioned to Quentin and he stood with her to leave.

Harris pulled a business card from his pocket. "Here. You might want this." The detective tossed it in his direction and it landed with a soft plop on the table in front of him. Quentin picked it up and tucked it in his breast pocket.

"I doubt we'll have any more need of your services, Detective Harris," Shackleford said, turning toward the door. "Or, for that matter, any of the rest of you either."

"I'm sorry to hear that, counselor," Tischler said.

"Not half as sorry as you're going to be after we've had our day in court. The state of New York will have to raise taxes just to keep up with the punitive award."

Thirty-Two

"What the hell was that all about back there?"

Garnell caught up with Hollister by the coffee machine after they'd all left the room.

"What do you mean?"

"You don't sandbag me in front of a suspect. We're all supposed to be on the same team here."

Hollister dropped a couple of quarters into the machine and pushed one of the buttons. He said nothing.

"Come on, Hollister, talk to me."

The big man turned and looked at Garnell. "You just don't get it, do you, Harris?"

"Get what?"

"It's us against them. The good guys against the scum bags. You can't go around accusing me and my partner in front of the captain and the DA of fixing a case and expect us to sit still."

"I wasn't accusing you of anything."

"No? If you're on our team, brother, you've got a funny way of showing it."

"That's not what I was trying to do and you know it."

"I'm telling you we can still get to Price. He's hiding something, I can feel it."

"Even if you're right, even if he is still somehow mixed up in these murders, we need to try to work with him. We need to find out what makes him tick. This many years later, it may be the only way left to find out what really happened."

Hollister stared at him for a moment before turning to pick his cup of coffee out of the machine. He inhaled and blew out a deep breath. "Maybe you're right. Maybe I overreacted in there."

"Look, man. I know how much work goes into a case like this and how much bullshit the system can be sometimes. You guys might have done everything by the book and gotten a solid conviction. But something must have been missed here. Maybe not by you. Not consciously, at least. None of us is infallible."

"Huh." Hollister almost smiled. "They teach you big words like that down in NYPD school?"

"No. My wife's a law student at Fordham."

"Oh, Jesus." The Binghamton detective rolled his eyes.

"Think about what you just saw in there. You honestly think Price is some kind of rapist serial killer?"

Hollister said nothing.

" 'Cause if he is, he must have some kind of magical spell he used to transport himself out of Auburn and down to the Bronx."

The white cop's expression softened. "Maybe you're right."

An hour later, Garnell was back across Court Square at the police bureau with Hollister and King. Still not the best of friends, but a barrier had been broken and they all had a job to do. They had a couple more old boxes to sort through in the evidence room.

"What's this?"

Garnell held up a bulging file folder full of what looked like greeting cards and some sheets of paper with writing. It was marked CRAWFORD CORRESPONDENCE.

Hollister looked up from where he was working. "Ah, it's nothing. Just some condolences Ruth Crawford, the vic's mother, said she received. None of them are signed. Probably some old coot, friend of the family or whatever, taking a shine to her."

"Really?"

Garnell began to read.

Thirty-Three

Sierra Lathrop was waiting for him on the front steps of the Broome County Public Library. Quentin thought she looked intoxicating framed against the midday Court Street traffic.

"How'd it go at the DA's office?" she asked as he stepped off the bus with a handful of other passengers.

"Okay up until the time your boss decided it was time for us to storm out."

"That bad, huh?"

He shrugged. "Could've gone worse."

"That's why I could never be a lawyer myself. Too confrontational."

"Is that right? What kind of confrontations do you prefer?"

She smiled. "The more nurturing kind."

Man, oh, man.

"We did learn something pretty critical though," he said. "They found a match with the DNA sample that freed me. From another murder five years ago downstate."

"While you were in prison."

"That's right."

"You're kidding."

"Nope. The girl was from around here."

"That's awful."

"Yeah."

"I mean, it's good news for you and all, but that's still terrible."

They headed on into the library together. He steered her toward the public computer terminals he spied as soon as they walked in.

She had a certain grace about her movement, he noticed, like a dancer.

"You ever done ballet?"

"Yes," she said, looking embarrassed. "When I was younger. How did you know?"

"The way you move. I tend to notice things like that."

They sat down in an empty carousel in front of one of the computers.

"What exactly are we looking for here again?" she asked.

He explained it all once more. Soon they were online, Sierra seated at the keyboard working the mouse while Quentin leaned over her watching the screen. She smelled of something tropical and exotic.

He was amazed at the speed of the link and the wealth of options available. He'd had monitored, heavily censored Internet access while at Auburn. Here they could search for whatever they wanted with virtually no one looking over their shoulders.

Sierra opened a popular search engine, typed in the date he'd long ago committed to memory followed by the words "Binghamton fatality river," then looked at the results.

It was halfway down the third page, just below a site featuring the supposed dangers of a particular brand of SUV. The *Press & Sun Bulletin* archives apparently contained an article about a driver who had died in a car crash on the date in question. A little more searching brought them to the article, complete with a black and white photo of the deceased— Caucasian, large ears, black-rimmed eyeglasses, a lick of dark hair across the forehead—along with a grainy action shot of a compact sedan being pulled from the river.

"Holy . . ." he muttered.

"What do you mean?"

So it was true. Gwen hadn't been dreaming. He glanced around the room to make sure no one was watching them. There were a couple of people at other terminals, but they seemed engrossed in their own surfing. He pulled out the single photo clipping he'd taken from the box in the park with all the cash. Even in its faded condition he could see it was identical to the one on the screen.

The story described the deceased as one Benjamin Alexander Cook and gave an address in the city. Cook, age twenty-eight, went by Alex, was single and worked as a copier repairman for a local office supply company. The accident had apparently occurred in the wee hours of the morning. Excessive speed was cited as the primary cause. It was not known yet whether alcohol was involved. The cause of death was thought to be drowning. At least Quentin had a name and a place to start. He was following a thin thread; where it might lead, he had no idea.

Just to be sure, he asked Sierra to continue searching for any other accidents that might have occurred on the same date. As he suspected, there were none. She printed a copy of the article for him. He folded the sheet of paper and stuck it in his pocket.

"Okay," she said. "You want to tell me what's going on with all this?"

"Just something I'm working on. Trying to help out Gwen Crawford's mother."

She stared at him. "Gwen Crawford's mother? The victim of the murder you were convicted for?"

"That's right."

"Quentin, are you sure you ought to be . . . I mean—"

"It's okay. Don't worry."

They headed back outside to the sidewalk in front of the building. Traffic was beginning to build.

"Ms. Shackleford says you have a really good case and all,"

she said. "You don't want to do anything—"

"I won't. Look, it's getting late. I'm sorry but I've got to run." He turned to go, but turned back. "I really appreciate your coming all the way down here to help me out with this."

She shrugged. "It was nothing."

"Maybe we can get together over a cup of coffee sometime and discuss the situation further. You look gorgeous, by the way."

"I . . . thank you, but I—"

He leaned over and gave her a quick peck on the cheek. Nothing sensual. Just quick and platonic. Enough to open a door.

"Thanks very much again," he said as she smiled. "Really."

"You're welcome."

Intoxicating.

Rain was forecast for later in the morning, but for now the sky was merely dappled gray and black. For some reason Quentin felt like he was losing time, even more than he had at Auburn, the nagging sense that important events affecting his life were occurring beyond his vision or reach. Freedom wasn't all it was cracked up to be when you still lived under a cloud of doubt.

He walked the several blocks to the address listed in the yellow pages for the office supply company where Alexander Cook had once worked. The building was sixties-style yellow brick with a plate-glass entrance in front. Inside was a showroom full of the latest copiers and other related office equipment.

"Can I help you?"

The woman was young and attractive in a midwestern, wholesome sort of way. She was dressed in dark slacks and a cream-colored oxford-cloth shirt with the company's logo emblazoned above the breast pocket.

"Yes," he said. "I was hoping to talk to a manager."

"Are you interested in office equipment?"

"No. Not exactly."

"Employment?"

"No. I'm a part-time student at Broome CC and I'm doing some research on traffic fatalities in the city. I was hoping to talk to him about a former employee."

He hoped the ruse would work. It had been a long time since he had been a part-time student, and research on traffic fatalities was a stretch but not that far out of the realm of possibility.

The woman gave him an odd look for a moment, then said "Sure. Let me see if someone is available."

She disappeared through an open doorway into a back office. Through a window he watched as she spoke to an older man with a chiseled chin and thick forearms seated in front of a computer terminal. The man said something back to her, then clicked a box on his computer screen before rising from his seat and walking through the door.

"My name's Kurt Bertram," he said. "I'm the owner here. Can I do something for you?"

Quentin repeated his story.

"And your name is . . . ?" the owner asked.

"Slater," Quentin lied. "Lewis Slater."

"A little old to be going to school, aren't you, Mr. Slater?"

"I spent some time in the army. Just getting around to finishing my degree."

"Well, good for you, on both counts. Come on back."

The man led Quentin into his office where the two of them sat down in vinyl office chairs.

"My older brother was killed in 'Nam, you know," Bertram said. "You ever deployed overseas?"

"No. I was in the eighty-second Airborne at Fort Bragg, but I didn't stick around long enough." Only part of this was true, but he hoped a vague answer would end this line of discussion.

"Oh, okay. Well, anyway, what kind of information was it you were looking for?"

Quentin opened his notebook and pulled a pen from his pocket. "It's a long shot, I'm sure. It's about an accident that occurred a long time ago."

"Well, I've been in business almost eighteen years. Used to be at another location over on Hawley Street. I might be able to help."

"One of your employees was killed, a young man by the name of Alexander Cook."

"Alex?" The man's forehead furrowed. "Oh yeah, hard to forget about that. Crashed right into the river."

"You knew him then?"

"Of course. It was a real tragedy. He wasn't a bad worker. Customers all seemed to like him."

"The information I have is that there may have been alcohol involved."

"That's what the cops said. It was a real surprise to me though."

"Why is that?"

"Alex was a Mormon. Or at least he'd grown up as one, from his family and all. I think he'd kind of lapsed, renounced the faith, or whatever you want to call it. But he still wasn't much of drinker."

"The alcohol would have seemed out of character for him then."

The man hesitated. "Yes, I suppose."

Quentin sensed there was something more so he waited.

Bertram said, "You know the cops never really talked to me about it at the time. I know the accident came as a real shock to Cook's family out in Idaho or wherever they were from. The father even called me here at work about it. Like I said, it was a big surprise to me too. But then again, there was a part of me that always wondered about Alex."

"What do you mean?"

"Well, let me tell you." The office man's voice grew conspiratorial. Maybe the sudden jolt to his memory had caused him to remember something else, or maybe he just needed to unburden himself of something he'd been keeping secret all those years. "I never told anyone else this because I didn't really think it mattered at the time . . . but I think the guy was a real narcissist."

"A narcissist?"

"Yeah."

"What makes you say that about him?"

"He was unloading his briefcase one morning while I was walking by and out fell a bunch of photos."

"Okay."

"The weird thing was, they were all photos of him. Some of them even in his underwear or maybe it could have been a swimsuit, I don't know. He quickly scooped them up so no one would see them."

"Was he gay?"

"No. At least, I don't think so. He'd mention something about going on a date with a girl once in awhile, you know, just guy talk."

"Maybe he was trying to get work as a model. He ever say anything to you about that?"

"No . . . but I just remembered, there was one more odd thing."

"What was that?"

"About a month after it happened, I got a call from the police. Apparently they had found some money in Alex's car, a couple of bills, that they said had been traced to some kind of drug bust. They wanted to know if I had any idea how he might have come by the money. I, of course, had no clue, and I never heard anything more from them about it."

"You remember the name of the person from the police who contacted you?"

The man scratched his head. "No. It's been so long. I pretty much forgot all about it until just now. But hey, all this stuff is probably way more than you need for your report, right?"

"Oh, no," Garnell said. "Any bit of information helps. I'm trying to compile as complete a record as possible. Profile of an accident. You know, that sort of thing."

"Then you also know Alex was coming here from his other job that morning, right? 'Cause the cops said they thought that might have contributed to the accident. Him being so tired and all."

"Other job?"

"Yeah. Poor bastard was ambitious, burning the candle at both ends. He moonlighted working maintenance at night over at the college."

"Binghamton University?"

"No, no. The small college over in Hamlick. What's it called . . . Merryweather, isn't it?"

THIRTY-FOUR

The rain began before Quentin fully awoke. He sensed its rhythm in some dim reach of his consciousness, a steady drumbeat of droplets overflowing the gutter outside the window of the back bedroom of his uncle's place.

He hadn't intended to fall asleep again before leaving for work, just to lie on the bed and read his mother's Bible. He heard the television blaring at the front of the house and Nelson with his big dog puttering around in the kitchen.

Two ideas nagged at him. First, the notion, finally foisted upon him by Christine Shackleford, that he deserved just compensation for his prison time. He'd signed the necessary papers back in her office after the meeting with the DA. Second, and much more disturbing, the revelation the DA had given them about the DNA match. The manageable truce with an evil that Quentin thought he knew was rapidly coming to a close.

There had been other victims. He should take what he knew to the cops. He and Ruth were really nothing but bumbling fools, weren't they, compared to pros like Harris and Hollister? What could they hope to accomplish?

"I thought you said that Crawford woman was coming to pick you up at eleven-thirty to give you a ride to work."

Uncle Nelson, still in his bathrobe, stood in the hallway outside the open bedroom door, the German shepherd panting faithfully beside him.

"Yeah." Quentin looked at the electric alarm clock on the

nightstand. It was only a few minutes after eleven.

"Well she must be anxious to get to work because her car just stopped at the curb out front."

He leapt out of bed. "Probably just wants to hear how the meeting went at the DA's office this morning."

"You and she are up to something, aren't you?"

"You don't want to know, Uncle Nelson. She's a troubled woman."

"Yeah? We all got troubles. You aren't trying to help her poke her nose into her daughter's murder case like she asked you, are you?"

"We're just talking. We're just friends."

"Like you was friends with that daughter of hers got herself killed and you in so much trouble."

"What are you so worked up about it for?"

" 'Cause I'm worried about you, boy, I really am. They could go ahead and bury me tomorrow, wouldn't matter. But you, you've been given another shot. Your big chance, you ask me. Why do you want to go poking around in this white lady's grief and troubles?"

"Maybe because they aren't just her troubles." He turned to head for the bathroom to get ready to go.

Outside at the curb, the rain had diminished to a drizzle. Ruth was sitting behind the wheel with all the windows down, reading the newspaper.

"I hope you don't mind me being early," she said. "I was waiting to come knock on the door."

"Don't worry about it," he said, opening the door and sliding into the seat beside her.

"Supposed to clear up and become nice by late this afternoon."

"Won't matter either way when we're in the restaurant," he said.

"Did it matter much whether or not it rained when you were in prison?"

He shook his head. "I used to like the bad weather more. Made it seem better to be inside."

"I was out trying to run some errands before work, but I couldn't concentrate on a thing wondering what you must be talking about with them down at the DA's office."

"They got a match on some other DNA."

"They what?"

He told her, as he'd told Sierra, about the report the DA had showed him and his lawyer.

"You mean to tell me whoever killed Gwen has done it again since?"

"Looks that way."

She folded up her newspaper and dropped it over the seat back, leaned her curls into the headrest. "What are we getting ourselves into here, Quentin?"

He said nothing.

"They must know for sure you didn't have anything to do with Gwen's murder now . . . God, why can't I just let it go?" she said. "I wish I could just trust the police to find whoever did this, to make it right."

"Maybe it's never going to be made right," he said. "You ever think of that?"

"What?"

"Maybe you're looking for peace of mind in the wrong place. Finding this guy isn't going to give it to you."

She was silent for a moment. "Your mother had it, didn't she? I'd sometimes sit listening to her talk with the others at the restaurant on Sundays and wonder in my heart which was worse, losing a daughter the way I did, or having a son still alive and in prison for murder."

"Sure. But you didn't see her downtown pounding on the

DA's door, did you?"

"She told me once it was all about trust. She had absolute faith, she said, that it was all going to work out all right for her. For you. Even for me."

"It hasn't been doing too bad so far."

"Yeah. Shame she's not here to see it."

"I'm not so sure that really matters as much as we think it does."

"Tell me something," she said, as if the thought had just come to her.

"What's that?"

"Tell me what you told the police. I mean back then. Tell me everything you remember about what happened the night Gwen disappeared."

"Why? You were there at the trial."

"I just want to hear it again from you. I want to see if I remember it all right."

The rain beaded muddy streaks across the windshield.

"Okay. I guess we've got time. Let's see, I was working the party that night. But you already know that."

Ruth nodded. She had already lit up a cigarette and blew the smoke out through the crack in the window.

"It was the usual affair. End of year bash, fairly subdued. Short-haired people letting their hair down."

"Had you worked a lot of parties like that?"

"Quite a few. When the faculty were present, we were mostly there just as window dressing. Sometimes some of the students would sneak out to the parking lot to smoke a joint or drink or whatever."

"Did you ever search students for drugs?"

"If they were right in our face with it, sure, or if we suspected there was some serious dealing going on. We didn't storm through the dorm rooms though, I can tell you that."

"Why not?"

"Policy from the administration—spoken, not written down anywhere."

"You mean like don't ask, don't tell?"

"Something like that, I guess. Yeah."

"Was Gwen doing drugs?"

He hesitated for a moment, not wanting to breach a confidence, even now. "She might have. She didn't seem like she had a problem with anything though. She told me her grades were good. She always looked healthy enough."

"Back to that night."

"Right. Anyway, like I said, it was the usual end of year shindig, a live band playing, people everywhere milling in and out, food, drink—alcohol officially only for those over age, but of course a lot of the kids, especially the seniors, were drinking too."

"When did you first see Gwen?"

"Around nine o'clock."

"Who was she with?"

"A couple of her friends."

"That would be Marcia Mulligan and Jenny Stubblefield who testified at the trial, isn't that right?"

"Yeah."

"They both said Gwen stopped to talked to you."

"And she did."

"What did you two talk about?"

"Nothing too dramatic. She said she was looking forward to the summer, had an internship lined up with a magazine in the city. She was excited about it."

"So she was supposed to be going to Manhattan. Did she say when she was going to leave?"

"Nope."

"At the trial they said she was supposed to be sharing an

apartment in the city with a couple other girls from her class. Did she say anything about that that night?"

He shook his head.

"Why do you think she stopped to talk to you then?"

Quentin stared down at his hands for a moment. "I think she was just being friendly. I truly do. I know a lot of people would like to try to read more into the situation than what was there, and I can't stop people from having wild imaginations. But . . . she was a friend."

"She talked to you again, didn't she? Later?"

"Much later. The party was starting to wind down a little, must have been way after midnight."

"Do you know what she was doing between the time she came in and stopped to talk to you and the time she talked to you later?"

He shook his head. "I saw her dancing with a couple different guys, talking with some of the girls."

"All of whom testified that the only thing unusual that night was her going over to talk with you."

"Like I said, I can't stop people's imaginations."

"When she came over to talk to you that last time, that was the last time you saw her that night?"

"That's right."

"Did she say or do anything that would lead you to believe she was in any trouble?"

He was treading on thin ice here. "She was tired," he said. "I think she also said she was a little nervous about heading down to the city."

"But nothing more specific?"

He shook his head.

"Others at the party testified you looked like you were having some strong words with her."

"I was giving her some advice, that's all. You know. About

how to handle herself down in New York. It's seriously different than Binghamton."

The lies had been delivered so often and for so long now that he'd almost convinced himself they were true. He'd read somewhere about how certain sociopaths were able to beat lie detector tests because they actually believed the falsehoods they were telling. He wondered if he might have passed into that category.

"So you have absolutely no idea what could have happened to Gwen after she left the party that night?"

"No. Not really." He looked at his hands.

"Not really?"

He glanced back up at her and her eyes lasered into his.

"Okay, look," he said. "She gave me some stuff to watch over a couple of days before she disappeared."

"Stuff? What kind of stuff?"

"Don't worry about it. I'm looking into it."

"You're looking into it? Why wasn't there anything brought up during your trial. Why didn't you look into it then?"

"Because I . . . because I couldn't."

"You couldn't." The hollows under Ruth's eyes seemed to be exaggerated in the pale interior of the car. Quentin wondered if she'd been drinking again the night before, if so how much. "Why not?"

"I don't want to get into that. The less you know the safer it is for you."

"I don't need to be safe anymore."

"Yes, you do."

"You sound like a cop."

"Sorry, don't mean to."

"You're just full of surprises, you know that, Quentin Price?"

He shrugged.

She looked at her watch. "Time for us to get to work." She

started the car. He watched as she crushed out the last of her cigarette in the ashtray, already filled with other butts. "It's a disgusting habit, I know."

"You try to quit?"

"Once—for six months. I started up again though, after Gwen died."

"You're still looking for something," he said.

She smirked. "You're really starting to sound like a detective to me."

THIRTY-FIVE

Garnell, King, and Hollister made their way along a tree-lined boulevard less than a quarter mile from Merryweather College in Hamlick. Professor David Karthoff's house was a well-kept English Tudor, flower boxes in the windows. Down the street, the hedges were all manicured, brightly painted crosswalks shone in the rain, and the single stoplight on the corner in front of the deli/service station blinked a lonely summer vigil.

"Lucky we caught this guy at home," Hollister said.

Garnell reached in his jacket pocket for a notebook. "Said he's anxious to talk with us."

"I remember talking to the professor back then," King said. "Don't remember he was all that much help."

"We'll see."

They climbed out of Garnell's Caprice and made their way up the sidewalk and beneath the awning of the front porch.

Karthoff had been Gwen Crawford's faculty advisor. He might have been considered a potential suspect but for his outstanding reputation as a teacher and mentor, not to mention his solid alibi. He'd been quite visible at the big end-of-the-year school bash and had moved on, equally visibly, to an after-party bash that didn't break up until nearly dawn. That was well after the time Gwen Crawford's car was discovered unlocked, empty, and alone, in the student union parking lot by a local Hamlick cop. The fact that Gwen wasn't even reported as missing by her roommates until nearly twelve hours later made piecing together the timeline somewhat difficult, but virtually everyone else at the party that night who might have been considered a potential suspect had some sort of alibi.

Garnell rang the bell.

"Hope we're not chasing phantoms here," Hollister said.

Garnell didn't comment. He didn't figure the big man as a bad cop, just a frustrated and humiliated one. But sometimes the combination could be just as dangerous.

The man who answered the door was not at all how Garnell had pictured him—some tweedy intellectual type with a pipe between his teeth. Instead, Karthoff was a strapping, nearly oaf-ish man, easily six-five or taller, whose high balding forehead was couched by thick eyeglasses. He was clad in dark tall-man trousers and an Icelandic sweater that seemed wholly out of place, even on a gray day in the middle of the summer.

"Good afternoon, detectives. It's certainly been awhile. Please come in."

Hollister introduced Garnell and the three cops entered the cool dry air of the front foyer. Karthoff pulled a handkerchief from his back pocket and dabbed at his elongated nose. "Excuse the get up." He pulled at a sleeve of his sweater. "You'd think it was January, the way I'm dressed, but this damned summer cold's got me eating chicken soup and spending lots of time reading under the covers."

Sounded to Garnell like a pretty pleasant way to have to while away a part of your summer, if you were a tenured prof like Karthoff.

"You still married, professor?" he asked. He remembered reading from the original witness notes that Karthoff had a wife and two children, a teenage son and daughter.

"Oh, yes, yes, of course. Connie is at our beach house in Rhode Island for the month. I'm joining her next week. And of course our two kids are both grown. Both married, I'm happy to say, with families of their own. My daughter just had her first child, in fact. They're in Seattle. We're planning a trip out there in August. Still getting used to the grandfather thing."

"You're a professor of economics?"

"That's right. Please, would you gentlemen like to sit down? Can I get you some coffee or hot tea? Or maybe you'd like something cold to drink?"

They declined the offer and moved on into the living room. There was a large grand piano framed by two wingback chairs, an impressive brick hearth, its glass doors closed and cool at the moment, a sofa, a pair of rocking chairs, and a coffee table. A pastel oriental carpet covered part of the hardwood floor. King and Hollister took the wing chairs, leaving Garnell and the professor to take the rockers.

"So you were Gwen Crawford's advisor," Garnell said.

"Yes, I was, I'm afraid. One of the sadder chapters we've ever had to deal with here at the college. The saddest, personally, I think I've ever encountered in my career. How are her parents, by the way? They were divorced, if I remember correctly."

Hollister cleared his throat to enter the conversation. "They were, that's correct. And as far as we know, they're both doing fine."

"Glad to hear that. You know I can't even begin to imagine how terrible that must have been, losing a child. It was bad enough for those of us who knew and cared about Gwen as a student."

"If you don't mind my asking," Garnell said, "how did you end up as Gwen Crawford's advisor. I thought she was an art major, studying photography and that sort of thing."

"Oh, well, faculty advisor assignments are made during the freshman year before students have even chosen their major, and the pairings are pretty much random. It doesn't really matter much. In fact, I found dealing with Gwen rather refreshing.

Not that my economics students are dull, mind you. Most of them. It's just that, well, Gwen had a certain sensibility and way of looking at the world that most social science students lack. Sometimes I wish more of them would study art history."

A grandfather clock in the den chimed out the hour.

"Your secretary told us you said you really wanted to speak with us when she gave you our message," Hollister said.

"Yes, that's right. I was a little surprised, frankly, to hear from someone after all this time. But then I'd seen the story in the newspaper a few days ago and got to thinking back about things."

"Did you remember something different from what you told the detectives ten years ago?" Garnell asked.

"More 'in a addition to' than 'different from,' I think. When I read the article that talked about the DNA evidence exonerating Quentin Price I started thinking again about who else, besides Price, might've had much contact with her that night. And I remembered something odd—I don't really know why it never occurred to me at the time. But then, I guess a lot of us here in the community were pretty much in shock for awhile, especially when it came out that Gwen had been murdered so brutally."

He sat up straighter in the chair. They waited for him to go on.

"Gwen stopped by my office briefly to pick up some papers a couple of days before the party. I was running between classes and was only there for a minute or two myself. And it wasn't unusual. Gwen would often stop by for a chat or just to say hello during my office hours—she was just that kind of a person. But I suddenly remembered after seeing the article in the paper that she mentioned something about the club at the party. I thought she was confused about the location and was referring to the faculty club or something, so I never gave it a second thought. But the other day it suddenly hit me. She was talking about the photography club."

Garnell looked at Hollister and King. There had been nothing in the witness files or anywhere else about a photography club. The look on the other detectives' faces told him this was news to them too.

"Was there supposed to be a meeting or something at the party?" Garnell asked.

"I don't think so, not exactly. But what I remembered the other day was that Gwen had mentioned something a week or two earlier about trying to organize a kind of area-wide club. She said she had talked to a couple of people about a potential kick-off event and was even trying to line up a speaker— something like that, at least."

"I guess it never got off the ground."

"No, I suppose not. It's just that, she'd mentioned it in conjunction with the party, that's all. Until I read the article in the paper the other day and started trying to remember who else might have known her and all. Then when you called, I thought I at least better let you people know about it."

"Of course." Not much to go on really, but at least it was a new thread. "This is very helpful, professor. We really appreciate your time today."

The professor dismissed the compliment with a wave of his hand. "Oh, you're most welcome."

"If you think of anything else, please don't hesitate to give us a call."

"Absolutely. And do you mind if I ask you all a question?"

"Why not?"

"I suppose we've all gotten used to the idea—those of us on the faculty, I mean—to the idea that Price was the killer. But . . . if he wasn't guilty, if there was—forgive me—some kind of colossal mistake made in prosecuting and trying him, that would mean whoever perpetrated the crime could still be among us, or among the alumni."

"It's a possibility."

"How could someone have lived with that? How could they just have gone on with their regular life all these years, especially knowing that someone else went to prison for their crime?"

Garnell looked at the professor, a fleshy, graying hulk of a man, more used to the rough and tumble rigor of academic debate and scholarship, the mentoring of young minds, a life of the intellect rather than a life of the flesh.

"I'm always amazed, professor, at how well we human beings rationalize our situations. That goes for even the lowliest of the lowlifes."

"Must be some kind of economic principle for that, isn't there, Doc?" Hollister said.

The professor looked at them for a moment. " 'It is not from the benevolence of the butcher, the brewer, or the baker, that we expect our dinner, but from their regard to their own interest.' Adam Smith said that," Karthoff told them.

"He did, huh?"

"Yes. And my advice to you gentlemen, for what it's worth, is that whoever raped and killed Gwen Crawford is going to keep finding new ways to act in their own self-interest. My question is, if driven to it, could they or would they kill again?"

The detectives exchanged looks with one another.

Karthoff looked curious. "Gentlemen?"

Garnell cleared his throat. "Let's just say, professor . . . it's not an academic question."

THIRTY-SIX

The man with the cup of coffee at the front booth looked vaguely familiar.

Quentin finished clearing the dishes from the large table where a group had just departed and hoisted the heavy tub on his shoulder. Ruth pulled him aside as he entered the kitchen.

"You see who is sitting up there?"

"Who?"

"It's Jack."

"What's he doing here?"

"Says he came to talk to you."

Quentin lowered the tub onto a conveyor belt leading to the dishwasher. "Why? You think he's planning to shoot me here in front of all the customers?"

"He's not planning to shoot you, Quentin. I think he just wants to talk."

"Talk. You think he wants to try to help us?"

"I don't know. Maybe."

"He's a private investigator, right?"

"Yes. That's right."

Quentin glanced at the oversized clock on the kitchen wall. "I've got a break coming up."

"Be careful," she said. "I know what he can be like."

A couple of minutes later he was standing next to the booth at the front of the diner shaking hands with Gwen Crawford's father. The man's stare was filled with barely concealed anger, his grip dismissive, as if he were all about telegraphing some kind of a message. Quentin had run across his type and then some up at Auburn. Didn't matter which side of the wall you were on.

"I guess Ruth has already told you what I think about you, Price." The man wasn't quite as tall as he but must have outweighed him by fifty pounds. Deep forehead, Roman nose. Deep scar on one forearm. Not too much flab on him either for a guy his age. He figured he could probably take care of the guy if he ever needed to, but he wouldn't want to have to find out.

"Not in so many words but I got the idea," he said, sliding into the booth across from the big ex-cop.

"I'm not here to mince words. You raped and killed my daughter no matter what the law says."

He stared at him across the table for a moment. "And if I didn't?"

"If you didn't then God help both you and the son of a bitch who, did because you allowed it to happen and you're both as guilty as sin as far as I'm concerned."

"Gee, Jack, I'm glad you and I could have this little chat." He started to pull himself back up out of the booth.

"Hold on a minute. Stay and drink some coffee."

He kept going.

"Please."

He paused, waited.

"The real reason I came by here is because I wanted to look you in the eye again."

Quentin thought back to all those vulnerable days during the trial with a younger Jack Crawford, sitting usually together but sometimes apart from his ex-wife in the visitors gallery, those cold gray eyes boring in on him.

"Why?" he asked.

"I wanted to see what in the world Ruth thought she was doing. I wanted to see if anything about you had changed."

"Well you've had your chance to do that now, haven't you?"

"I have."

"Good for you then."

"One word of advice."

"What's that?"

"Don't go trying to capitalize on that poor woman's emotions. She isn't all that stable."

"Oh really. Who says I'm trying to capitalize on anything?"

"Come on, Price." The man pulled a money clip from his pocket, peeled off and threw a five dollar bill down on the table as payment. "We both know the way this is going down."

He had no clue what the guy was talking about.

"You're looking to cash in a big payday from the state. You get the mother of the victim on your side, the better it looks for you."

"You're kidding, right?"

"I wish I were."

"You consider yourself a good judge of character?"

"Yeah. As a matter of fact, I do."

"Ever spend any time in the stir?"

"No. Why?"

"Gangs got a saying in there . . . 'Blood in, blood out.' Ever hear of it?"

"Yeah."

"You know what it means?"

"Means you have to stab somebody with a handmade prison shank in order to join the gang. And if you ever decide you want to leave, you're going to get cut yourself on the way out."

"Or killed . . . You got it."

"You in one of those kind of gangs, Price?"

He shook his head. "Never."

"What about it then?"

"Well, I just figured, after today you might want to remember that saying, Mr. Crawford."

"Yeah? Why's that?"

" 'Cause from now on, let's just consider you and me blood in, blood out."

"You want a ride home again?"

It was nearing the end of his shift. McGinnis's had closed an hour before and Ruth was standing at the kitchen door, a tray of clean water glasses in her hand. A crop of hair had worked loose from beneath her net in back. Quentin thought she looked bone weary.

"Maybe I'll just take the bus tonight," he said.

"You sure?"

"Yeah. Go on home, get some rest."

"Jack didn't get to you earlier, did he? You said he was an ass but you were fine."

"Nah. I gave him my best gangbanger impersonation. That ought to set him thinking."

"You need to be careful."

"Don't need to remind me," he said. "You need someone to walk you to your car?"

"No thanks. I'll be all right."

"Good night then."

"Good night."

He watched as she finished putting away the tray of glasses and disappeared out through the back. He still had one big pan to clean. He was in the middle of scrubbing out the encrusted remnants of scalloped potatoes when Ruth reappeared.

She had her purse in one hand and an envelope with a sheet of paper in the other. Her face had gone bone white.

"What's the matter? You forget something?"

She held out the paper with the envelope. "I found this on

the Chrysler."

Quentin reached for a towel to dry off his hands.

"Someone must have tucked it under my windshield wiper."

"What's it say?"

"Go ahead and read it," she said.

The envelope had her name on it. He took the paper from her hand. It was a plain sheet with a few computer-printed words.

MEET ME. SUSQUEHANA GORGE STATE PARK, ELEVEN P.M. LOOK FOR BLUE PICKUP. ABOUT GWEN.

"This from him? The same person who sent you those condolences in the mail?"

"I think it could be." She stared at him, wide-eyed.

"It's too convenient." He handed back the paper. "Something's wrong." The gorge was a remote strip of riverfront down US 17 a few miles from Binghamton; he'd visited it once with his parents when he was younger. He thought about the gray Toyota.

"What do you mean?"

"I don't like the sound of it."

"Will you go with me?"

He sprayed water from the sink to finish rinsing the last pan. "I don't think you should go at all."

"Why not? I mean, this could really be important. Maybe whoever this is knows something."

"And they suddenly just so happened to want to spill the beans to you? I don't buy it."

She glared at him, folded the sheet of paper back into the envelope, and slid it into her purse. "Well I'm going whether you come with me or not." She spun on her heels and began to walk out again.

"Hold on. Wait just a minute," he called after her.

She stopped to look back at him.

"All right," he said with a sigh. "Just let me punch out."

In the car, the defroster cleared a haze from the windshield as she drove. The rain had stopped, but the night was cool, the city lights and the surrounding hills cloaked in ground fog.

"I need to get my license again so I can start driving myself."

"Good idea," she said. "But you'll need a car first."

He thought about the stash of money he had secreted away. Couldn't use any more of that though. Not when it was potential evidence.

What kind of fool's magic were they headed into now? He remembered a little bit about the exit off the highway a few miles south and the access road that led to the gorge. If you wanted to escape detection, it was a good place to meet. It was also a classic setup. He checked the mirror for any sign of the Toyota, but saw none. Still, he worried about their chances.

"We need some kind of protection," he said.

"What?"

"What time is it?"

She looked at her watch. "Just about ten."

"We've got time then."

"Time for what?"

THIRTY-SEVEN

They were on Front Street a few blocks from Uncle Nelson's place. They passed a row of dilapidated wooden structures with stucco facades crammed in among a row of once-proud Victorian homes, their porches sagging, most of their paint and their pride long since departed.

"What are we doing here?" Ruth asked.

Quentin shifted in his seat, his eyes focused straight ahead. "Going to see my uncle."

"What for?"

He met her glance with his. "A gun."

"A what?"

"We need some kind of weapon."

"But don't you think, under the circumstances, with you just getting out of prison and all—"

"Here's how we play it. I'll get Nelson to loan you his pistol. Officially, that is. Then you can give it to me. It's an old .38, a Browning, but he cleans it religiously and keeps it loaded."

"You really think this is necessary?"

"We're not going to meet someone blind and unarmed."

She nodded and drove on.

At Uncle Nelson's, lights burned brightly from inside. The neighbor's houses on either side were dark and quiet. When he'd come home from work the past couple of nights, the old man had been sitting up waiting, watching television in his recliner the way his mother used to do. He fished for the spare key Nelson had given him, found it, and went to unlock the door. The dog was whimpering somewhere inside. Maybe the animal was getting used to him and recognized the sounds of his homecoming.

The door was unlocked.

Later, Quentin realized that should have been a warning, but he was so focused on getting the gun and the meeting at the gorge, he didn't give it much thought. Maybe Uncle Nelson was expecting him. Maybe the old man had just forgotten to turn the bolt.

Ruth was right behind him. He twisted the knob and pushed the door open.

"Oh, my God, what's that smell?"

He held out his arm to stop her from advancing.

"Something not good," he said.

A sharp metallic odor permeated the house. She started to say something more, but he raised his hand for her to be quiet.

From where they stood he could see that no one was seated in front of the TV. The set was off, in fact. The dog wasn't visible either, though you could certainly hear its plaintive cries, now rising to a crescendo.

He moved cautiously across the living room. Stopped a couple of times before the hallway that led to the kitchen to listen for any more sounds, but there were none.

The kitchen came into view. The brown linoleum floor was marred by something new, a dark stain spread across the tiles like a spilled glass of dark juice.

"Oh, no. Oh, God, no."

'His eyes began to fill with tears at the sight—the outstretched hand, the figure of Uncle Nelson's body curled into an almost fetal position. The dog was posted beside his dead master, gravely wounded and unable to move, still whimpering and searching Quentin's face for some kind of answer.

Ruth let out a tinny whine of shock. Quentin retreated inside himself, willed himself to move slowly, methodically, as if he'd somehow passed outside his body. He bent down to examine the corpse, careful not to touch anything.

Ruth knelt beside the dog. "Poor, poor thing."

"You have your wireless phone?"

"In the car."

"Use the phone over there on the wall." He pointed across the room. "Call 911."

They switched places and she went to make the call.

"It's okay, pup," he said, speaking to the dog, searching for an entry wound, a place to apply pressure. "It's okay."

Nelson. Why in the world would someone kill Nelson like this?

Cradling the shepherd's head in his hands, he heard Ruth talking to the dispatcher on the phone, heard the whirring motor of the refrigerator and the sound of cars outside. He didn't know how long he sat with the dying animal. A minute? Four or Five?

"They want me to stay on the line." Ruth turned the phone away from her face.

He tried to gather his thoughts. "Okay, but you need to do something for me first."

"What's that?"

"Stay with the dog for a minute."

"Why? Where are you going?"

"To get what we came for before the cops show up."

"I don't know. You sure?"

"I'm sure."

"What do we tell the police?"

He thought about it for a moment. "We tell them nothing. About the note you found on your car, that is. You were just dropping me back home after work when we noticed the door was open."

"Okay."

"Where's the note?"

"In my purse. Right here." She had tucked it on her arm as they entered house.

"Let me have it. I'll take care of it."

She did as he instructed and handed him the envelope with the note folded inside.

He rushed through a search of the rest of the house, knowing whoever had done this was long gone. The place, especially his room in back, had been tossed. Books and clothes and the contents of drawers were strewn everywhere.

Ruth looked up at him as he passed back through the kitchen. "I'm so so sorry about your uncle, Quentin. I hope it didn't have anything to do with—"

"We can't worry about that now."

"What about the gorge?"

"Can't worry about that now either. Whoever sent that note will find you again."

"I'm really getting scared. Maybe we should just tell the police everything, ask to be put into protective custody or something."

"You want to find out who killed your daughter or not?" The words sounded harsher than he meant them to.

She stared at him. The ride was about to get bumpy. Would she bail or was she ready to come along?

"Yes, I see. Of course, you're right."

He found the Browning and the ammunition in the case under Nelson's bed where he'd seen the old man put it. He took the case and the envelope Ruth had given him and went out and hid them in with the spare tire under the floor of the trunk of Ruth's car. The sound of the first siren approaching reverberated through the air as he reentered the house.

Ruth was back on the phone. She was explaining something to the dispatcher about the dog. She had found the worst of the wounds and was pressing on it. Her waitress uniform, like the front of Quentin's T-shirt, was now smeared with the animal's blood. The dog's eyes were calm but pleading for an explanation, its breaths becoming irregular.

Quentin wished there was something more he could do, wished he'd never come here, wished he'd bought himself a decent hotel room and sent his uncle a postcard instead. He looked again at Uncle Nelson's body, sat down next to Ruth, and put his arm lightly around her shoulder. The shepherd stopped breathing, its muzzle still resting against Ruth's kneeling form.

A police cruiser skidded to a halt on the street out front. A patrolman called Ruth's name through the open front door.

"Here. Back here." Her voice was no longer urgent, resigned it seemed, to the awful destiny that had befallen them. Tears were streaming down her face.

The first of the officers, a hook-nosed young man with dark hair and a dark mustache, came down the hall and entered the kitchen, his eyes wide and his Glock drawn. "Christ almighty."

"It's bad," Quentin said.

THIRTY-EIGHT

Garnell stared across the small living room at Ruth Crawford and Quentin Price, seated beside one another on a threadbare couch. They were each wrapped in a blanket provided by the paramedics. From the looks on the faces of the first responders, it was obvious this kind of killing was hardly your everyday occurrence in Binghamton.

Everyone did their job like the professionals that they were, though. As many death scenes as he'd worked, he'd never really gotten used to it either. The day you did was the day you should quit, Pappas, his partner, was fond of saying.

"Okay. Okay, let's just review what you're telling us again. Mr. Price, here, is working in the same restaurant with you, Ms. Crawford, and you were giving him a ride home from work."

The woman's eyes were red-rimmed and bloodshot. She dabbed at them with a tissue. "Yes, that's right."

"You both saw the door open. You came in and found Mr. Price's uncle and the dog dead."

"The dog wasn't dead yet," Price corrected him.

"Right, I'm sorry. But they'd both been shot."

"Yes, sir," Ruth said.

"Too bad we couldn't interview the dog," Hollister said with a smirk, obviously not buying their story. Garnell looked across at the two Binghamton detectives. Hollister was standing in the doorway with a toothpick in his mouth while King sat in a chair taking notes.

"So you didn't hear anything or see anything else as you approached the house?"

They both shook their heads.

Garnell kicked at a loose piece of linoleum on the floor. "Someone's torn the place apart pretty good."

"We saw that," Price said.

"Anything missing?"

"I haven't had time to look. Then again, I've only been staying here a few days. Not sure I would know if there were."

"Your uncle keep any valuables or big amounts of cash on the premises?"

"Your guess is as good as mine."

"Could be a simple robbery."

"Robbery gone to hell in a handbasket," Hollister said. "How come you haven't even been out of the joint for a week and we find you sitting on another homicide, Price?"

Price shrugged, said nothing.

"That's one whopper of a coincidence, you ask me."

Indeed it was.

Price still kept prison quiet.

"You're not suspects here," Garnell said. "The shooting looks like it took place a few hours ago. You've both got alibis."

A bright light flashed from the direction of the kitchen where the crime scene photographer was still at work. On the way down the hall, Garnell had almost tripped over an extension cord to a flash klieg light the man was using. Sloppy. But then it wasn't his crime scene.

He thought he'd try a different approach.

"Ms. Crawford, you've already had enough horror in your life, I know. But I can't help you unless you're willing to tell us the whole story here."

The woman looked up at him. "There's nothing more to tell. We came in and we found them like we told you. That's it."

He looked at the two of them on the couch. "Why don't I believe you?"

Heels clicked on the porch outside. The front screen door slammed and the voice of Christine Shackleford, Price's lawyer, told him that was the end of the questioning for now. They had nothing to hold these people for.

THIRTY-NINE

The city looked bleak and gray at seven a.m. when Garnell met with Hollister and King in the restaurant at the Holiday Inn. All three were unshaven and in need of showers, propped up by strong coffee.

After sending Crawford home and Price to spend the night in a motel, they'd remained at the crime scene until nearly two a.m. Hollister and King had even gone back downtown afterward to write up their reports.

"Not much to go on." Hollister picked at the plate of eggs in front of him. He took a long draught of his coffee.

"The old guy and the dog didn't look to have put up much of a fight," King said. "They must have been surprised by the attacker."

"Any usable trace evidence? Hairs? Fibers?" Garnell asked.

"Some." Hollister glanced at his notes. "We've sent it all off to the lab."

"How about footprints in the yard or in the driveway?"

Hollister shook his head. "I hade five officers with me going over every square inch with flashlights. I'll check again in the daylight, but it doesn't look promising."

The older detective flipped open another spiral notebook on the table beside his food and scanned some more of his notes. "Got a little bit of info from some neighbors. Closest one home was from two houses away. We'll canvas the street again this morning."

King, who was drinking orange juice and eating a sticky bun, said, "I talked to one lady, said she saw a stranger walking down the sidewalk an hour or two before what the ME says is the time of the shooting. Guy was carrying a bag over his shoulder."

"She give a description?"

He looked at his own notes. "Caucasian. Not tall. Dressed in a windbreaker. That's all she remembered. She said it was starting to get dark."

"She see where he went?"

"No. Said her phone rang and she went to take the call. When she went back to the window, the guy was gone."

"No one saw anyone leaving the house after the shooting or on the street later?"

They both shook their heads.

"Looks like you guys have your hands full."

"Second homicide this year," King said. "An elderly man shot down in his kitchen. Be a lot more people making sure they lock their doors tonight."

"You've worked a lot more of these kind of cases than we have. What's your gut tell you on this?" Hollister asked.

Garnell thought it over. "My gut tells me where there's smoke there's fire. And there's a lot of smoke around this Quentin Price character right now."

"Damn straight. He beats an old murder rap and the next thing you know his uncle is dead. Something sure ain't right."

"You think whoever did the shooting was looking for something in the house?"

"Like what for instance?" Hollister looked at his partner.

"I don't know. Maybe something having to do with Price. The place was tossed pretty good."

The older detective sighed. "We probably should have told you this before."

"Told me what before?"

Hollister related how he and King had followed Quentin Price the afternoon after his release from prison and what they had seen up at the Round Top picnic area.

"So you guys have been turfing me all along," he said.

"A little."

Garnell felt a swell of anger. He glanced into the murkiness of his creamed coffee, wondering if this were the beginning of even more revelations. It was natural that the two local cops would hesitate to tell him everything at first. How could they be sure of his motives? Still, he felt frustrated. Binghamton was as much a part of his sinew as theirs.

"What else are you not telling me?"

Hollister looked at him with an even stare. "Nothing."

"You could've screwed this whole investigation."

"Yeah? Well, the bodies are starting to pile up, and the tracers are all pointing back to Price and whatever happened or didn't happen ten years ago."

They all needed some rest. Anyone could see that. Still, there was no excuse.

"Burying something in a public park isn't a major crime, you know, unless it's some kind of illegal substance."

"What the hell was Price up to then?"

"Have you tried questioning him about it?"

"No. I mean, we talked to him, but we didn't want to tip him off to our surveillance. We've been hoping he might do something else."

"So you're still keeping an eye on him?"

"We've, uh, we've got somebody taking care of it."

He said nothing. The last thing he needed was to have to worry about whatever agenda the other detectives might have. Were they just doing their jobs? Maybe they still didn't trust him. But then how could he be expected to completely trust them?

Hollister drained the last of his coffee then put his mug back down on the table. "I just hope it doesn't turn out to be some random neighborhood speed freak did the old man and the dog."

King said, "Why's that?"

" 'Cause if there's a God, when it comes to Quentin Price, he can't be that cruel."

"Too much coincidence," Garnell said.

"You think we should bring Price in, try to shake him down again?"

"You're not going to get very far the way he's lawyered up."

"So what do you want to do, Mr. Homicide?"

"You guys stay on last night's murder."

"And what are you going to do?"

"Try to find a way to get to Price."

Quentin left the motel at first light. He was bleary-eyed and still in shock, his bones full of fatigue and an unspeakable sorrow. The sun was trying to break over the hills through a patchy, gunmetal sky.

He climbed on the first available bus out to Endicott and rode all the way back to the Friendly's. The walk up the hill through the neighborhood to the park made him uneasy. He kept glancing around and over his shoulder, looking for any signs of the Toyota or any other surveillance, finding none.

He wore only sweatpants and a T-shirt. He had barely slept at all. He kept replaying the last few days in his mind, wondering if there was anything he might have done differently. The conclusion was inescapable. If he hadn't chosen to show up on his uncle's doorstep, Nelson would still be alive.

By the time he reached the park, he had broken into a jog. Let anyone who might see him think he was just out for a morning run. When he got to the trailhead, he quickened his pace.

He had started to sweat. But he needed to know.

The landmark on the trail looked undisturbed. So far so good. He sprinted the last fifty yards, breathing heavily. There was the spot.

He dropped to his knees and leaned into the hillside in the dim early morning light, straining to see. Why any of this was happening.

The dirt, turned to mud from the rain, was fresh from someone else's digging. He knew what Uncle Nelson's killer had been looking for.

His metal box was gone.

FORTY

Jack met Ruth at her apartment, a place he didn't like to visit. He had only been there once before. It reminded him of all the years and all the things, good and bad, that he'd become since they'd been together. Her kitchen was clean and bright and despite the fact that she was a smoker the place smelled fresh enough. Jack wondered if she always made certain to take her habit outside on the deck or the front stoop. Wondered what she did in the middle of the winter.

"Would you like a beer or something?" She looked across at him as they sat down together around her small breakfast table.

"No. I really can't stay."

She nodded.

He took a good look at his ex-wife and his voice caught in his throat. She may have been beaten down, but no matter how many times he saw her again, there were echoes of Gwen all about her: the skin of her cheeks and the little indentation in her nose, the green-blue of her eyes, even the way her hair curved into her forehead. Mother-daughter resemblance in reverse. Ruth must have felt this too, her mirror a never-ending highway of dark memory.

"You said you really needed to talk to me," she said.

"Right."

"I have to get ready to leave for work in an hour."

"I know. Look, I just wanted to try to get to the bottom of this whole thing between you and Quentin Price."

"What did you say to him at the restaurant?"

"That I still think he raped and killed our daughter."

"You're unbelievable, you know that?"

"I warned you to stay away from the guy. Next thing I hear, you've gone and gotten him a job for Christ's sake and you're spending time with him."

"You don't control my life anymore," she said.

"What?"

"We haven't had anything to do with one another for what now, fifteen, sixteen years, and you think you can suddenly just waltz right in here and start telling me what to do?"

"That's not the point, Ruth."

"Isn't it? What, you still don't think I'm a big girl, Mr. Macho ex-policeman? You think your balls are so big you can still order me around?"

"No, I don't think that."

"Good, because you can't. The truth is you've never even taken the time to know me, Jack. Not even when I was sharing your bed."

This wasn't going at all in the direction he had hoped for on the drive down from Syracuse. In days past he might have lashed back at her, might have stood up for himself and told his side of the story. But he was beyond all that. His anger had moved deeper into his mind and heart to places sometimes he was no longer even aware of. He worried sometimes, because he had read somewhere that this type of catatonic calculation was indicative of psychopathic tendencies.

"I can't take back time, Ruth. I just came because I wanted to talk with you once again about what happened to our little girl."

"She wasn't a little girl, Jack. She was a full-grown young woman."

"She'll always be a little girl to me."

"Whatever," she said.

"Whatever? This guy you're hanging with rapes and strangles to death our only child and all you can say is 'whatever'?"

"He didn't do it, Jack. Can't you get that through your thick skull."

"Don't give me that bullshit."

"Someone murdered his uncle last night."

"That's why I'm here. I saw it on the news."

"I was there."

"You what?"

"We found the body together."

"Jesus, Ruthie. I told you that you needed to stay away from this creep."

"All I want to do is find out who really killed Gwen."

"Why?"

"You know why."

"Are we really going to have to go back through this again? All that stuff we went through with the grief counselor and that good-for-nothing preacher and everything."

"I think you may need it again more than I do."

"Look, you want to find our daughter's murderer, you don't have to look very far. You're practically holding the guy's hand."

"Won't you just listen and stop being so pig-headed for a change?"

She told him about her newfound concern regarding the condolences she'd received over the years. She told him about her discussions with Quentin, how she really believed he was innocent and was learning to trust him. He noticed she left out the part about the note he'd had dropped off last night though.

Somewhere along the way, he stopped processing what she was saying and found himself focusing again on her face. Those were Gwen's eyes. Gwen's hair. He wished he could have let her finish, wished he could have listened to all that she had to say, but her words set off such a firestorm in his brain he broke in:

"What kind of cockamamie schemes are you trying to come up with when the truth is staring you right in the face?"

"You haven't been listening to a single word I've said."

"How many times have we had this conversation?"

"Won't you ever give me credit for anything? Won't you ever recognize that I might just have as much or more intelligence and common sense as you?"

He had been listening for twenty years to all her BS. He hated to admit it had become another language to him, something far away and foreign from his own as if she were speaking Arabic. Her words, her voice, the very stink of her, only reminded him of the reasons he'd walked out the door in search of something better all those years ago. She was nothing more than an impediment, a barrier to the new life he had created from his own sweat and toil. The problem, as he saw it, was there was nothing more he could do about the paralysis of their coexistence, short of exposing himself and sharing with her the depth of his real anger, how he was dealing with it, everything he had planned.

Ruth pushed her chair away from the table and stood. "I'm sorry you had to drive all the way down here. But this whole conversation is pointless," she said. "You disagree with my decision to reach out to Quentin Price. Fair enough. But it's my decision, not yours. I'm not connected to you any longer."

"Oh, no? How's this for a connection?"

He did the only thing he could think of doing under the circumstances. He reached inside the pocket of his jacket and pulled out his wallet. Tucked there in one of the clear plastic housings was a wallet photo, his favorite, of Gwen. He opened the billfold and pulled the picture out. Flung it down on the table where it spun for a moment before coming to rest, as if it were lighter than air.

FORTY-ONE

Two days passed.

Quentin returned to Uncle Nelson's place just as soon as the police had finished their work and would let him in. He somehow reasoned he would be safer there, rationalizing that whoever had killed Nelson would be wary of returning to the scene of the crime so soon.

He spent most of the first morning dealing with a special cleaning company and straightening up the chaos created by the intruder's random search of the house. Ruth called him and told him Walt Oriskany said it was no problem for him to take off whatever time he needed.

That afternoon he walked down the street to a hardware store and bought a new set of locks, front and back. Took them home and installed them himself. He'd always been handy, and fortifying the house gave him something to do to take his mind off the rage and the sadness, the warring feelings of anger and fear smoldering inside of him.

By nightfall, eating dinner at Nelson's table, he felt the chill of aloneness, a loss so deep it went beyond words. For all his imperfections, Nelson had been the last link to the only family he had known. Nelson didn't have a lawyer, but apparently had left a will, so Quentin hired Christine Shackleford to come in and help with the probate. They found the duly signed and witnessed document in a fireproof box in the back of Nelson's bedroom closet. The house and much of the estate had been left to Quentin, the rest given to the church.

The cleaning service had done wonders getting rid of the blood and mess, but who was there left to clean up the mess in Quentin's heart? He talked to Ruth a couple more times—she'd heard no more word from her mysterious note passer.

The police and any other evidence of the crime seemed to have evaporated for the time being. But Quentin wasn't taking anything for granted. At night, he slept with the loaded Browning close by his side. He checked out the windows through the curtains every now and then for any sign of the gray Toyota or anyone else who might be watching. The young newspaper reporter, Kelly Miller, called and left him a message on Uncle Nelson's answering machine, but he didn't call her back.

Had Ruth's mystery note been a diversion to keep him away from the house a little longer that night? His thoughts circled round the various possibilities, but he wasn't yet ready to move—not yet. He was now more worried than ever but feeling out of control, unable to shake the feeling that he was caught up in a story much larger than himself; the same way he had felt on the night Gwen Crawford disappeared.

His uncle's will also specified instructions for Nelson's interment. No funeral, no ceremony—just cremation and simple placement of the remains at a local cemetery beneath a bronze marker Nelson had purchased years before, noting his purple heart earned in World War II. There was nothing in the will about what to do with the shepherd. A woman from the local SPCA had come around that first night, after a phone call from the police. They carted the shepherd's body away and the next morning the woman called him at the motel, asking him to come by and sign a form to allow them to incinerate the body.

Instead, he asked if he could have the body, and went and retrieved it from the shelter. He buried the dog in the backyard next to a lilac bush he remembered his Uncle Nelson planting the year Quentin graduated from high school. He found a couple of two by fours in the basement, a hammer and some nails, and fashioned a crude marker, promising himself to order a more proper monument when he found the time.

On the third night back in Nelson's house, the phone rang about ten o'clock. It was Sierra.

"Did I wake you?"

"Nah. Not sleeping much these days."

"I'm very sorry about your uncle."

"He was a decent man."

"You doing okay?"

"I'm all right."

"There's was no service? I just saw a short obituary in the paper."

"That's all Nelson he wanted. No fuss. He wrote it that way in the will."

"I see."

He said nothing.

"I've been thinking about our meeting at the library the other day . . . Are you, are you trying to find out what really happened to the girl they said you killed?"

"Something like that."

"You let me know if there's anything else I can do to help. All right?"

Fat chance. He wasn't about to bring one more person into the danger zone. "How about you?" he said. "How are you doing?"

"I'm okay. The articles in the newspaper say they think your uncle's murder was a robbery."

"Yeah. They've been asking questions around the neighborhood and have set up a tip line. Good for them."

"You don't think they're going to get very far?"

"No."

"Do you think his murder might be related to what happened to Gwen Crawford?"

"Yes, I do."

"That would mean . . ."

"That would mean all of us need to be very careful."

"Yes."

There was silence on the line again.

"I'd like to see you again," she said.

"I'll call you sometime."

"What about tonight?"

"Tonight? You mean right now?"

"Yes. Do you want me to, you know, come over?"

It had been a long time since he'd been with a woman. "Yeah," he said. "You know, I'd like that very much."

FORTY-TWO

On a table at police bureau headquarters, Garnell and Detectives Hollister and King spread out the photos of the Nelson Root crime scene before them. It was late again. In another corner of the oversized room, a man toting a camera bag set his burden down on a table and began to unpack his equipment. Another pair of detectives entered, also working. Apparently all three had just returned from working another incident.

"Hey, man," one of the other detectives said across the room. "Got anything new on your murder?"

Hollister sighed and shook his head.

"Stinks. But how'd you like the gig we just got? Guy beaten up behind a biker bar out on Route 11. Blood everywhere. Sent him off to the hospital. Lots of people around and no one saw a thing."

"They call it chicken-shit blindness," King said.

The man smirked and the three others, headed their separate ways, straggled out through a side entrance leaving Garnell, Hollister, and King to stare at their photos and notes.

"It's sure beginning to look to me like it really could be a random robbery," King said. "No matter what other connections you try to make, no matter who we talk to, that's the way it seems to be shaping up."

"Kids or drugs. Most likely, the latter," Hollister said.

Garnell shook his head. "I don't buy it. Speed freak would've been more sloppy. And nothing was stolen according to Price."

"The guy's been in prison. Only been staying with the uncle for a few days. How's he going to know everything that might have been in the house?"

Garnell scratched the growth of stubble on his chin. "I think the shooter was looking for something. Maybe that box you said he had buried in the park. The one you gave to Jack Crawford."

"Which puts us right back to square one and puts Price right back in the middle of our sights."

"And it means we need to talk with Jack Crawford. What do you think he's planning to do with the box?"

Hollister glanced at King. "Got no clue. I don't know if I want to know."

FORTY-THREE

Garnell turned into Ruth Crawford's apartment complex under a hot sun. Several kids streaked by on bikes. Others ran through a sprinkler across the street or played on the complex playground, a smoothed-out patch of dirt with a swing set, a rust-stained set of monkey bars, and a slide. He envied them their innocence.

Ruth's battered Chrysler was parked at the curb in front of her unit. As luck would have it, Ruth herself was just exiting her apartment in her waitress uniform. Garnell climbed out of his car.

Ruth locked the door behind her and turned toward the lot. She caught sight of him standing on the sidewalk.

"I've got nothing more to say to you, Detective Harris. I told you everything I know the other night."

"Looks like you're headed to work," he said.

"That's right. So I don't have time to sit here and chitchat."

"Just a couple more questions, please, if you don't mind. By the way, has Quentin Price gone back to work down there at the restaurant?"

She shifted her purse to her other arm. "Not yet."

Garnell shook his head. "Got to be a tough thing. Losing your uncle like that."

"Are you going to find out who did it?"

"Yes. Sooner or later, we will."

She stood with her hand cupped over her brow to shield her

face from the glare. He searched her eyes. Was she telling him the whole truth? He didn't think so. Anymore than he trusted Price to tell him everything. But Ruth Crawford could be worn down, he was sure. A drinker who was still a soul in torture—he just needed her to understand he was as much on her side as Quentin Price might be.

"Seems like you've done a lot for Mr. Price since he got out of prison, ma'am. I mean, setting him up with a job so soon and everything."

"Who told you that?"

He said nothing.

"Probably Walt, wasn't it? That man can't keep his big mouth shut sometimes."

"I understand you had a relationship with Price's mother too before she died."

"So what if I did?"

"I'm not trying to suggest anything in particular, Mrs. Crawford. Just trying to understand you better. We all want the same thing here, believe me."

"The same thing as Detectives Hollister and King? I saw what they did to poor Quentin the other day when I brought him into the restaurant. They went after him like it was an inquisition. That's not what we'd agreed to. You're a black man. You ought to understand."

He smiled. "Mrs. Crawford, let me put myself on the line here. We still don't know for sure what's happening, but I do think there's more than a strong possibility, in fact an absolute certainty, that whoever raped and strangled your daughter ten years ago also killed again not too long ago."

"I'm already aware of that."

"And maybe the same person killed Quentin's uncle the other night."

She said nothing.

"It's natural that you would be impatient. You want to know what happened and who really killed your daughter. But under the circumstances, are you sure you want to be hanging out with Quentin Price?"

"What are you saying? It's not his DNA that was found."

"That's right. But just to be on the safe side—"

"Seems to me I've spent my whole life on the safe side, especially since Gwen died. Not taking any chances, not willing to risk the pain. I'm not going to do that anymore. Quentin's exactly the person I want to be hanging around."

The woman had guts, he had to give her that; or maybe she really was a lunatic. Maybe she'd gone psycho because that was the only way she could help lead him to her daughter's killer.

"I understand you've received some strange condolence cards and notes since your daughter's death," Garnell said.

Her expression changed.

"I've read all of them, you know."

"Do you think they might be from Gwen's killer?"

"No way to be certain. They do seem odd."

"Is there any way to trace them?"

"Not really. We can try some things. Analyze the paper and ink and the handwriting."

"That would be good. You know my daughter's birthday is coming up again."

"So I understand."

"I've showed the copies of the condolences to Quentin too."

"Okay. Why don't you let me talk to him, see what I can find out?"

"Nothing's stopping you."

"I just want to make sure you understand I'm just as much on your side as he is. Maybe more so."

She looked at him for a moment and he let the meaning of

his words sink in. She started to speak but something stopped her.

"Why don't you trust me?" Garnell asked.

Her gaze drifted toward the ground. "It's Jack," she said.

"Gwen's father?"

"Yes."

"Okay," he said. "I get it. Are you saying he did something to you?"

"No. Not physically at least."

"And now that your daughter's case has been thrown wide open again you tried with Hollister and King, only to feel burned again."

"My ex-husband's not a bad man, detective."

"I haven't met him yet."

"You don't know what it's like though to lose a child. The things it does to you. It rips your heart out."

"So because of that you mistrust all cops."

"Don't you get it?" She shook her head. "I learned I could never trust Jack with my emotions. He stomped on them time after time. Worse, he didn't even realize when he was stomping on them. It wasn't that way when we were first married. Being on the force made him like that."

"That isn't true for everyone."

"Maybe not. But that's not the worst problem."

"What's that?"

She crossed her arms and her eyes bored into him. "The worst problem is that all you cops somehow seem to keep screwing up. You didn't do it right again. You see? And now I have to go back and start dredging up all these old feelings again, like it will be with me forever, like I can never move on."

"I'm sorry," he said. "I'm very sorry."

"Sorry stopped cutting it a long time ago, detective. You don't think so, ask Jack."

FORTY-FOUR

The NYPD detective in the coat and tie came around the side of the house as Quentin was putting Nelson's lawnmower back into the utility shed. The lawn was small and had taken him less than twenty minutes to mow.

"You again."

"Me again," Harris said.

Traffic swooshed by in the background. He could hear the sound of Nelson's old bedroom air conditioner running too. It cooled most of the house during the heat of the day.

"You know I remembered seeing you before here in Binghamton."

"Yeah. I grew up here. Even watched you play basketball a couple of times."

"I thought that was it . . ."

He didn't trust this man. At least with the homies at Auburn, you knew where they were coming from.

The cop looked toward the house. "I'm really sorry about your uncle. You get everything cleaned up okay?"

"I'm taking care of it." He turned and closed the shed door.

"You said the other night you've got a job working at the same restaurant where Gwen Crawford's mother works."

He looked back toward the man. "That so?"

"That's a little strange, don't you think?"

"Maybe." He shrugged. "Job's a job."

Where he worked was his business, not some nickel-plated

nigger's, no matter where the man had grown up or gone to school.

"I'm just wondering what your motivation is to even want to hang around here after all that's happened. If I was you, I'd be on the next bus out of town."

"Yeah. Well you ain't me, are you? Besides, you heard what the DA said about me trying to leave the area."

The two stared at each other for a moment. Quentin wondered if this guy, who must have spent more time working homicides than Hollister and King put together, could really make any difference now that the evil that seemed to have been dead and buried with him at Auburn had been set free again.

"You-uh, you've been doing a lot of work on the house?" the detective asked.

"Mostly inside. A lot of straightening up and running errands to get stuff to fix things."

"I'm glad I caught you at home then. Look, I'm sorry the way things ended up down at the police bureau the other morning. You don't have to tell me anything without your lawyer present, if you don't want to."

"Wasn't planning to."

"I just can't help feeling that something's left out, that whatever happened between you and Gwen Crawford the night she disappeared was a lot more complicated story than what it appears."

He said nothing.

"Am I right in my thinking that? Help me out here."

Quentin shook his head. "You're good."

"Thank you."

"No, I mean, you've got the empathetic hustle thing down pretty pat, man. They could use you up at Auburn. Talk to some of the Harlem Mafia Crips and Bloods they got holed up in there."

Harris folded his arms across his chest. "Exonerations like yours don't happen every day, you know."

"Tell me about it."

"I'm disappointed. I thought you were on the side of finally trying to make this whole business right."

"Yeah. Ten friggin' years of my life because you people screwed up your jobs."

"They'll be a comeuppance for that."

"There will, huh?"

"Yes. In the meantime though, they've sent me up here to try to help figure this whole mess out. Me. Not somebody else."

"Go ahead then, Mr. Detective. Solve away."

"Why won't you help?"

"I'm not helping nobody."

"But you might be helping Ruth Crawford."

"What business I have with Mrs. Crawford is between me and her." He turned his back on the man again and locked the padlock on the shed door.

"You know I could almost believe you really did do it, Price. I could almost see you talking to Gwen Crawford that night and grabbing her later on and doing everything just the way they said you did."

"No kidding," Quentin said. "Sometimes, when it gets really dark at night, and I start thinking about all the bullshit artists out there like you, I could almost see it too."

Forty-Five

Garnell leaned back in the desk chair, blew out a long breath, and slammed the yellow pages book down on the bed in his hotel room. It had been more than seventy-two hours since Nelson Root's murder. Neither the crime lab in Binghamton nor Hollister and King had come up with any solid leads. The ammunition used was standard 9mm, the kind favored by any number of gang drug dealers or others looking for an easy cannon to haul around. It was leading everyone to speculate the crime might just have been a random act of violence.

Besides talking to Price and Ruth Crawford, he had been camped out at the Holiday Inn, making phone calls, interviewing any other old witnesses he could find, even visiting the old Gwen Crawford crime scene a second and a third time, stopping by his old high school and visiting some of the old haunts asking questions, with nothing really new to show for it. But what gnawed at him more than anything else was an index card in a plastic bag on the bed.

He leaned over the bed and picked it up to examine the writing again.

I HAVE GWEN'S BIRTHDAY PRESENT FOR MRS. CRAWFORD AGAIN. A BIG ONE THIS TIME. ONE FOR THE NIGGER MURDERER AND THE NIGGER COP TOO.

He'd already dusted it for prints with a kit he'd brought along. Of course the results were negative. It wasn't the invocation of the "N" word or the threat that made him uneasy, though they were troubling enough, especially since Gwen Crawford's birthday was only a few days away. There was an even bigger problem. The card had mysteriously appeared beneath a stack of papers on the borrowed desk he had been using at police bureau headquarters. Someone inside the police bureau or with connections inside was trying to intimidate him off the case.

He needed to talk to Jack Crawford. Whether that would lead him any closer to Gwen Crawford's killer, he was beginning to wonder. His cell phone rang on the desk. He scrambled to answer it.

"Garnell."

It was Monique.

"Hi, sweetie."

"I've been worried about you. You haven't called me."

"I'm sorry, baby. How are doing?"

"I'm okay."

"How's Ivy?"

"Everything's fine. When are you coming home?"

Home. Was it still the boiling summer streets of the Bronx and Queens where his back-breaking caseload kept him constantly on the go, his heart thumping in his chest? Or was it back here in Binghamton now where the memories of his youth seemed to pique him from around every corner?

"Soon, I hope," he said.

"I got your last email. Any breakthroughs?"

He told her about the DNA match from Gwen Crawford to the Santiago case and about the Nelson Root murder. She went quiet as he was talking.

"We're making some progress though," he concluded.

"I'm worried, Garnell," she said. "Why do you have to be the one to stay there? Why can't the local police just handle it?"

"I want to try to see this thing through, honey."

"Can you get some time off to come home for at least a day or two?"

"Maybe this weekend." If they all lived to see the weekend, he thought.

"We miss you, Garnell. You wouldn't think Ivy would miss her daddy, being so young and all, but I think she really does. The way she looks at me and all . . . it's the cutest thing."

"Put the phone up to her ear, will you?"

"All right."

He spoke to his baby daughter. Not in baby talk the way some parents did. He used his best soothing voice, its pitch controlled by some invisible connection between him and the distant child. Ivy babbled something unintelligible. Monique came back on the line and he felt the weight of her breathless prose.

"Sweetie?"

"I'm here," he said.

"She giggled and reached out for the phone like it was you."

"At least she knows her daddy."

It made him think again of Jack Crawford.

Midday he drove up to Syracuse under a brilliant blue sky. Interstate 81 was a shining gray ribbon of asphalt, pockmarked with big rigs, cars, and motor homes heading north, the sun bouncing flares of light from their windshields and mirrors. The river-fed valleys of the Southern Tier soon gave way to the hard-scrabble glacier-scraped ridges and plateaus of the central New York snowbelt, now awash in summer green.

When he was a kid growing up, his parents used to take him shopping in Syracuse. The salt city was the big metropolis to him then. Now it seemed small in comparison to just the Bronx.

On those shopping trips as a boy he'd see other young black men idly listening to music outdoors or just hanging on stairways smoking. The way Garnell's old man saw things, there were two kinds of people in the world. He and his parents were not the kind to end up like those young men: with no hope, no future. You didn't complain, you overcame.

Word had it that Crawford was pulling down the big bucks as a private investigator. That, in and of itself, wasn't of much concern to Garnell. A man with his contacts and experience would make either a formidable ally or rival when it came to investigating his daughter's now apparently unsolved ten-year-old murder. And something told him not to just take Hollister and King's word for everything when it came to Jack Crawford.

The offices of Crawford Investigations were housed in an impressive-looking corporate park, a half dozen modern concrete buildings surrounding a manmade lake complete with spouting fountains. He entered through a glass door and showed his badge and ID to a secretary who quickly ushered him in to see the owner.

Jack Crawford was as formidable a figure in person as he appeared on his resume. Standing six-foot-three or more, piercing blue eyes, sandy hair, and a grip that seemed designed to let the other man know who was boss.

"So they got you humping after Gwen's old case."

"That's why I'm here."

"I'm glad they're at least taking seriously the fact that my daughter's killer is now running around free."

"Well I can see how you would feel that way, Mr. Crawford. And there have been some new developments."

"The DNA match, you mean?"

"You've heard about that then."

"I've heard it's got you people's panties in a bunch which well it should."

"That and Price's dead uncle."

"Heard about that too. Awful. Price seems to be around a lot of bad stuff, doesn't he?"

"Where were you the other night when Nelson Root was murdered?"

"At a Syracuse Chiefs game with a couple of clients. You want their names and numbers?"

He thought about it. "No. Never mind. The point is Quentin Price couldn't have killed our other vic and dumped her down in the Bronx. He was locked away up in Auburn."

"Oh, I know. I know."

"That doesn't make you want to revise your earlier statement?"

"How long you been a homicide investigator, detective?"

"Five years."

"And on the street, how long before that?"

"Four."

"Fast tracker. Good for you. Down there in the big city though, you must have figured out like we have up here that there's no such thing as infallible evidence. There's a lot more to the game than waiting on some dweebs in white coats sitting in some lab to spoon-feed you the answers. The real world's a lot messier than that."

"It can be."

"Serial killers might make good fare for movies and the once-a-year national news stories, but from what I read about the phenomenon, it's always wiser to lend higher credence to the more obvious suspects first."

"Like Price."

"He'd still be top of my list."

"At least you're consistent." He stood from the chair where he'd been facing Crawford across the desk and walked toward the window, glanced outside, then back at Crawford. "I understand you've been having some contact with Detectives Hollister and King down in Binghamton."

"Maybe." Crawford didn't miss a beat, although his voice dropped a notch.

"I understand they might have given you something, something that might belong to Quentin Price. A small, rectangular metal box."

Crawford's smile was strained. "Maybe."

"Tampering with potential evidence can be a serious matter. Do you have the object here?"

"Uh, no. As a matter of fact, I don't. I don't even have it in my possession any longer."

"Really?" He glared at the man.

"Really."

"Do you know where it is?"

"Not exactly."

"What's that supposed to mean?"

"It means I don't know where it is. All it is is an empty box, anyway. I passed it on to some people who might be able to do some good with it."

"Oh, is that right?"

"Yeah."

"What kind of people?"

"Look, Detective Harris. Where you come from they may like everything to be held by the public. But up here in the hinterlands, we like to keep some things private."

"Private."

"Yeah. Like it says on my door. That's why I get paid the big bucks."

"I want that box back."

"Okay. I'll see what I can do about getting it back for you," Jack said. "Not that it's going to help you with anything. May take a day or two."

Forty-Six

Garnell crossed the room, searching for any other angle that might help break down Jack Crawford's defenses. There was an arrangement of striking photographs on the wall there: black and white landscapes, portraits, and still-lifes. "Did you take these?" he asked.

"No. Those were taken by Gwen."

"Of course. I understand she was quite a photographer."

"That she was."

So far the lead provided by Gwen's former college advisor had led them nowhere. None of Gwen's other friends that they had been able to talk to so far remembered her saying anything about a photography club or meeting anyone at the party that night.

"You remember if your daughter ever belonged to any kind of a club?" he asked.

"Club?"

"Yeah. You know. For taking pictures."

"I don't know. I never heard her mention anything about it."

"One of her old professors, her advisor in fact, now remembers he thinks she might have been trying to start some kind of club, that maybe she was supposed to be meeting someone that night."

Crawford shrugged. "The first I've heard of such a thing."

The PI turned in his chair but made no effort to stand along with Garnell.

"Yeah, well, it's pretty sketchy and all. Hasn't led us anywhere."

"Right. Like a lot of other dead ends. Waste of time."

"You and your daughter were close, Mr. Crawford?"

"Reasonably so."

"I understand she wasn't getting along with your ex-wife at the time of her murder."

"Yeah. You should be asking Ruth about that though."

"But what's your father's opinion?"

"My opinion? I don't know, girls get into these things with their mothers sometimes. Like fathers and their teenage sons, you know?"

"You think it was just temporary then."

He shrugged. "I would have hoped so. But like I said, you should be asking Ruth. Seems like it tore her up pretty good."

"When you and she were divorced, how did Gwen handle it then?"

A cloud seemed to drift through his eyes. "Oh, I don't know. She was twelve going on twenty-one, if you know what I mean. She seemed to handle everything all right."

"You think she blamed her mother?"

"Maybe. There was enough blame to go around."

Scanning down the room, his eyes alighted on a framed certificate and some more photos, these of various groups of cops, what he assumed was Jack Crawford standing somewhere among the rows. "You ever miss being on the force?"

"Not really. I did at first, steady paycheck and all, but it passed. The kind of stuff I do's probably peanuts compared to a big homicide dick like you, but the pay's a hell of lot better and sometimes I run across some pretty interesting stuff."

"I guess you don't have to worry as much about doing things by the book either."

"What do you mean?"

"I'm talking about the box. You know, making sure to preserve the chain of evidence, that sort of thing."

"You're like a broken record. And the answer is yeah, if it's a criminal case we do. But if things start getting too gnarly, that's when I call you guys. Who needs the hassle?"

"How about when you were a cop?"

"I was disciplined once or twice. No secret—it's in the record. Sometimes I got a little overzealous, but I never broke any laws."

"Sure."

"If what you're asking is am I sitting on some other hot piece of evidence going to make your case, the answer is no. Why would I?"

"You made your opinion pretty clear about Price's guilt. How's it make you feel, him getting out?"

"I believe we've already established that's it pisses me off."

"Enough to do anything about it?"

"What are you talking about?"

"I'm talking about using your contacts and money to mount your own investigation which might start screwing with our investigation."

"I'm not going to do that," Crawford said. "I don't need to do that."

"So you don't have anything additional on Price or about this case that might help me?"

"No."

He moved back along the wall of photos done by Gwen Crawford.

"A man's only child. A daughter. There's something special about that," he said. "I know if it were my baby girl, if something happened, well, I don't know what might happen."

For a brief moment Jack Crawford's countenance turned zero dark thirty, a brooding glimpse. Then he smiled a tight smile. "That's why I really want you to nail whatever bastard it is, Price or whoever. Anything else I can do to help you, detective, you just let me know," he said.

FORTY-SEVEN

Night was falling as Jack turned his Seville into the deserted parking lot at Onondaga Lake Park. He shut off the engine and lights and climbed out, closing his door behind him. Fletcher was already there waiting beside the Toyota.

"I'm not happy about this," Jack said. "What the hell's going on?"

"You tell me."

"You know who off'd Price's uncle?"

"Not a clue."

Jack had hardly slept the past two nights, wondering just what kind of game Price might be playing. Bad enough to have wiped out Gwen's life. Now whatever Price was into had swept up part of his own family as well. Did it matter? Did it change anything? Not really.

"This NYPD detective's been snooping around," he said.

"Yeah?"

"Might be a problem."

Fletcher said nothing.

"I still want it done," he said.

"That's why we're here. I'm inclined to bow out at this point. Too much exposure."

"Like there wasn't any before? Look, I wanted you on this case 'cause I knew you could do the job."

"And because you knew you could put the screws on me."

"As always."

Fletcher stared at him for a moment. "The fee doubles," he said.

"Fine."

"That easy? Maybe I should have asked for more."

"You'll get your payment. But the timetable's moved forward."

"All right. You got another note for me to put on your ex's car?"

"No. Why don't you come up with something on your own this time."

"Sure," Fletcher said. "Didn't you say your ex had been getting cards in the mail she was obsessed about?"

"Yeah."

"How about I just mail her something myself this time then?"

"Okay, what are you going to say in it?"

"Don't worry. I've got some ideas . . ." Fletcher smiled. "Speaking of your ex, what do you want to me to do about her?"

"What do you mean?"

"Seems like she's been hanging out a lot with Price."

He had thought some more about Ruth. Whatever crusade she was on was delusional. "Ruth's made her bed," he said. "Let her lie in it."

Fletcher said nothing and Jack's words seemed to hang in the air for a moment. Out on the lake, the shadowy wings of a pair of frightened geese burst into flight.

FORTY-EIGHT

Quentin stepped off the bus a block away from his mother's old building. It was rush hour, but unlike the early morning commuters driving past, he was in no hurry. He'd seen no sign of any vehicle following the bus, but he needed to make certain he wasn't being watched.

Feeling the comforting weight of the Browning beneath his dark windbreaker, he walked slowly down the street, glancing over his shoulder once or twice, turned right toward the river, and made his way down to the end of the dead-end street before doubling back. Carrying a concealed weapon without a permit was, of course, a felony in New York State. He had weighed the consequences of making this trip unarmed and decided he'd rather risk a weapons charge than be found dead on the side of the road somewhere.

He turned right at the corner, and kept going until he reached the front entrance of the building. Checked again for any signs of surveillance.

So far so good.

Inside, he didn't bother with the elevator this time. He took and proceeded directly down to the basement laundry room where he ran into a problem. An older woman with bulbous eyeglasses and a silver front tooth looked at him in alarm and gave him the once over as she pulled her laundry from one of the dryers.

Start with a little truth.

"Afternoon, ma'am."

"Good afternoon," she said. "Do I know you?"

"I don't think so."

"Do you live here in the building?"

"No, but my mother used to. She passed away a couple of years ago. Carla Price?"

"Carla? Oh, yes. I remember Carla. I didn't know her all that well. I only moved down here from Utica a few months before she died. You say you're her son?"

"That's right. Just looking for a few things she left down here in storage."

"Of course. Did you see the super?"

"Nah. I'm hoping her old key will work." He produced a copy of his mother's old key he'd placed in his pocket for just such an eventuality. He had no idea whether or not it would still get him into the wire storage cage area.

"But they're new tenants in her old apartment."

"I know. I was here and spoke with Mr. Ambrose the other day."

"Oh, all right then. What did your mother leave behind?"

"Just a couple of old blankets and some clothes. Not really worth anything. I just wanted them for sentimental value."

"That's nice. My kids will probably incinerate all my stuff as soon as I'm in the ground."

He smiled, not really knowing what to say.

The woman finished loading her basket. "Tootle-oo," she said, trundling off toward the stairs with it tucked beneath her beefy arm. "Have a good day."

He breathed a sigh of relief, waited until the sound of her footsteps climbing the stairwell had disappeared, and instead of heading for the tenant storage area, pushed through the opposite door into the boiler room.

The sheets of plywood were just as he'd left them. He

breathed a sigh of relief, found the loose brick and his roll of money intact, put everything back the way he had found it, and was upstairs and back out on the street before the woman probably even had time to begin folding her laundry.

What to do now? Who had been looking for the box at Nelson's house and why? It was someone close by, he had a feeling. Within range but out of touch. He felt like a fish underwater looking upward at a murky, unidentifiable form.

He caught another bus and rode it out Vestal Avenue to a shopping center, where a salesman just opening the store was more than happy to sell him a new cell phone and a prepaid service plan. Eventually, once he started making payments, it would help build up his credit, the man explained.

Just what he needed—credit. He dropped the phone in his bag and left the store.

On the bus back downtown, he tried for the umpteenth time to piece together Uncle Nelson's murder with Ruth's obsessions and idiosyncrasies and with what he'd learned so far. It just wouldn't quite fall together. He had money and he had time and it was a beautiful summer day. Strange, but he no longer felt the urge to run. Him sitting here a free man, it wasn't for no reason. With Ruth Crawford or without, Gwen's and Nelson's killer or killers were out there waiting.

Let them come.

FORTY-NINE

It was nearly a two-hour drive from Syracuse into downtown Albany. Garnell used the time in the car to talk to Clyde Watford, the old railroad man who'd found Gwen's body, on his cell phone. He spoke with Quentin's old boss at the college too. Neither man could offer up anything new. He reached the attorney general's office a little before three.

This time the summons had come not from Deputy Attorney Bollinger himself but from Betty James, the AG based in Binghamton. They wanted to meet with him in person to discuss the new developments in the Gwen Crawford case as well as the Nelson Root murder.

Garnell had only been to the capitol building once before, on a field trip when he was in the seventh grade. He remembered the Moorish-and-Gothic-Revival-style ceiling in the main lobby, the magnificent sandstone staircases with their famous carved faces. It gave him a sort of perverse pride to be returning here, this time showing his ID on official business and being directed to the deputy attorney general's office.

James was already seated in a wingback chair speaking with Bollinger when Garnell was ushered in.

"Detective Harris. Right on time. Good of you to come." Bollinger rose from behind his desk and stepped around to shake Garnell's hand. A silver-haired fox of a man in an expensive suit. Plastered across his face was what might pass for a wry Irish grin. "I trust you had no trouble finding the place?"

"Right." He smiled at the man's tepid attempt at a joke.

"Ms. James here has just been filling me in on the investigation down in Binghamton."

"Yes, sir."

"If you don't mind . . ." Bollinger gestured toward another wingback next to James opposite his big desk. "Why don't you brief me on your version of events as well."

He glanced at James, who crossed her legs and gave him an expectant look. He and Bollinger took their seats and Garnell began a recitation of the events and discoveries he'd made since arriving in Binghamton on Sunday, including the Nelson Root killing.

When he finished, Bollinger asked, "So what's the bottom line, detective? Are we dealing with some kind of serial killer here?"

"If you look at the DNA match with the Santiago murder. Two cases. Same MO. I'd say yes, it's likely."

"We're considering asking the FBI for help."

"That's your call, sir," he said.

"Nothing against the local detectives or your investigation, of course."

"I understand."

"How do you think Tischler's office and the Binghamton police will take the news?"

"I can't speak for them, sir," he said. He had been on the case for less than a week while Tischler, Hollister, and King had lived with it for ten years. They hadn't exactly welcomed him with open arms; then again, they hadn't totally rejected his assistance either.

"A wise answer," the DAG said, looking at his assistant attorney general from Binghamton.

Betty James cleared her throat and began: "There's another element to this investigation we need to make you aware of,

Detective Harris."

Another element? He waited.

"We've managed to keep it quiet so far. But the plain fact of the matter is we've already had an FBI profiler looking into this case, even before we found out about the second DNA match."

"Okay."

"And one of their primary hypotheses is potentially very disturbing."

"What's that?"

"They believe the perpetrator may well be someone within law enforcement."

Garnell nodded.

"You don't seem surprised."

"What's the profile based on?" he asked.

James reached down into a briefcase on the floor next to her and pulled out a manila folder. She opened it and began reading.

"The location of the body. Gwen Crawford was found on private property in an area railroad security and the police were supposed to be patrolling regularly. Unfortunately, that wasn't happening at the time, which was one of the reasons it took so long to find the body. Someone who was aware of the problem would have been able to exploit that."

"Or it could have been just happenstance."

"Yes, but—" She read on. "Of even greater concern is the case against Mr. Price. Price claimed all along he had never seen the rope and the other materials that were found in his garage. There were, however, a number of other items found along with rope—all documented with the cash receipt that was discovered. Very sloppy for Price, a security guard who was supposedly studying criminology."

"You're saying it was a setup."

"Yes."

"I've already been through that idea with Hollister and King."

"It would take someone with an intimate knowledge of the system to know exactly how to manipulate the evidence. Of course the federal report concludes with the usual disclaimer. 'None of this may be seen as definitive proof of police or law enforcement involvement.' "

Garnell looked at the deputy attorney general.

The DAG looked back at him. "Well?"

"Well what, sir?"

"If you want to bow out of the investigation now, here's your opportunity."

The thought of bugging out was tempting. Anything that smacked of internal affairs went against his grain, not to mention what it might do to his reputation. He could simply turn over his notes to the attorney general's office and be on the road back to the city, where Monique and Ivy and his everyday job were waiting for him.

On the other hand, there were his old ties to Binghamton. There was Ruth Crawford. There was the fact that the perp or perps had already reached out and touched him personally via the index card. And there was Quentin Price.

"Thanks for the offer, but if it's all the same to you, I think I'll stay on the case," he said.

The DAG nodded. "All right then. I was hoping that's what you'd say.

"But from now on your main contact is to be Ms. James here. You'll want to keep interfacing with the detectives and the DA Tischler, of course. We don't want to be tipping our hand to whatever insider or insiders might be involved."

"You think there might be more than one, sir?"

Bollinger shrugged. "I have no idea. But if we're dealing with some kind of cover-up, there well might be."

"You and Tischler are friends, right?"

"Not exactly friends. More like old acquaintances. Like I told you, we knew each other in college."

"You thinking he could somehow be involved?"

"I'd find that very disturbing."

James, who'd been flipping through some pages in the report while they spoke, interjected: "I've known Randall Tischler for more than ten years. In my experience he's as straight as they come."

"Trust me, counselor," the DAG said with a chuckle, "he wasn't so straightlaced back when we were in college. Not that that means much of anything at this juncture."

"So let me get this picture clear in my thinking," Garnell said. "You want me officially reporting to AAG James here but still acting like I'm consulting with all the other Government Plaza folks down in Binghamton because you, or at least the FBI anyway, thinks there might be a killer loose somewhere in the system."

"It's possible—that's all we're saying," the DAG said.

Of one thing he was certain: when it came to attorneys general, if trouble happened, he was going to be the expendable one, not the other way around.

"All right," he said. "I report in by phone?"

James nodded.

He glanced across at the folder on the AAG's lap. "You going to let me take a peek at that?"

"Of course," she said turning the folder around and handing it over to him. "Knock yourself out. The rest is just a bunch of stuff we sent them—photos and such."

"One other thing you should be aware of, detective," the DAG said.

"What's that?"

"This afternoon Quentin Price's attorney filed a five-million-dollar wrongful incarceration lawsuit against the State of New York."

"Lovely."

"Every trial lawyer between Buffalo and Long Island must have been salivating over this one. At any rate, I'm sure you'll be able to read all about it in the paper tomorrow morning. And I'm sure I don't need to remind you about the kind of extra heat this kind of litigation puts us all under. Of course it should go without saying if any reporter tries to contact you our policy is strictly no comment."

"Yes, sir."

The DAG looked at his watch. "I've got another appointment coming in."

"Sure," Garnell said.

"Betty here will keep me in the loop. I understand you may be working up against some sort of deadline?"

"Well, not a deadline exactly, sir. While I was interviewing Gwen Crawford's mother she revealed that ever since her daughter was murdered she's received an anonymous condolence letter or flowers on the girl's birthday. With Price in prison and the case supposedly solved, at first she chalked it up to a well-meaning acquaintance, coworker, or neighbor."

"Which it very well still could be."

"Yes, but for the last couple of years Mrs. Crawford has begun to think differently. And if you look at the cards, sir—she's saved them all and—"

"You think they might be from the killer."

"Yes."

"What are the postmarks?"

"Different post office branches. All from the greater Binghamton area."

"None from Auburn prison, I take it."

"No, sir. But if we know a new one's bound to come in, we

might be able to work with the post office to intercept it."

"That'll take a court order."

"I can handle it," James said.

"But we may have an even bigger problem," Garnell said. "Now that you've told me what the Feds are thinking, you need to see this. . . ."

He reached in his pocket and pulled out the baggie with the index card that had shown up on his desk. Through the clear plastic, he showed them the writing on the card and told them how he had discovered it on his borrowed police bureau desk. He also read the card. The DAG took a deep breath and leaned back in his chair.

"Somebody couldn't have just walked in off the street and happened to have dropped this on the right desk," James said.

"Not hardly," Garnell said.

"Looks like the FBI may be on target then."

"There's the racial element too," the DAG said. "Whoever sent this was obviously trying to taunt you."

"I got the message," Garnell said.

"Who else in Binghamton knows about this?"

"No one. I checked it for prints myself."

"When's Gwen Crawford's birthday?"

"Next Tuesday."

"Then you better get cracking, detective. We need to find this fiend before he tries to kill again."

FIFTY

Quentin was in the back yard sawing a piece of wood to repair a broken section of Nelson's deck when the phone rang inside. He stepped across the weathered boards and in through the sticky sliding glass door.

"I got another message," Ruth told him when he answered.

"Okay."

"This wasn't like the first one. It came in the mail. A letter."

"Postmark?"

"Here in Binghamton."

"Like the ones before."

"Yes."

"What's it say?"

"Dear Mrs. Crawford." Reading now. "I know you must be in anguish. Anguish is misspelled." She read on. "I know some things that can help you and your friend find out about your daughter."

"Your 'friend,' huh?"

"That's what it says."

Who was this person? He felt an odd tingle up the back of his neck. "Must have been keeping an eye on you for awhile," he said. "What else does it say?"

"It gives detailed instructions on a place and a time to meet. A wayside on some road up in Chenango County."

"Where there's no cell phone coverage, I bet. What time?"

"Same as before. Eleven p.m."

"What day?"

"Tonight."

"No mention of what happened to Nelson?"

"Uh-uh."

"Stupendous." His gaze moved through the glass to the corner of the decking where he'd left the Browning, propped between a pile of wood and an old coffee can. He needed to buy a waist holster. Didn't know how the gangbangers he'd known in prison had ever done it when they were on the street, stuffing their Glocks or whatever into their blue jeans like they were squirt guns.

"You still there?"

"Yeah."

"Are you coming in to work today?"

"No. Got some things to take care of first."

"What should we do?"

"Don't see that we have much choice. You swing by here and pick me up after you punch out and we'll go."

"All right. I should be there a little after ten."

Darkness filled the empty living room. Quentin waited inside by the door. Despite all the cleaning, he could still smell Nelson's breath and Nelson's sweat, not to mention the scent of the dead German shepherd in the upholstery, in the rug. Every now and then he would peek out through the curtains to look for the Chrysler. He really should look into buying a car of his own, he thought. Just a run-of-the-mill used vehicle that would be dependable. He felt for his cell phone in the pocket of the sport coat he'd bought and checked inside the new shoulder holster beneath the jacket for the Browning too.

He sighed as her headlights appeared from down the street. He walked out to meet her at the curb, locking the front door behind him as he went.

"Aren't you a bit overdressed?" she said as he slid into the seat beside her.

He lifted the flap of his jacket to show her the gun. She grimaced. He slammed his door shut. "Let's go."

She handed him a map, a small flashlight, and the letter she'd received.

Half an hour later they were miles north of the city and well into Chenango County. Following the instructions in the letter, they left the main Route 12 and headed west in the general direction of Cortland. Except for their headlights, the county highway was pitch black. There was little shoulder and the sides of the roadway were overgrown with weeds. Lights from passing houses were few and far between.

"I'm not much of a fan of these directions," he said. He pulled out his new phone and checked the signal. "No service. You got any coverage on yours?"

She looked at hers and shook her head.

"Just as I figured."

"How much farther?"

"About a mile up this road."

She kept the car moving at a steady clip. He closed his eyes momentarily, feeling the rhythm of the cars motion and the night.

"I suppose it's too late now to—wha—?"

The catch in her voice caused him to open his eyes again.

"Oh, no," she said. She was looking in her rearview mirror. "I can't believe this."

"What is it?" The flashing glow of blue lights on the dash gave him the answer. He swore under his breath.

"What are the police doing way out here?"

"You're not speeding, are you?"

"In Bertha? Are you kidding?"

The last thing they needed was another encounter with cops.

"Is your license and registration current, all that?" he asked.

"Yes."

"What about your tail and brake lights?"

She glanced at her controls. "There's no warning light and they were all working fine last I knew."

"Great," he said. "This is just great." He thought about the loaded, unpermitted gun beneath his jacket. He drew in a deep breath, steeling himself for yet another encounter with the man.

The blazing lights were closing fast. Ruth dropped their speed, easing the car toward the grass at the side of the road. He looked in the side mirror. For a moment he thought the cruiser might be planning to blow on past them, maybe a local sheriff or cop on the way to an accident or a 911 call. But no such luck. Matching their maneuver, the patrol car slowed too, its nose pointed directly at their rear bumper.

The road widened to a pullout in front of a driveway and a darkened farmhouse. Ruth edged the car off onto the shoulder and brought them to a stop. The cruiser, Quentin could see now, was a big unmarked Ford. It careened to a halt about fifty feet behind.

"It'll be all right. I've never even gotten a ticket before," she said.

"Oh, that'll help." He was wondering if they were going to be late for their mystery appointment, wondering about their reason for being out here in the first place, wondering about the cops who were pulling them over.

The farmhouse lay just ahead, a single streetlight illuminating the driveway to their immediate right. Behind them, two uniformed men pushed open the doors of the Ford and stepped out, and he could make out the silhouette of a third person in the back seat of the cruiser. The lights flashed on the car's roof, he noticed, but not on the grill.

Something wasn't right.

He unbuckled his seat belt, slid slowly across the seat toward Ruth, and, without turning his head, shifted his gaze to her mirror to get a better look.

"What are you doing?"

"Be cool now. Just be cool."

He edged toward the middle of the seat. The men were approaching together, both apparently intending to take up position on Ruth's side of the vehicle.

"Put your foot on the brake," he said.

"What?"

"Put your foot on the brake and shift the car into drive. Do it. Now."

She did as he instructed. The men in the mirror froze. For a moment, the Chrysler's brake lights turned their faces a faint shade of red. They were less than twenty feet from the car and Quentin could see the dark intent of their eyes. The blue lights continued to whirl behind them.

"We need to get out of here," he said.

"What? Are you crazy?"

The men behind were reaching for their guns.

"Go! Go now!"

"What?"

He squeezed his foot across the divider, pushing her out of the way.

"What are you doing?"

He grabbed the wheel and slammed the accelerator to the floor. The Chrysler's huge V-8 hiccupped before catapulting them forward, spewing stones from beneath the tires as they fishtailed back onto the road.

A deafening crack split the air. Ruth screamed. Their rear window had been shot out.

"You're going to get us both killed!"

"Those aren't cops," he said.

"What?"

The car whipsawed and growled. Still leaning across the dash, he fought to keep it under control.

"I said those aren't cops! C'mon. Take the wheel and drive."

Her face had turned ashen, but she did as she was told. They jolted through a series of potholes. Quentin looked back and saw the two men leap into their car and peel out after them.

"Keep it to the floor. We've got to try to find some help or a place to lose them."

They were rumbling back up to speed now, approaching fifty. No more dwellings were in sight, only fields and woods leading on one side and steep hills and forest on the other.

"Come on. Come on. Can't this thing go any faster?"

"No." She glared at him for an instant.

Around a curve and over a rise, another road appeared in the swath of their beams.

"Okay, good, good. Take this road to the left."

"You sure?"

"Yes, I'm sure."

She barely slowed as she jerked the wheel around. They lurched on to the second road, throwing him against the door.

"Nice turn," he said.

"I could do without the sarcasm."

They were headed into deep woods on a narrower paved thoroughfare. A large yellow sign read DEAD END. She had to slow considerably.

"Cut your lights."

"Did you see that sign?"

"Yes. Cut the lights."

"But I won't be able to see where I'm going."

"Do as I say, and keep moving. Go slow if you have to, but try to keep us rolling. And keep your foot off the brake."

She flipped the switch on the dash and they were plunged

into darkness, a blind juggernaut of rumbling steel and glass. They bounced on and off the shoulder. The sides of the car scraped weeds and branches.

Quentin turned to look behind them again. Sure enough, the cruiser roared by on the bigger road, its spinning beacons no longer illuminated. There was no siren either.

"They'll figure out what happened in a couple of minutes, but at least this buys us a little breathing space."

"Great. This road must end pretty soon. I think it's getting narrower."

"I know. Just keep going."

"What makes you so sure they weren't cops?"

"You hear a siren?"

"No."

"That tells you something, especially when we ran."

"But how'd you know when they pulled us over?"

"There were two of them, plus there was a third person in the back seat. State troopers or local cops out here normally patrol alone. That got me curious, and then I noticed the handgun in the driver's waist holster. It was big, forty-four magnum maybe, way too big for most cops on the job. I knew for sure though when I got a good look in the glow of your brake lights at their shoes."

"Shoes? You decided to get us shot at based on somebody's shoes?"

"Yeah. They were light colored, brown maybe."

"Light brown."

"Right. Cops in uniform always wear black shoes."

Ruth checked her rearview mirror again. "They'd turned off their flashing lights when they went by too. What does that mean?"

Good, she'd seen it too. At least she was observant.

"It means two things," he said. "First, like I said, they're definitely not cops. And second, they're probably out to kill us without drawing any attention."

"This can't be happening. Who sent them?"

"Probably whoever sent you that note."

"I still don't believe this."

The car bumped hard through a pothole and scraped against the side of an evergreen. Where were they now exactly?

"Stop the car and let me drive," he said.

"Huh?"

"Stop the car, I said. I want to drive."

"Okay. Okay. What about the brake lights?"

"Let it roll to a stop."

They coasted along for several seconds, finally coming to rest against a bush overgrowing the narrow shoulder. A large grove of trees, shadows of maple and oak and beech, towered all around them in the darkness. Ahead, from what Quentin could tell, the road started to drop more steeply. Unfortunately, there were still no more dwellings in sight here, either, no lights of any kind.

His eyes had adjusted some to the light. Ruth's blue waitressing outfit and fiery hair faded to gray in the dimness. With the back window gone, the odor from the bad exhaust began to seep into the cabin.

"Shift it into neutral," he said.

She did as he told her. "Should I get out and come around to the other side?"

"No. They probably wouldn't see us through the trees, but we don't want to risk any inside lights coming on. Just crawl over top of me."

"All right. You sure?"

"C'mon. They might come barreling back down this road at any second."

She climbed over his lap, and as she did Quentin caught

some of the scent of her, a soapy hint of apricot. He did his best to avoid making contact, but couldn't help it when her thigh brushed against his. Made him think of Sierra. He realized he'd forgotten to call her earlier as he'd intended.

As he took the wheel, it occurred to him he hadn't driven a car in over ten years.

No time to worry about that though. A quick glance in the rear revealed a faint glow of headlamps in the woods behind them.

"Here come our friends again."

Ruth spun around to look. "Maybe it's someone else."

"I wouldn't count on it."

"What should we do?"

He fingered the gun against his waist and tried to figure the odds. The growing light in the trees overhead told him their pursuers were getting closer.

"All right. Here's what we need to do."

FIFTY-ONE

Ruth trembled on the seat beside him. She had a glassy-eyed vulnerability that made her all the more dangerous. Probably from the drinking. Would she collapse on him now just when they needed each other the most? They'd each folded their body below the seat and were invisible to anyone approaching from behind. For Quentin this was no easy task, due to his size and the fact that he wanted to keep his foot on the gas pedal, the gearshift within easy reach.

He lay halfway across the seat with his head nearly in Ruth's lap, listening to the Chrysler's engine and her breathing. They weren't touching, but he could sense the rhythmic rise and fall of her chest. The clamor of the night sounds from the woods washed over them again too, one creature calling to another. Was that how it had been with Ruth and Gwen ten years before? Two creatures calling out to one another, lost in the darkness?

"We have to wait until they're out of the car and almost on top of us," he said softly.

"I'm sorry for getting you into this. I should have just left you alone."

He said nothing. His fingers curled around the Browning.

Soon the roar of the Ford's engine, approaching through the woods, overwhelmed the sound of their own idling motor. Still no flashing lights, but shadows waned as the light from their beams grew in the trees overhead until it was almost as bright as day.

He could tell when they spotted the Chrysler too, the pace of their rolling tires slowing as soon as they came around the curve. He was counting on the fact they'd be wary. He hoped they'd bring their vehicle in a little closer than before. But not too close.

It sounded as though they were doing exactly that.

Cautiously, however—at one point Quentin was almost afraid one of them might have slipped out his door without them hearing.

But then he heard their car brake to a stop as if it were right on top of them. The driver shifted into park. The glare from the Ford's headlights shone everywhere inside the cabin above the seat.

He'd give them two or three more seconds at best.

"Price! Quentin Price, you in there?"

The voice was deep and plaintive. Not one he recognized. Ruth stirred, but he touched her hip to urge her to keep still. Maybe the men suspected he and Ruth were also armed. They wouldn't just start blasting away without knowing what they were shooting at. He felt certain at least one of them was leaning out his window though, his handgun trained on the seat tops of the Chrysler.

"We just want to talk, Price. That's all . . . . What about you, Ms. Crawford, you there?"

"What if they left?" Another voice, more baritone than bass, coming from the other side of the car. "What if they took off running into the woods? We'll never find them."

"Shut up," the first voice said.

An alarm chime sounded. One of the Ford's doors had opened.

That was it. Quentin depressed the brake pedal, reached up and popped the gearshift lever into reverse. He took his foot off the brake and mashed down on the gas.

Two muffled shots sounded as the Chrysler rocketed backward and crashed into the front of the Ford. He and Ruth bounced against the dash.

More shots. Like blunt darts striking. They must have been using sound and flash suppressors. Military issue? One round punched through part of the radio, sending sparks flying.

Dust was flying everywhere. He shoved the gearshift into drive and they flew forward. He jammed on the brakes, reversed again. Shots peppered all around as they slammed even harder into the cruiser. A bullet whizzed past his ear and struck the dash.

He shifted again and hit the gas.

One of the men leapt on the back bumper as they began to accelerate.

Quentin twisted the wheel and flipped on the headlights so he could see. They fishtailed back and forth for several seconds, but the man hung on, no doubt trying to free his gun for a shot.

Another three or four seconds until they got up to speed. Another shot, just missing.

He slammed on the brakes. Felt his chin strike the wheel. Ruth had somehow managed to fasten her belt but still hit hard against the dash. A sickening thud sounded too as the man who'd been hanging on the back flew forward, striking the edge of the roof where the glass had been shot out, and tumbled off the trunk.

Quentin shook himself to clear his head.

He cut the lights again and open his door, rolled out into the dirt. It took a few seconds for his eyes to adjust to the near darkness once more. The only light came from the now distant glow of the Ford's a couple of hundred yards behind them.

The man who'd been clinging to the bumper lay spread eagle. Tall and muscular with short cropped brown hair, a thick neck, and an ugly blood purple at the top of is neck. Quentin crawled over and checked him for a pulse. He was dead or about to be.

Where was the guy's gun? He felt around in the dirt beside the body but came up empty. He finally spied a large dark shape lying among the weeds a few feet away, scrambled over and grabbed the piece, a big .45 with a silencer, just as another shot from the guy's partner blew into the ground about ten feet behind them.

He returned fire with the big Colt, two quick rounds to send the remaining shooter a message. He wanted to search the dead man for ID too, but that would have to wait. He checked the clip on the bigger gun and found four rounds left and one in the chamber. Unless the other guy was packing an arsenal, at least now they wouldn't be outgunned.

He shimmied around the side of the Chrysler, opened Ruth's door. "You okay?"

She sat up and nodded, but barely. Her eyes darted back and forth, scanning the darkness as if she were searching for threats from all directions.

"Stay down, crawl out if you can, and get around in front of the car with me."

They were still in the middle of the road. The engine block offered the best protection. Another shot came from the direction of the cruiser, this one missing badly. Great, let him waste more bullets. He helped her moved around in front of the car.

"I'm all right," she said.

"You sure?"

"Yes."

Something else was worrying him. He only saw two men now. No sign of the third man he was sure he'd seen in the rear seat back there on the road.

The shooting had stopped for the moment. Had the other man given up and fled? Unlikely. He probably figured his best approach was advancing toward them on foot off the road, using the cover of the trees and the darkness. Unless the guy was using night vision goggles, it was going to come down to a close-quarters gun battle in low light.

"What about him?" Ruth asked, looking back at the body on the ground behind them.

"Dead."

"Dead?"

"Right."

She was silent for a moment.

"You recognize him?" he asked.

She shook her head.

"Me neither."

"What are you going to do?" She stared at the .45 in his hand and the Colt he'd tucked back into his holster.

"Whatever I have to to keep us from ending up like that dude on the ground over there."

The silencer screwed into the barrel of the big handgun added a bulk to its weight. He strained to hear any sounds from the woods, leaves moving or twigs cracking, anything that would indicate the approach of the second assailant. He peered over top of the hood toward the glow of the cruiser's lights.

"Did the plan work?" she whispered.

"Not exactly the way I'd intended. But it looks like we smashed in the front of their car pretty good. And I see some steam rising so we must've taken out their radiator and water pump."

"What do you know." She almost managed a smile.

"At least this old tank is good for something."

"Bertha." She patted the car's grille. "She's ruined. I don't even carry collision insurance."

"Let's just hope Bertha keeps going long enough to get us out of here."

A small creek ran under the road between them and the

cruiser. There was a faint whiff of moisture in the air, a trace of mist rising through the trees. They were just outside the entrance to what looked like a state park. He could make out a stone-littered parking lot and a picnic area. An indecipherable sign hung from a chain across the entrance to the lot. Probably shut down for repairs.

"Why don't we just get back in the car and drive away?"

"And go where? He's got the road blocked and I don't see any other way out."

"You think this has something to do with whoever killed Gwen and your uncle?"

"Gee, now there's a thought."

"If we're lucky, maybe someone heard the car crash or the shots you fired."

"Luck's got nothing to do with it." He looked around at the surrounding woods and his mind raced back to his years of military training in the North Carolina woods. "These guys planned this well. It didn't look like there was anybody home at that farmhouse back on the main road. And there doesn't seem to be anybody else around here either."

She looked around and nodded. "Okay."

"You ever fire a handgun before?" He reached for his holster.

She slowly shook her head.

"Well you're about to learn." He handed her the Browning.

"This is like some horrific nightmare, worse than you could ever imagine."

"Yeah," he said. "Welcome to my world."

FIFTY-TWO

From across the pond, Jack heard the call of a whippoorwill, an ancient mournful sound. He swirled the ice cubes in his nearly empty tumbler of scotch, its pentagonal base resting comfortably in the palm of his hand. It was a cool moonless night on the back deck of his house, but with the warmth of the liquor flowing through his veins Jack felt no need for a sweater or a jacket.

Alone again tonight. Jack loved the darkness of summer here, the warm temperatures and low humidity—parties in the Plaza downtown, movies at the old Palace Theater in Eastwood. He would miss all these if he left.

Now though his gas grill and hot tub sat unused. After his two days with Hannah, she had gone back to the security of Cazenovia, to the bed of a man she didn't love. It was her choice—the choices we make come to define us. His choice to call Quentin Price to account was about to define him. How and in what way he was still not sure. But he could sense the momentum rising, the perilous hope of gain, accompanied by the fear of all that might be lost.

Through the panes of the French doors, a light still glowed from his office and his war room in the bowels of the house. Was it a night like this when Gwen had been murdered? Had Price been fueled up on alcohol too? Though there was never any evidence of such, and it never came out under Price's cross-examination by the prosecutor, Jack had always wondered.

He checked the face of his Rolex. They would be in the middle of shaking down Ruth and Quentin Price now. What must be going through Price's mind, realizing he hadn't gotten away with murder after all, that he would never get away with it while he, Jack Crawford, was still around?

He finished the last of his scotch just as the cell phone burbled in his pocket. He pulled it out and answered.

"Jack?"

It was Hannah. "Hi."

"He's snoring upstairs so I thought I'd come down here to the porch and call you."

"It's a nice night, isn't it?"

"Beautiful."

"I was just finishing a scotch."

"You sound tired."

"Just sitting here missing you."

"I had such a great time the last couple of nights. I miss you too."

"Sometime we should talk about making our arrangement more permanent."

"What do you mean?"

"I don't know. Maybe going away somewhere together."

"It sounds nice." The line was silent for a moment. "But I don't know."

"It's just a thought," he said.

"Business keeping you awake?"

"Yeah."

"Maybe you should sell your agency or bring in someone younger to help you."

"What, and miss out on all the midnight stake-outs and hopping over fences to shoot low-light video?"

"What time did you get home tonight?"

"A little while ago."

"I rest my case."

He couldn't tell her what he'd really been up to. He grunted but said nothing.

"I better go. Don't want him to hear me."

"Sure."

"Goodnight, Jack."

"Goodnight," he said and hung up.

Maybe, if he somehow got through all this with Gwen's death avenged and his career and his life mostly intact, he would be able to tell her goodnight on a more regular basis. The gargle of a distant tractor trailer carried through the night. Jack shifted in his deck chair, checked the time again, and watched the darkened woods.

FIFTY-THREE

Quentin lay still in the blackness, the gun poised in his hand. They'd moved about fifty yards into the woods where they'd found a slight rise and the natural shelter of some fallen tree trunks. He surveyed the area again, Ruth at his back. It was darker here away from the cars, a good place to make a stand.

There'd been no sounds and no signs of movement from the other shooter since they'd left the road. He knew that was soon to change.

They wouldn't have long to wait.

Ruth tapped him on the shoulder and pointed in the direction of the park.

A stick cracked from that direction. The remaining shooter was trying a flanking maneuver, maybe to make absolutely certain again there was no one else in the area before mounting a surprise final attack. Whoever he was, he didn't seem very familiar with the concept of moving quietly through the woods. His track was bringing him to within thirty feet of their position. They had the advantage of surprise and cover.

Quentin turned his body around and moved Ruth into position behind him. A minute later, the dark shape of a man came into view from behind a huge oak. The figure hesitated for a moment, the shadowy length of his gun pointed forward, before continuing.

There would be no hesitation on Quentin's part.

Once he had the shooter in comfortable range—prone firing

position, double tap, triple tap if needed, square to the middle of the target. He might be a little rusty and the big .45 would have some kick to it. Nothing he couldn't handle.

The man continued moving straight toward them.

In the movies there might have been more melodrama, a musical accompaniment, maybe some kind of crazy heavy metal. At fifteen feet Quentin zeroed in his target. The silencer was deadly. The guy never knew what hit him. Two quick rounds, one of which looked like it blew through the man's neck.

Quentin was up and on his feet in an instant and moving to check out his target.

"You killed him. Did you have to do that?"

"What did you think I was going to do, stand up and yell, 'stop in the name of the law'?"

"I don't know, I just . . ."

The overweight man, much more flab than muscle compared to his partner, Quentin could see, heaved what appeared to be his last breath. His uniform was obviously imitation—a good-enough knock-off for the dark maybe, but not up close. A black seam of blood flowed from beneath him.

Quentin rooted around the man's pockets and pulled out a wallet.

"You got any kind of light?"

"No. Wait. There's a small penlight on my spare key." She fished through her own pockets and came out with it.

They used it to examine the wallet. A New York State driver's license told them the man's name was Carl Bataglio. He had no police shield or any other kind of identification, not even a credit card. Quentin shook his head.

Ruth turned and stared at the dead man, as if she could barely believe what they had done. She seemed on the verge of tears.

"You okay?" he asked.

She wiped her nose and nodded.

"We did what we had to do."

"I know."

He stood and turned away from the body. "There was a third person in the back of their car earlier when they stopped us, I was sure of it."

"What do you think happened to him?"

"No clue. That's what worries me."

He looked round cautiously. The man's gun had fallen somewhere, but Quentin's foot brushed up against something else, another solid object. He bent down on one knee, felt recognition in its smooth surface, and plucked it from the leaves. Ruth shined the penlight on the dull surface of the metal box.

"What is it?"

"Something I've been missing."

She gave him a curious look.

"Never mind. We need to figure out how to get rid of these bodies before it turns light."

"Don't you think we should be calling the real police?"

He shook his head.

"But it's obviously self-defense. They were trying to kill us and we had to stop them."

"So?"

She looked at him in the near darkness. A con fresh out of prison. A gun with his prints on it. She, as the only witness maybe with an agenda of her own, and her own set of prints on another gun. Did he have to spell it all out?

Ruth looked at her watch.

"Okay," she sighed. "Got any ideas?"

FIFTY-FOUR

Later, they sat together on a picnic table, drinking coffee from foam cups next to an all-night convenience store on the outskirts of Binghamton. Well past two in the morning. The clerk inside had glanced at the smashed-in trunk of the Chrysler, but not for long.

Quentin looked over at the car in the artificial light. The tires wore a fresh coat of mud and sand on top of the old layer of dirt, the result of pushing the big Ford with its windows rolled up and the bodies of the men in the back seat over an embankment into a pond they'd found down the road. His back ached from dragging the bodies at arms length to keep from getting blood on him.

Ruth cupped her hands around her coffee. She had grown strangely quiet since their narrow escape and the gruesome cleanup after, almost as if she needed to withdraw from the horrific intimacy that had been forced upon them. The metal box lay on the table beside them.

"They called out your name," she said.

"What?"

"Back when they stopped right behind us the second time. They called out your name."

"Yes. Yours too."

"I never expected it to come down to killing."

"Your note writer's pretty desperate."

"Gwen. How could she . . . how could she have ever gotten

mixed up with people like this?"

He said nothing.

"What did you do with their IDs?" she asked.

"Tossed 'em in with the bodies. The cops will find them when we're ready to let them know."

"If you don't want to go to the police, what next?"

"I don't know. I need time to try to figure this all out."

He had never had to kill other human beings before—not even in the army. He still needed to be careful how much he said. He put down his coffee and ran his hands across his face.

"What is it?"

"Nothing. Forget it."

"No," she said, clutching his arm and staring into his eyes. "Tell me."

He tried to see what lay beyond her ragged emotions. A truck whizzed by on the highway behind them. "All right," he said. "I guess it's about time I told you the real reason your daughter wasn't speaking to you when she was murdered."

FIFTY-FIVE

Jack thought he must be having a heart attack.

He opened his eyes. There was no pain, but his chest felt heavy, as though he were swimming upstream and getting nowhere, fighting for every breath. The air seemed to have grown heavy too and been sucked from the darkness of his bed. An antiseptic smell filled his nostrils.

There was someone else in the room.

"Bad dream?"

A wave of fear pulsed through him. He went to reach for the Beretta on the bedside table.

"Uh. Uh."

He turned his head to see Fletcher seated in the lounge chair near the bed, a large handgun of his own pointed straight at Jack.

"Oh, Fletcher, it's you. Jesus, you scared me. What the hell?"

"I know, it probably pisses you off a little to have someone like me get the jump on you, Jacko. But hey, look at it this way. You're far from the first."

The smell must have been coming from Doyle's breath. He wasn't stupid enough to try to challenge a man with a loaded semiautomatic pointed at his head.

"You don't need that thing." He indicated the gun.

"Don't I?"

"What are you talking about?"

"I'm talking about the fucking screwup of all screwups. We

went after Price and I don't know what the hell happened."

"What? What happened? You mean you don't have him?"

"I don't have jack-shit right now." He finally lowered the gun and Jack breathed a little easier. "I had a scam all set up to take him, my two guys dressed up as state troopers. Your ex was with him too. But Price made us before we could move."

"Where are Price and Ruth now?"

"I have no idea."

Jack sat up in bed.

"What about the guys working with you?"

Fletcher hesitated. "Don't know about them either. They, uh, they seem to be out of the loop."

"Out of the loop?"

"Gone. Missing. And the fake cruiser they were driving with them."

"What?" Jack pushed back the covers, climbed out of bed, and donned his robe. Not a good way to start his morning.

"You sneak into my bedroom in the dark just to tell me how bad you and your boys messed up?"

"Hey, listen. This dude Price is one bad mofo."

"Yeah, and you're supposed to be too."

Fletcher said nothing, but a hint of fierce desperation passed through his eyes. Jack folded his arms across his chest. This was a complex little man he never had been able to fully figure out. Like a few of his other snitches and contacts, only Fletcher was different. Still, he recognized a challenge when he saw one.

"Have we got a problem here?" he said.

"No." The photographer jammed his gun back into his waist-band.

"Let's get one thing straight." Jack was more angry at himself than anything else. "If you ever sneak in here and try to get the jump on me like that again, I'll either shoot first and ask questions later or beat the fucking crap out of you."

"All right. But you're going to have to take Price down yourself. It's not worth the risk for me. I'll put eyeballs on him from now on, but that's as far as it goes."

"What about how much I paid you?"

"Here." He reached into his jeans pocket and came out with the roll of hundreds, which he tossed across to Jack who caught it. "Keep the rest of your money. I subtracted some for my expenses."

Jack looked at the cash in his hand. He had a pretty good idea Fletcher had subtracted more than just expenses, but he said nothing. The day was just beginning to grow light outside. He needed strong coffee and time to think.

FIFTY-SIX

Garnell turned beneath the sheets in his hotel room and glanced at the clock on the bedside table. Eight twenty-five Saturday morning. He'd been up half the night trying to piece things together since getting back late from Albany. Even made a stop by the Binghamton Police Bureau and checked his temporary desk again, just in case there were any more communiqués; he found nothing at the bureau but the usual busyness of the typical summer Friday night crime blotter you might find at any midsized American city police department.

The clock gave him an idea. A creature of habit, his NYPD partner, Jane Pappas, would be just finishing her morning workout at the gym. Weekdays, it would be an hour and a half earlier, but not on Saturdays. He thought back to the Santiago case from a few years before. It hadn't been their case, of course, but there was some detail he remembered hearing about . . .

His cell phone lay next to the clock. He reached across, pulled it into the palm of hand, and pushed the speed dial for Pappas's number.

She answered on the second ring.

"What are you, a masochist?" He could hear health club Muzak in the background, her breath coming in short bursts.

"Talk to me ten years from now when you're busting a gut behind some desk somewhere while I'm still lithe as a minx."

"A minx?" He chuckled under his breath. Even Pappas herself liked to refer to her build as "sturdy."

"You still stuck up in the north country?"

"Yup." He described in more detail the pleasant banality of his surroundings and the circumstances, which took awhile because she kept interrupting and trying to ask questions.

"So what," she said. "You calling to apologize for leaving me holding the bag on all this work? We solved the Lee case, FYI. Got the girl's ex-boyfriend cold."

"That's great. Really great, but listen. I had a meeting with the deputy attorney general up in Albany yesterday."

"My, my. The competition must not be so stiff once you get up past Rockland County."

"Would you shut up and listen to what I'm trying to tell you. He showed me this FBI report. You know how they're always trying to Bigfoot everything. Anyway, they've apparently taken a look at the Crawford case at the DAG's request, and guess what?"

"What?"

"They think the perp could be a cop."

"Based on what?"

"I don't know, patterns maybe. Whatever it is, kind of stuff they look at . . . So anyway, I was trying to think back to the Santiago case, trying to remember if there was any whiff of any such thing. I remember Johnson or Keiper telling me about some detail, but I can't seem to come up with it."

"So you were hoping I would remember it?"

"Yeah. It's just bugging me, that's all."

She gulped in another deep breath. "Nothing I can think of either offhand."

"Then maybe you could get a hold of one of those guys or at least go by the office and check the file for me?"

"What's the rush?"

"I don't have time to get into it right now, Pap, but it's urgent."

"Okay, okay. I'll get on it, along with a million other things I got to do. Where are you going to be, lover boy?"

"Busting my ass up here in Binghamton."

"All right, but you owe me," she said. "Hurry up and solve your case and get back down here to work."

FIFTY-SEVEN

They slept for a few hours in the car—Ruth in the front seat, Quentin in the back. A little while after sunrise they drove the half hour back to Uncle Nelson's house, where Quentin ran in and out quickly in order to pick up extra ammunition for the gun. They were headed for the college in Hamlick. Quentin told Ruth he wanted to talk to her back at the site of Gwen's disappearance.

The groundswell of adrenaline gone, he had to fight to keep from dozing while she drove. Ruth looked worn out as well. Her window was cracked open while she smoked, one hand on the wheel. The village of Hamlick was still in the throes of its summer slumber. Quiet shady streets. Empty parking spaces as they passed through the small downtown. At the brick-columned entrance to the college, Ruth drew in a deep breath and turned in to the campus.

Quentin sat up and looked around. Maybe it wasn't such a great idea to come back here again—he remembered what Christine Shackleford had told him about staying away. Images of his life before the murder came rushing back to him from every direction. A few things had changed on the campus, of course, but by and large the place looked just the same as the day he had left it for the last time. He watched as a crew of groundskeepers stared at their unsightly car, the unlikely return of a prodigal.

The snack bar grille at the student union opened at eight.

They had arrived in time for the morning rush and had to wait behind a large group of summer campers calling out their food orders to their counselors.

The good news was the kids were getting their orders to go; they cleared out as soon as they received them. With their own breakfast in hand, Quentin and Ruth sat in an empty booth in a remote corner.

"Why bring me back here?" Ruth's voice had an edge to it that bespoke her weariness and maybe her functional alcoholic's need for a drink.

" 'Cause this is where it all began," he said.

"For both of us."

"Yeah." He scooped a big bite of his eggs.

"Well?" she said. "You acted like you were going to give me some big revelation about Gwen."

Quentin paused and reached inside the paper bag they had brought along with them. He pulled out the metal box they had found in the men's car and placed it in front of her. An organic musty odor rose from the table.

"Sorry about the smell," he said pushing their food to the side. "But this thing was buried for a few years."

"You said you'd seen it before," she said.

He nodded. He had come this far. Might as well give it to her one step at a time. He pulled out the thick of wad of hundred-dollar bills from his pocket.

Her eyes narrowed. "Quentin, what . . . I mean, where did you come up with that kind of money?"

"It was Gwen's," he said. "She gave it to me for safekeeping."

"How much is there?"

"Over three thousand dollars."

"Gwen was killed over this money?"

"Maybe. I don't know."

"Where did it come from?"

He picked up the empty metal box and opened the lid. Examined the inside carefully.

"What are you doing?"

"Just a second." He reached inside the base of the container and ran his fingernail along its edges. It took some doing, but after a minute he managed to puncture the seal and loosen the base a little. Then it was just a matter of prying and coaxing the edges up until the entire base lifted up to reveal a thin slot beneath the main compartment.

"It has a false bottom?"

"Uh-huh." He stared in at the revealed contents: another waterproof bag, this one containing a stack of photos. He lifted the bag out to show to Ruth.

"Pictures? Of what?"

"Take a look," he said. He split open the bag and fanned out the stack. The photos had deteriorated some, but the images were still visible and as striking as the moment they were taken.

"They're of Gwen."

He nodded.

A number of the photos were head views but several were full-body shots of Gwen smiling in somewhat provocative poses. Not fully nude but in a revealing bikini that left little to the imagination. Call them soft porn.

Ruth's countenance darkened. "Who took these?"

"My guess is whoever killed Gwen."

"Why?"

"Good question."

"How did you . . . How did you know about these photos and this box? Who were those men last night? What's going on here?"

Quentin glanced around to make absolutely certain no one was within earshot. "I'm not sure how they got a hold of the box exactly."

"Okay, but you must have some idea."

He told her how he had gone to retrieve the box at the park in Endicott the afternoon he was released from, how he had taken the money but reburied the container.

"Someone had to have seen you."

"That's the way I figure it."

"When did you bury the money and these pictures?"

"After Gwen went missing and I began to suspect that something might have happened to her."

"But why? Who took these pictures and where did she get this money?"

"Gwen told me she was in some kind of trouble. She said she'd visited the place of some guy she'd met at a photography exhibit in Binghamton and while he was out of the room she found these photos together with the money, so she took them. She came to me the day before she disappeared and gave me the cash and the pictures and asked me to hold on to them for safekeeping. That's what I was trying to talk to her about the night of the party."

"Why didn't she confront this person or ask you to talk to them?"

"I don't know. Maybe she was scared."

"You're saying the photos were taken without her knowledge."

"I think so."

"But how?"

"We'll get to that."

"Gwen wasn't stupid."

"No. But it gets worse," he said.

"How?"

"She said the guy was someone from law enforcement, maybe a detective."

She stared at him for a moment. "Which was why you never said anything or told anyone at your trial."

"I didn't think I would be convicted. By the time I realized it might happen, it was too late."

"And you spent ten years of your life in prison because of it."

He said nothing.

"Does your lawyer know about any of this?"

He shook his head.

"Why didn't you ever tell anyone before now?"

"Who was I supposed to trust? Besides . . ." Outside in the bright sun, a group of maintenance men went to work with mowers and trimmers on the hedges and the main student union lawn. Quentin looked around at the quiet shadows of the snack bar then down at the table. "Look at the bottom photo."

She reached under and lifted the last photo from the bottom of the stack. She let out a quick involuntary breath. "Oh, my gosh."

The picture was almost too hideous to comprehend. It showed Gwen, her eyes closed, with a hangman's noose around her neck. A photo of Gwen after her death?

"Look at it closely," Quentin said.

"It looks like it's been doctored."

"Exactly. That's Gwen's face pasted onto a photo of someone else's neck and body."

"Who would make such a hideous statement?"

"Someone who wanted to send a warning. This was how he planned to murder Gwen."

"Did she show you the photos when she gave them to you?"

"No. They were in a sealed envelope and she asked me not to open it. But I opened it and took a look after she disappeared."

"Why didn't you go to the police then?"

"Because of what Gwen had said about one of them being involved. But that wasn't all. A picture like this last one, only it was of my mom, showed up in my cell right after I was arrested."

"Of your mother? What happened to it?"

"I destroyed it, flushed it down the toilet."

Ruth put her hand to her mouth. "He was going to kill your mother too."

"Unless I took the rap for Gwen's murder. Since he didn't find the photos or the money he had given Gwen, he must have guessed Gwen had given them to me. The threat was pretty clear."

"And he planted that rope and those other things in your garage to frame you."

"I didn't put them there. And they sure as heck didn't get there by magic."

Ruth leaned forward in her seat and rubbed her temples with both hands. "This is . . . I don't know . . . This is all pretty overwhelming."

"Yeah, well there's more, and I've got another idea about what might be going on."

"Go on."

"We were just stopped by a couple of guys posing as cops, right?"

"Yes."

"Well what if whoever killed Gwen was posing as a cop too?"

Ruth lowered her voice. "You think it might have been one of those two men we just dumped in the bottom of the pond?"

"No. But there was a third guy there when they stopped us, like I told you."

"What happened to him then?"

"They must have dropped him off down the road some-where."

"Why didn't he come after us with the other two?"

"For the same reason he was staying behind in the back seat when they pulled us over. Because either you or I would have recognized him."

"So it's someone you or I know then."

He nodded. "Or at least one or both of us have met him."

"He sent the note I just received then?"

"Probably. Either him or someone working for him."

"Do you think he could be Gwen's killer?"

"I'm not sure yet. But whoever he is, he's trying pretty damn hard to silence us."

Ruth sat back in her seat for a moment. "But what does any of this have to do with Gwen not speaking to me before she was murdered?"

"That's why I wanted to talk to you here," he said.

FIFTY-EIGHT

Jack placed the phone back in its cradle. He sat back in the chair behind his desk and stared out at the wind-blown reeds on the pond behind his office building. This whole Price business was way out of control now. It had begun to play with his head.

Hollister and King were no longer returning his calls. He'd told Fletcher to go sit on Price's apartment, but had heard nothing. Price and Ruth, if they were still alive, could have bugged out anywhere for all he knew.

To top if off, he was way behind on his work. He was supposed to be coordinating a surveillance operation at a corporate client's warehouse this morning in Liverpool, but he'd had to farm the job out to someone else, giving up a big portion of his fee.

The need to avenge what had happened to Gwen, not just to settle the score but to make it right, was as real as anything to him now. It was accelerating a wholesale change in his life, crossing a line from good into evil, and what scared him the most was how easily he had made the transition, how close he had been traveling to that line. For what now, years?

He had enough in ready cash and money market funds. Plus he held a sizeable portfolio in stocks and bonds he could cash in. A plan began to take shape in his mind. He picked up the phone again and called Hannah Marx. She answered on the second ring.

"It's me."

"I was just thinking about you," she said.

"Are you free to talk?"

"Yes."

"What are you doing right now?"

"Lying back in bed reading a magazine."

"Sounds serious. What are you wearing?"

"Blue negligee."

"I like that one."

"I don't know why but I've felt vaguely depressed all morning, ever since George left for work. I'm glad you called."

"Something has happened," he said.

"What?"

"I can't get into the details right now. The thing is, well, I may need to do some things in the next couple of days and I may need to disappear for awhile."

"It's about Price, isn't it?"

"Like I said, I really don't want to get into the details."

"Where are you going to go?"

"I don't know yet. Maybe Mexico. But I'd like you to come with me."

There was a long silence on the line and before she even spoke the words he knew her answer.

"I'd like to. I really would . . . I mean . . ."

"If it's the money, I've got plenty of that. I'm talking about a whole new life here."

"Somewhere else."

"Yes."

"What about my son? How will he be able to find me?"

"He's old enough. We can send him a postcard. He'll find us."

"I can't. I couldn't do that to him."

"Things are already in motion, Hannah. I'm sorry to have to

put you on the spot like this, but it can't be helped—the die is already cast."

"I . . . I can't imagine life without you."

He waited.

"Still I . . . I need to think . . . I just can't—"

"Can't what? Chuck it all? Walk away? Don't you see? This is our moment, the moment we've been building toward all along."

"But what are you planning to . . . I mean what are you going to do that is so drastic, that means you have to change all this? I thought we had a good arrangement."

"It's business. Believe me, sweetie, it's best for you if I don't tell you any more."

"And you, you expect me to live like that?"

It was pointless to go on. He felt another section of his world collapse. Whatever combination of experience and misery that had piled up in her life, however they might have helped each other heal—it was now, suddenly, unexpectedly, all adding up to an untenable house of cards, a beautiful mirage.

"Jack?"

"I'm really sorry, honey." His eyes welled up, but he wasn't about to lose it on the phone with her.

"Give me your number, Jack. I'll call you tonight. Let me just think about this, will you?"

"You have my cell number. After tomorrow, it won't be working."

"I'll call you later tonight. I promise I will. I love you, Jack."

"I love you too."

He broke the connection.

Theirs would have been a strange new life together, full of exotic possibility. He had never really allowed himself to dream about it because he had always known it might come down to this kind of stark moment, this kind of choice—go or no go. For a moment he felt as if his mind were detaching from his body, as if he were on surveillance, watching himself.

Like a robot, he went through the motions of closing the office. He drove the few miles to his house, went to the bedroom, and packed a small suitcase as if he were only leaving for an overnight trip. He sat at his home computer, moved through the other necessary steps, made a few phone calls and screen clicks—accounts closed, passwords deleted. The bank and the post office were the only places left to visit.

His last job was to tear down the sanctuary of his war room— every map, every article, every photo—and run them all through the shredder. It took awhile, but he dwelled over nothing, stuffing it all into a large plastic trash bag. On his way to Binghamton he would find a dumpster somewhere, or better yet, a place with an incinerator.

He carried everything out to the Seville. Locked the house and set the alarm, almost pausing to look back but thinking better of it. He climbed into the car, started it up, and backed out of the garage with the door closing into the stark light of day.

FIFTY-NINE

Gwen's old dormitory was built into a hillside, a multistory, apartment-like complex that looked pretty much the same as it had when she was alive.

"You going to tell me now why we're here?" Ruth said.

Quentin stopped and pointed to a third-floor window.

"Do you remember what's up there?"

Ruth looked at the building. "It's Gwen's old room, isn't it?"

"That's right. Inside that window is where she slept the night before she was murdered."

"I remember. I remember visiting here with the police."

"Hollister and King."

"Yes, they brought me to have a look. Gwen wouldn't let me visit after she finished her junior year. I wasn't welcome, she said."

"Yeah, well, maybe that was because she was already worried by then and wanted to protect you."

"Worried? About what?"

He sighed. "A couple of years before Gwen was murdered, there'd been some reports of a peeping Tom on campus."

"Was the person caught?"

"No. The reports stopped once we boosted security patrols and improved some of the lighting around the dorms."

"And no one ever thought to link any of this to Gwen's abduction and murder?"

"Oh, I'm sure it was brought up. But the timeline didn't fit."

"And you think this person, maybe the same person Gwen told you she had met, may have taken those photos of her through the window?"

"No, the pictures are too clear. I think they may have used some kind of hidden camera, and I don't know, maybe Gwen saw something or someone that made her suspicious. Or maybe she just had some kind of sixth sense and was feeling vulnerable."

"But we still have no idea who this person might be."

"No, but I think I might know who may have set up the camera."

"Who?"

"A guy named Alex Cook who worked maintenance here for awhile before he was killed in a car accident."

"Did you know him?"

"No. You might have noticed, they've got a pretty big staff around here to take care of the grounds and all the buildings. I knew a few of the guys over there, but I don't remember ever seeing him. I just learned about Cook a couple of days ago."

"Wait a minute. You're telling me you think Gwen's killer died in a car accident?"

"No. Again, the timeline doesn't fit. Cook died some time before Gwen's disappearance. And his death was written off as an accident, although I'm not so sure it was. I just think Cook may have been working with whoever took those photos, probably helped set up the camera or cameras for him, at least initially."

"So the killer had taken secret photos of other students?"

"Maybe. I'm still just guessing about some of this."

"What made you look into this person Cook in the first place?"

"Gwen. She must have found out something about Cook herself. She never gave me his name, but when I pressed her for more details about what kind of trouble she was in, she said I should keep in mind a date from a couple of years before. That there had been an accident in the river."

"The river?"

"Yeah, Cook's car went into the river over in the city. I remembered the date, but I wasn't able to find out anything before I was arrested. I finally went to look into it a couple of days ago. That's when I found out about the accident and I went and talked to his old boss at an office supply company and found out that Cook moonlighted over here."

"So you think Cook was working with someone else who took the photos of Gwen?"

"Yes."

"And this someone else was either a cop or someone pretending to be a cop."

He nodded.

"If Cook's death wasn't an accident, why was he killed?"

"I don't know exactly, but when his car was dragged from the river, apparently he was found with some large bills in his wallet that were matched to some money from a police drug bust."

"So there's a link to the police." Ruth sat dumbfounded for a moment. "Who can we trust?"

"Maybe no one."

"But you . . . you could have gone to someone, couldn't you? Before you knew all this, in the beginning, I mean."

"I could have, but I was stupid. I should have gotten some outside authorities involved before I was known to the killer and the threat came to my mother."

"Could there be more than one? More than one, killer, I mean."

"I don't know. But I am sure nobody but me knew those photos were in the box, because the seal hadn't been broken again. So whoever killed Nelson was either after them or the money."

The sun had climbed higher in the sky. It was beginning to grow hot standing on the grass. There appeared to be no summer campers housed on this side of the campus. Another groundskeeper mowing the lawn beside the dormitory had finished the job and moved off over the hill, the sound of his engine fading in the distance. There was still a small patch of woods, scrub pine and cedar mostly, on the hillside above the dorm.

Quentin sensed a small movement among the pines. A pinprick of light. What the . . . ?

"Get down!"

He grabbed her by the sleeve and pulled her roughly to the ground. She screamed as the first shot pierced the air. There was no loud crack from the rifle, sound-suppressed and masked by the roar of the distant mower, just the sickly thud of a bullet striking the soft earth beside his head, the shattering of the turf into fragments raining over them. He pulled the Browning from inside his jacket.

"The tree," he said.

She followed his lead and they crawled toward the safety of the large maple. Two more shots came at them, one grazing his wrist, but they made it to the trunk safely. The shooting ceased as abruptly as it had begun.

"You okay?" she said. She was breathing heavily and her legs were streaked with dirt.

"Fine. I think we'll be all right here." His wrist was bleeding but not too badly. The edge of the sleeve was torn. "Don't know if I can say as much for the suit."

"Why didn't you shoot back?"

"Shoot at what? He's got a high-powered rifle at seventy-five yards and I've got an old handgun. Besides, he's done here for now. I'm not even sure he was trying to kill us, because he probably could have easily enough. Maybe he just wanted to send a message."

"Should we go after him?"

Quentin's mind created a mental map of the far side of the hill behind the dorm back when he'd worked on campus. A parking lot. Another row of dorms. Of course there was no way to say for sure if changes had been made or new buildings added.

"No. He knows the terrain and is already bugging out by now. He's not going to risk being seen."

"Let me see your hand," she said. She took his large fingers in hers and turned the wrist over. "It grazed you. This needs a bandage."

"I'll be all right."

"So what do we do now?"

"We get the hell out of here. But before we do, I'm going to see if I can dig one of those rounds out of the grass here. Someone's bound to notice the holes and report them."

"Well that may help for the future, but what's to stop this person or whoever sent those men last night from coming after us again? We need help and protection. We should call someone else if the police can't be trusted."

"No. I've got a better idea," he said.

SIXTY

Garnell sat in his car parked at the curb on the street in front of Price's uncle's house. No sign of Price or Ruth Crawford or anyone else, for that matter. He'd talked with Hollister and King again about the Nelson Root murder, trying to ferret out any hidden motives they might have, but had come up empty. He'd put a request in with the captain's office for departmental records on current and past employees, but was told by a less-than-cooperative assistant that, being the weekend, it might be several hours before anything could be pulled together for him.

Now, past dinner time, the day had almost gotten away from him, and he was still no closer to catching his killer. He had a feeling something was going down and he was three or four steps behind, running to catch up. What he needed was a break, something to tip the balance in his favor.

He thought of Monique, alone for another weekend with their baby, down in the city. He was justifiably proud of his little family. Monique had gone through a difficult pregnancy, suffering back spasms and Braxton Hicks contractions from the seventh month on, before giving birth to a healthy normal baby girl. Part of him still felt like a traitor being away from home at a time like this. Each day Ivy changed. A week was like an eternity—something else that he missed. He laid her over his shoulder to burp her when Monique was done feeding her, breathing the infant's smell, soap, and safety. It calmed his fragile nerves. Her chubby little arms clutching his bicep must have made him look like the village idiot, sitting there with a silly grin plastered on his face. He didn't care.

He pulled out his cell phone and pushed the speed dial for home. Monique answered on the third ring.

"Hey, stranger."

"Hey yourself," he said.

"You sound tired."

"Yeah. It's the case. How's the baby?"

"Fine, she's asleep."

"Okay. I miss her. I miss you even more."

"You still haven't told me much about your case."

"No I haven't, have I?"

"I've got an ear and I can listen."

He brought her up to speed on all that had happened so far.

She was a great listener, even on the phone, interrupting only to interject, "that's awful" under her breath when he came to the part about Nelson's Root's killing and gave her a summary of the FBI profiler's report.

"Sounds like you've got a real mess up there," she said when he finished.

"You could say that."

"The DAG going to back you if you have to start peeking around under official panties?"

"He gave me the option to back out."

"Which you didn't take of course, having no sense of professional decorum toward your fellow law enforcement professionals."

"Who says I don't have decorum?"

"I do, but never mind. Just looking at what you've told me from afar, there's no way this fresh killing of Price's uncle isn't somehow related to the other murders."

"You'd think so, wouldn't you? But nobody up here's come

up with anything so far . . . There's one other thing I haven't told you."

He told her about the index card he'd found on his desk.

"That's pretty scary, don't you think?" she said.

"I suppose."

"If it turns out to be one of your brothers in blue performing the killings, they might not exactly be foaming at the mouth for answers. The two detectives up there—what are their names, Hollister and King—could they be in on it too?"

I don't want to know, Hollister had said.

"I really don't think so," he said. "But they might be guilty of overlooking something. People learn to start looking the other way sometimes. After awhile, they're not even aware that they're doing it anymore."

"Have you been able to talk to Quentin Price alone?"

"Yes."

"What's he got to say about everything that's happened?"

"He won't talk. Not that I blame the man. And a funny thing's been going on. He's been hanging around with Gwen Crawford's mother."

"The girl he was supposed to have murdered?"

He nodded. "She even got him a job at the restaurant where she works."

"Anything physical between them?"

"Doesn't look like it. She's a bit too old for him."

"Hey, you'd be surprised."

"The whole thing's raised a few eyebrows though."

"So what's her motive? Christian kindness, you think?"

"I've talked to her. She seems a little off, like she may be on the bottle or something. Cops up there say she's always been a little kooky. Claims she's been getting these strange condolence cards every year from some anonymous person."

"More notes. Have you seen them, the condolence cards, I mean?"

"Yeah."

"They seem strange to you?"

"A little, yeah."

"I hear you say that and I think they must be really spooky."

"Maybe."

"Whatever you do, please be careful," she said.

The phone beeped in his ear. He pulled it away to look at the call ID on the menu screen. What was that he'd wished for about a break?

"Sweetie?" he said.

"I'm here."

"I'm sorry, but I've got another call coming in."

"All right. I hope it helps."

"I hope so too. It's Quentin Price."

Sixty-One

A couple of hours after sunset, with a cool fog hovering over the interstate, Ruth and Quentin pulled into the truck stop south of Binghamton. A dozen or more tractor trailers were parked in the rest area; their amber running lights glowed like slumming stars among the dark hulks of steel. After leaving Hamlick, Ruth and Quentin had spent the remainder of the day holed up in Ruth's apartment, taking care of Quentin's wound and talking over what to do. They both called in sick to work. Ruth told Walt they'd been involved in a traffic accident. Detective Harris had wanted them to sit tight until he got there, but Quentin told him he preferred to meet in a public place.

Ruth had changed into jeans and a brightly colored print blouse. Her face tightened when she saw Harris's car parked in front of the convenience store and food court. "Did you tell him everything?"

"Almost everything."

"Do you think he'll want to take us into protective custody or something?"

"Not if I can help it." The last thing Quentin wanted was to ever see the inside of a jail cell again.

They climbed out of the Chrysler. In the harsh halogen light of the lot, the back of the car really did look like a mess. Like at the college, they'd drawn more than a few stares each time they'd hit the highway. Amazing the thing kept going.

Quentin carried a paper bag containing the metal box,

photos, and money. He waited while Ruth locked the doors.

"How do we know we can trust this man?" she asked.

"Right now, he's the best that we've got."

The inside of the truck stop was a cavernous mall filled with shelves of snack foods, supplies, and sundries, clothing, books, and movies for sale or rental. To one side was a row of fast food concessions, pizza, burgers, and the like. On the end of a long row of tables and chairs, sipping a cup of coffee, sat Detective Harris.

From across the space, Quentin took the NYPD investigator's measure. He appeared to be alone, as Quentin had asked. They walked over to his table.

"Glad the two of you are okay." Harris stood and looked them over. He and Quentin shook hands.

"Yeah. But if we stopped for every so-called pair of cops who tried to pull us over we wouldn't be."

The detective nodded. "Already checked with the state police. You were right on about your suspicions. I'd like to retrieve the bodies and the car though, see if we can try to figure out who they really are."

Ruth looked apprehensive.

"Do whatever you gotta do," Quentin said.

He and Ruth declined the offer of coffee or anything else to drink. The three of them sat down around the table. Quentin placed the paper bag on the floor next to him.

"You said on the phone someone was shooting at you too."

Quentin reached inside his pants pocket and pulled out the bullet he'd dug out of the dirt at the college. Soft nose, power point, designed to deliver maximum energy on impact. It had degraded from striking the soft earth but not as bad as it might have if it had struck a body or a more solid object. "You'll find a couple more of these with the ground chewed up over by Gwen's old dormitory on the Merryweather campus."

"Looks like a thirty caliber. That would have done a world of hurt."

"Uh-huh." He handed the cartridge to Harris and described the exact location.

"What were you two doing over there at the college?"

There was no use belaboring the point. Quentin grabbed the bag, lifted it onto his lap, and pulled out the dirty rust-streaked metal container. He placed it on the table.

"I had this stashed away. Buried it in a park over in Endicott for the whole time I was up at Auburn."

"Okay."

He opened the lid and poured out the contents. Hundred and fifty dollar bills and grainy, faded photos fanned onto the tabletop.

Harris lifted a brow, looking impressed.

He told him what he had told Ruth about the box and his last conversations at the college with Gwen before she disappeared.

When he finished, Harris asked, "Why didn't you go to the police with any of this again?"

"Like I said, from what Gwen told me I figured a cop, maybe more than one, was involved."

"But now, after the fake state troopers last night, you're not so sure."

"Right."

"Well it just so happens I've got an FBI report says they think it might be a cop." Harris stroked his chin.

Quentin pointed to the doctored photo. "All I know is, just like this picture, the threat against my mom was real."

"You mother's passed away now, hasn't she?" Harris asked.

"Yeah."

"So whoever had you bottled up has lost that leverage."

Quentin watched as he idly flipped through the stack of

money on the table.

The detective's eyes narrowed. "You spent any of this cash, Price?"

"A little."

"The serial numbers on the bills are sequential. You ever notice that?"

In fact he had noticed but hadn't known what to make of it. Was the cop playing games? "Yeah, so?"

"Just a little curious. Means it was most likely taken out of the bank all at one time."

"You mean like maybe drug money or something?"

The detective narrowed his eyes. "Not necessarily. But I'd like to do some checking on the numbers all the same."

"If what Gwen said was true, what was a cop doing carrying around all these benjamins?"

"Good question. And why give them to Gwen?"

"So what are you going to do? Round up everyone who has anything to do with the Binghamton Police Bureau?"

"At least it narrows the list of suspects."

"Maybe you need some more backup," he said.

Harris looked annoyed. "The attorney general's office is aware of the situation."

"What about Jack?" Ruth asked.

"Your husband?"

"Yes."

Harris stared at her. "Are you trying to tell me the man raped and murdered his own daughter?"

"No. But he might know something more than he's telling. He's convinced Quentin is still guilty. More than convinced. He's obsessed over it."

"So I gathered from talking with him. You think he's out to harm you people?"

"I don't know. I wouldn't put it past him."

"And tomorrow's your daughter's birthday."

"Yes, it is. Do you believe me now about those notes I received?"

"I'm starting to." The cop hesitated. "If anything comes through the post office, we'll try to trace it."

Quentin stared at the younger man, who was looking idly at the table. He wasn't much for reading minds, but the detective was telegraphing concern over tomorrow's anniversary. "You know something else, don't you?"

"What?"

"I said you know something else."

Harris sighed and rubbed his eyes. He paused for a moment before pulling out the baggie containing the index card threat, from the inside pocket of his coat. He laid it on the table and smoothed out the clear plastic for them to read.

Sixty-Two

Jack sat alone in his car outside Ruth's apartment complex again. From the opposite side of the street, he had a good view of her front door, but there'd been no sign of her Chrysler or activity from inside the apartment.

Worse, Fletcher had stopped answering his cell calls, and Jack was afraid the guy was becoming unreliable. He'd gone by Price's uncle's house and seen no sign of Price or Ruth, not to mention Fletcher. Several hours of staking out Price's uncle's house had proved fruitless so he had decided to try over here. But it was after dark by the time he arrived, and Ruth wasn't home either. What was going on? Where could she be at this hour of the night? Still with Price? Were she and Price injured or dead?

He chewed on the last of the French fries from his drive-thru meal, took a sip of his lukewarm coffee. He hated himself for what he was about to do. He hated himself even worse for having gotten himself into this situation in the first place. He could end up in jail. Wouldn't that be ironic? Him in the slammer while Price ran around free as a bird.

He half-turned the ignition key in order to roll down the power window in the Seville. He needed to feel the cool night air on his skin. A muscle car with two teens in the front, a boy driving and a girl next to him, rumbled toward him. Muted music thumped from behind its windows. The music was turned down, though, as they approached the apartment complex. The young man angled the car to the curb a dozen or so yards in front of the apartment buildings. Oblivious to Jack's presence, the girl undid her seat belt, leaned over to the side, and held a long, hot kiss with her boyfriend. Then she pushed open the door and jumped out, short blue-jean cutoffs, brown hair, tanned skin. She turned and waved as she ran in the complex entrance and hustled over to the nearest apartment, unlocked the front door with a key, and disappeared as the muscle car edged from the curb and rumbled off down the street to the thump of the music again.

Still no sign of Ruth. Jack needed information and he needed it now. He reached for his cell and pushed the speed dial. Finally, Fletcher answered his phone.

"It's me," he said.

"Oh, hey."

"Where have you been? I've been trying to call."

"Sorry. Had to do some other work."

"I went by Price's place and there was no sign of you. Ended up having to sit on the place myself."

"I picked up their trail again."

"Ruth and Price?"

"So they're both okay. What happened to your boys you sent to shake them down?"

"That I still don't know. Price ducked into the house for a minute while I was watching. But he came back out right away, and they took off again, so I followed them."

"Where'd they go?"

"Back over to Hamlick, to the college."

"What the hell were they doing there?"

"I don't know. A security guard, some woman, surprised me, and I lost them."

"That's just friggin' great."

"I was going to call you in a little bit, see if you wanted me to go back over to Price's place. I tried the restaurant a little while ago, but the place had just closed. Didn't see the Chrysler in the parking lot, but people were still working inside, so I went and knocked on the door. Pretended I was a customer who'd lost his cell phone and they let me in to look. Different people. Your ex definitely wasn't there. Neither was Price. Then I had to head over to the newspaper to get some photos ready for tomorrow's paper."

"Anything else?"

"That's it for now. You want me to go by and check out her apartment?"

"Already taken care of. Can you work the rest of the night?"

"No problem."

"Good. Go back and sit on the house on Front Street."

"Will do."

"And this time call me right away if the black guy shows up."

"All right."

"And Doyle."

"Yeah?"

"Nice work on the college. You did good."

"Thanks."

"Only next time don't lose them."

"You know what?"

"What?"

"I just thought of something. I got another hunch as to where your ex and Price might be."

"Yeah?"

"Why don't you take the house?"

"I've already been over there. I'm sitting on Ruth's apartment."

"Okay, stay where you are, I don't care. But let me play this thing out. See what develops. If it doesn't work out, then I'm back on house stakeout till they show somewhere."

"Okay. You've got my number," he said.

"It's already after midnight. You know what day it is, Jack?"

"It's Monday."

"That's right. June first."

"June first. Right. That was—"

"Your daughter's birthday, Jack."

"Yeah. How'd you know that?"

"You said I was good."

SIXTY-THREE

Quentin awoke in the unfamiliar hotel room he now shared with Detective Harris, the first light of a new day making its presence known on the ceiling and through the curtains. Ruth had been booked into the room next door. They shared a connecting door, which Harris kept cracked open.

Harris was already out of the other bed and nearly dressed. "I've got to get downstairs to the coffee shop to meet with Hollister and King," he told Quentin.

"They know we're here?"

"Not yet."

"You sure you can trust them?"

"Yeah." Harris finished knotting his tie. "They're not bad cops. Just wrong ones."

"From my experience it's hard to tell the difference."

"There's a difference. Trust me."

"Maybe I should call my lawyer," Quentin said.

"What for?" Harris said. "We're not taking you into custody. I just think the two of you will be safer here until we can figure this whole thing out."

"Which could take forever."

"If so, then we might have to consider other options. A safe house or even a jail cell is better than being dead."

"Easy for you to say."

"I checked on Ruth. She's still asleep."

"Okay."

"You've also got an extra room key. I'll be back in half an hour." Harris picked up a notebook and turned toward the door. "And I'll keep an eye on the elevator and the entrance to the emergency stairs. Any problems, call me on my cell."

Comforting, but Quentin wouldn't mind having some extra protection of his own. Unsure what to do with the Browning with the detective in tow, Quentin had left it locked in the glove compartment of the Chrysler in the parking lot outside. He was beginning to wish the sound-suppressed .45s they'd taken off the faux state troopers hadn't gone into the pond with their bodies.

"What about food?" he asked.

"I'll bring you some back. And there's a coffee maker in the bathroom."

"How long do you think we'll have to be here?"

"If this guy makes a wrong move with the birthday thing, hopefully not long." Harris strode toward the door and put a hand on the knob. "Okay? You good?"

"For now," he said.

The detective nodded and disappeared out the door.

Quentin sat up in bed and stared around the empty room. They had cable, free movies, even free Internet access. All the comforts of home. He didn't like it one bit. Being caged up reminded him too much of Auburn. He peeked through an opening in the curtains.

What would have been Gwen Crawford's thirty-first birthday was dawning with a bright sun in a cloudless sky. He climbed out of bed, used the bathroom, and dressed. After splashing water on his face and brushing his teeth, he put on a pot of coffee. From the next room, he could still hear the faint sounds of Ruth lightly snoring. Curse of the drink maybe, or maybe it was just age.

Half an hour, Harris had said. Was it doubt he had seen in

the cop's eyes? They'd come this far, hadn't they? They'd trusted each other, at least a little. But maybe Harris knew, as he did, that trust only lasted as long as actions warranted. Now the detective was headed downstairs to talk to Hollister and King, and maybe other cops, more people in the loop, more potential for disaster. He'd seen the kind of screwups that could happen at Auburn, how one or two guards talked to an inmate and then the message got garbled up the chain of command.

Ruth stirred in the next room. Quentin went to the door and nudged it open. She was lying on her side with a sheet over top of her. Her eyes opened.

"Time to wake-up, sleepyhead. Coffee's on."

"What?" Her voice was raspy from sleep. "What time is it?"

"I'm not liking the way this situation is shaking out. It's time for us to get out of this place," he said.

Sixty-Four

"What's going on, Harris?"

Garnell felt Hollister's eyes on him as he and King took chairs across the table. He had purposefully picked one in the far corner by the window, away from the regular traffic flow. The coffee shop at the Holiday Inn was busy this time of the morning.

Garnell finished a sip from his cup of coffee. "Quite a bit, actually."

"Yeah?"

"Someone's been trying to kill Price and Ruth Crawford."

"Say what?"

He told them what Ruth and Quentin had told him about the two men impersonating state troopers. A waitress approached with a steaming coffeepot, ready to turn over and fill the two empty mugs in front of Hollister and King, but Hollister waved her away.

"Do you know all this for a fact or are you just taking their word for it?"

"They've given a description and exact directions to where they dumped the car and the bodies. We can go drag the pond."

"Where are Price and Ruth Crawford now?"

"I've got them stashed safely for the time being. The local AG's office has also been informed."

Hollister picked a toothpick out of a bin on the table next to the ketchup and stuck it in his mouth. King, who looked like he could use another cup of coffee, glared across the table.

"The DA or our chief or our captain know anything about it?" Hollister asked.

Garnell shook his head.

"Why not?"

"Because someone who knows how to work the system may be behind all this. Maybe an insider."

"A cop?" The elder detective's brow furrowed.

"Exactly."

"But you said the guys who went after Price last night were impersonating cops."

"Yeah. Price thinks that could be a possibility here too." He told them about the FBI profile and about what Price said Gwen Crawford had told him.

"Be a friggin' nightmare if it's another cop," King said.

"This guy, whoever he is, probably killed Gwen Crawford. Price says he thinks Gwen knew something about the killer and that the killer also threatened his mother."

"Him thinking it was a cop . . . What was in the box?"

"A big wad of cash Gwen Crawford had given him. The bills are sequential so we can run a check on them. And there were revealing photos of Gwen Crawford stored in a false bottom. Price says someone secretly took the pictures."

"Photos?" Hollister glanced at his partner.

He explained the scenario further and what Price had said about how Gwen told him she came by the photos and the money. "Not only that. One of the pictures was clearly a threat. It was a mutilated corpse with Gwen Crawford's head doctored on top of it."

"Price had these all along and he never brought any of this up at trial, not even to his lawyer?"

"He said he didn't trust anyone, especially the cops, and he didn't think he'd ever be convicted."

"How do you know Price didn't take these pictures himself, kill Gwen, and now is fabricating this whole scheme?"

"Be a helluva scheme, especially considering the DNA. I believe Price. He says Gwen told him a cop was involved and he received the same kind of photo threatening his mother after he was arrested."

King was shaking his head.

Garnell went on. "Price says Gwen Crawford told him about what might have been another killing. A man named Cook. It happened a couple of years before Gwen Crawford's murder and got passed off as an accident."

Hollister looked at King and they both shrugged. "Never heard of the case."

"Apparently, there had been reports about a peeping Tom at the college. Price thinks this guy might have set up some hidden cameras in the dorm."

"Which were never found when Gwen Crawford's dorm was searched," King said. "How can that be?"

"Our real perp could have already gone in and removed them."

"Security was pretty lax on those dorms back then," Hollister admitted. "But what you're talking about is some kind of serial killer walking around right under our noses."

"Or one who wants us to think he's a serial killer. Maybe playing cop too. Could be almost anyone working around the courthouse, for the Feds, or at the bureau across the street."

"That narrows it down to only a few hundred."

"You can see why I'm trying to keep the need-to-know loop small on this," Garnell said.

"Then let's go pull this car out of the water and start trying to find out what's going on."

"Yeah, but we need to keep a low profile."

"I know a guy with a wrecker we can trust. I've used him before."

"Good."

King cleared his throat. "You're so sure it's someone with law enforcement, how do you know Bill or I isn't the killer? Maybe we're even working in tandem."

Garnell studied the younger man's face. "I'm giving you the benefit of the doubt," he said.

"Shut up," said Hollister to his partner. "Look, Harris. This whole cop thing could just be a ruse to pull our attention away from Price. You consider that?"

"What, you think he's got Ruth Crawford and FBI profilers on his side now too?"

Quentin's cell phone rang and he looked at the number on the display. "Excuse me a second, fellas." It was Jane Pappas.

"Hey, Jane. You get a hold of Johnson or Keiper?"

"Good morning to you too," she said. "And no I didn't talk to either one of them, but some of us have to get into the office early. I'm looking at the Santiago file now."

"What have you got?"

"Thought I would have remembered . . . The vic was found with a fake sheriff's shield pinned to her clothing. Johnson and Keiper figured it was just the perp's idea of taunting the cops."

"That's it. I knew there was something. Thanks, Jane. Now I really owe you."

"Don't mention it," she said.

He hung up and replayed the conversation for Hollister and King.

"Okay," Hollister said. "But are you saying we're going to have to start turning over everybody who works downtown here?"

"Unless you've got some hot new lead or evidence about the Nelson Root murder, I don't know about."

The three detectives stared at one another.

"Fake state police cars, old hidden cameras, a pile of cash with some kind of sniper over at the college, and now we've got fake badges . . . I sure hope you're right about all this, Harris. Because if you're not and Price is somehow guilty, all of our careers are going down the toilet," Hollister said.

"Going to be pretty hard to keep this quiet once we start nosing around in people's business," King added.

"We'll just have to do the best that we can. If we spook our target, it may be to our advantage."

"Or get somebody else killed."

"It might even be more urgent than that," he said.

"What do you mean?"

"Remember the condolence letters on her daughter's birthday Ruth Crawford talked to you guys about in the past?"

"Yeah, the ones I showed you. What about them?"

"They may be material. She's been getting more mysterious notes. That's what led Crawford and Price into the trap with the two supposed cops. But that's not all . . ." He showed them the note he'd received at the bureau and told them where it had come from.

"Someone couldn't have just walked in off the street with this," Hollister said.

"No. And today just so happens to be Gwen Crawford's birthday."

"Then we're way behind in the count."

Sixty-Five

Jack's mouth tasted like drywall. His back hurt and he needed to piss. He struggled to keep his eyes open, glancing at his watch. Half past seven. Ruth had to return to her apartment sooner or later, didn't she? Wherever she'd spent the night, it wasn't here. He pounded his fist on the dash of the Seville.

At a McDonald's across the street, he ducked in to relieve himself and fortify his brain with fresh java, glancing every now and then down the block toward the apartment.

There'd been no answer on Ruth's cell number all night. Back in the car, he tried her phone one more time. This time though, she answered after the fourth ring.

"Ruth?"

"Jack? Is that you?"

"Yeah."

"Where are you?" she asked.

"I'm around." He had to play this cool. "Are you going to be at work today?"

A hesitation. "Maybe. I'm not sure. Why?"

"I was hoping to get together with you a little later to talk some more about the situation with Price."

"I thought we already talked enough about that, Jack. You're not going to change my mind about it."

"I'm not going to try to change your mind, Ruth. Never could do that. I just wanted to try to appreciate your position better. Maybe I'm missing something. Maybe there's something I don't understand about Price."

"What are you up to?"

"Where are you? At home?"

"No. I'm . . ." Another hesitation. "I'm out."

If he had time to make the calls and paid off the right people, he could find out exactly where she was by the GPS locator embedded in her phone. He hoped he wouldn't have to resort to that.

"I would really like to talk. Just talk. Can I meet you somewhere? I can even come to the restaurant later if you want."

There was a much longer pause this time. Long enough to know she was with someone and discussing the options. He could hear muffled noises that sounded like voices. Finally she spoke into the phone again.

"I'm sorry. I can't do that right now, Jack. I don't want to talk to you."

He felt the white-hot flash of anger rise up within him again. But just as quickly he assessed the prospects. "You mean I drove all the way down here to Binghamton for nothing?"

"You're in Binghamton?"

"Yes."

Silence.

"C'mon, Ruthie. Just five minutes. That's all I'm asking."

"No. Please don't call me anymore, Jack. And please don't go by my apartment. I want you to leave me alone."

He had to wrestle with his emotions to keep from crushing the phone in his hand. It was important he left her with the idea he was going to go away. He didn't want to leave too quietly though. That wouldn't sound plausible. "I'm not happy about this, Ruth. I'm not happy at all."

"I know. I'm sorry. But that's the way it has to be."

"She was my daughter too you know."

He could tell he'd struck a chord with that one when she

answered with a slight quiver in her voice. "I know she was."

"You're a fool, Ruth."

"No I'm not."

"Whoever's got you is filling your head full of bull. They're using you." It would take a couple of hours, but by late morning he would have an exact location of Ruth's phone at the time he'd placed his call.

"No they're not."

"Good-bye, Ruth." He pushed the button on his phone to end the call.

You're dead to me, he thought. Like Hannah. Like everybody. Like Gwen.

Sixty-Six

It was too nice a day for dragging dead bodies out of ponds. Sun high overhead. Sky a brilliant blue. They were all in shirtsleeves too since the temperature had climbed into the seventies. Garnell leaned against the front fender of the wrecker and watched as the winch began to draw the car out of the water.

He had been afraid they might need to call in divers. But the car had been in such shallow water that the tow truck driver, obviously possessing a talent for this sort of thing, had been able to snag the vehicle's bumper by wading out to where the water was only chest deep. Hollister and King stood next to Garnell, the older detective smoking a cigarette.

"I didn't know you smoked," Garnell said.

"I don't." Hollister tossed the butt into the dirt and crushed it out with his shoe.

"From the story Price and Ms. Crawford told, this was a pretty clear-cut case of self-defense."

"That remains to be seen, doesn't it? Especially since your star witnesses have decided to disappear."

"Let's just see what we've got," he said.

The car was a late-model Crown Vic that could have passed for an unmarked state trooper's. Price and Crawford's directions had led them exactly to the spot. Garnell had interviewed them separately, digested their testimony about what had happened out here, and decided they were most likely telling the truth. It was stupid of him to have left them alone in the room like that.

Just as they had told him, there were two men in the car. One was slumped over the steering wheel, the other face down in the passenger seat. Both dead of course, apparently from gunshot wounds. From the condition of the bodies, it appeared they'd been in the water for a day or so, jiving with Price's and Ruth Crawford's stories.

"We got any clue who these guys are? Maybe one of them is our local Binghamton cop type." Garnell looked in through one side of the car and watched as King and Hollister leaned in through the other.

Hollister turned the head of the man on his side with his gloved hand and looked at the face. He then looked across at the driver.

"Never seen either of them before. Not working downtown or anywhere else. You, Sean?"

King repeated Hollister's examination. "Nope. Me neither."

Garnell looked at their clothes more closely. "One thing's for sure. They're definitely not the state cops they were pretending to be."

King was feeling around one of the bodies. "Got a wallet here." He jumped to check the other body as well. "Here too."

"Good. Price said he left them with the bodies."

They extracted the contents, spread them out on the roof of the car, and checked out the licenses.

"Still never heard of them?" Garnell asked.

They both shook their heads.

"Out of towners though," Hollister said. "Looks like from Buffalo way."

"A couple of goons from Buffalo dressed up like cops show-ing up here on the right back road in the middle of the night," Garnell said. "Pretty damn curious."

"That took some planning." Hollister shot a worried look across the car at his partner.

Garnell stared at them. "You two guys are still holding out on me about something, aren't you?"

"Christ almighty." Hollister whipped out his phone, looked at the screen, then slammed it shut again. "No coverage."

Garnell was a half a step behind, but closing rapidly. "What's going on, Hollister? Talk to me."

Hollister brought his hand down on top of the dripping car, eyes boring into his. "We need to find Jack Crawford pronto and bring him in for questioning."

"What for?"

"Because I'm pretty sure he can help explain what these two stiffs are doing here," Hollister said.

SIXTY-SEVEN

"You miss me?"

"Yeah, but that's not why I'm calling," Quentin said.

"Okay."

Just the sound of Sierra's voice made him feel something he had been missing for a very long time. "I need your help. Looking for some specific information."

"Anything. But maybe I should let Ms. Shackleford know about it too. I haven't said anything to her about what you told me the other night, but—"

"All right. She might even be able to help."

"What do you need?"

"I need to know about money that may have been recovered from a local drug bust about the time of that accident we read about. I need to know if any of it went missing or somehow disappeared."

Maybe Detective Harris had been on to something about the money. This was one way to find out.

"I'll probably have to talk to the police chief or the DA."

"All right. But try to keep the reasons for questions vague. Maybe tell them it has something to do with another case or something."

"Sure. I can do that."

"I need this as soon as possible."

"I'll get right on it. Can you give me any more to go on?"

"It's best for you if I don't."

"You're not . . ." She hesitated. "You're not in any danger, are you?"

"Let's just say I've had better days."

"I don't like the sounds of that, Quentin. If Ms. Shackleford hears that you—"

"Don't worry. I can take care of myself. Just please get me this information as soon as you can."

"Where can I reach you?"

Quentin gave her his cell number and hung up the phone.

He tucked the phone back the pocket of his jeans. The Super 8 Motel on Front Street was a step or two down from the Holiday Inn, but since neither he nor Ruth wanted to risk going back by the house or Ruth's apartment, it would have to do. Their room was in the back of the main building facing a Dumpster and the interstate. They had parked the Chrysler in a commuter lot a quarter mile down the street, hoping it wouldn't be noticed. Ruth had tossed her small bag on the bed closest to the bathroom and sat down at the table by the window to smoke.

"Are you hungry?" he asked.

"I could eat something."

"I'm going to go down and pick up a couple of sandwiches from the restaurant. You okay with that?"

"I . . . I suppose so."

Quentin felt under his jacket for the Browning. "I'm going to leave you the gun then. I shouldn't be gone long. Anybody comes to this door who looks suspicious, shoot first and ask questions later."

He pulled out the gun, grasped the barrel pointing it away from them, and placed the grip in her outstretched fingers. She held onto it with both hands.

"What about you?" she asked.

"The restaurant looked pretty busy. Plus, I've got the cell. Nobody's going to bother me down there."

"Maybe we should just go back down to the Holiday Inn and talk to Detective Harris."

"I told you. I'm not sure we can totally trust him. And even if we can, by the time he's up to speed with everything, it may be too late to keep whoever's been writing those notes from delivering Gwen's birthday present."

"Just be careful."

"Always."

Downstairs in the lobby, another guest was checking in. Quentin moved with a sense of urgency out the front door and across the parking lot, scanning the perimeter as he went. The waitress at the restaurant was more than happy to take his order for sandwiches, fries, and drinks to go. While he waited, he searched out the late lunch crowed for any sign of a familiar face or anyone who might be watching him, but everyone seemed too involved in their own meals and conversation to pay him much attention.

A different idea had begun to gnaw at him, but he couldn't put his finger on it. He retraced the events of the last couple of nights in his mind, the two men on the late-night highway up in Chenango County, the shooting at the college. His thoughts drifted back to the shadowy figure of the man in the back seat of the fake state police cruiser. Something about his profile reminded him of something or someone—he wasn't sure who.

The waitress brought his order in a paper bag with a cardboard drink carton. He paid her and made his way out of the eatery, across the parking lot, and back into the motel.

The hallway was quiet as he exited the elevator. Too quiet maybe, but Quentin dismissed the idea as paranoia. Housekeeping must have finished up their work on this level for the day.

He knocked on the door of the room. "It's me."

"Okay." He heard Ruth shuffle around inside.

"Can you open the door? My hands are full."

"Coming."

More shuffling, the door was pulled open, and Ruth's face appeared.

"Everything okay?"

She nodded and he stepped into the room as the door was pulled further open.

He should've noticed the strained look on her face, but he was distracted with the food. There was a flutter of movement from the darkened bathroom. Ruth started to say something, but her voice caught in her throat as the door of the room closed behind him. Before Quentin could move, Jack Crawford stepped calmly from the bathroom with a Beretta pointed at them. He was dressed in crisp khakis and a collared short-sleeve shirt, his big arms bulging through the sleeves.

Quentin glanced at the Browning which he saw lying uselessly on the bed.

"Don't even think about it." Jack tilted the gun and shook his head. "Either of you makes a sound, I blow out someone's face."

Quentin still held the food in his hands. But he couldn't risk tossing it at Jack with Ruth there. For a moment the three of them regarded one another.

"Why don't you set the food down on the other bed there." Jack pointed with his free hand.

"I'm sorry, Quentin," Ruth said. "He came to the door and he said he wanted to talk. I didn't know what to do. I—"

"It's okay," Quentin said. He turned toward the barrel of the Beretta. "What's this all about, Jack?"

"What the fuck you think this is all about, Price? It's about you finally coming clean about how you killed our daughter."

"I didn't kill her, you should know that by now." He kept his tone even.

"Is that the line of horseshit you've been feeding Ruth here?"

"I want to find out who killed her just as bad as you do."

"Oh yeah? Well who is this mysterious masked man then?"

"He's killed at least three other people including my uncle. There was also a part-time maintenance man who used to work at the college and another woman named Santiago who the cops say was dumped down in the Bronx. There could be others. Gwen had found some pictures he secretly took of her and some money and she was scared. She thought he was a cop."

"Oh, gosh. Must be a serial demon working right downtown," Jack said. "You're certifiable, Price." But his eyes registered some doubt.

"Look," Quentin said. "I know how it feels to lose someone close to you. Like someone's ripped your guts out. Like there's a big hole in your chest, worse than any gunshot hole because you can never get rid of it. It gnaws at you all the time."

Jack stared at him for a moment. The gun didn't waver. "You know you're pretty good at this line of baloney, Price. You learn all this psychobabble shit in prison? Studying to be like a lawyer or a psychologist? No, wait. A cop, wasn't it? . . . Oh, Jesus." Jack rolled his eyes. "There we go. This fucking country's going down the toilet so fast now we're going to put the killers on the streets as cops. Like communism, the fucking secret police or something."

"Jack," Ruth said. "Look. Maybe you should talk to the police. We've just come from a meeting with Detective Harris from NYPD and he was going to meet with the Binghamton detectives."

"Who? Hollister and King? Wastes of a suit. None of 'em could make a case if their lives depended on it."

Ruth took a step toward her ex-husband. "What's gotten into you, Jack? You're talking like a crazy person. Think of your business. Think of your future."

"I have no future. Not since Gwen. And neither do you. Not unless it's inside some bottle."

"That's not fair."

"Don't try to tell me it isn't true. And while you've been busy gallivanting around the countryside with our daughter's killer, I've been trying to figure out a way to elicit a real confession."

"Just what are you planning to do?" Quentin said.

Jack took a breath. "Simple enough. I take you and Ruth here someplace real private and you and I will have a friendly discussion about what went down ten years ago. Nobody else seems to be able to shake you down. Now it's my turn."

"We've already been down that road, Jack," he said.

"Yeah? I don't think so." The PI lifted a dull metal object from his pocket. He cupped it in his fingers, stepped forward, and whipped it across Quentin's jaw.

Quentin felt the jolt of pain all the way into the back of his neck, and he started to swing back until he caught sight of the gun pointed at them again.

"I was just getting warmed up on you the first time. You haven't seen me when I really get angry."

Quentin said nothing while his head cleared. He tasted blood in the corner of his mouth.

Ruth said, "This is insane, Jack. None of this is helping what happened to Gwen."

The big man glared at her. "How would you know? You don't know dick about my life."

"I don't, huh?"

"I got money. I got clothes, a great car, a great house. I got a girlfriend who's beautiful and is so nuts about me she'll ball me almost anytime I want except she won't leave her hubby. But what I don't got is what this prick stole from me ten years ago. What he's supposed to still be rotting up in Auburn for."

"Did you send those three men after us the other night?"

Jack hesitated for a moment. "Who else do you think sent them?"

"They were trying to kill us, Jack."

"They what?" He squinted at her.

"One of them may have murdered your daughter," Quentin said.

"What the fuck you talking about?"

"One of them got away."

"What happened to the other two?"

"We shot them in self-defense. Two of them anyway. Hollister, King, and Harris are probably out there picking up their bodies now. But the third one disappeared."

Jack's face went stone-cold blank.

"Do you hear what I'm telling you."

"It doesn't matter," Jack said, but he sounded less convinced than before.

"What do you mean it doesn't matter? Who was the third person in that car?"

Jack shook his head. "I don't know what the hell you're talking about. Both of you must be drunk. I got the jump on you easy enough."

The room fell silent for a few moments. The air conditioning kicked on and the vent in the ceiling began to pour out cold air.

"C'mon. Enough of this garbage," Jack said. "Time to move."

Quentin studied the man. He'd been threatened with death before, at Auburn a couple of times and once on the streets in Queens, but this was different. It almost seemed beyond anything of this world, as if the menace had grown out of another dimension. What more could Jack Crawford do to him? Torture him? Kill him, unless he told the man what he wanted to hear?

"All right," he said. "Let's go."

Ruth eyes began to fill with tears. "Please don't do this, Jack."

Jack reached back into the bathroom and came out with a roll of duct tape. Looked at the two of them and tossed Ruth the tape. "Rip off a couple of lengths of tape. About three feet each ought to do it."

She did as he instructed.

Jack took the first piece from her and looked at Quentin. "Hold out your hands."

Quentin did and, keeping the gun steady, Jack proceeded to wind the tape tightly around his wrists. Then he did the same to Ruth. When he finished he checked the restraints.

"You're missing the real killer," Quentin said.

"Shut up." Jack switched hands with the gun and reached behind him to slip on a light windbreaker he must have brought with him. Then he moved to the hall door and cracked it open to peek outside before pulling it open and stepping outside to hold the handle. He motioned with the gun. "After you, people. We'll go down the emergency stairs. Keep your hands down in front of you so it looks natural."

Quentin moved slowly past Jack and into the hallway. For a moment he considered diving into Jack's midsection, but what good would that do? Jack would start shooting, and Ruth might get hit.

The hallway was still empty. Jack hurried them along to the stairwell entrance then down a couple of flights to the bottom. He held the gun at waist level tucked in close so that it was covered by the jacket.

Quentin was hoping they'd have to pass near the lobby, but Jack was too smart for that. At the bottom of the stairs, they reached an emergency exit that appeared to head out the back of the building. The door was propped open with a small block of wood.

"What if I really didn't murder Gwen?" Quentin asked.

"Then you have nothing to worry about, do you?" Jack said.

"Wait until we get someplace where we can talk."

"Someplace where you can shoot us, you mean?"

There was no reply. They were hustled out the door into a small alleyway that led to the parking lot. Jack's Seville was parked right at the entrance to the alley.

Ruth walked ahead of Quentin. He felt the presence of the big man right behind him. "You've got some cajones doing this in broad daylight, I gotta give you that."

"What part of 'shut up' do you fail to understand?"

Another stinging blow, this time to the side of his head, almost staggered him.

After Auburn, after all the years of disappointment and hope, was this how it was going to end? In the hallucinogenic rage of a grieving father? Quentin was a little surprised Jack hadn't made them put their hands behind their backs to restrain them. He had been moved around shackled for years and he knew what advantage arms bound in front offered him. Maybe the PI feared it would look more unnatural if they were seen. Whatever else happened, he had just about decided, he would not let Ruth or him get into a car with this man. Their captor would get off at least one or two well-placed shots before he could grab his wrist and the gun. But Quentin had the advantage of age and size on the man, not to mention a prison-chiseled body and reflexes.

As if reading his mind, Jack seemed to drop back a pace or two, giving himself more distance. Quentin kept moving, wondering if Jack were weighing the situation the same way he was, thinking about how he was going to maneuver them into the Seville.

They passed a storage bin and were almost to the car. Something wasn't right. Quentin glanced back, ready to move, when, in an almost surreal moment, the goateed photographer from the newspaper, dressed in a black jumpsuit, burst from behind the bin—the same shadowy profile Quentin had seen from a distance in the back seat of the Crown Vic, he suddenly realized. The little man slammed a tire iron into the back of Jack's head. Ruth yelped. The big PI grunted like a bull on a picador's lance and went down heavily, the Beretta skittering out of his hand.

Quentin dove for Jack's gun. But the photographer was carrying too, and despite being occupied making sure he'd neutralized Jack, he managed to fire a muffled round that just missed Quentin sprawling across the alley floor. Quentin clutched the Beretta and rolled to point it up at the man, just in time to see him grab Ruth by the hair and pull her in front of his body.

"You aren't going to be able to fire that cannon worth a damn with your hands trussed up like that."

"Try me." Quentin managed to slide his finger inside the trigger guard.

Ruth started to cry out again, but the man squeezed his arm around her neck and cupped his hand across her mouth. Her eyes were wild with fear.

The man checked behind him and starting dragging Ruth by the neck around the back of the Seville.

"We'll finish this when the time comes. You know what I want. And no cops, or she gets buried next to her daughter."

Quentin managed to struggle to his feet, but by the time he did, they were on the far side of the Seville. He could make out a sliver of another car through the glass. Still couldn't risk a shot. Their heads disappeared behind the bigger vehicle, a door slammed, and an engine roared.

He ran to the end of the alley just in time to catch sight of the gray Toyota careening in a cloud of smoke and spinning tires from the lot.

Sixty-Eight

Midafternoon and Garnell sat with Hollister and King in the small conference room down at Government Plaza. They'd just come from an emergency meeting with AAG James. The serial numbers on the bills from the box Price had given them indicated the money was part of fifty thousand dollars from a drug bust that had mysteriously disappeared from an evidence locker more than ten years before.

On the table in front of them lay six large cardboard boxes containing computer printouts and files on all full- and part-time employees of the city police bureau, the DA's and sheriff's offices, and all other attendant agencies, as well as stacks of phone and radio call messages. The word had gone out a couple of hours earlier for all personnel to check in and verify their whereabouts for the day.

Like the person they were seeking was about to volunteer the truth.

But at least it might shake his tree, let him know they were on his trail, Garnell figured. Bulletins had also gone out on Price and Ruth and Jack Crawford, but so far to no avail.

Hollister's cell phone rang. He fished it out of his pocket and answered, grunted a couple of times. "Really," he said. Finally he said, "Thanks for getting on it so quickly," and hung up.

Garnell and King looked at him.

"Got more info on the jokers in the fake state police cruiser. Couple of goons from out Rochester way. One a former schoolteacher and convicted sex offender."

"Stellar," King said.

"Guess they were in over their heads."

"You could say that," Garnell said.

They sorted and sifted through the material for another twenty minutes. Nothing promising. Then King, who'd been reading through the phone and radio check-ins, looked up. "Hmmmmmm."

"What have you got?" Garnell slid his chair a little closer.

King pushed the piece of paper over at him.

The phone message had come in a half an hour before.

It wasn't a regular check-in, however. The crime scene unit supervisor had been trying to find the main photographer he used, a freelancer named Doyle Fletcher, who also did work for the newspaper and a couple of other local publications.

Fletcher hadn't shown up at a scene he had been paged about, so they had had to find someone else. The photographer wasn't a full-time department employee—it wasn't all that unusual. But the supervisor said Fletcher's boss at the newspaper told him Fletcher hadn't shown up for work there either this afternoon, and he hadn't been answering his cell phone. The supervisor said this was unlike him.

"A photographer," Garnell said under his breath.

"Like Gwen Crawford." Hollister stood and came around to have a look as well. "And the photography club the professor was talking about."

It was like a tumbler in a lock being tripped, the entire mechanism beginning to shift. Garnell remembered standing in Jack Crawford's office examining his shrine-like memorial to his dead daughter's photography. The look and feel and texture of the photos. Somehow they eerily reminded him of something and now he knew what: the crime scene photos of her own death. Had some of those photos been taken by the same person or at least under that person's tutelage? Could Doyle Fletcher have been the person Gwen was supposed to be meeting at the party the night she disappeared? Her faculty advisor had said he thought she was trying to line up a speaker for the club.

Hollister's forehead wrinkled in concern. "This guy Fletcher. I've seen him around here hundreds of times."

Garnell looked again at the supervisor's note. "We know our perp is someone working inside or around the department. What's this guy's address?"

Sixty-Nine

Jack stirred as he swam back into consciousness. He was in the back seat of his own car, trees flowing past, bright sunlight streaming in. The back of his head throbbed. His stomach lurched and he felt like he might throw up.

"That was a nasty hit you took, man."

He looked across the seat to see Quentin Price at the wheel of the Seville.

"What happened?"

"What happened was you got jumped by this little photographer dude works for the newspaper and now he's got Ruth. I need some answers from you and fast."

"Fletcher."

"What?"

"His name is Doyle Fletcher. And he doesn't just freelance for the newspaper, he works crime scenes part time for the Binghamton Police Bureau."

"Crime scenes? He a cop?"

"No. Freelancer, but they all trust him."

"He's the guy you hired, right? He's been following me around and he was in the back of that car with those guys pretending to be state troopers."

"That's him."

"And you even had him go to try to talk to my mother when she was dying."

"Yeah. It was when I first got wind that anyone was seriously considering letting them test for the DNA and maybe letting you out." He felt ashamed all of a sudden, especially hearing it from Price. He'd considered, at the time, that Carla Price was dying, but his fear and his anger at her son had won out.

"Fletcher killed your daughter, Jack."

"What?" He felt dizzy.

"And if Harris, the NYPD detective is right, he's killed a bunch of other women too."

"He couldn't . . . I don't . . ." But even as he heard the words, Jack knew it was the truth. He'd been wrong about Quentin Price, wrong about Ruth, wrong about everything.

Worse, he'd known Gwen's killer and at least something about his underhanded dealings all along. Even made the worthless piece of scum work for him because he had the dirt on what he thought was Fletcher's minor trade in illicit photos. Blinded by his smug fury, played him like an idiot.

He tried to think some more but his thoughts became jumbled fragments, things present and past. Memories of Gwen and Ruth. Gwen when she was little on her bicycle riding around the neighborhood in Camillus, brown hair trailing in the sun. The final blowup with Ruth. Fight, almost put his hand through a wall, broken finger. Moving. Plants dying in his big new house, the place dry and dusty. The touch of Hannah's skin on his.

"Jack. Jack, you with the program here?"

"Sure. Yeah, sorry. Can I get a drink of water?"

One hand still on the wheel, Price fumbled for something and dropped a container of bottled water over the seat. He reached for it. His head whirled and his stomach protested, but he managed to get the top off and drink some, cough, then drink some more.

"Thank you," he said.

"You're welcome."

"You said Fletcher's got Ruth?"

"Yeah. I need you to tell me where I can find them."

He tried to organize his thoughts. "He's got an apartment in the city, but I don't think he'll take her there."

"Where then?"

"Fletcher's into trading dirty pics. He likes to pretend he's a cop to impress people too. I think he's been doing it a long time. No kiddie porn or shit like that though. Thinks he's some kind of artist."

"How do you know this?"

"I found out about it when I was investigating a Canadian business owner for a client in Syracuse . . . I can't believe I was so stupid. I thought I had Fletcher pegged."

"And you figured you could leverage what you knew about this Fletcher into getting him to work for you."

"Yeah. But this is only the third or fourth time I've used him in maybe five years. He always did a good job. I had no idea he'd . . ." He couldn't finish the sentence. The rage that had fueled him for so long went searching for a different target.

"Where is he, Jack? Where's he taken Ruth?"

His head spun. He felt himself begin to vomit, leaned forward, but managed to hold it down.

"Hang in there, Jack. Where do you think he's taken her?"

"There's a place," he said. He coughed out the words. "A tract home out in Vestal. I tailed Fletcher there one night when I first found out about him. He could be there." He gave Price the address—he was good at remembering such things—at least he could still hang on to that.

"Okay. I got it. Okay."

The car rolled on through a neighborhood with tall trees. Jack watched the tops of them sail past through the windshield.

"Price."

"Yeah?"

"I'm sorry."

The driver said nothing. The car was slowing down. They were entering a driveway and some sort of lot next to a large building.

"What's this?"

Price still didn't speak. He braked the car to a stop, put it in park, and pushed open the driver side door.

"Where are we? I'm going with you, right?"

"I'm sorry too," Price said. "But I'm taking you to an ER."

SEVENTY

Ruth sat blindfolded and alone in the dark. She was in some sort of basement, listening to the hiss of a dehumidifier. All her searching, all the drinks over the years, and soon she'd be with Gwen. This monster was cunning, cunning enough to have fooled her daughter and framed Quentin. He must have even fooled Jack. What was there to do now but wait to die?

She could no longer feel her hands and feet. She'd had nothing to eat or drink for hours and she badly needed to urinate. She could use a shot of whiskey, anything. At least she was still alive, which was probably more than she could say for Jack. Poor Jack—her captor was going to go on killing until he got what he wanted and maybe even after that.

She heard the hollow thump of what might have been a screen door followed by the creaking of the man's footsteps on the floor overhead. A click sounded and a pale light appeared behind the blindfold. The man clomped down the basement stairs.

"Are we happy down here?"

She remained silent.

"No pouting allowed. At least until we take care of your friend Mr. Price."

"I need to use the bathroom."

"Hmmm. Now that does pose a problem for us, doesn't it?"

She sensed him moving around behind her. Felt the vibrations as he began to untie the knots. The rope loosened and she groaned at the first stab of pain from her arms and legs. Her back felt like it was on fire.

"Oh, yeah. Should've warned you. It'll hurt like the dickens for a couple of minutes until you get the feeling back in your extremities . . . C'mon. Stand up."

It hurt so much, she almost passed out. But she gritted her teeth and pushed with her legs to a standing position. The room, or what she perceived of the room through the blindfold, seemed to spin. She heard the dull snap of the safety on a handgun close to her ear.

"The bathroom's straight ahead and to your right. I'll direct you."

She was afraid of where this might be leading, what he might do, but the last thing she needed was to soil herself. She allowed him to direct her into the bathroom where she was able to squat on what smelled like a foul toilet.

"You got a nice ass for an older bitch."

Would he try to grope her, or worse? Thankfully, he left her alone.

A minute later, feeling better, she let herself be directed back into the big basement room where her hands were re-tied.

"You're gonna have to help me find your big black boyfriend. That's one thing you and your daughter had in common. A taste for dark meat."

"You're sick," she said.

"Am I now?"

"What business did you have with my daughter?"

"Your daughter was special. An artist like myself."

She almost started to cry. She heard his feet scuff along the floor a few steps, then the sound of a door swinging open from the far side of the room. The unmistakable odor of gasoline filtered through the air.

"What are you doing?"

Fletcher moved back beside her. "I'm tired, Ruth. Tired of all of this."

"What's your name?"

"Doyle."

"Why are you so fixated on Gwen's birthday, Doyle?"

"Well, I want to honor her. Just like I need to honor everyone who's touched my life, people I've taken pictures of."

"So you sent me those condolences every year."

He said nothing, but she heard him chuckle to himself.

She needed to try to keep him talking. "You're a photographer then."

"Among other things."

"Do you kill people so you can take pictures of the dead?"

"Oh, please." There was disgust in the man's voice. "I'd get a job as a forensic photographer in a bigger city if all I wanted to do was trade in smut."

"You took those pictures of Gwen though. Do you deal in pornography?"

"That's just someone else's twisted label for something I see as beautiful. I don't dehumanize my subjects. I bring them into a new kind of existence, infuse them with an immortality they never could have achieved in real life. Like Gwen. Which is why I need those photos and my money back."

"Did you steal that money, Doyle? Quentin told me Gwen thought you were a cop. Was she beginning to suspect you? Is that why you killed her?"

"I showed her a badge and my ID from when I'm working downtown. I've got lots of money from different places."

"One of the detectives said there were others you may have killed. How many have their been all together, Doyle? Do you even know the number?"

"I'm very good at what I do, Ruth. I keep meticulous records, thousands of images I've created. You would be amazed to see the organization and the detail. But of course I can't show any of it to you."

"Does Jack know about any of this?"

"Jack's a fool. A smart fool, but still a fool. He looks at everything and everyone except himself and what's right in front of him."

"Those men you sent to try to kill us, are there others?"

"No more questions, Ruth," he said.

She smelled the gasoline again. "So now you're just going to what, Doyle, burn all this down and disappear? You're going to destroy all your masterpieces?"

Fletcher gave no reply.

"You said you were tired. Couldn't you just give up and turn yourself in?"

"No. I can't ever be caught, Ruth. I've seen what the system does to people like me. They'll humiliate me and grind me up with all sorts of psychologists, and in the end they won't even kill me, which would actually be more merciful."

The man was fumbling with something. Then she heard the click of a shutter, and a flash blinded her through the cloth.

"Just a few photos, Ruth. You don't even realize how magnificent you look with your hands taped behind your back."

The flash exploded through the blindfold again.

Seventy-One

The building was less than a five-minute ride from downtown. Contemporary-style brick and glass. Sixteen apartments total built around a center stairwell, four stories, eight apartments on either side. Alternative rock, acoustic, nice harmonies, floating from a lower window. Someone cooking out on a charcoal grill in back. Fletcher's apartment was on the third floor.

Two squad cars and four uniforms were already there, having parked down the block and made their approach before Garnell, Hollister, and King arrived. The news wasn't bad, but it wasn't good either. Nobody home.

One red flag began waving after another.

Inside, Fletcher's place was sparsely appointed. A thin layer of dust on the furniture, otherwise spotless. Antiseptic. Unlived in. The neighbor across the stairwell confirmed that Mr. Doyle was hardly ever there. She'd only seen him once or twice in the past year.

Another puzzler. One of the uniforms came pounding up the stairwell to report they'd discovered a green Chevy pickup in the lot with plates that matched the one registered to Doyle Fletcher. Wherever he was, then, he was driving another set of wheels.

"So the guy's got a front pad," King said as they trotted back down the stairs.

Garnell turned to Hollister. "Front life's more like it. We need to find out where he is really living. What is he driving?

How about the newspaper?"

"I just talked to the crime scene super and his boss over at the paper. They say he's been driving a gray Toyota, but they don't have a plate number. Only address the paper has on file is the same one we've got."

"How about more information from the other members of the crime scene unit team or other people at the paper? You said yourself you've seen him hundreds of times. He must hang out with somebody."

"We're checking on it. Word I'm getting so far though is that the guy never fraternizes much outside the office. People don't seem to have to much to say about him. He's good at his job. He's meticulous, methodical. Not at all flamboyant."

"An easy guy to overlook," Garnell said.

His phone buzzed on his belt clip. He picked it up and answered.

"Detective Harris?"

"Yes."

"It's Beatrice Tover, head of security over at Merryweather College."

"Right. Sure, how are you?"

"I'm calling about an incident that happened over on the campus here yesterday. I caught a strange man heading out of one of our dorms. Said he was working for the phone company, but that turned out to be untrue. He showed me ID, but I thought it might be fake too, so I started doing a little checking and ran the license plate from a truck he was driving. Ever hear of a man named Doyle Fletcher?"

Seventy-Two

The afternoon sky was a brilliant blue as Quentin made his way down the tree-lined sidewalk. Sierra Lathrop lived with a room-mate in a brick, colonial-style townhouse less than a ten-minute run from the emergency room where Quentin had deposited Jack and the keys to his Seville with a concerned intake nurse. Quentin's call had brought her home from work early. Sierra's eyes flashed at the sight of his sweaty face as she opened the door.

"I've been worried about you." He tried to give her a hug, but she pushed him away. "What's going on here, Quentin? Why are you using me to get all this information?"

"I'm not trying to use you," he said.

"Look. I like you and I thought you liked me. I don't care about your situation or your lawsuit, but I'd like to know what's happening before I go sneaking around behind my boss's back any more to help you."

"Why, you don't think Ms. Shackleford would approve?"

"I don't know of any lawyer that would approve of you trying to solve an old murder you've already been exonerated for."

"Fair enough."

She glared at him.

"Look," he said. "Ruth Crawford's in serious trouble."

"What?"

"Someone's kidnapped her." He told her about the ambush up in Chenango County, the shooting at the college, and moving to the hotel, then he and Ruth being taken by Jack Crawford, and finally Ruth being taken by the photographer.

"Where's Jack Crawford now?" she asked.

"I left him at the hospital emergency room."

"I don't know what else is going on, but you were right about the money thing. As I was headed out the door a call came in from the DA's office. The girl there said that a couple of months prior to the dates I asked about a large amount of cash went missing from an evidence storage locker. It was drug money and they managed to keep it quiet. The perpetrator was never caught."

Fletcher had to be the thief, the mystery photographer, and Gwen's killer. Maybe paid Alex Cook with some of the tainted money too—he must have killed him in order to silence him about their little photo operation at the college, drugged him or maybe forced him off the road, or at least Gwen was convinced of that. Cook and Gwen could have been the first victims, or they may just have been part of a long line.

"Okay. I need to ask you a big favor."

She looked at him. "You name it."

"You have a car?"

"Yes, of course."

"I need to borrow it to go after Ruth."

"Are you crazy? Why don't you call your friend the NYPD detective again?"

"I'm still not a hundred percent sure I can trust him, let alone the other cops. What if this photographer dude is working with some of them?"

"So what, you're just planning to charge into this madman's house like Vin Diesel or something?"

"Not exactly. Fletcher won't recognize your car. I've got Jack Crawford's .45 and my uncle's old Browning."

They stared at one another.

"I don't believe in guns."

"This isn't the time to debate the Second Amendment."

"I'm going with you."

"No way."

Sierra folded her arms across her chest. "I still think you ought to call in the police."

"Think about it. This guy sees the cavalry show up, who knows what he's liable to do. He might kill Ruth. We're running out of time. Besides, I screwed up and didn't do enough to try to help Gwen Crawford when I knew she was in trouble in the first place, and now I let Jack Crawford get the jump on me. It's my fault Fletcher has Ruth. I'm going to be the one to get her back."

"Fine. But Fletcher won't recognize me either. I can drive the car."

She did have a point. She could get him in close and still keep the car available if they needed to make a getaway.

"It could be dangerous," he said.

"All the more reason for me keeping watch with a phone."

"All right," he said finally. "But you have to promise to stay with the car."

SEVENTY-THREE

The house was easy enough to find. An over-under ranch with curtains pulled over the windows, it occupied a double lot at the end of a cul-de-sac ringed with similar houses, a basketball hoop in front of one neighbor's driveway, a child's tricycle and other toys scattered on the lawn in front of another. The gray Toyota was partly visible, its tail poking out from inside the garage with the door three quarters of the way down. Lower-middle-class suburbia. What struck Quentin was the banality of it all. No flashing neon sign advertising that a serial killer lived here.

Sierra U-turned her small Nissan in the center of the cul-de-sac while Quentin, in the back, peeked over the seat at the street. Cars filled several of the driveways. Kids battled with squirt guns only a couple houses away from Fletcher's. That wouldn't be the name he went by here, of course.

"This isn't going to work. We need to find another way in."

Sierra kept her eyes on her driving. "Looks like there is a patch of woods in back, houses on the other side, but they're newer. Another development being built."

"Okay. Let's give it a try."

"Long as I can figure out how to look like a realtor." She drove to the end of the street, turned a couple of corners, and swung back in the direction of the house. A minute later, she turned the car into another street. "It is a new development. No one working here today though."

"Perfect."

"I can see the back of Fletcher's house. There are two bigger houses under construction here."

The car was slowing.

"Okay," he said. "Can you find someplace to park where you can keep an eye on the back of Fletcher's house without easily being seen?"

"How about beside this Dumpster?" She braked the car to a halt. "I can see over the top of it through the woods. It's only about fifty, sixty yards."

"Anybody else around?"

"Not that I can see at the moment."

"Sounds good."

"This would be easier, you know, if we waited until dark."

"That's what Fletcher's bound to be thinking too. He doesn't know anybody else knows about this place. Probably figures he has a little time to plan his next move. Plus, if anybody else sees me walking around in broad daylight, I can always tell them I'm with the cable company or something."

He took the clipboard he'd borrowed from Sierra's house to make him look semi-official.

"So go over this with me one more time. Once I see you reach the back of the house, I give you five minutes. If I don't see either you or Ruth Crawford coming out by then, I call 911. And if I see you coming before that, I also call 911."

"That's it. Pretty simple."

"One problem. I don't know what Ruth Crawford looks like."

"You see any woman coming out of there, you get on the phone."

"Got it. What if you don't find anything? What if the house is empty?"

"Then I'll be back and we can try to figure out what to do next."

Before she could ask any more questions, he was out of the car and crossing somebody's future backyard toward the woods. He saw with relief that the construction area was quiet, just as she had said. The trees would provide decent cover and Fletcher's back yard was little more than a narrow strip of grass. Hidden in the brush, he paused for a second to reconnoiter. A blue jay and a few sparrows flushed from the bushes beside the house. He could smell burning charcoal, someone down the block firing up the outdoor grill. There was a concrete patio beneath a wooden deck, a set of sliding glass doors with heavy-looking curtains, no sign of life from anywhere in the house, either above or below.

Then, in the flicker of an eye, he caught a faint flash of light through the curtain beneath the deck. He thought it might have been a trick of the approaching dusk, heat lightning maybe, but there . . . he saw it again. Someone was shooting photos.

It was still Gwen's birthday, although the evening was rapidly approaching. He crossed the narrow yard in a couple of strides, moved beneath the shadow of the deck, and flattened himself against the brick wall outside the sliding door. The intermittent flashes continued. He pulled the Beretta from inside his jacket and freed the safety. This was no time for subtlety.

Ducking low, he leapt in front of the opening. He led with his foot through the door—the plate glass shattered with a boom. Inside, the dehumidifier was deafening. Ruth screamed as he rolled through the curtain and onto a carpet with his gun trained on the room. He caught a glimpse of Fletcher leaping up a stairwell and fired once at his retreating legs. The man yelped in pain, but slammed through a door at the top of the stairs. The sounds of him bolting it and banging around upstairs filled the basement.

"Who's there?" Ruth sat bound to a chair by heavy tape and blindfolded, an expensive-looking camera, the same one Quentin had seen Fletcher using when he was taking pictures for the newspaper, lying on the floor behind her. She sounded like she was in shock.

"It's me."

"Quentin, oh, my God."

"Gotta get you out of here."

He ripped off the blindfold and went to work on the tape around her arms and legs with his free hand, keeping a wary eye on the stairs. Fletcher was still thrashing around upstairs. Quentin noticed the smell of gasoline.

"I'm afraid he's going to try to firebomb this place," Ruth said.

"Then we don't have much time." He was almost through with the tape binding her to the chair and around her ankles. The noises from upstairs had stopped.

Ruth was able to stand now. He helped her to her feet.

"Goddammit, Price, you broke my plate-glass window."

It was Fletcher's voice, coming from the other side of a door that looked like it led into another room at the base of the stairs next to some ducts, perhaps leading to a furnace. There must have been another way for him to drop into the basement.

"Not to mention shooting me in the knee," Price went on. "That hurts, you know."

He pushed Ruth. "Run," he said under his breath. "Get out now."

"What about you?" she whispered.

"Run." He shoved her hard and she turned and stumbled outdoors through the broken glass just as the door to the other room flung open and the basement was sprayed with bullets from an automatic rifle. Quentin dove to the ground and returned fire at the darkened door.

"Aghh!" The little man bellowed. "Dammit! Hit again."

Quentin said nothing, kept his gun pointed at the darkness

inside the door. He figured he had a few more rounds in the clip.

"Now I'm really fucking bleeding. Cocksucker . . ." The voice sounded weaker.

"Throw out your weapon."

"I can't, asshole. I can't pick it up."

"Kick it out through the door then."

He heard a grunt and a shoe striking something. A dull thud sounded as the stock of an M-16 appeared on the carpet partway through the door.

"Look. I'm bleeding bad. Going to die here. I'm coming out. I'm giving up."

"Both hands where I can see them," Quentin said.

Fletcher appeared limping out of the darkness, his hands raised high in the air. He was smiling from ear to ear though, his white teeth gleaming through his dark goatee.

"Either way, you lose, nigger."

Strapped to Fletcher's shoulders was a backpack. From one of his fingers dangled a thin wire.

Too late, Quentin started to pull the trigger. But he barely had time to register what was happening before Jack Crawford, the bulk of his legs driving low and hard like the linebacker he'd once been, appeared as if out of nowhere from behind Fletcher, tackling the little man and throwing himself over top of the bomb. The room disintegrated, thunderous fire-like white needles, and Quentin was pulled down into darkness and a void like none he had ever known.

Seventy-Four

A pale, institutional light crept into Quentin's vision as he awoke. He was in the hospital room where they'd kept him for observation overnight. He'd been lucky. The blast had leveled a section of Doyle Fletcher's house, killing Fletcher and Jack Crawford and causing a blaze that took a fire crew nearly an hour to extinguish, but thanks to Jack, Quentin had been spared the worst of it. The concussion he'd suffered was minor. The lacerations, burns, and bruises on his body would heal soon enough.

"Feeling better?"

Ruth Crawford rose from a chair in the corner. She'd sat there through the night, dozing through the pearl dawn and so, in a chair opposite, had Sierra, who, with Ruth's help, had pulled him out of the fiery rubble and called 911.

"I'm fine," he said.

"Can you get out of bed okay?"

He swung his legs off the side of the bed and sat up. Felt a momentary vertigo, but it passed. "No problem."

Across the room Sierra opened her eyes and smiled. "Hey stranger, you're up."

The door to the room creaked open and a middle-aged nurse bustled into the room. "You're looking pretty chipper this morning, Mr. Price," she said.

Quentin looked at the biggest of the bandages on one of his arms. "I'm feeling fine."

"That's good." She stuck a thermometer in his ear for a quick reading and slapped a blood-pressure cuff around his arm. She pumped up the cuff and waited, watching the gauge. Everything was apparently normal. "That's very good."

"Where are my clothes?" he asked.

"There wasn't much left of them, I'm afraid," Sierra said. "I went back to your uncle's house while you were sleeping, used your key, and got you a fresh set. Hope you don't mind. They're hanging on the back of the door in the bathroom."

"Thanks very much," he said. "I need to get out of here."

"Not until the doctor sees you and okays it," the nurse said. "And I think there are a few policeman waiting downstairs who want to continue their discussions with you as well."

He'd been so groggy the night before, he had managed only a brief interview with Detective Harris. Hollister and King had been there too, a couple of people from the DA's office, and a woman from the FBI.

"Is my lawyer around?"

"She said she'd be back by seven," Ruth said. She looked at a watch on her wrist. "That's in thirty minutes."

"You guys mind if I take a shower?"

"Be my guest," said the nurse. "Long as you're feeling up for it. Just try not to get that big bandage too wet."

"Don't worry. I'll manage."

He tucked his gown around him and pulled himself off the bed.

"Cute buns," Sierra said.

"Woman, have you no shame?" He tried but failed not to crack a smile.

Sierra giggled and gave him a look. "You want some privacy, we'll be out in the hall."

He nodded and the three women disappeared from the room. Quentin entered the bathroom and closed the door. He used the toilet and turned on the shower. He paused for a minute to look at a few of his cuts and burns in the mirror. They didn't look as bad as he'd feared. Who'd of thought among Fletcher, Jack, and Quentin that any of them would have made it out of that basement alive? But there Quentin stood.

The water took a minute to get hot but finally made a nice steaming stream. He moved into the shower and, holding his bandaged arm to the side, stepped underneath the warm flow, hung his head, and closed his eyes. He thought about all that had taken place leading up to the explosion. He thought about all the wasted years in prison, jail cells, real and imagined. He didn't know what he was going to do now, didn't know how many more sessions he was going to have to endure with the police, how his lawsuit against the state would go, or where exactly he wanted to end up with his life.

But he knew one thing for certain: he felt a strange new kinship. His mother's faith had been redeemed because in spite of all that Jack Crawford had done, in spite of every law of physics and reality, Gwen's father had flown across that basement to his rescue like some dark wounded angel. Quentin had been there to see it happen. It was fitting, wasn't it? He picked up a bar of soap from the shower tray and began to scrub.

Blood in, blood out.

ABOUT THE AUTHOR

Andy Straka is a burned-out medical equipment salesperson who turned to writing in order to finally justify his college English major of many years before. Featured by *Publishers Weekly* as one of ten rising stars in crime fiction, his debut novel, *A Witness Above,* garnered Shamus, Anthony, and Agatha Award nominations for best first novel. His second book, *A Killing Sky,* was nominated for an Anthony, and his third, *Cold Quarry,* won a Shamus Award. A native of upstate New York and a graduate of Williams College, he lives with his family in Virginia.

2,800
1,600
1,600
0

5,200
3,800
6,200